The
PEACEMAKERS

A NOVEL BY

RICHARD HERMAN

Willowbank Books
San Francisco   Los Angeles

Willowbank Books
www.willowbankbooks.com

FIRST EDITION
2011

ISBN-13: 978-0615573090
ISBN-10: 0615573096

Also by
Richard Herman

Caly's Island
(writing as Dick Herman)
A Far Justice
The last Phoenix
The Trojan Sea
Edge of Honor
Against All Enemies
Power Curve
Iron Gate
Dark Wing
Call to Duty
Firebreak
Force of Eagles
The Warbirds

In memoriam

David "Bull" Baker
Brig. General, USAF (Ret.)
He led and made a difference.

Blessed are the peacemakers:
For they shall be called the children of God.

Matthew 5:9

PROLOGUE

Rancho Cordova, California

David Orde Allston sat in the backseat of the small Toyota and bit his tongue. It was hard being a passenger and keeping quiet while his kids did the driving. He rearranged his legs in a futile attempt to be more comfortable, but the rear seat of the Toyota wasn't designed for someone six feet tall. The former fighter pilot was forty-five years old, and thanks to hard effort, still lean and fit. That helped somewhat, but he was convinced a sadistic contortionist had designed the rear seat.

Allston made small talk mainly to relax Ben, his sixteen-year-old stepson, who was behind the wheel and learning to drive. "Heavy traffic for a Saturday."

"Piece of cake, Pop," Ben replied.

Allston smiled as his slightly misshapen jaw offset to the right and his hazel eyes flashed with amusement. Ben's one goal in life was to be a fighter pilot, and he was going through a World War II phase and imagined himself flying in the Battle of Britain, which explained his current vocabulary.

"He wants to fly a Spitfire," Lynne said from the front passenger's seat. She turned around to face Allston. Lynne was Allston's twenty-one-year-old daughter and tall and beautiful like her mother, his first wife. "See what you've done, teaching him to fly."

"Spits can be arranged," Allston said. He tried not to think what Ben's mother, his former third wife, would say about that, but at sixteen Ben was already an excellent pilot flying high-performance aircraft.

"Yes!" Ben shouted. The teenager's enthusiasm was infectious and Lynne smiled at Allston, enjoying the moment.

The car slowed as the traffic on Sunrise Boulevard piled up. Ben didn't quite make it through the last traffic light before they hit Highway 50, the freeway leading to Sacramento's airport thirty-five miles away, and had to stop short of the intersection. They were first in line and caught in the right hand lane. Once past the intersection, it was a clear shot to the freeway. Lynne was worried. "Will we make Ben's flight to Los Angeles?" Her step-brother was booked on Southwest for one of his periodic visits to see his mother and didn't want to go.

Ben smiled. "Ain't that a shame?" He hummed a few bars of the song and beat the steering wheel in rhythm.

A quarter mile ahead, Allston saw the traffic sign pointing to the freeway's on ramp. Automatically, he checked his watch and ran the numbers. It would be close. "Piece of cake," he said.

The last three cars making a left hand turn in front of them slammed to a halt, blocking the intersection. "Gridlock," Ben announced, happy their forward progress had come to a halt.

"You're not getting out of this," Allston told him, "so quit smiling." Then, "Lock your doors." Lynne and Ben heard the change in his voice and quickly depressed their lock buttons. "At your four o'clock," Allston said. His words were short and clipped, a sure indication his situational awareness had kicked in. Lynne shot a look to her right. A tall, skinny, raggedy, gaunt-looking man was standing on the corner less than ten feet from her door. His eyes darted from car to car and his hands twitched with anticipation. Their light changed to green, but no one could move because of the three cars still blocking the intersection. "Ben, heads up," Allston ordered.

"Roger."

The man bolted for the last car in line trying to make the left hand turn. He grabbed the driver's door handle and jerked the door open. Allston hit the release button to his seatbelt as the man dragged a young woman out of the car by her hair. "Car-jacking. Lynne, get out and call 9-1-1." His words were crisp and clear with no sign of panic.

"My baby!" the woman cried, holding on to the man. He threw her to the ground and kicked at her.

Allston and Lynne were out of the car. "Ben, block the car so it can't back up." Ben understood immediately. If the hijacker backed up, he could turn the car and would have a clear shot at the freeway for a quick escape. Allston slammed the door and ran for the woman lying in the street while Lynne ran for safety, her cell phone in her hand.

Allston bent over the woman as the hijacker jumped into the driver's seat. "My baby's in the rear seat!" the woman cried. At the same time, Ben

2

stepped on the accelerator and twisted the wheel to the right. Allston leaped for the hijacker as Ben slammed his Toyota to a halt behind the woman's car, his front bumper against its rear bumper.

"Ben!" Allston shouted. "Get out." The teenager bolted out the door and ran for the woman still lying in the street.

Allston was a blur of motion as he reached into the open car window and grabbed the hijacker's hair. Allston drove his left fist into the man's face with three short pile driver jabs as Ben scooped up the prostrate woman and carried her to safety. The man managed to shift the car into reverse and stomped on the accelerator, pushing Ben's Toyota. There was no bang, only the sound of grinding metal on metal as the two cars shot backwards. Allston stumbled but held onto the hijacker's shirt and hair with both hands. The car had room to turn and the man hit the brakes as he twisted the wheel to the right. It was enough for Allston to regain his balance. He braced his left foot against the door and pulled the hijacker out the window. He banged the hijacker's head against the pavement, stunning him.

Two other men were there and it was over. "Nice going," one of the men said in admiration. Lynne and the young mother ran for the baby still in the car. The baby was fine and the mother cried with relief. The wail of a police siren echoed in the distance, growing louder by the second.

Ben and Lynne stood by Allston in the street. "You did good, son. Real good."

Lynne affectionately ruffled Allston's short dark hair. "You never change, Dad."

"When something goes wrong, get aggressive," Allston replied. It was one of the basic rules of survival he had learned long ago flying fighters.

Lynne understood. "You've just got to get involved – no matter what."

ONE

Abyei, South Sudan

BermaNur scrambled to the top of the low hummock as the sun rose above the eastern horizon and established its dominion over the ancient land. Dust swirled around his feet as his eyes narrowed and swept the eastern horizon. He knew the airplane bringing food would come from that direction. Behind him, the first of the refugees swarmed out of the compound, clutching baskets and large pots.

He burned with hatred when he saw the Dinka who followed the two UN relief workers and mixed in with his fellow tribesmen. Neither the Dinka, the two Europeans, nor the Americans who flew the big white airplanes, deserved to live, but food and the three went together and his hunger was stronger than his hate. BermaNur was seventeen-years old, scrawny from malnutrition, and old beyond his years.

He looked over the ragged mob and saw his mother and older sister pushing their way to the front. With him, they were the last survivors of his family. Again, his hatred flared. He knew his mother had sold herself for food and he promised himself that someday he would blot out that dishonor by killing her. And he would immediately kill his sister if she ever sold her body. Jahel would honor him for the honor killing, and his tribe, the Rizeigat, demanded no less. BermaNur swelled with pride. The Rizeigat were Fursan, the cavaliers, or horsemen, of the Baggara, and honor was more important than life. For now, the age-old rules and traditions were in abeyance, but only until the western intruders and their big white airplanes were gone.

His small wireless, the modern version of the walkie-talkie, vibrated in his hand. He pressed the receive button and held it to his ear. It was Jahel. "Do you see anything?" The sheik had spoken in the same quiet way when he had chastised BermaBur for his mother's misconduct. That conversation had ended when Jahel had taken BermaNur's horse, his most valuable possession. Without a horse, BermaNur was not able to join the marauding bands of Rizeigat and increase his family's wealth. But once his family's honor was restored, Jahel would return his horse, and with it, his personal honor. That was the way of the Rizeigat and the Baggara. BermaNur fumbled for the transmit button. "Nothing, sire."

"Watch closely," Jahel said. "We must stay hidden until the last possible moment. All depends on your warning."

BermaNur's heart beat fast. "I see it! It is far to the east."

"Is it coming this way?"

The young Sudanese paused. This was the test he had been waiting for and he had to be right. Then, "Yes!"

"Good." Jahel broke the connection. Now the teenager had to wait.

The white C-130 Hercules descended to 1200 feet above the ground and entered a racetrack pattern around the strip of road on the southern side of the ravaged village that served as a landing strip. The Hercules was an old workhorse of the United States Air Force and this particular aircraft had entered service in 1976. A coat of white paint belied the aircraft's thirty-four-years of age and it was nearing the time when it would be consigned to the bone yard.

One of the UN relief workers made sure the villagers were clear of the road and fired a canister, laying green smoke to indicate wind direction and signal the four-engine cargo plane that it was safe to land. The pilot saw the smoke, entered a downwind leg, and called for the before landing checklist. The copilot started the flaps down and lowered the landing gear. The C-130 turned onto the base leg and the pilot marked the spot where she would touch down. It was a much-practiced routine. The pilot turned onto final approach and flew the big bird, nose high in the air, towards the touchdown point she had selected.

The copilot placed his left hand over the pilot's right hand that controlled the throttles. It was a technique they had developed to prevent the pilot's hand from bouncing off the throttles on a hard landing. She planted the C-130 hard in a controlled crash. The large tandem main wheels absorbed the shock, sinking a foot into the hard earth. The pilot slammed the nose onto the dirt road and jerked the throttles aft. The four propellers went into reverse as she stomped on the brakes, dragging the Hercules to a stop in less than 2000 feet.

BermaNur's eyes followed the landing C-130 as it hurtled down the road, blasting dust out in front, and coming directly at him. His jaw went rigid when he thought the left outboard propeller would hit him. He closed his eyes and refused to move. But his perspective was wrong and the plane passed by with over twenty feet to spare. He breathed a sigh of relief as his communicator vibrated. He pressed the receive button. "Did you think it would hit you?" Jahel asked. His laughter filled BermaNur's ear.

The teenage Baggara knew he was being watched, part of the test. "*Insh' Allah,*" as God wills, he replied. It was one of the few Arabic phrases he knew. He turned towards the airplane as it backed up, its powerful props in reverse. The cargo door under the tail was raised and the loading ramp lowered to the horizontal position. A crewman wearing a headset stood on the ramp and directed the pilot. Inside, the teenager saw pallets piled with food. Again, he refused to move as the plane backed down the road and the wing passed over him. For a brief moment, he looked directly into the face of the pilot – a woman! Her blonde ponytail bounced as she turned and waved at him.

He could only stare at the nose of the big aircraft when it finally stopped far down the road and the starving villagers swarmed around it. The anger that threatened to consume him burned with a white-hot intensity. Because of a woman pilot Jahel was laughing at him! It was too much for any Fursan. He keyed the communicator. "It is a woman who pilots the airplane," he told Jahel.

"Why do you speak of this?" Jahel asked.

"Do the Rizeigat beg from women?"

"Never," Jahel said. There was no laughter in his voice now.

"It cannot be tolerated," BermaNur said.

"Tell me when the airplane takes off," Jahel said. The boy sat down to wait.

Exactly twenty-four minutes later, one of the propellers started to turn as the villagers who had swarmed near to get the food shipment, moved away from the airplane. Soon, all four engines were turning as the pilot called for the before takeoff checklist. She set the brakes as the engines spun up and the propellers bit into the air. The nose lowered as the roar of the turboprop engines beat at him. The nose came up when she released the brakes and the Hercules surged forward. The teenager didn't move as the plane lifted off well before it reached him. The landing gear came up as it passed overhead. He made the radio call. "The infidels have taken off." The Hercules climbed into the sky and turned to the east. "The infidels will fly directly over you," he radioed.

BermaNur watched as the distinctive smoke trails of two shoulder-held surface-to-air missiles streaked from the ground, chasing down the lumbering aircraft. But someone on the Hercules saw the missiles and decoy flares popped in the aircraft's wake. The aircraft took evasive action and jerked wildly, surprising him by its agility. He held his breath, afraid the aircraft would escape the fate Allah had willed. The two missiles missed and went ballistic. His eyes opened wide when the Hercules's right wing folded up on its own and the plane rolled to the right.

The plane spun into the ground as a feeling of pure vindication flooded through the starving teenager. He shouted *"Allahu akbar!"* God is most great, at the top of his lungs as a pillar of smoke and flames mushroomed into the sky and a thundering roar momentarily shook the ground. He stood up and headed for the mob of villagers now running for the compound. He ran to find his mother and sister to ensure they had all the food they could carry. If not, he would have to beat them. His family's honor demanded no less. It was the will of God.

E-Ring, The Pentagon

Every head turned when Fitzgerald entered the conference room. Since there were six lower-ranking generals present, the room was not called to attention, per Fitzgerald's instructions. But everyone stood anyway. General John "Merlin" Fitzgerald, the Air Force Chief of Staff, commanded that level of respect. Fitzgerald was tall and solidly built, his face care-worn, and his salt and pepper hair cut short in a military haircut. The Chief of Staff's bright blue eyes often danced with amusement – but not this morning.

Brigadier General Yvonne Richards stood on the opposite side of the table and studied his body language as he sat down, trying to read his mood. Fitzgerald was a much-studied commodity in her world, and she considered the way he used briefings to keep his staff on the same page, not to mention on edge, hopelessly old-fashioned.

"Seats, please," Fitzgerald said. He turned to the large computer-driven display screen at the front of the room and the officer standing beside it. "Good morning, Colonel. Let's have it." Everyone knew what was on Fitzgerald's mind.

"Good morning, sir," the colonel said, starting the Power Point presentation. "I'm Colonel Robert Banks, chief of the Policy Division of the Office of Military-Political Affairs. As you know, the Air Force lost a C-130 yesterday morning in the Sudan." A stylistic photo of a C-130 flashed on the screen. "The Hercules was part of the 4440th" – he pronounced it 'forty-four fortieth' – "Special Airlift Detachment providing support and flying relief missions for the United Nations peacekeeping force to the Sudan out of

Malakal." He had just told Fitzgerald what he already knew, not the best of beginnings, and missed the narrowing of Fitzgerald's eyes. But not Richards. The general's body language told her that he was not hearing what he wanted. Colonel Banks was a key member of her staff she was grooming for command, but he was in danger of suffering a professional death by Power Point. She gave him the high sign to move on.

"There were no survivors," the colonel continued, "and an investigation team is en route to the crash site." Again, it was something Fitzgerald knew. "Moreover, the Administration has determined that no change in our peacekeeping operations is warranted because of the crash." That also was not news.

Fitzgerald's fingers beat a tattoo on the table. A colonel's job was to think, evaluate, and react accordingly. This one was wasting his time, and the general firmly believed in three strikes and you are out. "Clear your desk and pack your bag, Banks." The colonel gulped and stifled a reply. He had been relieved and any chance of command had just gone up in smoke. He walked out with as much dignity as he could muster.

Fitzgerald turned to his staff. "Next." His chief of staff hit a button to summon the next briefer.

The door opened and a woman entered. Her blue eyes were still wide from learning the fate of Colonel Banks. Her auburn hair was cut short and framed a lovely face. She was short and stocky, big busted and big hipped with an hourglass figure. She would never be fashionably thin, but Renoir would have painted her with admiring gusto. She stepped to the podium and picked up the remote control. "Good morning, sir. I'm Major Gillian Sharp. I work for the African Desk at the DIA as an intelligence analyst, and will be briefing you today on the current situation in the Sudan."

She cycled to the first display and started to talk. A slight flicker of light caught her attention when the image on the screen behind her changed for no reason. At the same time, she noticed that Fitzgerald was holding a remote control. He pressed the button again, and the display again changed. She waited quietly while he ran through her entire briefing in less than twenty seconds. Satisfied, he nodded, willing to cut a junior staff officer more slack than a colonel. "Go ahead, Major."

"Sir, as you know, the detachment commander, Lieutenant Colonel Anne McKenzie, was among those lost in the crash." She announced the names of the other four crewmembers in a way that made Fitzgerald think of an honor roll. "The exact cause of the crash is not known at this time, but satellite photography down-linked two hours ago indicates it might be structural failure." The general was impressed and he bombarded her with questions.

9

He grunted in satisfaction when she gave him the exact latitude and longitude of the crash site. "Both Abyei and the crash site," she added, "are in the disputed border area between Sudan and the new Republic of South Sudan."

Then he hit her with the heavy stuff. "How unstable is the situation on the ground?"

"The recent increase in attacks indicates the Sudanese government in Khartoum has unleashed the Janjaweed in a new, but still low-intensity round of genocide in the area. We are expecting a repeat of the violence in Darfur. Khartoum is fighting desperately to hold on to the area, and the external violence seems to be quieting their internal dissidents, insulating them from the 'Arab Spring'."

"Who are the major players? I'm looking for names and faces, Major." For Fitzgerald, conflict was a personal thing and leadership made the difference between victory and defeat.

She typed a command on the podium's keyboard, and a photo of an overweight officer wearing a medal-bedecked uniform that stretched over his potbelly materialized on the screen. "This is Major Hamid Waleed, the commander of the Sudanese Army garrison at Malakal. While Malakal is nominally part of South Sudan, the Sudanese have not withdrawn their army, adding to regional instability." She didn't remind Fitzgerald that the 4440th was based at the airfield at Malakal. "Waleed was a key player in Darfur." She quickly recapped how the Government of Sudan had armed Baggara horsemen, the Janjaweed, in Darfur and implemented a program of genocide, murdering African tribesmen. When the task proved too big for the Janjaweed, the government sent in the army with armed helicopters to complete the killing in that part of western Sudan.

The image on the screen changed to a tall, bearded man in a ceremonial robe and riding a magnificent horse. He clutched a gold-plated AK-47 in his right hand. "This is Sheikh Amal Jahel of the Rizeigat, a tribe of the nomadic Bedouin Baggara people. He leads the Fursan, the cavaliers or horsemen of the Baggara, who form the core of the Janjaweed. Unlike Waleed, Jahel is reported to be fearless and commands the absolute loyalty of the Fursan and the Janjaweed. The AK-47 was presented to him by a Chinese peace delegation."

"How does all this affect our mission in the area?"

"Sir, that is beyond my pay grade, but I can offer an opinion."

"Offer."

"First, we are in the process of re-evaluating the threat. If the crash was caused by hostile action, we may have to pull back from the forward relief area and confine our operations to more secure areas. Second, the accident aircraft was delivered to the Air Force in 1976 and was the low-time airframe of the six Hercules deployed to the Sudan. If the crash was caused by structural failure, we may have to ground the remaining five pending an inspection, or replace them with more modern aircraft."

"And if we can't do any of the above?"

Her eyes softened. "Then expect more losses, sir."

"Thank you, Major Sharp. Stay on top of the situation. A daily briefing." Notes were made all around and she was placed on the schedule. The major set the remote control on the podium as Richards caught her eye and signaled for her to wait in the corridor. She hurried out.

Fitzgerald looked down the table. "The 4440th needs a commander. Any names?" Normally, the selection of a detachment commander would have been made at the wing and numbered Air Force level, far below the Pentagon. But the 4440th was in a unique position and outside the normal hierarchy and chain of command. His staff had been expecting that question and a list with five names was passed to him. He quickly read it and the short description after each name. They were all dedicated, highly educated, competent, and superbly trained professionals who were deathly afraid to say or do anything that anyone might find objectionable. He wasn't impressed. A name came to him from the time he commanded Air Combat Command. "Lieutenant Colonel David Orde Allston."

Around the table, fingers danced on BlackBerries to research the name. The lieutenant general who served as Deputy Chief of Staff for Manpower and Personnel studied the readout in front of him. "He made the news last week and certainly had an interesting career. Over two thousand hours flying F-15s, and a top gun at William Tell." William Tell was the Air Force's live-fire fighter gunnery competition held every other year. The general quickly scrolled down, scanning Allston's career. "He was later reprimanded as a squadron commander when a sexual discrimination complaint was filed against him. The charges were dismissed, but he was relieved of command and put out to pasture flying C-130s." As an afterthought, he added, "He was married and divorced three times, and has a daughter and stepson who live with him."

"And he shot down a MiG," Fitzgerald replied.

Richards sensed Fitzgerald knew more about Allston than he was letting on and tested the waters. "He has an interesting nickname."

"Mad Dawg," Fitzgerald replied.

"There is another problem," the director of personnel said. "He retired two months ago."

"Un retire him."

"Sir," Richards said, "may I ask why you selected this Mad Dawg?" She deliberately stressed Allston's nickname to make her point. "I would have thought an officer with experience interfacing with our allies would be more suitable."

Fitzgerald gave her high marks but it was time for the shock treatment. "If you mean more politically correct, you thought wrong, Brigadier." He studied Richards for a moment. She was among the best the Air Force had, yet he doubted she understood. Allston was a fighter pilot and could lead men and women in combat, a personality type that had long been driven out of the Pentagon and an increasing rarity in the Air Force. And there was no doubt in Fitzgerald's mind that his five C-130s in the Sudan were in combat and harm's way. He relented and gave her a reason that was true, as far as it went. "He'll do what it takes to get the job done." The meeting was over.

Richards waited until Fitzgerald had left before gathering up her notes. As expected, Gillian Sharp was waiting in the corridor. "Walk with me, Major," she commanded. "Do you go by Gillian?"

"I prefer Jill, ma'am." She fell in beside the one-star general, all too aware they looked like a female Mutt and Jeff team. Richards was everything she was not; tall, slender, graceful, and movie star beautiful. She was also well connected politically and rumored to have a sponsor who trumped any four-star general.

"You impressed the general. What's your background?"

"Thank you, ma'am. I've spent most of my career with the DIA working the African Desk as an area specialist. I did a tour teaching Geography and Geopolitics at the Air Force Academy, and a year in Afghanistan." She didn't mention the numerous times she had been to Africa on temporary assignments as that went with her job.

"May I ask how old you are?"

"I turned thirty-eight last month."

"Married? Children?" A slight shake of the head answered her. "Well, Jill, you're old enough to understand your situation. You have the general's attention and are in a unique position to make a difference."

"Thank you, ma'am. I'll do my job as best I can."

"We have a problem. Fitzgerald is a dinosaur who should have been put out to pasture twenty years ago." Anger edged her words. "Look who he selected to command the 4440th. Unbelievable." Her voice echoed with disgust. "It was a chance to demonstrate to the world we have changed and are team players. But what do we get? An over-the-hill fighter jock, an absolute throwback. Fitzgerald doesn't understand the world has evolved and our place in it. World opinion counts because it conveys legitimacy. That was the big lesson of the Iraq fiasco. Fortunately, our political masters understand that." She pulled out the big guns. "That is why the Speaker of the House created the Office of Military-Political Affairs and made sure I headed it."

Jill glanced up at the general. She understood all too well what Richards was telling her and didn't like the implications. Richards was a political general on the make, and generals on the make used subordinates like Jill as stepping-stones to promotion.

"The way we employ our Air Force," Richards continued, "requires legitimacy in the court of world opinion, and every command decision we make must reflect that reality. Your job is to help make sure Merlin understands that. Everything you tell him must be filtered through that prism." She gave Jill a quick smile. "I hope I can rely on your help . . . and discretion." Now the carrot. "I think you would make an excellent member of my team and help bring the Air Force into the Twenty-First Century."

"I hope it's not a breech birth, ma'am."

The general laughed. "Jill, I think we are going to get along just fine."

* * *

The captain held the door leading into the Office of Military-Political Affairs. "We're in the E-Ring now," he told David Allston. It was a gentle reminder they were in the command section of the Pentagon. "Brigadier General Richards is expecting you." Allston suppressed a groan. He was still suffering from jet lag and a lack of sleep after catching the red-eye from San Francisco. The recall to active duty had come as a total surprise and he was still wondering what had driven that decision. The Air Force was full of active-duty lieutenant colonels and colonels who would jump at chance for an independent command, no matter how small. Still, there was no mistaking the urgency behind the order to report to the Pentagon. This was his fifth stop as he worked his way through the staff receiving a series of briefings on his assignment. "The General expects you to report in a military manner," the captain said.

"I think I can remember how to do that," Allston reassured him. The captain spoke to a secretary who buzzed Richards' inner sanctum. She motioned them to chairs to wait. Allston smiled at her. "Is it still fifteen minutes for majors, ten minutes for lieutenant colonels, and five minutes for colonels?" he asked. The time kept waiting was an old Pentagon pecking-order game many generals still played.

The secretary gave him an angry look only to be met with his lopsided grin. Something softened inside her. "Can I get you a cup of coffee? Tea?"

"Now that's a first," the captain escorting Allston grumbled.

"Thanks, but no thanks," Allston replied.

Exactly ten minutes later, the secretary ushered Allston into Richards' office. The secretary gave Allston a sweet smile, hoping he would ask her out to coffee. Allston snapped a sharp salute. "Lieutenant Colonel Allston reporting as directed." It wasn't "as ordered," which was his way of reminding the general that she was not in his chain of command.

Richards returned the salute and let him stand at attention. It was her way of establishing control. It was also a mistake since it gave Allston time to size her up. His eyes roamed around her office, taking in the plaques and photographs. There was not a single item indicating she had ever been close to operations, or an airplane for that matter. "You're wearing the retro service dress jacket," she told him. "It was phased out last year." The jacket was a throwback to the 1940's with a belt and patch pockets.

Allston played the game. He went to parade rest, his hands clasped behind his back. "Permission to speak," he said.

She smiled indulgently. "Permission to speak is not necessary, Colonel. We're not the Marines."

"Thank you ma'am. At least this looks military and reminds folks of our heritage, and not a bus driver."

"I take it you wouldn't be caught dead in the new uniform?"

"Only if I wanted to be laughed out of the nearest bar."

She gave him the tight smile. "I designed it, Colonel."

Not the best of beginnings, he thought. "My apologies, ma'am, but I believe it is counterproductive."

"How so?"

"The new uniform is a fashion statement. No staying power, which is what the military is all about."

She dropped the subject. "Well, Colonel, I'm your last briefing." That wasn't true, and Allston had one more stop that she didn't need to know about. "It's critical that you understand the 4440th Special Airlift Detachment's unique position. You fall under the operational command of the United Nations Relief and Peacekeeping Mission, Southern Sudan." Allston already knew that. "That command arrangement is part of the quid pro quo for our participation in the United Nations Sudanese relief operation. That means you are outside the normal command and control of AFRICOM and the NMCC." AFRICOM was US Africa Command, the unified command

14

in charge of US forces in Africa that reported directly to the NMCC, the National Military Command Center.

"That does not mean you are a free agent. You take direct logistical support from the Air Force and you are to consider yourself part of the Air Force at all times. However, operationally you will respond to the UN Relief and Peacekeeping Mission. As this is part of the White House's new foreign policy initiatives, you will liaison with my office."

"Yes, ma'am," he replied.

"There is one more thing," she said flatly. "You have a reputation for singing rude drinking songs, smoking cigars, and drinking, all of which must stop."

"I only sing in the shower now, gave up cigars years ago, and hardly drink."

She frowned. "And womanizing."

"I did do market studies between wives."

"Today's Air Force strongly discourages that type of conduct. Do you understand?"

"Completely."

"Good. Dismissed."

"Thank you, ma'am." He threw a sharp salute and beat a dignified retreat, glad to escape the lion's den.

Outside, Allston checked the time. He thanked the captain escorting him and said he wanted to join a friend for dinner and could find his own way. The captain was glad to escape and took off. The secretary looked at him expectantly, hoping she was the friend. Allston gave her his best grin and ambled down the hall towards the riverfront. He walked into an outer office and was immediately ushered into General John "Merlin" Fitzgerald. The general returned his salute and came to his feet, extending his right hand. "Welcome back aboard." Fitzgerald pointed to a couch and sat down beside him.

"Dave, I inherited a can of worms on this one and have dropped you into it. I would have never let the 4440th be placed under the operational control of the UN and cannot think of a surer way to hang our people out to dry, especially in an area that is coming apart." His jaw hardened. "I'm not going to let that happen, but the Air Force has been effectively sidelined. Right now, I only have one dog in this fight – you." He spent the next eighteen minutes detailing Allston's marching orders and what he expected.

When he finished, Allston shook his head. "General, this sucks. You've got better things to do with your time than have me reporting directly to you through a back channel. You need to set up a special directorate for this type of thing."

"Unfortunately, that directorate is the Office of Military-Political Affairs that Congress created. I believe you've met Brigadier General Richards."

Allston leaned back and groaned loudly.

TWO

Over South Sudan

Captain Marci Jenkins didn't know what to make of her new commander. The 4440th had received word he was coming and his reputation had spread like wildfire through the detachment. The reaction was universal – they had been lumbered with a broken-down fighter pilot, the last thing trash haulers needed. The acting commander of the detachment, Major Dick Lane, had bit his tongue and detailed her to fly a C-130 to Bole International Airport at Addis Ababa in Ethiopia and pick him up. Once on the ground, Allston had simply walked up to the waiting Hercules and introduced himself. Surprisingly, he was wearing a gray-green ABU, the Airman Battle Uniform, and not a dress uniform. He wasn't what she had expected.

The flight from Bole was just over ninety minutes and she asked if he would like to sit in the copilot's seat and fly the Hercules. He gave her his lopsided grin, settled into the seat, and took control. She was impressed with the smooth and instinctive way Allston flew the C-130. Even Technical Sergeant Leroy Riley, the flight engineer, noticed the way he brought the old bird onto the step with ease, increasing their airspeed and lowering fuel consumption. Most pilots only talked about it, and many denied it could be done. But their airspeed and fuel flow were ample proof it could. "How's she feel?" Marci Jenkins asked from the left seat.

"Just like old times," Allston replied.

"I thought you flew fighters," Marci said.

"I did, until I got my" – he almost said "tit in a wringer," but caught himself in time – "my sweet young body in trouble and was put out to pasture flying Herks until I retired. It was a great assignment and I love the C-130. It is one fantastic bird, probably the closest thing there is to a four-engine fighter."

"Not this one," she cautioned. "It belongs in the Boneyard."

"I don't know about that," Allston replied. He fell silent. By his standards, it was a relaxed flight. They were on a westerly heading, flying at 18,000 feet, and making a groundspeed of 320 knots. The terrain below was a mottled-brown grassland with clumps of low trees and bushes, much as he had expected. Ahead, he saw the green corridor that marked the White Nile as it snaked its way north. It was all he needed to find the airfield. "There, on the nose," he said. Marci leaned forward and looked over the instrument panel, but couldn't see what he was seeing. "The air patch – on the eastern side of the dogleg where the river turns north again," Allston explained, talking her eyes onto the airfield. She checked the GPS and looked again. Her eyes followed the green corridor, still not finding the airfield.

"You got good eyeballs," Riley said. He was sitting between them and aft of the center console. He liked their new boss, but sensed that Captain Marci Jenkins was not a happy camper. She had worshipped their former commander, Lieutenant Colonel Anne McKenzie. Everyone had liked the popular McKenzie and had despaired at her death, especially Marci, and he understood why the captain would be reluctant to give her allegiance to any newcomer, much less a macho fighter pilot.

"I've got it," Marci said, taking control of the aircraft. She still couldn't see the airfield at Malakal, but she was the aircraft commander. "Before descent checklist," she called. It was the copilot's job to read the checklist and she wanted to see if Allston would stay in the right hand seat and play copilot. He did and started through the checklist.

The flight engineer realized Allston was reciting the checklist from memory. "Damn, Colonel, when did you do that?"

"Do what, Riley?" Allston replied.

"Memorize the checklist."

"I reviewed the tech manual on the flight over. It all came back."

"I'd prefer you to read the checklist," Marci said, establishing her authority.

"You bet," Allston said. He scrolled down the checklist. Then, "Captain, do you mind circling the area and pointing out the local landmarks?"

"Besides the river and the town, there's not much," she answered. "You'll see it all during the approach."

"What do you use for an I.P.?" The Initial Point was an easily identifiable geographical reference a few miles from the end of each runway that pilots used to enter the landing pattern.

"We don't have one," she replied. "We use the GPS. There's no control tower."

18

Allston made a mental note. He had some work to do. "Thanks for the stick time. I'll give it back to Bard." Allston crawled out of the copilot's seat to let First Lieutenant Bard Green do his job, and strapped into the empty navigator's seat. He made another mental note. He watched the crew as they entered the landing pattern and landed on Runway 23, to the southwest. The approach and landing were okay but nothing to write home about.

Malakal, South Sudan

Marci rolled out long. "The compound is at the southwestern end of the field," she explained. Allston stood behind the copilot as they taxied to the end of the 6600-foot runway and turned off to the left into the parking area with a big hangar on the far side. "Let me be the first to welcome you to Malakal," the loadmaster said over the intercom, "the garden spot of the Sudan, or South Sudan, or whatever."

"Some garden," Bard Green snorted. "Now we got the heat, a hundred to one-oh-five every day. But the humidity ain't too bad, around thirty percent. Wait until August when the Nile floods and the humidity hits eighty-percent and the bugs come out. At least it cools down a little but it's still not pleasant. Everyone wants to get the hell out of here."

Allston listened to the crew complain as they taxied into the parking area. That in itself was not a bad thing, and he expected a lot of bitching and moaning. A single crew chief came out to meet them and motioned them to a corner of the square ramp. Allston automatically counted three other white C-130s parked in a ragged line with little semblance of order. "Where's the fifth bird?" he asked. Marci said it was flying a relief mission and the three C-130s on the ground were down for maintenance. He made another mental note. He climbed off the flight deck as the loadmaster opened the crew entrance door, on the left side of the aircraft, immediately aft of the flight deck. Rather than deplane, Allston walked past the hatch and into the cargo compartment. It was filthy. He turned to the loadmaster, only to discover he was alone on the airplane. "What the hell?" he muttered.

He clambered down the crew entrance stairs and the heat hit him. A worried looking major wearing a sweat-stained flightsuit was waiting beside a battered pickup truck. He threw Allston a sloppy salute. "Welcome to Malakal, hell's half acre. I'm Major Dick Lane, acting honcho and your Ops Officer." The Operations Officer was a key member of any flying unit and Allston returned his salute.

He introduced himself and they shook hands. "Glad to meet you, Major. You look like a man carrying the weight of the world."

Relief flooded over Lane as he unloaded his problems on his new commander. "Colonel, this place is falling apart and no one gives a damn. We got three birds down for lack of parts, and the UN changes the rules daily, make that hourly. We haven't got a clue if we're coming or going, and morale is in the dirt." He jutted his chin in the direction of the hangar. "I've got an accident investigation team inside headed by a bird colonel who is chomping at the bit to get to the crash site. But I can't get permission from the UN to fly them into Abyei. That's the village near the crash site. We haven't even recovered the bodies yet . . . this place really sucks."

Allston took command. "Then let's do something about it. First things first. Get this bird refueled, the accident investigation team ready to board, and a crew out here." Another thought came to him. "And load a pallet of relief supplies, anything that's handy. While that's happening get all the crew chiefs and the Maintenance officer out here ASAP."

"You're gonna love Lieutenant Colonel Malaby," Lane said. He keyed his hand-held communicator to make it happen while Allston walked around the three C-130s parked nearby. They were as dirty as the aircraft he flew in on. He didn't even want to look inside. He paced the ramp and waited. Ten minutes later, eighteen airmen and sergeants managed to find their way out of the hangar and cluster under a wing taking advantage of the shade. But there was no Lieutenant Colonel Malaby. Allston checked his watch and walked over to the group. A sergeant called them to attention, turned and saluted.

Allston returned the salute. "At ease. This is a work area and we're in less than friendly territory, so don't salute. I don't need someone taking a pot shot at me. He might be able to shoot and that would ruin my day." He gave them his crooked grin and saw them relax. But they didn't know what was coming. He spoke in a low voice, making them strain to listen. "I'm Lieutenant Colonel David Allston, your new boss." He paused for effect. "I just got here and so far, I'm not impressed." His tone was soft and friendly, his words were not. "And it's your fault. Since you don't know me, this is your lucky day and you get a second chance." He motioned to the Hercules being refueled. "I'm taking that bird up for a few hours and when I get back, I expect to be impressed."

He studied their body language. He hadn't gotten through. "You're crew chiefs and these are your birds." His voice hardened, challenging them. "You own them, not the Department of Defense, not the Air Force, not me, not the Maintenance officer, not the flight crews. You! Line 'em up and make this ramp look military. Then wash 'em down and clean 'em up. Hose out the cargo compartments. Make 'em shine." He let his words sink in. "They deserve better. A lot better."

"Colonel," a hesitant voice called, "how do we wash them down? There's no water supply on the ramp and we need a pumper truck, which we ain't got."

"I saw a fire station with two trucks at the main terminal when we taxied in. One looked like a pumper to me. Use it."

"Sir, they won't let us use it. We . . ."

Allston cut the speaker off. "Start a fire. Then bribe 'em after they get here. You're in Africa, Sergeant."

An African-American sergeant came to attention and boomed, "Yes, sir! We'll make it happen." A big smile spread across his face revealing a magnificent set of teeth. "Welcome to the Forty-four Fortieth, sir."

"Your name, Sergeant."

"Staff Sergeant Loni Williams."

"Sergeant Williams, as of now you're in charge of this detail. Make things happen." Allston motioned the sergeant over, surprised by his muscular build. He was short and reminded him of a fireplug. "Please tell Colonel Malaby to be waiting when I get back," he said in a low voice.

"Yes, sir," Williams replied, his smile wider still. "She ain't gonna like that. She thinks she should be the detachment commander."

Allston arched an eyebrow. "Tough tacos, Sergeant." He sensed he had an ally. "Hey, I could have said 'tough shit.'" He spun around to check on the C-130. Refueling was complete and the pallet of relief supplies loaded. A very unhappy Captain Marci Jenkins and her crew were walking back out to the aircraft. He motioned her over for a quiet word.

"I'm taking the accident investigation team to Abyei and need your help."

"Sir," she said, "we can't land anywhere but here without clearance from the UN. You're asking me to violate our standing orders. I won't do that."

He nodded. "I'm not asking you to. I'm asking you to be my copilot."

"Sir, when was the last time you flew a Hercules?"

"About an hour ago. I had my last flight check five months ago, before I retired. It's still good."

"But you have to be checked out by an instructor pilot to be current, sir. And we don't have an IP now." McKenzie, the dead commander, had been the only instructor pilot in the detachment.

"You've just been upgraded to IP, Captain, and I'm your first check out." Marci bit her lip, not sure what to do. "You'll miss all the action," he

21

coaxed. She nodded, still chewing on her lip. "Great. Get the investigation team on board and let's go have some fun."

Abyei

"That's the village," Marci said from the right seat. "We normally land on the road on the southern side, about three-thousand feet of hard pack." Allston leaned forward in the left seat and studied the area. He made a decision and called for the before landing checklist. "Sir," Marci protested, "we don't have clearance from the UN to land."

"Right," Allston replied. He turned to the flight engineer. "Riley, did you see the Door Warning light flash?"

"Sorry, sir. I missed it."

"Right. But it's a safety of flight item. We need to land and check it out."

"At the nearest suitable field," Marci cautioned, quoting from the flight manual.

"This one looks suitable to me," Allston replied. "Before landing checklist." Marci shook her head and read the checklist. Allston turned over the village at 2000 feet to announce their presence and saw smoke from cooking fires hanging in the air. There was no wind to worry about as they entered a short downwind to land on an easterly heading towards the refugee compound. Allston flew a classic short-field landing and planted the Hercules hard. He reversed the props while the nose was still in the air and rolled out in less than 1400 feet.

"Nice landing," the flight engineer murmured. It had been years since he had seen an approach and landing that precise. Even the reluctant Marci was impressed.

They came to a halt as two white pickups from the village raced out to meet them. "That must be the welcoming committee," Allston said.

"They're UN relief workers," Marci replied.

"Loadmaster," Allston said over the intercom. "Tell the investigation team I'm going to arrange transportation to the crash site and they've got four hours to get back here. I will leave without them." He grinned at Marci as he unbuckled. "That should get their attention. Okay folks, let's go make it happen."

"No way I'm gonna miss this," the flight engineer said. The entire crew followed Allston outside to wait for the surprised relief workers to arrive. Within minutes, Allston convinced the four relief workers that they had made a precautionary landing to check out an unsafe condition, traded the pallet of supplies for use of their trucks, and sent the investigation team on their way to the crash site. "Four hours," he yelled at them. "Let's go look at the refugee camp," he said to Marci.

Nothing in Allston's experience had prepared him for what was waiting inside the compound walls. Dirty, gaunt-eyed children with swollen bellies sat in the dirt as flies swirled through the still, stifling, acrid air. Their eyes followed the Americans in silence. A mother nursed a dying infant, and Marci looked away, the only way she could handle it. Without a word, a relief worker led them to a makeshift hospital. "There's not much we can do," the woman explained. She bent over a three year-old child lying in a cot. Her right arm had been blown off by an AK-47 round and her stomach ripped open. "What you brought today will help and we might be able to save her."

The little girl looked at him, her beautiful dark eyes calm, not begging, not pleading for help. She reached out with her left hand and held his right index finger. Something deep in Allston turned. "Who did this?" he asked.

"Janjaweed." The relief worker related how the Baggara, Arabized nomads from the state of Western Darfur, had been organized into militias by the Sudanese government and unleashed in a campaign of genocide against the non-Islamic African tribes of the south. "At first, the killing was limited to Darfur, but the Baggara have moved eastward and brought their families with them. The South Sudanese are fighting back as best they can but this is more typical."

Allston looked at the wounded child. "I mean, who specifically did this?"

"The villagers say it was Jahel. He's the leader of the local Fursan, or horsemen of the Rizeigat tribe. About one-fourth of the village is Rizeigat. The Fursan consider themselves the elite warriors of the Baggara. They openly brag they shot the C-130 down." She looked at the infant. "I don't know why he does this."

A burning sensation clawed at Allston. "Apparently this Jahel likes to kill and maim innocent children."

"And you never dropped a bomb on civilians?" the relief worker asked.

"Not knowingly," Allston replied. Strangely, he was not upset by her question that was really an accusation. "And they were always doing their damnedest to kill me at the time." He paused, thinking. "The Rizeigat and Africans seem to be getting along here."

"Only because we're here," the relief worker replied. "We're all that's between them and starvation. The moment we pull out, the Rizeigat will massacre the Dinkas."

The burning sensation in Allston grew more intense. "Is the child Dinka?"

The worker's simple "Yes" pounded at Allston. He had to walk away. Marci stared at his back. "Let him be," the worker counseled. She had seen it before when the barbarity of the Sudan tore a person apart. "He has to make a decision."

Allston made it. There were no second thoughts or doubts, and he knew it was right. He turned to the two women, forever changed. "I'll do what I can. Let's go." He spun around and walked out of the camp, back to the waiting Hercules.

Marci hurried after him, not understanding what had happened to him. "There's nothing you can do, Colonel."

Allston kept walking, his eyes sweeping the village, taking it all in. He fixed her with a hard, challenging look. "I didn't sign up to ignore this. Did you?"

* * *

BermaNur squatted in front of his mother's hut and shoveled the last of the sorghum porridge into his mouth. He used a finger to wipe the pot and sucked it clean. The teenager froze when the two Americans walked past. The man was wearing an army style uniform and the woman the flightsuit he had seen so many times before. He came to his feet and ran into the hut for his communicator. He hit the transmit switch. "Jahel, the Americans are in the village now." He had already warned the sheik that the C-130 had landed.

"How did this happen?" Jahel asked. BermaNur heard the clatter of trotting hooves in the background.

"There was no warning the Americans were coming this time." He had to make Jahel understand. "There is always warning."

"They must not take off," Jahel replied.

"I will stop them," the teenager said. He ran after the Americans, determined to keep his promise. He reached the road and scrambled up the same low hummock as before. The Hercules was parked on the road, two hundred meters in front of him. He sat down to wait. His eyes narrowed as children from the village swarmed around the Americans, begging for food. With nothing left to give, the tall American pilot picked up one of the children and carried him piggyback as he walked around the big plane, giving the flock of older boys an impromptu tour.

24

* * *

Allston sat the child down when the accident investigation team returned. The colonel leading the team climbed out of the lead pickup, weary and dirty. "How did it go?" Allston asked.

The colonel shook his head. "We didn't have near enough time. We took photos and what measurements we could." He paused, obviously upset. "We found the graves. Someone had buried them." He reached into his pocket and handed Allston a handful of dog tags. "One of the relief workers had these." Allston read the five names and handed them to Marci.

Her face was a mask. "They were my buddies." She handed the dog tags back to the colonel.

"Any idea what caused the crash?" Allston asked.

"The site has been looted and even with a full-blown investigation, we'll never know for certain now. But it wasn't a surface-to-air missile."

"That means pilot error," Allston said, "or mechanical failure."

"It wasn't pilot error," Marci said, conviction in her voice. "Anne was too damn good a pilot."

"Lieutenant Colonel McKenzie?" Allston asked, a little surprised by the familiarity. Marci nodded. Allston thought for a moment. He nodded. "Okay, lets go." He shook hands with the boys who still surrounded them and led the way onto the C-130. The loadmaster pulled up the stairs and locked the hatch.

* * *

Apprehension swept over BermaNur when a propeller started to turn. By the time all four engines were on line, he was on his feet and filled with worry. When the big aircraft reversed thrust and backed down the road for takeoff, he panicked. He keyed his communicator, "Jahel! They are leaving!"

"We're almost there," came the answer. "Stop them!"

The teenager didn't know what to do but the aircraft had stopped at the far end of the road. The nose lowered as the engines spun up and the props bit into the air. The aircraft started to roll. In the distance, far behind the aircraft, he saw a cloud of dust that had to be Jahel and his band of Fursan. Now the Hercules was roaring down the dirt road, coming directly at him and away from the charging horsemen. BermaNur ran out into the road and held up his arms, willing the plane to stop.

*   *   *

"Colonel!" Marci shouted. "There's a kid on the road!"

"Got him," Allston replied. He had a problem. There was not enough room to stop or to swerve. Luckily, the aircraft was lightweight and they were accelerating smartly. But could they come unglued from the dirt road in the distance remaining? Allston pulled back on the yoke and willed the Hercules to break free of the shackles that bound it to the earth. It did. "Gear up," he ordered. Marci's left hand flashed and snapped the gear lever on the instrument panel to the retract position.

BermaNur wanted the aircraft to hit him. He firmly believed Allah would honor his sacrifice and wreak vengeance on the Americans. But the plane passed safely overhead. He turned to the north and saw the band of horsemen charging towards him. It was Jahel. He faced the riders and steeled his will to resist any blame for not stopping the Americans from leaving.

On board the Hercules, the gear was moving. Allston leveled off at 200 feet above the ground and turned out to the east, avoiding the village. He looked back and saw the boy standing in the road, unhurt. The gear clunked into place. "Who were the guys on the horses?" he wondered.

Malakal

The C-130 turned off the runway and Allston taxied slowly into the compound. "Sweet Jesus," Riley, the flight engineer, said. "I was certain we were gonna hit that kid."

"It was close," Allston said. He gave them his crooked grin. "No harm, no foul. Feather the outboards." Riley shut down engines one and four. "Check that out," Allston said. The area was a beehive of activity. The four Hercules were marshaled into rows, two on each side of the ramp, their noses pointed inward. A fire truck was washing the last one down and the Herks gleamed in the sun, their white paint clean and radiant. A smiling Loni Williams threw them a sharp salute when they taxied past. A crew chief and two wing walkers ran out to meet them and backed them into an open spot on the left. The fire truck drove up, closely followed by a fuel browser.

"I'll be damned," Riley muttered. "The place looks like military."

A white pickup slammed to a stop in front of the nose and a bird-like woman dressed in the same style ABU that Allston wore got out. Her UN blue beret was perched jauntily on her short and curly brown hair and she wore big sunglasses, reminding Allston of a chipmunk. She stood five foot two and paced nervously back and forth. "Is that our Colonel Malaby?" Allston mused.

"The one and only," Riley replied.

They shut the engines down. "Loadmaster," Allston said over the intercom, "stay on board and help the crew chiefs sweep out all the crap on the cargo deck. Then clean the bird up, make it shine." He got out of the seat and deplaned to meet Malaby.

She was more than ready for him. "Lieutenant Colonel Susan Malaby," she snapped, introducing herself. She charged ahead. "Colonel, you've managed to drive whatever morale that was still hiding around here into the dirt, and are now the most hated man south of the Pentagon. And you did all that within twenty minutes after getting here. That's got to be a record."

Allston cocked his head and thought for a moment, sizing her up. "Tell you what, Colonel. You worry about getting the planes flying and I'll worry about morale. And that's south of Bumfuck Egypt, not the Pentagon."

"Bumfuck Egypt? I never heard of it."

"According to legend, Bumfuck was the worst assignment in the whole fucking Air Farce." He looked around. "In fact, that's what we're gonna call this place, Bumfuck South. See if you can get a sign painted."

"My job is fixing aircraft, not painting signs. Get me the parts we need and I'll get 'em flying."

"Will do. For now, cannibalize like hell." She looked at him in shock. Removing parts from a downed aircraft to keep others flying took special permission that required reams of paperwork. Getting a Papal Dispensation was easier and faster. Before she could answer, the colonel in charge of the accident investigation team joined them.

"Colonel Allston, a word. I've talked to my team and we're going to report the most probable cause of the accident as structural failure, not pilot error or hostile action. We're going to recommend your aircraft be grounded pending inspection."

"Well," Malaby said, "that ends this discussion."

"Not hardly," Allston said. "Get 'em fixed and make 'em shine. And I still want that sign. That's all, Colonel."

He headed for the air-conditioned offices attached to the side of the big hangar to meet the rest of his staff. Major Dick Lane, his Ops Officer, and two other majors were waiting for him. One was his Logistics Officer who managed supplies and moved cargo, and the other was the Facilities Commander who took care of everything else. They escorted him on a quick tour as they briefed him on his detachment: five C-130s and 162 personnel, counting Allston. Thirty-four were aircrew, eighty-two were maintenance, twenty-two were logistics, and sixteen were facilities who took care of the mess hall, billeting, communications, administration, and the buildings. Finally, there were eight security police. The big hangar was shared by maintenance and logistics for handling relief supplies. Behind the hangar, twenty air-conditioned personnel tents along with four sleeping trailers and three huge white tents were scattered haphazardly around the area. The personnel tents were used for billeting, and two of the big tents were for warehousing relief supplies. The last white tent served as the mess hall and recreation center. The fuel dump was set well back from the hangar and near the main gate and the road that led into town. The two black, and very big fuel bladders made Allston think of giant amoebas poised to mate.

They were back in the offices within thirty minutes where an e-mail was waiting on his laptop. His United Nations masters in Addis Ababa, Ethiopia, demanded his immediate presence. He checked the time. It had been a long day and the hour was late. He replied that he would be there as soon as airlift permitted. Next, he called up his secure line and sent an e-mail to Fitzgerald.

> Some magic is needed here. Three Herks non-operational for parts.
> Need to X-ray the wing spars ASAP or will ground the fleet.
> Request an airdrop-qualified navigator.

Allston hit the send button and went to dinner in the big mess tent. He had to turn morale around and the best place to start was with the working troops.

THREE

African Union Headquarters, Ethiopia

The driver spoke English non-stop on the four-mile drive from Addis Abba's Bole International Airport. "We are here, Mr. Colonel. This is the headquarters for the African Union. The United Nations stays here." He pointed down Menelik II, the broad avenue with a wide tree-lined median, "and there, at the Hilton hotel."

"Why the Hilton?" Allston asked.

The driver laughed as he pulled to a stop in front of the steps leading to a modern office high-rise. "For lunch and afternoon activities when there is no work. Which is every day. Follow the signs to the UN Economic Commission for Africa in the third building." He turned around in his seat and gave Allston a serious look. "Hey, mon, they are not going to like seeing you in that uniform." Laughing at his own wisdom, the driver gunned the engine and shot into the heavy traffic. Allston trotted up the steps and into the main foyer. He immediately felt out of place as well-dressed men and women hurried past, all holding folders or briefcases and wearing looks of purposeful resolve.

The beautiful woman at the information desk frowned when he signed in. She gave him a visitor's badge. "Follow the signs," was all she said.

The marbled-floored halls were well marked, and he had no trouble following the brass plaques that guided him to the UN Economic Commission for Africa. He noticed a distinct pattern to the people. The men were all middle-aged or older, all African, and dressed in expensive suits. The women were more racially mixed and approximately three-fourths were young, beautiful, and dressed in high fashion. His ABUs were totally out of place. Judging by the looks he received, he assumed they had never seen a warrior in the building. The public elevator in the third building was out of order and a security guard denied him access to the elevator reserved for VIPs. He trotted up three flights of stairs and found another brass plaque that announced he had found the offices of the United Nations Relief and Peacekeeping Mission Southern Sudan. He pushed through the door and into an opulent reception area. This receptionist was even more beautiful than the first, which led to some mild speculation about the UN's hiring policies on his part. "The commissioners are expecting you." She motioned at a massive hardwood door. He shoved his blue UN beret into a pocket and pushed through.

Three civilians were sitting in easy chairs around a low circular table, drinking coffee. Reports and memos littered the table. The distinguished-looking man in the center, the head of mission, set his coffee cup down and fixed Allston with a long look, his dark face impassive. "We do not allow that type of uniform, especially when worn by a European or American," he finally said.

"My apologies, sir. I wasn't told and only directed to report here as soon as possible."

"Common sense should have told you to not wear a combat uniform. It is a reminder of our colonial history and past oppressions." The other two men nodded in agreement.

Why does everyone have a hang-up on uniforms these days? Allston wondered. "So noted," he said, sitting down.

"You were not invited to sit in our presence," the man on the left said. Allston gauged him to be a Zulu. "Please stand until you are invited to sit."

"Certainly," Allston said, coming to his feet. "Forgive me for asking, but is this why I was summoned here? For a lesson in UN protocol?"

"Your attitude is counterproductive," the Zulu said.

"May I ask counterproductive to what?" Allston replied. "My job is to fly relief for you, not look pretty."

"Counterproductive to good order and discipline," a voice from behind said. Allston turned to see a man standing against the back wall and sucked in his breath. The speaker's resemblance to the long-dead Idi Amin, the monstrous Uganda dictator, was startling. He stood well over six feet tall and wore the immaculate service dress uniform of the French Foreign Legion. The gold braid on his cuffs announced he was a colonel. He held his white kepi in his huge left hand and large medals decorated his broad chest. A double fourragère encircled his left shoulder.

"May I introduce Colonel Pierre Vermullen, La Légion Étrangère," the head of mission said. "Colonel Vermullen is the new commander of our peacekeeping forces."

30

"The side with the simplest uniform always wins," Allston said under his breath.

"Do you believe that?" Vermullen asked.

"It's a lesson of history," Allston answered. It was one of his favorite maxims.

The head of mission shook his head in disgust and moved ahead. "First, we called you here so there would no misunderstanding about your duties and obligations while serving in the Sudan." He handed Allston a folder. "These are your standing operational orders. You are to deliver supplies to refugee camps we designate and to support Colonel Vermullen in his peacekeeping mission. You will consider a request from Colonel Vermullen for support as an order from this Mission." He waited while Allston scanned the single page. "Second, we are very concerned with your unauthorized landing yesterday at the village of" – he fumbled through his notes – "Abyei."

"I had just arrived in-country and was receiving an area check out when the unsafe door warning light flashed at us. As that is a safety of flight item, I landed at the nearest suitable place to check it out, which just happened to be Abyei."

"Which caused incalculable political harm," the third man at the table said. He reminded Allston of a Nigerian general he had once met who was charming, educated, well spoken, and totally corrupt. This man was also a Nigerian but lacked the charming and civilized exterior.

"And you just happened to have an accident investigation team on board," the head of mission said.

"Since we had not received clearance to land the team for an on-site investigation, I intended to do an aerial survey. Once on the ground, it seemed logical to take advantage of the opportunity."

"It would have been much wiser," the Nigerian said, "to have continued your flight rather than land. Once on the ground, the investigation team should have never left the airplane. Discipline is critical as we withdraw our relief workers and peacekeepers to safer areas."

Allston was stunned by the news the UN was pulling back. The three men at the table stared at Allston and his anger flared. What the hell is going on here? he wondered. He forced himself to calm down and looked at the Frenchman for clues. Unfortunately, Vermullen's face was a blank. A hard silence ruled the room. The Zulu finally spoke in a low voice. "I find your attitude both arrogant and unbearable. I must recommend that you be immediately replaced."

"Fine by me," Allston said returning their stares. "I'll contact my superiors and recommend that the United States immediately withdraw all support, personnel, aircraft, and funding, for your mission. I'll be a civilian the day I get back and I'll go public with my recommendation. Given the current sentiment in the States about the UN . . ."

The head of mission interrupted him, suddenly wanting to compromise. "Lieutenant Colonel Allston, you don't understand how delicate our situation is. We are here to keep the two warring factions apart. By landing without prior permission, you appeared to be showing any favoritism to the Dinka, and violated the sovereignty of the Sudan, thereby adding to an already volatile situation."

"And exactly who holds sovereignty over that area?" Allston asked mildly.

The head of mission ignored him and checked his notes again. "The governor of Western Kordofan has filed a complaint."

"Was the governor appointed by Khartoum?" Allston asked.

"Of course. Please remember that as long as you are at Malakal, you must not show favoritism to the Government of Sudan, to any tribe, or the Republic of South Sudan. It is our presence and neutrality that keeps them apart and at peace."

Allston almost said that what he had seen did not look like neutrality or peace. An inner voice warned him to caution and he remained silent. "Thank you for coming so promptly," the head of mission said. Allston was dismissed and he quickly left, glad to escape. Outside, he asked the gorgeous secretary to please call for a staff car. He waited while she made the call in case she forgot the moment he was out of sight. Vermullen came out of the office and they walked in silence until they were out of the building and on the steps.

"You must learn to handle our UN masters," Vermullen cautioned, seemingly undisturbed by the peacekeeping mission's abandoning the southern tribes to the Sudanese. "As for the standing operational orders you were issued, I view our relationship as collegial and not as a commander and subordinate. We must work together to be effective."

"Sir, have you been out in the field?" Allston asked.

"In the Sudan? Not yet. Like you, I just arrived, but I have been on peace keeping missions in other parts of Africa many times." A staff car pulled up and a much older legionnaire hustled to open the door. "Ah, there's Hans. On the spot, as always. By the way, you were right about the uniforms." The private held the door and snapped a sharp open-handed salute as the colonel squeezed his bulk inside. The car drove off and another staff car arrived, this one a black Mercedes flying a UN flag. The head of the peacekeeping mission came down the steps with the gorgeous secretary from his office on his arm. They ignored him and got inside.

"Over here, Mr. Colonel," a voice said. It was Allston's driver.

"Any idea where they're going?" Allston asked.

"The Hilton, where else?" the driver replied. "For lunch and afternoon activities." He led the way to their car. "Where to, Mr. Colonel? The Hilton?" He laughed uproariously, enjoying his own humor.

Allston never considered it. "Where do they sell hats?" The driver pulled out into the traffic, and, within minutes, they were inching their way past crowded stalls in an open-air market. Allston saw what he wanted. "Over there." The driver stopped and Allston pointed to a stall with hats. "The stall with the tan Australian bush hats. Can you negotiate for me?" He pointed to the rugged, wide-brimmed hats with a leather chinstrap and the right side of the brim folded up and snapped to the side of the low crown.

"You want one of those?" the driver asked.

"Not one, two hundred."

Malakal

"Colonel, there's a C-17 ten minutes out," the Ops Officer, Dick Lane, said. He was monitoring the UHF radio in airlift operations, the closest thing they had to a control tower, and checked the meteorological display before keying the mike. "Roger Dumbo Four. The wind is calm, altimeter 29.99. Recommend Runway Two-three for landing, no other reported traffic."

It was Allston's first full day after returning from Addis Ababa and was still learning the ropes. "A Dumbo, isn't that unusual?" Dumbo was the call sign for a C-17 Globemaster III, the Air Force's primary heavy lifter cargo aircraft.

"Very," Lane replied. He explained that their normal logistical supply line was by truck out of Ethiopia. "The UN contracts for civilian trucks to haul all supplies. I'd guess that over half the loads are stolen or hijacked along the way. They even take JP5, which they can't use." JP5 was the jet fuel the C-130s burned. "We buy it back from the bastards who stole it. According to rumor, the three UN commissioners get a couple of million euros a month from kickbacks outta the arrangement. Needless to say, someone is gonna be very pissed." The two men walked out to the ramp to watch the Air Force's main cargo lifter taxi in. "That's what I want to fly," Lane said, his voice wistful.

"But you're stuck in Herks," Allston said. Lane nodded in reply, a less than happy man.

The C-17 taxied into the compound, its 170-foot wingspan barely clearing the parked C-130s. Sergeant Loni Williams and two wing walkers guided it through a tight turn and, by judicious reversing of thrust, were able to turn it around. Lieutenant Colonel Susan Malaby, Allston's cantankerous maintenance officer, was beside herself as the cargo was offloaded. "Colonel," she called, "we're golden! We even got the engine we needed." A new Allison T56 turboprop engine on its dolly rolled down the huge aircraft's cargo ramp under the high T-tail. Maintenance crews quickly rolled it over to a parked C-130 that had been grounded waiting for an engine change. The old engine was already off and mounted on a dolly for return shipment.

Then pallet after pallet of supplies was offloaded, effectively doubling their stocks of essential parts and supplies. "Can you believe that?" Allston's Logistics officer said. He actually bounced in excitement. Allston berated himself for being so slow. His troops wanted to do their job and all he had to do was to supply the wherewithal. But could he take them to the next level? He didn't know, but he had to try.

A four-man maintenance team got off the C-17 with a pallet of equipment for X-raying the wings. Finally, a strange looking captain wearing a flightsuit walked down the ramp loaded with bags and an old leather suitcase strapped closed with a belt. 'Mandrake the Magician' was stenciled on the side of the suitcase in faded gold letters. He seemed to wilt in the heat as he struggled with his load. Sergeant Loni Williams took pity on him and shouldered part of the load. Williams pointed to Allston and Lane and the two made their way across the ramp. The newcomer carefully set the suitcase down. He threw Allston a salute. "Captain Glen Libby reporting for duty."

Allston studied the man, not sure if he should send him back. Libby stood five feet six with a potato-like body and toothpick arms and legs. His face reminded Allston of a bulldog. Then it hit him. Libby was a remake of a young Winston Churchill. "Don't salute outside," Allston told him, returning the salute. He glanced at Libby's nametag. There was no star over his navigator wings, which meant he hadn't been flying that long, and his full name was Glen G. Libby. "What's the G. stand for?" Allston asked.

"It's Glen Gordon," Libby replied. "Everyone calls me G.G." It sounded like Gigi and Lane suppressed a chuckle. He considered navigators a hold-over from the past and no longer needed in the modern Air Force.

Allston's and Lane's communicators squawked simultaneously. The gate guard was calling with the news that two Sudanese Army trucks had barged through the gate without stopping. "Well, we better go howdy those folks," Allston said. He headed for the detachment's offices but didn't get far. Two weapons carrier type trucks sped around the corner of the hangar and headed directly for the C-17. Two soldiers stood in the back of each truck manning a machine gun mounted over the cab. The trucks slammed to a halt, and Allston's eyes narrowed as an army major got out of the lead truck. He was heavyset and his potbelly strained at the buttons on his uniform. A web belt was strapped around his middle with a holster holding a large, well-used automatic.

"The commander of the army garrison in town," Lane whispered. "A real bastard."

"Major Hamid Waleed, Army of Sudan," the newcomer announced in a rapid-fire, staccato bark. "Don't you salute your superior officers?" Allston extended his right hand. "I'm Lieutenant Colonel David Allston, United States Air Force. At your service." The major ignored the outstretched hand. "And, yes, I do salute my superior officers." He almost added a 'Don't you?' but thought better of it.

Waleed flushed at the rebuke that he had not recognized Allston's rank and was out-ranked. "Colonel Allston," Waleed said, "I'm here to investigate an unauthorized landing and possible smuggling." He gestured at the C-17.

"Just routine resupply," Allston explained.

"Still, I must investigate. Orders, you know. As a military man, I'm sure you understand I have no choice." He spoke to his men in Arabic and gave them lengthy instructions.

Libby walked calmly over to Loni Williams and spoke in a low voice. Williams nodded and quickly disappeared behind the C-17. The pudgy captain then joined Allston. "I speak Arabic," he said in a low voice, his back to Waleed. "He just told his men that he wants the engine that came off the Globemaster."

"What the hell for? What can they do with it? That doesn't make sense."

"It does if you're an Arab. He's establishing his authority. He figures that the engine is the most valuable thing that was offloaded."

"Crap! So I've just got to stand here and let him take it?"

"Maybe not," Libby said. "Let me talk to him. While I distract him, tell the C-17 to start engines and be ready to taxi when I give the high sign. Tell the aircraft commander to kick up dust and hose the place down with his jet wash."

Allston didn't hesitate. "Do it." Lane spoke into his communicator to make it happen. "Major Waleed," Allston called. "May we speak for a moment? May I introduce my protocol officer, Captain Libby?"

Libby made a big show of saluting Waleed and broke into a torrent of Arabic as the C-17 started engines. The surprised Waleed could only stare at Libby as he gushed on, an unbroken torrent of words as he waved his hands. Both Allston and Lane caught the 'chocks out' signal and Lane spoke into his communicator. Immediately, the huge cargo plane started to move as its big turbofan engines spun up. The aircraft commander rode the brakes as he taxied out and swerved back and forth, blasting the ramp and kicking up a huge cloud of fine dust. The C-17 turned onto the runway and stopped. The engines ran up and the big plane surged forward, taking off.

One of Waleed's soldiers ran up, still coughing from the dust, and spoke rapidly. Libby translated for Allston and Lane. "He says the aircraft was empty."

Waleed wiped his face with a grimy handkerchief. "My sergeant says that the only unauthorized item was an engine that was brought in." Libby immediately protested in Arabic but Waleed only smiled. "It is not for me to determine what is contraband. I am only following orders." Libby gave up and pointed to a dolly with the engine. Waleed spoke to his men and they quickly hitched it to the lead truck. Waleed barked a command and climbed on board. The two trucks sped away, towing the bouncing engine.

Malaby drove up in her pickup and got out. "What did they want with the old engine?" she asked.

Allston and Lane turned to Libby who only shrugged with a sheepish look on his face. "We distracted 'em while Sergeant Williams did the old switcheroo." They all stared at the strange looking captain. "Hey, if you're not cheating, you're not doing your job," Libby said in his own defense.

Allston knew when he was in the presence of a warrior, no matter how he looked. "Welcome to Bumfuck South, G.G. You wouldn't happen to be drop qualified, would you?"

"Done a few," Libby replied, "and won a few bucks." He had been on countless airdrop missions delivering everything from paratroopers to bulldozers. In his small world, he was the king of drop-qualified navigators and had won so many bets about whose load landed the closest to the mark that only the unknowing bet against him. He thought for a moment. "You want the old engine back?"

"You can do that?" Malaby asked.

"I think Sergeant Williams and I might be able to arrange something."

"Don't get your ass in a crack," Allston replied.

The Peacemakers

* * *

Allston and his small staff walked into the big hangar just after midnight. The four-man maintenance crew that had flown in on the C-17 had been working since they had arrived and were exhausted. They had erected a high framework on wheels that arched over the wing. A large black box was on the topside of the framework and mounted on a track that moved fore and aft as the framework traversed the length of the wing. The sergeant in charge explained that it was the very latest in X-ray technology combined with sonic scanning, and that when fully assembled and calibrated, they could scan the wing spars for cracks and traces of metal fatigue. "Normally it doesn't take too long to do the actual scan, but since the hangar here is not air conditioned, heat buildup is going to be a problem. Keeping the equipment in calibration is going to be a bitch."

"Do we have to prep the aircraft?" Malaby asked. The sergeant explained in detail that the aircraft had to be totally defueled as the fuel tanks were in the wings, and which inspection panels had to be removed. "That will take some time," Malaby conceded. "I'll have to stand them down to get them ready."

Allston thought for a moment. "Prep and scan our two OR birds first" – OR meant operationally ready – "and get them back into the air ASAP. Do the three hangar queens last. How long before all five will be OR?" Malaby and the sergeant conferred. They agreed they could have all five C-130s flying in six days, provided the wing spars all scanned clean and free of cracks. "We need to talk." Allston led Malaby, Lane and the other two majors into the offices on the side of the hangar. The air conditioner ground noisily, barely able to hold the temperature down to eighty-five degrees.

"We're going to hustle the next six days," Allston told them. "We're going to fix the Herks while we keep flying, and we're going to make this place look military. Move the tents and trailers into straight rows. Clean everything up. Cut down all the brush. Paint everything you can. Inventory the supply tents and find out exactly what we've got in the way of relief supplies. And get the tents organized." The four officers stared at him in astonishment. "And set up a decent laundry service. I'm tired of everyone smelling like a goat and looking like they crawled out from under a rock." He paused and smiled. "Hey, at least no one needs a haircut. Next, we got a problem with the fuel dump. We need to build a berm around the bladders to contain any leaks. Hire a local with a Bulldozer. Make it happen."

"Finally, I'd like every Dick and Jane here to fly on a relief mission. I want them to see what I saw at Abyei. But it is voluntary." He looked at

37

them. "Any questions?" Four very unhappy officers left him alone as he turned on his laptop computer and called up his secure line to send an e-mail to Fitzgerald.

> Logistics delivered. Scanning equipment being assembled and calibrated. Estimate fully operational in six days. Need more Security Police and 200 side arms.

He hit the encrypt/send button and went to bed.

FOUR

Malakal

*T*he early morning shadows retreated across the parking ramp and the five C-130s gleamed in the growing light. It was the coolest part of the day as the compound came to life, and the big hangar doors accordioned back to reveal a vacant and spotless interior. The floors had been painted and the maintenance stand used for X-raying the wings disassembled. The inspection team stood by their loaded pallet, looking very pleased with themselves. Outside, Allston and his staff walked around the aircraft. "Colonel Malaby," Allston said, "well done."

"Thank you, sir. Please tell the troops." Then, "Oh no!" She pointed to a big banner stretched high across the front of the hangar announcing BUMFUCK SOUTH. "Who did that?" Allston suppressed a laugh. He suspected a gremlin named Loni Williams had been at work. "I'll get it down," Malaby said.

"Leave it," Allston replied. They walked into the hangar as it filled with men and women, all wearing freshly laundered flightsuits or ABUs, and the UN blue beret.

"Well," Dick Lane said, "this may be the first Air Force open ranks inspection ever held in Africa." The four halted as the detachment formed up in ragged groups. Lane groaned loudly. "You can dress 'em up, but you can't take 'em out."

"Call the detachment to attention," Allston told Lane. Malaby and the two other majors stood behind Allston as Lane marched forward. He stopped and came to attention.

"Flights!" Lane bawled. "A-ten-HUT!" The 4440th more or less came to attention. Only the eight-man security police detachment had a clue and looked military. Allston told Lane to give them parade rest and the order was dutifully relayed.

Allston stepped forward. "Good morning," he said in a loud voice. "This is a new day and there should be no doubt you are in the Air Force. You are the proud aircrews and keepers of five of the finest aircraft ever built. I have told the UN Relief Mission that we are ready to support them to the max and prepared to move cargo. Our mission is to keep as many people as we can from starving, and that is exactly what we are going to do. Seven days ago, I asked that you volunteer to go on a relief mission and see what I saw. Since then, eighty-seven of you took me up on the offer. Would all of you step forward and form up in four ranks." He turned to his staff standing behind him. "You've all been on a relief mission," he reminded them. They marched out to join the others.

Allston looked over the four ranks of men and women, a mix of aircrews, maintenance, logistics, support, and security cops. "By flying on a mission, each of you has earned the right to trade in your UN beret and wear the hat of a small group dedicated to bringing hope and peace to this devastated land. It is your choice to wear the hat, but if you do, wear it with pride." He motioned for G.G. and Williams to come forward. Both were wearing an Australian bush hat with the right brim folded up and snapped to the crown, and each pushed a cart filled with the same hats. Libby selected a hat from his cart and walked over to Allston and handed him the hat.

The pudgy navigator snapped a salute. "Welcome to the Irregulars, sir."

The name surprised Allston as he returned the salute. He handed over his blue beret and donned the hat. "Carry on," he said. G.G. and Williams passed down the ranks and the UN berets were quickly exchanged for bush hats. Only Malaby hesitated. Finally, she shook her head, keeping her blue beret.

Allston faced the seventy-four men and women standing in the rear and still wearing a blue beret. "You're more than welcome to join the Irregulars. Fly a mission and see for yourself why we are here. Then trade in your beret with Captain Libby or Sergeant Williams."

Williams came to attention. "Ih-reg-u-LARS! Let's hear it. Ooh-Rah!"

On cue, the Irregulars bellowed "OOH-RAH!" It echoed over the ramp and the compound.

"Okay," Allston said. "Let's go to work. Dismissed." The hangar rapidly emptied but Malaby stood there, shaking her head.

"Rather juvenile and stupid," she told Allston.

"Hey, if it's stupid but works, it ain't stupid." He couldn't remember where he had heard it, but he hoped it was true.

E-Ring

Major Jill Sharp stood at the front of the conference room nervously fingering the remote control. Briefing General John Fitzgerald every morning was not an easy task, and most mornings she felt like a fish trapped in a barrel as he blasted her with questions. A few of his staff filtered into the room and talked easily as they waited. Brigadier Yvonne Richards swept in majestically and silenced all conversation. Jill gave a silent sigh of regret. Richards was absolutely gorgeous in the new uniform, which looked like it had been specifically designed for her. Jill knew she could never look half as good. At exactly 0700 hours, Fitzgerald entered and sat down. "Please be seated," he said. He gave Jill his friendly look, which meant it was testing time. She bit the bullet and went to work.

"Good morning, General."

"Good morning, Major. Tomorrow morning, I'd like to hear about oil and South Sudan. Okay?"

"Sir, that's my area of expertise, and I have a briefing that I updated two days ago."

Fitzgerald nodded. That was exactly the response he wanted from his staff. "Let's hear it."

Jill's fingers danced on the keyboard at the podium and a map of southern Sudan flashed on the screen. "By 2007, the ethnic cleansing of Darfur was mostly complete. The government of Sudan has now turned its attention eastward." An overlay of rectangles and squares appeared on the screen and overlaid large sections of southern Sudan, all to the east of Darfur. "The prize is oil. These are the oil concessions that the Sudanese have parceled out to foreign consortiums." She pointed to the two most southern oil concessions. "However, the border between Sudan and the Republic of South Sudan is under dispute and both governments are fighting for control of the area and the concessions."

This was what Fitzgerald wanted to hear. "Stakeholders," he asked.

She answered without missing a beat. "China holds the most concessions, Canada second. With Darfur on its western flank secure, the Sudanese government is now clearing the oil concessions of the African tribes, to reinforce their claim. They consider the Africans infidels and therefore not entitled to a single cent of the oil revenues. To that end, the Government of Sudan has again unleashed the Janjaweed, and we can expect the Sudanese Army to start operations at any time in a repeat of what we saw in Darfur. We have monitored elements of the Army moving into the states of Western Kordofan and Northern Bahr el Ghazal where the Janjaweed are active." Annotations overlaid the map on the screen correlating the Sudanese Army's movement with Janjaweed activity.

"Is the 4440th in harm's way?"

"Not at this time." Jill used a laser pointer to highlight Malakal. "While Malakal is in the disputed area, no oil had been discovered in the southern most concessions. However, there are currently four Chinese exploration team working in the area. If oil is discovered, we predict . . ."

Fitzgerald interrupted her. "Who's the 'we,' Major?"

"Every area specialist I talk to." She rattled off a list of names that ran from the CIA to the State Department. "If oil is discovered, we predict that the entire area will be a major objective for the Sudanese government and ripe for ethnic cleansing."

"What's the UN doing?" Fitzgerald asked. "Sitting on their fat thumbs as usual?"

"Yes and no, sir." Every eyebrow in the room went up. It was common knowledge that Fitzgerald held the UN in deep contempt and the major was telling him something he didn't want to hear.

"This had better be good," he growled.

"The UN mission is withdrawing its relief teams from Sudan. However, the UN peacekeepers appear to have a different agenda." A photo of Vermullen in battle dress filled the screen. "The new commander of the UN's peacekeeping force is Colonel Pierre Lavelle Vermullen of the French Foreign Legion. He commands a company-sized peacekeeping force of 200 legionnaires."

"My God!" a voice at the far end of the table blurted. "He looks just like Idi Amin."

"Yes, sir," Jill said. "But he's no relation. Colonel Vermullen is 41 years old, born in Senegal and orphaned when he was three months old. A French family adopted him and took him to Paris. After graduating from St. Cyr at the head of his class, he joined the French Foreign Legion. His men nicknamed him 'Idi' and it stuck." She went on to describe how he was independently wealthy and the closest thing to a renaissance man the French military had produced in over a hundred years. He was considered by many to be the army's finest intellect and the youngest colonel since World War II. He was also a battle-hardened veteran of nine peacekeeping missions with a reputation for returning fire when fired on. "There is a rumor that al-Qaeda has placed a bounty of 50,000 euros on his head, but we cannot confirm that."

Richards glanced at the notes on her communicator. "He also has a reputation as a womanizer. At least he has that in common with Mad Dawg Allston."

"Yes, ma'am," Jill replied. "Vermullen is also married with three children." She keyed her remote and a picture of a pretty blonde Parisienne with three beautiful children flashed on the screen. It was followed by a photo of Vermullen marching at the head of the 2nd Foreign Parachute Regiment based in Corsica. "He is brave and unflinching in combat and has been wounded three times. He is the most highly decorated officer on active duty in the French Army. His men revere him and say they would follow him into hell. The French government appears to have given him wide discretionary powers to use force that far exceeds anything the UN will allow. Given his record and disposition, we expect him to use those powers regardless of what the UN Mission tells him."

Fitzgerald's fingers beat a tattoo on the table. He had to make a phone call and find out what the French were up to. Fortunately, he still had a channel to the Ministry of Defense in Paris. "Thank you, Major," he said, dismissing the intelligence officer. Richards caught Jill's attention and glanced at the door, signifying she wanted to talk after the briefing. Jill placed the remote control on the podium and went outside to wait in the hall.

"General Fitzgerald," Richards said as she stood. "My office received a complaint from the United Nations Relief and Peacekeeping Mission Southern Sudan in regards to an unauthorized landing made by Lieutenant Colonel Allston on" – she checked her notes – "Thursday, January 7. He landed at Abyei, a village in the disputed border area, and in violation of the Mission's standing directives." She paused for effect.

"That's the village where we lost a C-130," Fitzgerald said. "And?"

"Our personnel cannot flout the UN's established procedures, and my office will have to respond."

"Respond to what?"

Richards' mental warnings were in full alarm. She had pushed the wrong button, and while Fitzgerald had never fired a flag ranked officer before, at least six had found themselves looking at career-ending assignments when their tour at the Pentagon ended. She quickly consulted her notes and went into a recovery mode. "It happened on the day he arrived at Malakal and was on a local area checkout flight. The aircraft experienced an unsafe door warning light and he landed to check it out."

"It's too bad your UN compatriots have no clue as to what constitutes flight safety," Fitzgerald replied.

"However," Richards said, "he just happened to have the accident investigation team on board, which had not received permission from the UN to examine the crash site. Once on the ground, Colonel Allston arranged for the team to survey the crash site, again, without clearance from the UN."

"And that's a bad thing?" Fitzgerald asked. In his world, the information gained was critical to continuing operations and Allston was protecting his aircrews.

"In itself, no," she answered. "However, the incident may prove to be counterproductive in the long run to our mission in the Sudan."

"Do you think so?" Fitzgerald replied.

"Of course, that remains to be seen," she said, conceding the argument.

Fitzgerald wasn't finished. "In your response, remind your UN counterparts that we lost five personnel and one aircraft supporting their mission, and that flying safety must remain paramount if we are to continue operations."

"Yes, sir." She sat down, careful to conceal her anger and frustration. Seven minutes later, the meeting was over and she hurried out of the conference room. Jill was waiting for her. "Walk with me, Major," Richards said. "You did very well in there today. Unfortunately, I didn't. But I think I made my point. Your prediction about the discovery of oil was brilliant, but I would appreciate a heads up in the future."

"Yes, ma'am. I will if I can." They walked in silence for a few moments.

"I hope you will forgive me," Richards said, "but there is, ah, a personal matter we need to discuss. A few of my counterparts in there are, well, lecherous old bastards. They couldn't take their eyes off your breasts."

Jill blushed. She was very sensitive about her breast size. "Sorry, ma'am. This is what Mother Nature gave me."

Richards nodded in sympathy. "I do understand. But career-wise, you may want to think about a breast reduction." Richards stopped outside her office. "Jill, you are a most unique and gifted officer with a future. I'd like to help, but it may require that you step out of your traditional role."

Jill carefully masked her reactions and gave Richards the serious and concerned look she had practiced and refined over the years. "Thank you, ma'am. I hope I don't disappoint you."

* * *

Fitzgerald hit the intercom button to his secretary. "Mary, if there's nothing pressing on my schedule, can you clear an hour?" She told him there was nothing that couldn't be slipped. He gave her a number to call. "Call

44

me when you get through," he added, wondering how he could do the job without her. He kicked back in his chair and folded his hands across his chest. His eyes never closed as he processed Jill's briefing and what Richards had said about Allston's unauthorized landing at Abyei being counterproductive to their mission in the Sudan. In Fitzgerald's world, Allston's job was to carry out the mission, and Fitzgerald's job was to provide the support Allston needed to do it. He typed a brief message into his computer, but hesitated before hitting the send button. He humphed, the decision made, and hit the button. Exactly eight minutes later, Mary buzzed him. The spook he had summoned was waiting outside. "Please show him in," Fitzgerald said. The civilian who came through the door moved with an easy motion that belied his bulk. He was a 'gray man,' perfect for his profession and nondescript to the point of invisibility. "How are things in the basement these days?" Fitzgerald asked.

"Holding tight." The spook headed The Boys in the Basement, the elite band of covert intelligence operators who hid in the Pentagon's basement. On paper, they were part of the military and escaped the scrutiny of the congressional committees on intelligence oversight. More importantly, they escaped the constant leaks that bedevil all congressional committees. In the world of heads-on head intelligence, hard experience had taught the Boys that no secret was safe with a politician. As long as the Boys were 'holding tight' they were safe from politicians and could do their job. But they could never drop their guard.

Fitzgerald came right to the point. "The 4440th is operating in the blind in the Sudan and I suspect the UN is hanging them out to dry. We've got the big picture and know what the Sudanese are up to, but we need to fill in the details on the ground or the 4440th will be blindsided before I can get them out. In short, we need better operational intelligence, which we don't have at this time."

The spook had worked with Fitzgerald before and trusted him to follow the unique rules of his trade. Everything was highly compartmentalized and access to the product, and how it was gathered, was based on a strict need-to-know. "We've got a few gremlins who speak the lingo."

"Yours or mine?" Fitzgerald knew that the Boys recruited and used Air Force personnel, but the spook would never reveal their identity.

The spook laughed and didn't answer the question. "Fitz, you haven't changed. Always worried about your folks." He thought for a moment, calculating how much he could reveal. Part of his job was to give Fitzgerald credible deniability, but at the same time, the general had to be told enough to keep him in the loop. "We have a few sources in Addis Ababa we can exploit. The bad news is that the best source in the Sudan, Dr. Tobias Person at Mission Awana, won't talk to us. He can't risk compromising his neutrality." He gave Fitzgerald his good old boy grin. "But we can always backdoor that one."

"Do it," Fitzgerald said.

"We'll get on it."

The intercom buzzed. "General," Mary said, "your call to France is on the secure line."

"I need to take this," Fitzgerald said. The spook smiled and excused himself.

Malakal

Allston walked through the hangar that was packed with maintenance equipment and cargo pallets ready to be loaded on relief missions. He stopped and stared at the engine dolly holding an Allison T-56 turboprop engine parked at the end of a neat row. Where did that come from? he wondered. Outside, he heard a C-130 taxi in. He glanced at his watch. It was the last mission of the day and all his aircrews and aircraft were safely recovered. The unyielding tension that bound him tight yielded a notch and he breathed easier. But it would all repeat itself the next day, and every day after that as long as he commanded the 4440th and sent his aircrews into harm's way. It was a burden few sane men or women chose to carry, and fewer yet who could do it successfully. He walked into operations.

Inside, G.G. was sitting behind the counter monitoring the radio, his feet up on the desk, the microphone in his left hand. He keyed the mike. "That's it for the day, Marci." He noted the C-130's landing time on the big tracking board and turned to his commander. "All five birds back, OR, and good to go."

"G.G., did you have anything to do with that engine out there?"

"Guilty. Me and Loni, er, Sergeant Williams, convinced a few misguided souls they didn't really want it."

"How did you do that?" Allston asked. He wasn't really sure he wanted to know.

"Magic, sir, pure magic." G.G. laughed. "I did a few slight-of-hand tricks and then offered to not tell their futures." He flicked his fingers and produced a big coin from nowhere. "No Muslim wants to know the day he will die." Now Allston was sure he didn't want to know any more.

The office rapidly filled as a sergeant and four airmen filed in. They threw their blue berets on the counter and stood there, big grins on their faces. "We flew with Captain Jenkins today," the sergeant announced. They had come for their bush hats. G.G. rummaged in a nearby cardboard box.

"Learn anything?" Allston asked.

"Yes, sir," a young airman answered. She looked all of sixteen. "The Dinka are hurting." Her eyes filled with tears. "I've never seen starving children before." G.G. handed her a hat and she held it, caressing the brim. "I gotta do something."

"That's why we're here," Allston said.

She slung the hat over her head, and let it hang on her back. The others quickly fitted theirs and did the same. The sergeant stood tall. "Irregulars, a-ten-HUT!" The five came to attention and threw Allston a salute.

"Welcome aboard," Allston said, returning their salutes. They quickly filed out, eager to wear their hats outside.

"The hats are working, Boss," G.G. said.

"It's not the hats," Allston told him. "It's about unit identification and having a mission." He walked into his office and opened the safe to get his laptop computer. He sat down to answer the mail. As usual, he had over a hundred messages. He scanned them, looking for the important ones. Richards in the office of Military-Political Affairs had sent six pages of detailed and revised Rules of Operations he was to adhere to. However, the important message was a one-liner from Fitzgerald.

Coordinate with and support Col Vermullen to max extent possible.

"What the hell is going on?" he wondered to no one. He warned himself to quit thinking out loud. He returned his computer to the safe and went to the mess tent for dinner.

* * *

The knock on Allston's trailer door came after midnight. "Colonel," G.G. called. "You're needed in Ops." Allston came awake with a rush and sat on the edge of his bed. He turned on the light and checked the time - 0135 hours. He pulled on a flightsuit and staggered to the door. G.G. was waiting anxiously outside. "The French peacekeepers have got their ass in a crack," G.G. explained, "and a Colonel Vermullen is here talking to Major Lane. They need to talk to you." The two men hurried for the big hangar. "Vermullen is one big mean-looking dude and his driver is some old Kraut who looks like he was left over from World War II."

"They're French Foreign Legion. Sort of like a cross between our Rangers and Special Forces."

"I wouldn't want to mess with them."

The Vermullen waiting for Allston was far different from the uniformed dandy he had met in Addis Ababa. He was dressed for combat and carried a stubby FAMAS G2 assault rifle that had been modified with a day/night optical sight and a laser range finder. A Browning 9mm automatic hung from his webbed equipment belt and two cords led from his helmet, one to a radio/GPS on his belt and the other to the optical sight on his assault rifle. The way he stood and his quiet manner left no doubt that he was a warrior. His driver and constant shadow, Private Hans Beck, stood at his back. "I understand you've got a problem, Colonel," Allston said.

Vermullen pulled a map out of a thigh pocket and spread it out. He pointed to a village. "This is Wer Ping, 305 kilometers to the west of here. I sent a patrol, twelve men and three trucks, to investigate a report the Janjaweed had tortured and murdered the villagers. The patrol was ambushed and are trapped on a road outside the village." Vermullen drew a small square on the east side of the village. "According to their GPS, they are here."

Allston automatically converted the 305 kilometers to 190 miles, less than an hour's flying time from Malakal. The threat was getting closer. "Is Wer Ping a Dinka village?" Vermullen confirmed it was. Allston studied the map for a few moments. "Not much to go on."

G.G. typed a command into his computer and a high-resolution satellite photograph flashed on the screen. He turned it towards the two men. "Based on those coordinates, it looks like they're caught on this north/south section of road next to the river." An expectant look crossed his round face. "Airdrop? If the legionnaires secure the area, we can land on the road to extract them."

It was obvious Vermullen was thinking the same thing. "All my men are *parachutistes* and are preparing now."

Allston made a decision. "Let's do it. How many troops are we talking about and where are they?"

"I'll have 120 ready in an hour. They are at our base in Beica."

Allston was shocked. "In Ethiopia? A hell of a lot of good you're doin' there." He was angry. By positioning Vermullen's peacekeeping force 200 miles away to the east, the UN had left his small contingent of Americans totally exposed to the threat coming from the west.

"That's where the UN placed us," Vermullen replied. "I am aware that you are uncovered here. But then, our UN masters are not concerned with the tactical situation on the ground."

Allston made a decision. He turned to his Ops Officer, Major Lane. "Dick, lay on two Herks to bring the paratroopers here ASAP. While that's happening, I want two crews to start briefing for the airdrop." He ran a mental list of his pilots. "I'll lead in number one with Bard Green in the right seat. G.G. gets to earn his money and does the airdrop. The aircraft commander for number two is Marci Jenkins. You pick the rest of the crews and hold things together here. If we hustle, we can drop at first light."

Lane looked doubtful. "We're winging this. Too many unknowns. It's gonna get tricky."

"*Demerdez-vous!*" Allston said. Vermullen roared with laughter.

Lane was totally perplexed. "Whaa?"

"*Demerdez-vous!* is the Legion's unofficial slogan," Vermullen said. "It means 'Make Do.'"

"I might add," G.G. said, "roughly translated, *demerder* means to get out of the shit."

"It sounds more like we're jumping into it," Susan Malaby said from the doorway. No one had seen her arrive. She jammed on her blue beret and stormed out.

FIVE

Wer Ping, South Sudan

*T*he chatter on the flight deck died away as the C-130 descended to 800 feet above the ground. G.G. sat at the navigator's station aft of the copilot and typed a correction into the navigation computer. The symbology on the navigation display in front of the pilots moved a fraction of an inch as the computer integrated the latest GPS inputs. "Release point on the nose," he told the pilots. He jumped up and stood beside the French captain who was standing behind the copilot and picked up the visual references he was looking for. His eyes narrowed. He wasn't happy with what the GPS and computer were telling him. Trusting his own instincts, he sat down and typed in another correction. "Ten minutes out."

The aircraft shifted as the sixty-one Legionnaire paratroopers in the rear stood and snapped their static lines to the overhead cable. Allston slowed to 120 knots, their drop airspeed, and automatically trimmed the big aircraft. The French captain pressed his earphones to his head to hear better. "Colonel Vermullen says they are ready," the captain said.

"Is he always the first man out?" Allston asked.

"Always," the captain replied. He keyed his FM radio and contacted the trapped patrol on the ground. He spoke in rapid-fire French. "*Merde*! They are taking incoming fire. The drop is unsafe."

"SAM! SAM! SAM!" the loadmaster in the rear of the aircraft yelled over the intercom.

Bard Green's right hand flashed out and hit the flare button, popping a trail of flares into their wake in a desperate effort to decoy the surface-to-air missile. Allston jinked the big transport to the left and then to the right as he cut a spiral in the sky. A Grail, a Russian-built shoulder-held missile, flashed by on the right and missed the Hercules. The men standing in the rear of the aircraft were tossed about like bowling balls in their heavy equipment, crashing into each other. "Everyone okay back there?" Allston asked over the intercom. The loadmaster reported that the legionnaires were picking themselves up off the deck and sorting out their equipment, but other than a few bruises, no one was injured.

Again, the French captain contacted the legionnaires on the ground. The news was not good. "The incoming fire is growing more heavy, now from all sides," he told Allston. "It is small caliber only, no heavy weapons." He relayed the information to Vermullen and the jumpmaster. G.G. announced they were ten miles out with five minutes to go, which the captain relayed to the waiting legionnaires in the rear. A deep frown crossed the captain's face as he listened. "My colonel says they are ready."

Allston didn't hesitate. "Abort the drop. Repeat, abort the drop." It was an easy decision, honed by years of experience and countless combat missions. "The jump is on hold until we neutralize the threat. We don't need the bastards using you for target practice when you're in your chutes. Everyone strap in. Loadmaster, that includes you and the jumpmaster." The aircraft shifted as the legionnaires sat back down in the canvas jump seats along the sides of the aircraft. Allston firewalled the throttles and dropped to 200 feet above the ground. "Listen up, it's fire suppression time. It's gonna be one pass, haul ass. Captain, tell your troops on the ground to keep their heads down. Stay in contact with them and I want a constant update on what the Janjaweed are doing." Another thought came to him. "Colonel Vermullen, I'm going to buzz the livin' hell out of the bad guys and get their attention. They're gonna shoot at us. You okay with that?"

"*Demerdez-vous*," Vermullen answered.

"Stalwart soul," Allston replied. He hit the com switch under his left thumb to transmit on the UHF radio and called the second Hercules behind him. "Marci, break it off and hold west of the river. I'll call you in when needed."

"Will do. I can't keep up with you, anyway." Allston glanced at his airspeed indicator. The needle was bouncing off 165 knots and the turbulence was increasing. He throttled back to 140 knots and the turbulence eased.

"Sir," Bard Green said from the right seat, "I'm not sure if the Herk can take this."

"Yeah, she can," Allston replied. "Can we?" He gave the copilot his lopsided grin. "When things go wrong, get aggressive." G.G. announced they were inside two miles just as Allston saw the legionnaires' three trucks stopped on the road. "Tallyho," he called. "Target on the nose. Riley, hit the fuel dump switch when I tell you." He dropped the C-130 down to 150 feet above the ground and inched the throttles back as he jinked the big bird with short heading and altitude changes. Allston was careful to watch the acceleration meter and not pull over two gs as he dropped another 50 feet. "Riley, dump." The flight engineer reached for the overhead panel and hit the two fuel dump switches with both hands as they flew straight and level over the legionnaires. "Dump off," Allston called. He pulled up to 200 feet and again jinked the aircraft, but this time more gentle.

"Colonel!" The French captain called, "The patrol wants to know if we are using chemical weapons."

"No way," Allston replied, "but that's what I want everyone to think. Let's do it again and see if we can convince the bastards that they are about to die." He turned to the left and circled back to run it at ninety degrees to the first run. He dropped to 150 feet and inched down to 100 as he rolled out and flew over the target. "Riley, dump." The flight engineer hit the fuel dump switch. "Dump off."

"Colonel Allston!" the French captain called over the intercom. "All gunfire has stopped and they are running away."

"How about that," Allston said. He climbed to 400 feet and circled back, this time to the right.

"I can see horsemen," Green called from the copilot's seat. "Three o'clock, on the road, keep the turn coming and you'll bring 'em to the nose." He laughed. "That got their attention. They're going at the speed of smell!"

Allston rolled the big transport out with the horsemen on the nose. "Tallyho. Loadmaster, lower the ramp to the trail position. Colonel Vermullen, can you get a couple of shooters on the ramp to act like tail gunners?" He heard Vermullen rattle off commands in French over the intercom and felt the movement in the rear as the legionnaires shifted. He automatically trimmed the aircraft and Vermullen said that four shooters were in position. "That was quick," Allston said. "Horsemen coming under the nose now. Fire!" Short bursts of gunfire echoed to the flight deck as the legionnaires opened fire. Then as quickly as it started, it was quiet. This time, Allston circled to the left as he climbed. He saw three horses on the ground and two bodies. "Let's do it again," he said. He found the retreating horsemen and rolled in. "Ready in the rear."

Again, the galloping horsemen came under the nose as the tall rider in the lead turned in the saddle and raised his AK-47. Allston caught a glimpse of the bearded man and a flash of teeth as he fired his submachine gun in defiance. "That's one gutsy bastard," Allston admitted. The rider never flinched and kept firing as the Hercules flew overhead. "Time to return the favor," Allston muttered. "Ready, ready, fire."

The gunfire from the rear was more sustained as the legionnaires got the hang of it. Then it was quiet. "That pissed off some folks down there. Check for battle damage." He climbed to 500 feet and circled the area. He counted five bodies and nine horses on the ground and played the numbers game. Had they killed enough of the enemy to force a withdrawal, but were they still strong enough with the will to regroup? It was one of the intangibles of combat the brass would second-guess from the safety of their headquarters every Monday morning for the next year. Allston looked for telltale clues and saw three dismounted horsemen scrambling through the brush and away from the legionnaires. A sixth sense urged him to press the attack.

Riley ran his checklist and reported the systems on the aircraft were fully functional and appeared undamaged. "If the gear comes down, we're golden."

"A-okay in the rear," the loadmaster said.

"Sounds like we got lucky," Allston said. He instinctively sensed the odds had shifted in their favor and they had a window of opportunity. It was his job to keep it open and the best way to do that was to get more firepower on the ground. "Captain, ask the patrol if the area is secure enough for the airdrop." He still expected the legionnaires to take some casualties when they parachuted in.

The French captain spoke into his radio and grunted in satisfaction. "*Oui*, Colonel, the area is secure." There was a deep respect in his voice.

Allston continued to circle as he called Marci's C-130 to join on him for the drop. "I have you in sight and will join on you in three," she radioed. "What were you guys doing over there?"

"Just having some fun," Allston replied.

"Colonel Vermullen," G.G. said over the intercom, "I'm using a new program I developed for airdrops and need to validate its accuracy under actual conditions. The computed air release point where I give the green light is based on where I want the first man to land – on the road and less than fifty meters from the trucks. If possible, can the lead jumper not maneuver and land wherever the wind blows to verify the accuracy of the system?" Vermullen replied that he was the lead jumper and would not maneuver if it looked close.

Six minutes later, the two C-130s over-flew the legionnaires. Allston's aircraft led and Marci's was offset 500 feet behind and 200 feet above his. Jumpers streamed out both sides of Allston's aircraft, shortly followed by sixty more from Marci's Hercules. Allston immediately circled back to track the accuracy of the drop. "Vermullen in sight," he told G.G.

"Got him," the navigator said.

"Oh no!" the French captain shouted. "He will land in a tree." The men watched transfixed as Vermullen disappeared into the top of a tall tree next to the road.

"I'll be damned," Green said. "It looks like he's fifty meters from the trucks and ten meters off the road." He groaned. "Bird colonels don't like landing in trees."

"He will not be happy," the French captain predicted.

"Well, you know what they say about a bird in the bush," G.G. quipped, making the best of it.

The two C-130s continued to circle the area as Vermullen's legionnaires went through a well-rehearsed routine and secured the area. They were out of their parachutes within seconds after hitting the ground and formed up into firing teams. There was no attempt to join up with their assigned squads and as soon as a sergeant had five or six men, they moved out, securing the perimeter. From his perch in the tree, Vermullen had an excellent view of the action and made no attempt to lower himself to the ground. One fire team ran down the road in the direction the fleeing horsemen had taken. Whenever they came across a horse or Janjaweed lying on the ground, they fired a short burst of gunfire, making sure the unfortunate animal was out of its misery and the man was no longer a threat. It was quick, efficient, and brutal. Exactly sixteen minutes after Vermullen had landed, the area was secure and two sergeants from the patrol were waiting for Vermullen to lower himself out of the tree. They quickly briefed him on the situation.

Allston landed first in case they had taken battle damage to the landing gear and might block the road. He eased the big aircraft onto the road and reversed the props. A cloud of dust roared out in front of them, blocking his view. He stopped and waited for the dust to settle. A bruised and battered Vermullen walked out of the dust with two sergeants and the ever-present Hans. A ragged and gaunt boy from the village followed them. The colonel's uniform was torn and his left cheek was bandaged. He fixed the C-130 with a hard look. "There is one angry dude," Allston said. He keyed the radio. "Marci, we're okay. You're cleared to land behind me. You've got about 4000 feet." A flying safety officer could cite chapter and verse about what could go wrong with one aircraft landing behind the other without a clear rollout, but Allston knew she could handle it. He set the brakes and quickly shut down the engines. "Come on, G.G. I think the Colonel wants to talk to us. And please, no jokes about a bird in the bush. He won't think it's funny." The two men clambered down the boarding steps and marched towards the waiting Frenchmen. Much to their surprise, Vermullen smiled at them.

"Captain G.G., I must apologize. I maneuvered to land in the tree. Otherwise, I would have landed on the road."

"Why?" Allston asked.

"The tree was a good place to observe if my men can operate independently of command. Forming up and grouping for action after landing is the most difficult and critical phase." He motioned at the two sergeants and the boy. "These men were on the patrol. The boy is the only survivor from the village. He hid in the bush and saw what happened. He speaks some English. There is something you need to see." He spoke in French and the sergeant in charge of the patrol led them into the nearby village of Wer Ping. The boy followed, shaking with fear.

The smell of burning flesh assaulted them well before they reached the village. "The Janjaweed camped here," the sergeant said. He walked over and kicked a body lying in the dirt. Hard. "This one didn't get away." He fired a short burst of submachine gun fire into the dead body. Allston shot a warning glance at Vermullen. The legionnaire had crossed the line and had committed a war crime. Vermullen only stared back. The sergeant led the way to a shallow pit a few feet from the campsite. The bodies of two young girls were staked out over a bed of charcoal. "They were roasted alive. Do you have a camera to document this?" G.G. pulled a small digital camera out of a pocket and started to take pictures.

"Janjaweed laugh," the boy said in halting English.

"They laughed when they did this?" Allston asked. The boy nodded in answer.

"It took a long time for the girls to die," the sergeant added.

"How do you know that?" Allston asked.

"Janjaweed watch," the boy said. "Janjaweed talk, talk, talk, laugh when die."

Vermullen spoke softly. "*Il y a plus.*" There is more. He led the way into the smoldering ruins of the village. A line of nineteen bodies were stretched out on the ground. All were male with bloody crotches. "They were castrated before they were shot." The sergeant checked the mouth of the nearest corpse. The man's genitals were shoved down his throat. "The women and girls were made to watch this before they were raped and killed."

"Where are the women?" G.G. asked.

"In the huts," the sergeant said.

"But they're all burned down," G.G. said, not understanding. Vermullen gestured for him to examine one and take a photograph. The navigator walked slowly to the charred ruins of the nearest hut. The stench of burning flesh was overpowering but he snapped four photographs before retreating.

"*Il y a plus*," Vermullen said. His small tactical radio buzzed with a message. "They found the body of the village chief." The boy looked at them, his emaciated body shaking. Not able to take anymore, he turned and ran.

"The chief was his grandfather," the sergeant said. The five men walked deeper into the destroyed village and found two legionnaires standing guard over the body. The village elder had been dismembered and his legs and arms thrown to waiting dogs. His stomach had been ripped open and his head shoved inside. G.G. bent over and vomited. Then he took more photos, his face deathly white.

"*Il y a plus*," Vermullen repeated.

"There is always more," the sergeant added. "Have you ever seen a baby impaled?" He pointed to the body of an infant dangling from a stake fence.

Allston stared at the baby, his whole being shaken to the core. There was no rationalization for what he was seeing, no justification, no explanation, no understanding. For the first time in his life, he understood what it meant to have an epiphany. This was reality and it was evil. Like most Americans, Allston had convinced himself that evil was a primitive belief that only existed in the ignorant. But the ignorance was his. The evil that the Allies had experienced when they stumbled across the death camps in World War II was still very much alive. It had taken a new form in Bosnia and now Africa, and it was the curse of the modern world, challenging civilization.

"*Il y a plus*," Vermullen said.

Allston breathed deeply, not able to speak and vent the emotions shredding his humanity. By any standard, he was a well-educated and superbly trained professional warrior, yet nothing had prepared him for this, not even what he had seen at Abyei on his first day in the Sudan. That had only been a prelude, a small sample of what he was witnessing. Perhaps a more urbane and sophisticated man could play the intellectual and find refuge in the abstract, but when faced with the horror of genocide, Allston could not mute it or turn away. This was the here and now and he had to physically engage. Anything less would be a denial of what he was and everything he believed in. A burning hate swept over him, threatening to consume him, and from that moment, he was willing to risk his life to kill the evil before him.

"Are you okay?" G.G. asked.

Slowly, Allston regained control. "No, G.G., I'm not okay. And I doubt that I ever will be." He swept the village with his hand. "If this doesn't put some hate in your heart, nothing will."

"It's there, Colonel," G.G. assured him.

"Good. Don't ever forget it."

"So now you understand why my sergeant reacted as he did," Vermullen said. He fell silent as he led them out of the village. The boy was sitting in the shade of a bush, waiting for them, his arms wrapped around his knees.

Allston extended a hand and pulled him to his feet. "Who did this?"

The boy froze in fear. Slowly, his lips moved, forming a single word. "Jahel."

Beica, Ethiopia

It was dusk when the two C-130s landed to discharge the legionnaires. Allston made his way through the cargo compartment as the legionnaires deplaned, impressed with the good order they left behind. They may have been societal misfits, but they were not slobs. His crew joined him as they walked around the aircraft, inspecting for bullet holes in the fuselage. Tech Sergeant Riley, the flight engineer beamed in relief when they only found three holes in the beavertail, the underside of the empennage beneath the vertical and horizontal stabilizers. Riley crawled inside and quickly reported that nothing critical had been hit and they had only taken superficial damage. Gauging by the size of the holes, they had taken fire from an AK-47.

"It had to be that Janjaweed we over flew who shot at us," Bard Green decided. "He didn't use enough lead."

Vermullen overheard them. "It is very difficult to shoot from a galloping horse. My *tireurs* could not hit him as he cut back and forth. It was an outstanding display of horsemanship. Do not underestimate this man." He let it sink in. "It is late. May I extend the hospitality of our mess for the night? I have a good chef."

"Why am I not surprised?" Allston asked. The arrangements were quickly made and the four pilots and G.G. were billeted in the officers' quarters while the two flight engineers and two loadmasters joined the NCOs.

An hour later, Vermullen was waiting for the Americans in the officer's mess. Like them, he was showered, but he was wearing a fresh uniform. His officers were clustered behind him and two immediately escorted Marci Jenkins and her copilot into the dining room. "Shall we join them?" Vermullen asked, playing the gracious host. As promised, the dinner was excellent and the surroundings on the elegant side. "The UN built this for the relief mission," Vermullen explained, "but the commissioners prefer Addis. They gave it to us instead." The big man thought for a moment. "It is not for the Legion. My men are losing their edge – too much of the good life. We need to be nearer to – what do you Americans say? – to the action."

"There's always Malakal," Allston said. "But I don't think our masters in Addis Ababa will approve."

"Tactically, that would be a good move. Unfortunately, you are correct; the head of mission will not approve. I believe he wants you Americans in harm's way." He changed the subject. "It appears your Captain Jenkins is most popular with my officers and is enjoying her dinner."

"She didn't see the village," G.G. said.

"Food will never taste the same," Allston added.

"You must learn to handle it," Vermullen said.

"I'll try," Allston replied. "But I never want to hear *Il y a plus* again. How do you handle it?"

"By relying on my men. For them, it was a successful mission with no casualties. In our business, there is no better result. Perhaps, we should see how they are getting on."

"Sounds like a plan," Allston said. "G.G., Bard, come on and join us." He looked around for Marci and her copilot but couldn't find either. Vermullen led the three Americans to the NCO mess where they could hear singing. "That sounds like German."

"Indeed it is," Vermullen admitted. "There are many Germans in the Legion, and they do love to sing." He listened for a moment. "It is an old World War II Wehrmacht drinking song." He sang in English, "Hurry, hurry to the whorehouse before the prices go up." They listened for a moment as a new song broke out. "Ah, I like this one better. 'Tonight We March On England.'"

Allston laughed, liking the big Frenchman more and more. "I imagine you would." The four entered the mess and a loud cheer echoed over them. There was no doubt that Vermullen was extremely popular with his men. Big water glasses filled with red wine were pushed into their hands and the noise grew even louder.

"Colonel," a legionnaire with a thick German accent called, "what are you going to do to the American who dropped you in the tree?"

"Let him do it to you," Vermullen shouted back. "Be sure to keep your ankles crossed to protect your Kraut balls." More cheers deafened them. Vermullen drained his glass and banged it on the bar for attention. The room quickly quieted. "It is obvious we are growing soft here. What would your mothers think? They will never forgive me, and we must rectify the situation." He looked out over them expectantly. "What? No suggestions?"

"Bloody hell!" a Cockney sergeant shouted. "We're moving to Malakal to save the Americans' bloody ass."

Vermullen pulled a face. "Well, if you insist, Sergeant Abbott." He turned to Allston. "Can you provide airlift?"

"So sayeth my standing orders. But what about the UN?"

A broad smile spread across the Frenchman's face. "If we do it quick enough, they will have no say in the matter. Tomorrow is Saturday and they never work on weekends." He laughed, enjoying the moment. "And very seldom on Mondays."

SIX

E-Ring

"*P*lease have General Richards come right in," Fitzgerald told his secretary. He glanced at his watch. They had less than ten minutes before his morning staff meeting. "Good morning," he said as Richards entered. He waved her to a seat. "Is this going to be one of those Mondays?"

"I'm afraid so, sir." She handed him a leather folder. "I received this by special courier from the State Department twenty minutes ago. We will have to respond. May I suggest we alert Public Affairs for pre-emptive damage control?"

Fitzgerald groaned inwardly. The Secretary of State detested the military and never missed a chance to slap the Pentagon around. He accepted it as part of the give and take of power politics in Washington and never took it personally, although the Secretary of State treated the Joint Chiefs as an evil cabal. He opened the elegant leather folder that was Richards' trademark and quickly scanned the thin document. He sat upright and slowly read it again. It was a formal complaint filed by the Government of Sudan with the United Nations charging the 4440th with using weapons of mass destruction on innocent nomads at the village of Wer Ping. "Did they specify what WMD they employed?"

"Apparently it was some type of nerve gas."

"And exactly how did they do that?" It was testing time and he wanted to know if Richards had the technical and operational expertise to analyze the accusation. Thanks to the internet, any rumor, opinion, or accusation had the weight of fact. While it amused him that modern society was confused over the difference, that type of sloppy thinking was not tolerated on his staff. In this particular case, the C-130s deployed to Africa were veteran E models equipped with flares to decoy heat-seeking missiles and totally unarmed.

However, the engineers at Lockheed had designed an airframe that was readily adaptable to a variety of missions that ranged from gunship to reconnaissance.

She hit the ball out of the park. "Sir, I'm aware that the C-130s at Malakal are unarmed cargo transports. However, it wouldn't take much for an enterprising commander to install crop-spraying equipment on the ramp at the rear of the aircraft. A concentrated insecticide could function as a degraded nerve gas. How effective that would be is questionable, but it does raise a possibility we can't ignore."

"Are you suggesting we have a rogue commander on our hands?"

"It has been known to happen. Our information is fragmentary, but given the current climate in the UN, I would not be surprised if they arrested Colonel Allston and turned him over to the International Criminal Court to be tried for war crimes. I'm recommending that we recall him immediately and place him under house arrest for his own protection."

Fitzgerald didn't answer as he rapidly cycled through his waiting e-mail, looking for a message from Allston. It was number 132 in his private encrypted account with forty attached photographs. Because of a public appearance and traveling over the weekend, he had missed it. Fitzgerald was a realist and knew he was too involved with the 4440th and had to work out a new command structure to handle it. He scanned the message and forwarded it to Jill without opening the attachments. He checked the time. "Thank you, General Richards. Let's see if Major Sharp has anything for us." He stood and led the way to the conference room next door.

Richards took her seat in the conference room and checked her personal communicator. The CIA had just confirmed that concentrated forms of agricultural insecticide were available in Malakal. It only remained for her to slam the door on Allston and replace him with a responsible commander who understood that operations were driven by policy. She smiled at the waiting major.

Fitzgerald caught the look on Jill's face as she concentrated on the computer screen at the podium. He waited until she looked up before nodding for her to start. "Good morning, General," she began. "Last Friday, two C-130s under the command of Lieutenant Colonel Allston airdropped 121 legionnaires near the village of Wer Ping in South Sudan to rescue a French patrol that had been ambushed by a marauding band of Janjaweed." She kept glancing at her computer as she recapped the operation and described how Allston had dumped fuel over the Janjaweed to simulate chemical weapons, and then directed small-caliber submachine gunfire from the rear of the aircraft onto the Janjaweed, killing five.

"Now that's an interesting use of jet fuel," Fitzgerald allowed.

Richards caught the irony in his tone. It was time for damage control. "Major, are you saying this was a deliberate pollution of the environment by Allston?" Even to her ear, it sounded trivial.

"At the present time, we have no reports of environmental damage. But I will pursue it."

"That's not necessary," Richards said, regretting she had mentioned it.

"Do you have anything else for us?" Fitzgerald asked.

"These photographs," Jill answered, "were taken at the village of Wer Ping, which was destroyed by the Janjaweed. " She typed a command into the computer and the photos of the carnage in the village slowly cycled on the big briefing screen. It was the first time Jill had seen them and she instinctively stopped on the photo of the impaled baby. A colonel hurried from the room, his hand over his mouth.

Richards changed her tactics. "Do you know who did this?"

Jill kept glancing at her computer as she answered. "Yes, ma'am, we do." She typed a command and the screen split, showing dead horses and bodies on a road. "These are the bodies of Janjaweed who attacked the legionnaires. Two of them were carrying pouches made from women's breasts."

"And how do you know these pouches came from women of this village?" Fitzgerald asked. Without a word, Jill cycled back to the photos of the burned hut. The charred body of a woman filled the screen. Jill hit a button and zoomed in on the woman's breasts. Fitzgerald closed his eyes and clamped a steel fist over his growing anger. "Thank you, Major. We've seen enough."

He turned to his staff. "I want a full-court press with the media on this one. Make sure these photos get to the right news outlets. I don't want them buried. Stress the heroism of the legionnaires and the professionalism of the aircrews in extracting them." He turned to Richards. "Please relay to your contacts in the UN that at the first mention of arresting Colonel Allston, I will recommend to the President that he implement the American Service-Members Protection Act of 2002. In case those clowns don't get the message, remind them that ASPA allows the President to use all means necessary and appropriate to free any of our service personnel who are detained or imprisoned by the International Criminal Court. Tell them we call it 'Invade the Hague Act' for a damn good reason." The meeting was over.

Richards was pleased that Jill was waiting in the hall for her. "Well done, Major. I assume you had just received those photos and intelligence update."

"Yes, ma'am."

Richards wanted to know the source of the photos but assumed that Jill was too low-level an intelligence officer to have access to that information. She paused, thinking. "We're dealing with too many unknowns and need more information. Have you ever been to the Sudan?"

Jill answered with the truth. "No, ma'am."

"I want to send you there on a fact-finding mission. Can you handle it?" Jill nodded. "Good. We need to get you there soonest. Pack your bag."

"Yes, ma'am." Jill turned and hurried down the hall.

Richards thought for a moment and pushed through the door into Fitzgerald's outer office where the tall and lanky, gray-haired lieutenant general who served as the Deputy Chief of Staff for Manpower and Personnel was waiting for an appointment. They exchanged pleasantries and she asked if she might segue in for a quick word with Fitzgerald. Since she was the subject of his meeting with Fitzgerald, the three-star readily agreed. Contrary to protocol, he held the door for her and followed her in. Once inside, the three-star let Richards do the talking. She came right to the point. "Sir, we're operating in the blind in the Sudan and getting blindsided. We must be more proactive and need our own eyes and ears on the ground reporting directly back to us. I want to send Major Sharp on a fact finding mission to Malakal."

Fitzgerald steepled his fingers and thought for a moment. "An excellent suggestion. Make it happen. I want a report back ASAP. After that, I want Major Sharp to stay as the Intelligence officer for the 4440th and keep the reports coming." Richards thanked the two men and beat a hasty retreat.

Fitzgerald tapped his fingertips. "What do you make of that?"

"The Brigadier wants to call the shots on this one. I don't know where she's coming from, but she has her own agenda."

"I know, Brad. Unfortunately, she's got political cover."

"Good luck with that one," the three star said. "She has potential and I'd hate to lose Richards. But she thinks the Pentagon and Washington are the Air Force. She needs a reality check."

"Roger on the reality check," Fitzgerald replied.

Malakal

The heat bore down on Jill as she walked in from the C-130 that had brought her from Addis Ababa, and the air-conditioned office in the big hangar was a welcome relief. She dropped her bag and asked the pudgy looking captain sitting behind the scheduling counter for Lieutenant Colonel Allston. She glanced at the nametag on the captain's flightsuit. "G.G.?" she asked.

"For Glen Gordon," G.G. replied. He motioned her towards Allston's office. He watched her as she walked down the hall, admiring the cut of her ABUs. An image of her lying naked in his bed flashed in front of him. Reluctantly, he focused on the moment. "Welcome to Africa."

Jill knocked twice on the open door. "Colonel Allston?" she asked. Allston looked up from his laptop where he was hammering away at the never-ending paperwork that went with his job. "Major Gillian Sharp reporting for duty." She snapped a salute and he waved one back.

"Been expecting you." He quickly took her measure; Five-foot three with an hourglass figure, hippy and big busted, and incredibly appealing. Her short red hair was cut to frame a lovely face and her big blue eyes immediately captured him. He felt an old urge in the lower parts of his body but quickly suppressed it. Major Gillian Sharp was going to cause a stir among the troops. He had seen it before and it shouldn't be a problem, if she understood what was going on. However, long experience indicated he would have to wait to see how she handled it. He hoped he didn't have to explain it to her. He locked the computer in his safe and grabbed his bush hat. "Come on, let's go."

She was confused. "Go where, sir?"

"You've got an investigation to conduct, right?" She nodded. "Well, Colonel Vermullen and a few of his legionnaires are waiting and I've got a C-130 standing by to fly us to Wer Ping." She followed him out, rushing to keep up with his long strides. "Come on, G.G.," Allston called.

"Never thought you would ask," G.G. replied, reaching for his bush hat.

* * *

Jill sat at the dinner table in the mess tent and picked at her food. She wasn't hungry after seeing the village and knowing what had happened there. Allston and Vermullen exchanged glances. They knew what she was going through. "Sorry for the shock treatment," Allston said. "Nothing can capture the reality of it . . . the smell, the dogs, the insects . . ." His voice trailed off.

"The first time is always the hardest," Vermullen said. He appreciated Jill's no-nonsense attitude and knew his officers were going to like her. Although he enjoyed the company of intelligent and beautiful women, he would never understand why Americans totally missed a basic truth of combat. When bullets started to fly, and real danger and real death ruled the day, Mother Nature sent an overpowering urge to procreate. He listened as they talked, and, judging by her body language, sensed she was attracted to Allston, not that he was surprised.

G.G. joined them and stood between Allston and Vermullen, shifting his weight uneasily from foot to foot. He held a new bush hat in his hands. "Colonel Vermullen, Colonel Allston, I believe we have a new Irregular." He nervously fingered the brim of the bush hat. "Ma'am, maybe you noticed most of us wear these." He held out the hat. "Anyone who has flown on a mission like you did today can wear one. Colonel Allston came up with the idea. We call ourselves the Irregulars. It's strictly voluntary and you don't have to wear it."

Jill took the hat. "Thank you." She tentatively tried the hat on and tilted it at a jaunty angle. She gave the men a little smile.

Allston sucked in his breath. She was one of those women who looked beautiful in hats. Vermullen studied the two officers. There was no doubt that Allston liked what he saw, and she was a welcome contrast to the wiry and intense maintenance officer, Susan Malaby. "Welcome to Bumfuck South," Allston said.

Jill pushed the hat back and let it hang between her shoulder blades like she had seen others do. She stood. "Thank you, gentlemen. Please excuse me, but I have a report to write." She walked out, leaving a wake of silence.

* * *

Allston hit the 'page down' button as he read Jill's preliminary report on the incident at Wer Ping. It was amazingly concise and complete. She had gotten the operation absolutely right, and, as she was not an aviator, that impressed him. "I wish I could write half as good," he told her.

"Thank you, sir. I had a lot of practice in Afghanistan debriefing missions."

"I appreciate you showing me this," he said. He knew that she was under no obligation to show him the report of investigation. "Will you go final with this?"

"I need to interview the UN relief mission in Addis Ababa before I do that."

"I'll lay on a C-130 to take you there ASAP. Don't wear ABUs."

"I don't have a Class-A uniform," she said. "My other bag hasn't caught up with me."

"Well, good luck with that one." He smiled at her perplexed look. "Our masters in Addis Abba are not used to seeing a working uniform." He changed the subject. "I hope you don't mind sharing a trailer with Colonel Malaby and Captain Jenkins." They were the only other female officers in the detachment.

"It's okay," she said. "The other girls are all sharing one of the smaller tents."

"Well, there is safety in numbers." Psychologists have different names for the problem of fraternization on isolated assignments, which Allston preferred to think of as 'the only available woman syndrome.' Most women officers had no trouble handling the attention that came their way, but young girls on their first enlistment often fell victim to the situation and got into trouble, pregnancy being the most common result. He wasn't running a Club Med and knew the havoc a bikini could cause.

Jill sensed what was bothering him. "Not to worry, sir. The studs have all been identified." She was honest with herself and admitted that under different circumstances, and in a different place, she would be interested in the tall and lanky lieutenant colonel. Very interested. But their differences in rank and position were insurmountable barriers, and she had heard of his reputation. "Besides, I've seen what pair bonding can do to a unit."

Allston was even more impressed. Like the Marines, she understood it was loyalty to your buddies and your outfit that mattered in combat, and that a pair bonding of any kind weakened that loyalty, usually with one result – increased casualties. "Good luck in Addis and hurry back. We can use an Intel officer around here."

SEVEN

Wer Ping

*B*ermaNur reined in his horse and joined the other recruits at the rear when the large band of Janjaweed entered the village. He was resigned to the dust and the biting jabs at his manhood the veterans flung at him because he was certain that Allah's wrath would descend on his tormentors and he would be raised high above them. The teenager made a show of it and imitated Jahel's laughing manner and the way he rode his horse. Unfortunately, BermaNur's mount sensed the teenager's exhilaration and responded, prancing and kicking in excitement, making it hard to control the animal. BermaNur sawed viciously at the reins as the other recruits laughed, adding to his chagrin. He ignored them for, regardless, he was riding with the Fursan, the cavaliers of the Baggara. Nothing else mattered and he was where he belonged. His honor had been restored. In his euphoric state, he didn't understand that Jahel had changed his tactics and was massing the Janjaweed to challenge the Americans and the French peacekeepers. In Jahel's scheme of things, the recruits were cannon fodder.

Jahel stopped at an open area and pointed out the nineteen patches of dark, blood-stained earth that stretched out in a neat row. Many of the stakes that bound the men were still in the ground. He laughed when he described how the men had begged for mercy and then shrieked in pain when they had been emasculated and left to bleed out. Each pool of blood marked where a man had died. "We found a way to stop their screaming," Jahel said, relishing the memory.

"Who buried the vermin?" a rider asked.

"The French pigs," Jahel replied. "They buried everything, even the animals. But we will not bury them." He laughed. "We will leave them for the jackals." He nudged his horse and cantered deeper into the destroyed village, finally stopping at the charred remains of a hut. He spoke in the boring voice of a teacher as he described how two girls and their mother had been raped and then burned alive in their home. "It was a tiring day proving our manhood." He laughed. "BermaNur, be patient. You will have your chance." He moved on. BermaNur ignored the patronizing jibe and paused as he rode by the hut. He had never had a woman and he breathed heavily in anticipation. His brow furrowed as his eyes swept the blackened remains of the hut. It looked vaguely familiar, but he never made the connection that his mother and sister lived in one just like it. He moved on, following the others.

Jahel shouted in jubilation when a white C-130 flew past the village as it descended. "It will lead us to the Dinka!" He spurred his horse into a gallop and led the Janjaweed out of the village, following the aircraft.

Near Wer Ping

Bard Green turned two miles short of the village and rolled the Hercules out on a heading of 125 degrees. It was his first solo mission as an aircraft commander and he was worried. He couldn't find the relief camp. "They said it was ten miles southeast of Wer Ping," the copilot said. "It should be on the nose."

The flight engineer unbuckled his seatbelt and stood with his head against the overhead panel to get a better view of the terrain. A hot wind was driving dust into billowing, rolling ripples along the ground. "Eleven o'clock," he said. "North of the river. Two clearings shaped like a dumbbell."

"Tallyho," Green said. He gave a thumbs-down gesture indicating they were going to land, and called for the before landing checklist. Green entered a tight orbit around the clearings. Now he could make out an area that had been cleared of brush and rocks for a landing strip. It was short and narrow but he could land. "Damn, where did all the people come from?" Tribesmen were streaming out of the bush and blocking the landing strip. "Where do they expect us to land?"

"Fly a low approach," the copilot said. "They'll get the idea."

"Flaps fifty percent," Green called, slowing the Hercules to approach speed. He turned final and descended to 200 feet as he flew over the startled tribesmen. Their upturned faces were a blur, but the flight crew had all experienced the look of hunger and despair that haunted their existence. "On the go," Green called, fire walling the throttles. He circled to the left so he could see. "I think they got the idea."

"I don't know," the copilot said. "Do we have enough room?"

Green studied the makeshift landing strip. "Yeah, I think so." The copilot rechecked the landing gear and placed his left hand over Green's right hand on the throttle quadrant. Green flew the Hercules onto the exact spot where he wanted to land and planted the big aircraft in a controlled crash. The main gear absorbed the landing shock as he slammed the nose down. He jerked the throttles aft and lifted them over the detent, throwing the props into reverse to drag the big cargo aircraft to a stop.

Suddenly, the Hercules jerked and skidded to the right, running off the packed dirt landing strip. "Differential thrust!" the flight engineer shouted over the intercom. One of the propellers on the left had not gone into reverse, which let the two propellers on the right create more drag, flinging them to the right. Both pilot's hands bounced off the throttles, and before Green could regain control, they hit a large boulder, shearing off the nose gear.

Green managed to grab the throttles and throw all props out of reverse as they skidded into the fleeing tribesmen. They felt a quick series of bumps before running over a four-foot deep depression in the ground. The left wing dipped down and the outboard propeller hit the ground. The recoil of the impact rocked the plane to the right and the right wing went down causing that outboard propeller to strike the ground. But this time a prop blade shattered and ricocheted into the wing, puncturing the fuel tank. Fuel streamed out as the Hercules rocked back to the left. The right wing lifted high into the air as the fuel ignited and the left wing crumpled under the impact. The aircraft came down again as the nose plowed into a deep gully. Now the tail came up and stood the Hercules on its nose. For a fraction of a second it stood there, poised on the verge of going over. Then it fell back on its belly, still right side up as flames engulfed the right wing.

Staff Sergeant Loni Williams was strapped into a parachute jump seat on the cargo deck and the first to react. The moment the aircraft stopped moving, he was out of his seat and checked on the loadmaster, Louise Colvin. She was stunned but conscious. Williams grabbed her by the arms and dragged her over the cargo pallets to the crew entrance door aft of the flight deck. He pulled the emergency handle and jettisoned the door. He pushed her out and crawled onto the flight deck as smoke filled the aircraft. The two pilots and the flight engineer were slumped forward, bloody and unconscious. Williams pulled the flight engineer back, released his straps, and heaved him towards the ladder leading to the crew entrance door.

"Lou!" he bellowed. "Gimme a hand!" Williams was all motion as he did the same with the copilot. Now he was coughing and couldn't see as he fumbled for Green who was still strapped into the left seat. He managed to drag him out of his seat and over the flight engineer and copilot who were lying on the deck.

Williams scrambled down the ladder still holding onto Green and threw him out the open crew entrance. He turned and reached into the smoke that had engulfed the flight deck. He grabbed both men and pulled for all he was worth. He stumbled out the hatch backwards dragging the two men and tripped over the inert Green who was still lying on the ground. "Lou! Get your ass over here!" He dragged the copilot and flight engineer clear of the smoke billowing out of the aircraft as the loadmaster came running back. "About fuckin' time!"

Williams fell to his knees coughing and retching from smoke inhalation. He looked up as the loadmaster disappeared into the crew entrance door. A moment later, she emerged out of the smoke carrying a first aid kit and her survival vest. Together, they carried the two pilots and flight engineer to safety.

* * *

BermaNur bent over the saddle's pommel, his cheek against his horse's neck. It had been a long run and he had carefully husbanded his mount, varying the gait, yet always urging it on. He sensed the horse still had more to give, and he was determined to outdistance the others. Even Jahel had waved him past, shouting his approval. Now only Jahel's second in command, a superb horseman, was in front of him. Ahead, he saw the burning wreckage of a Hercules and his spirits soared. Allah was most great and his justice certain. The rider in front slowed to a canter and then to a walk. BermaNur slowed and rode beside him, wise enough to know the race was over and not to shame a superior.

The rider stopped when he saw two Americans standing over their comrades lying on the ground. He leaned forward, his arms resting on the pommel, as a cunning look spread across his face. One of the Americans was a woman and the other a short African. "A *kafir*," the rider snorted. He turned and ordered BermaNur to stop. "This is not for you." He waved his AK-47 at the teenager, making his point. BermaNur reined his horse around and trotted away. He had made a mark and that was enough for now. He turned to watch – and to learn.

Alone, the rider cantered up to the Americans, still waving his AK-47. He smiled wickedly as he circled the Americans. Then he reined his horse into the *kafir*, pushing him away from the woman.

Malakal

G.G. sat at the scheduling desk in his normal position, chair rocked back, feet up on the desk, and practicing a card trick that required a difficult sleight-of-hand movement when a loud wail came over the radio's loudspeaker. He bolted upright, dumping the cards on the floor, and hit the mute button. Automatically, he copied the numbers on the readout as he hit the transmit button to call Allston and his staff. "Boss, the emergency locator beacon on Bard Green's Herk has activated."

"Be there in three," Allston replied. "Call Lane and Malaby. And notify Colonel Vermullen."

Near Wer Ping

The Janjaweed grabbed Lou by the collar and dragged her backwards while still waving his AK-47 at Williams on the other side of his horse. But Louise Colvin was not another hapless victim of rape by the marauding Janjaweed. She twisted and dug in her heels just as the horseman squeezed off a short burst at Williams. The three shots went wild, high above Williams' head, as she grabbed the Janjaweed's arm and pulled him out of the saddle. The horse reared as Williams pulled a combat knife out of his right boot. He scampered under the rearing horse, going directly for the Janjaweed. "Let him go!" he shouted. Lou released her grip, allowing the man to regain his balance and come to his feet. The Janjaweed spun around, bringing his AK-47 to bear. But Williams was on him and grabbed the back of the man's neck as he brought his knife up in a hard thrusting motion, cutting deep into the Janjaweed's chest below the sternum. Williams pulled the Janjaweed onto the knife, driving the tip into his heart. Lou grabbed the reins of the rearing horse as the Janjaweed died.

BermaNur saw his comrade go down and fired a long burst from the saddle. "Hit the dirt!" Williams roared as he dropped to the ground. Lou released the horse's reins as she fell. It was the first time BermaNur had ever fired an AK-47 and the barrel lifted, sending the rounds high over the Americans' heads. BermaNur dismounted and fired again. This time, two slugs cut into the horse. It bucked in terrible pain as Williams rolled clear and scooped up the dead Janjaweed's AK-47. He squeezed off a short burst.

He missed, but it drove the teenager back, who was now more concerned with saving his horse than avenging his fellow Fursan. Williams selected single-shot on the AK-47 and carefully aimed at the retreating teenager. He squeezed the trigger. He missed again and roared in frustration.

"You can't hit squat with an AK-47 at this range," Lou told him. She grabbed the weapon and shot the dying horse, putting it out of its misery. "Gimme an M-16 any day of the week." She had been raised on a ranch in Oregon and grew up with horses and guns. Williams methodically stripped the dead Janjaweed and horse of weapons and ammunition. He deliberately focused on the task, ignoring the tears streaking Lou's cheeks. "Damn," she muttered over and over, stroking the dead horse's ears.

Williams stood and looked around. The Dinka had all disappeared and they were alone. "We need to find better cover. The bastard will be back. With his buddies."

Malakal

G.G. spread the chart out for Allston and Vermullen and quickly plotted the coordinates. "This is the location of the crash. It's accurate to three meters." He typed a command into his computer and showed the men a detailed satellite photograph of the area. "But we don't know the status of the crew."

"We assume they are alive until we know otherwise," Allston said.

"Weapons?" Vermullen asked.

"The UN doesn't allow us to carry weapons," Dick Lane, the ops officer, said.

Vermullen was stunned that the Americans could be so stupid. "An order from the UN is only a point of discussion," he told them. "Time is of the essence. We have two or three hours at the most. The clock is running."

"How many men do you have and when?" Allston asked.

"I have eighty preparing now." He checked his watch. "They should be ready to board in twenty minutes."

"Paratroops?" Allston asked.

"All of them."

Allston was impressed. He knew what it took for a paratrooper to suit up for a combat jump. He turned to Malaby. "The birds?"

"We got two on station. Both are OR and good to go. Sir, I must protest. We need to coordinate this with Addis Abba."

"That will take a couple of days," Allston told her. "Configure the birds for a personnel drop." Malaby jammed her blue beret on and disappeared out the door. Allston watched her go. She was a good maintenance officer, but inflexible and short on imagination, two traits essential for success in any emergency. "I'll lead in number one. G.G. you're with me." He thought for a moment and turned to Lane. "Dick, I want you in the left seat of number two. You fill in the crews. We brief at the aircraft and in the air. We're like Gumby on this one – max flexibility."

"Marci Jenkins in your right seat," Lane said. "She'll give me a ration of shit I don't need if she gets left out." He rattled off a list of names, filling in the other crew positions. "Boss, we're pushing this one."

"Tell me."

Near Wer Ping

Allston throttled back and the C-130 descended, trading altitude for airspeed. "Go Guard," he told Marci. The copilot punched at a button on the UHF radio, selecting the emergency radio channel. Allston hit the transmit button under his left thumb. "Any Irregular, this is Gizmo One on Guard. How copy?"

Williams's faint voice came over the radio. "Read you five by, Gizmo One. Is that you, Boss?"

The worry that bound Allston yielded a notch. At least one of the crew was alive and transmitting on a handheld emergency radio. "Affirm. Is that you, Loni?"

"That's a roger, Boss. Me and Lou are okay, the pilots and engineer are messed up a little, but conscious. No broken bones and we got the bleeding stopped."

Allston allowed a satisfied grunt. "Say location." On cue, a bright flash on the ground flickered at them. An old-fashioned survival mirror from Lou Colvin's survival vest had worked its magic. "Got it."

"Boss, there's over a hundred Janjaweed in the area. I morted one and they're pissed."

"Help is on the way," Allston told him. He keyed the intercom. "Loadmaster, please have Colonel Vermullen come to the flight deck. Marci, go common." Again, she punched at the radio and switched to the UHF frequency the C-130s used to communicate between themselves. He keyed the radio. "Gizmo Two, how copy?" Lane confirmed the radio transmissions were loud and clear. "Roger," Allston replied. "Hold clear of the area, above the cloud deck. I don't want the Janjaweed to know you're here." Less than a minute later, the big Frenchman climbed onto the flight deck. He had shed his parachute and most of his gear in order to move around. Allston quickly briefed him on the number of Janjaweed Williams had seen. "We may have to fight our way in."

Vermullen snorted. "What is this 'we,' Yank?" He hunched over the navigator's table with G.G. and studied the chart. "I'll parachute in with my team to secure the area and evaluate the situation on the ground. Hold the other aircraft in reserve." They were on the same wavelength.

"May I make a suggestion?" Marci said. "It would be nice to have some firepower on board when we land to extract you."

"What are you thinking?" Vermullen asked.

"Leave a few shooters on board." She pointed to the emergency escape hatch above their heads. "We can put one in the top hatch, sort of like a nose gunner, and have a couple more on the ramp, like last time."

Allston reevaluated the young woman. She was definitely showing fangs, which he liked, and was much more aggressive than many of her male counterparts. Allston turned to Vermullen. "We can do that. Colonel, what do you think?"

Vermullen studied the overhead hatch. "How will he get up there?"

"The loadmaster can rig a ladder," Allston told him.

"I'll detail three shooters to stay behind," Vermullen said.

"No volunteers?" Allston asked.

Vermullen snorted. "No *parachutiste* trusts a pilot to safely land. It is much safer to bail out."

"Tell them not to shoot off a prop," Allston replied.

Williams voice came over the Guard channel. "Gizmo One! We're taking fire from the brush and tree line north of our position."

Vermullen studied the terrain below. "Where exactly are they located?"

Allston keyed the Guard channel. "Loni, give us a flash." Again, Williams used the survival mirror.

Vermullen pinpointed his location. The Americans were in an open area with a clear field of fire between them and the Janjaweed. The legionnaires would have been sitting ducks if they had parachuted in as planned, but Vermullen was a master tactician and quickly worked the problem, his eyes darting from the chart to the terrain below. It was time for Plan B. "The wooded area behind the Janjaweed blocks their field of fire." He pointed to an open area. "Captain G.G., can you insert us in that small clearing behind the Janjaweed?" G.G. assured him he could. "*C'est bon.* We will attack them from the rear. Once we have their undivided attention, Major Lane can insert Major Mercier and his *parachutistes* to secure the Americans and the landing area. If our luck holds, we can drive the Janjaweed towards Mercier."

"The old hammer and anvil works every time," Allston said. He relayed the plan to Lane who was orbiting fifteen miles to the south. "Gizmo Two, you're cleared to ingress the area. Drop on Williams when I clear you."

"Turning inbound now," Lane replied.

G.G. stood behind the copilot as Allston maneuvered the big aircraft, lining up on an open area north of the brush where the Janjaweed were hiding. When G.G. had his bearings, he jumped into his seat and drove the crosshairs on the radar display over the small clearing where Vermullen wanted to be inserted. "Sandwich time," the navigator said. At exactly four nautical miles out, G.G. called, "Two minutes." The loadmaster, Staff Sergeant James MacRay, reported that Vermullen was standing in the jump door and the legionnaires were ready to go. Allston dropped the Hercules to 800 feet above the ground. "One minute," G.G. called.

"We're taking ground fire," Marci said.

"Colonel Allston," MacRay said, "the jumpmaster said to descend to 600 feet. They want minimum time in the chutes."

Allston descended 200 feet, and was flying straight and level as G.G. counted down. "Green light," the navigator said. The C-130 shifted as the forty paratroopers marched swiftly out the two jump doors, twenty to a side. Allston jinked the bird hard to avoid ground fire as he climbed.

"*Merde!*" the French jumpmaster in the rear shouted over the intercom. "MacRay fell out the door! I see his parachute."

"Fuckin' lovely!" Allston roared. "I thought he was tethered in."

Vermullen's paratroopers were out of their harnesses and advancing on the Janjaweed in small groups within seconds after hitting the ground. It wasn't the glamorous, shoot from the hip, Hollywood portrayal of combat but a methodical and purposeful clearing action. The legionnaires directed their fire in mutual support, rapidly reloading, and always moving forward.

Lane's voice came over the radio. "Two minutes out. Got you in sight."

"You're cleared to drop," Allston radioed. "Get as close to Williams as you can."

"I've got a bright flash from the ground," Lane replied.

"That's your target," Allston told him. He was well clear of the Janjaweed and orbited to the north as Lane's C-130 ran in, also at 600 feet and 120 knots.

G.G. watched Lane's C-130 as it over flew Williams' position. "He's not dropping." A parachute popped open in the Hercules' wake. "No! No!" the navigator shouted as more parachutes deployed. "They blew it," he moaned. "They're gonna land a half-mile long."

Unaware the Americans were uncovered, Vermullen and his legionnaires drove the Janjaweed out of the brush. "Vermullen's driving 'em towards Williams," Marci warned.

"Got 'em," Allston replied. His eyes narrowed as he calculated the distances. The Janjaweed would overrun the survivors before Mercier's legionnaires could reach them. "We're landing," he announced. "Jumpmaster, I need a shooter on the flight deck and two on the ramp."

"I'll rig the ladder." G.G said. He disappeared onto the cargo deck as the French jumpmaster climbed onto the flight deck with his snub-nosed FAMAS G2 assault rifle and two bandoliers of ammunition. G.G. shoved a ladder onto the flight deck and worked to erect it as Allston turned short final, the aircraft's nose high in the air. G.G. reached up and opened the top hatch.

"Hold on!" Allston ordered. He planted the C-130 hard and reversed the props with the aircraft's nose still in the air. A cloud of dust roared out in front of them as Allston stomped on the brakes. They were still moving when he turned the nose toward the approaching Janjaweed. "Shooter in the top hatch." The jumpmaster scrambled up the ladder and braced himself as he fired in short bursts. "Cease fire!" Allston shouted as he played the throttles and brakes to pivot the aircraft around. The C-130's tail swung towards the Janjaweed and the shooters on the ramp under the tail opened up as Vermullen's legionnaires reached the brush line and joined in, catching the Janjaweed in a deadly crossfire.

However, the Beggara were skilled fighters and returned fire as they mounted their horses and ran for safety. Two horses and their riders went down. One horse was up without its rider and bolted clear. Its tall rider stood up, unhurt, and looked calmly around.

* * *

BermaNur saw Jahel's horse in full gallop with no rider, and without thinking, chased after it. He saw Jahel stand and veered to his right, racing for the tall sheik. Bullets zipped over his head and one ripped across his shoulders, barely breaking his skin. Jahel saw him and stood rock still, not moving as round after round missed their mark. He casually extended his right arm as BermaNur closed the distance. At the last possible moment, BermaNur slowed his horse and grabbed Jahel's hand. The sheikh swung up in an easy motion and straddled the horse behind the saddle as BermaNur dug his heels into the horse. They raced for safety. "From today," Jahel said, "you will join my bodyguard and ride beside me."

* * *

Allston was on the radio. "Williams, get on board ASAP. Jumpmaster, tell everyone to get on board." The Frenchman sat in the top hatch and keyed his handheld radio to relay Allston's order. The two groups of legionnaires converged on the Hercules.

"Colonel Allston," the jumpmaster said. "Colonel Vermullen wants to destroy the wrecked Hercules."

From her side of the flight deck, Marci could see the wrecked C-130 and scanned it with her binoculars. "It's pretty much burned out," she told Allston.

Allston made a decision. "Leave it. We need to get the hell out of Dodge, like now." He was worried the Janjaweed might circle back and catch them when they were taking off and at their most vulnerable. Again, the jumpmaster relayed the order to Vermullen. Loni Williams scrambled onto the flight deck, a very relieved man. "Got all your crew aboard, Williams?"

"Yes, sir," Williams replied. Now they had to wait for the legionnaires to board. In the lull, Williams handed Allston a cell phone. "I got this off the bastard I morted."

Allston examined the cell phone as the first of the legionnaires piled on board. "What the hell?" Allston wondered. "It won't work out here."

"Check the antenna," G.G. said. "I'm guessing it's for satellite communications. I've never seen a satcom that small. Pretty damn sophisticated." Allston handed the satcom back to Williams.

The loadmaster's very shaken voice came over the intercom. "Everybody is on board except Colonel Vermullen and four legionnaires holding the perimeter."

"MacRay, are you back to stay?" The sergeant said that he was. "Good decision," Allston replied. "Do another headcount while we turn around." He played the throttles and turned the Hercules, aligning it on the narrow dirt path. Then he slowly backed it into position. "MacRay, get Vermullen and his shooters on board. Before takeoff checklist," he told Marci. They quickly ran the checklist as the last of the legionnaires boarded.

"All accounted for," MacRay said.

"Strap in," Allston ordered. "We're going home." He pushed the throttles up and they were rolling. The big aircraft bounced over the rough terrain as they accelerated and the main gear thumped loudly in protest. The nose gear came unstuck and they were airborne. "Gear up." He turned out to the east. "Marci, you got it." He slumped into his seat and took a long pull at a water bottle as they climbed out and Marci cleaned up the Hercules. "Damn," he muttered to himself.

"What's the matter?" Marci asked.

"We're down to four birds."

"But we didn't lose anyone," she replied.

Not this time, Allston thought. How much longer would their luck hold?

EIGHT

E-Ring

*T*he sharp click of Yvonne Richards' heels echoed down the deserted halls of the Pentagon. It was early Saturday morning and she made a mental note to make sure her staff was at work. She pushed through the doors that led into Fitzgerald's office. "The General is expecting you," Mary said. "Go right on in."

"Is he in a good mood this morning?"

"Yes ma'am." The secretary beamed. "I heard him laugh." Fitzgerald had coached her on how to react if Richards asked that question.

Richards didn't want to be the person who spoiled the General's day and re-evaluated her strategy. She gave the secretary the knowing smile that they were sharing an inner secret. "Thanks for the heads up." She knocked on the general's door and entered.

Fitzgerald waved Richards to a seat and kicked back in his chair. The Boys were starting to deliver and he knew what was on her mind. "What's so urgent?"

"NSA intercepted a secure telephone call between the head of the peacekeeping mission in Addis Ababa and the Secretary General of the UN early this morning." Both generals knew the National Security Agency had the UN wired for sound. "The Secretary General appears to be very upset." She tried to read Fitzgerald's body language, but there was nothing there and that bothered her. The way he concealed his reactions made it difficult for her to control the conversation. "It seems that Colonel Allston armed a C-130 and used it as a gunship." She opened her leather folder and handed Fitzgerald a small-scale chart of the Sudan. "It happened at a makeshift refugee camp for Dinkas. It's circled in red. The camp is located 180 miles west of Malakal, where the 4440th is based." Fitzgerald's left eyebrow twitched. The distance from Malakal was important, but he didn't need to be told where the 4440th was based. She missed the twitch and plunged ahead. "The UN head of mission in Addis Ababa wants the 4440th withdrawn. He claims Allston's aggressive actions have put the entire operation in jeopardy, and it is an incident the Government of the Sudan cannot, and will not, tolerate."

"Are you aware the 4440th lost a C-130 at the same refugee camp yesterday?"

Richard's eyes opened wide. "I hadn't heard. Did we lose anyone?"

It was the right response. "No one was killed or seriously injured, but two Janjaweed almost took the loadmaster, Staff Sergeant Louise Colvin, hostage. One of the Janjaweed was killed and the other driven off. Later, over a hundred Janjaweed showed up." He paused to let that sink in. "That number indicates they are now operating in force and growing. Luckily, Allston and a company of legionnaires arrived in time to drive them off. From this end, it appears that Colonel Allston's 'aggressive actions' saved a few lives." He didn't remind her that a commander never loses the right of self-defense.

"Sir, this may be a chance to get our people out of there."

"Not if the President wants to maintain a presence in the Sudan, which he does. Tell your contacts in the UN that if they want our support in the future, not to withdraw the 4440th."

"Sir, we're receiving too many contrary signals to make a commitment one way or the other. The UN wants us there but doesn't like what we're doing. The President wants to maintain a presence there but can't tolerate casualties. And Allston seems to be a trigger-happy cowboy shooting up the place. We need stability if we're going to support the UN in the Sudan."

"Which is exactly why I'm sending you over there to evaluate the situation and report back with recommendations."

Richards fought to control the panic that ripped at her. It was one thing to move in command circles and be a player in creating policy, but it was an entirely different matter to be caught up in actual operations where bullets were flying. The first stroked the ego and got you promoted, the second got you killed. "Sir, I know we haven't heard from Major Sharp, but let me touch base with my contacts and find out what's happening."

"By all means. But I want you over there ASAP."

Richards fought to keep her voice from shaking. She hadn't joined the Air Force for this, but she knew there was only one answer. "Yes, sir. I'll get right on it." She fought for time. "I'll need clearance from Khartoum, and that might take a few days." A name came to her and she calmed.

"Make it happen," Fitzgerald replied, "but get over there." He watched her as she rushed out of his office. "Welcome to the real Air Force." He opened a folder and went back to work. It was an unsigned authorization to provide the 4440th with side arms. He ground his teeth in exasperation. He had down-channeled Allston's request almost three weeks before and not one officer in logistics had the balls to authorize it. He scribbled his signature in bold letters and wrote 'Action today. Delivery within 72 hours.' He crossed out the seventy-two and wrote '36.'

Malakal

"It's unusually cool this morning," Allston said as he joined Dick Lane and Susan Malaby on the ramp as a C-17 taxied in.

"Right," Lane agreed. "It must be all of eighty. Down right tolerable. Won't even break a sweat today." The two men laughed.

Malaby didn't join in and was all business. "The C-17 wasn't on the schedule."

"Indeed," Allston replied. I'm hoping Major Sharp is on board." They hadn't heard from the Intelligence officer in four days and he was worried. The thought of what could happen to a pretty redhead running around Africa alone was very disturbing. The C-17 swung around and came to a halt, its nose to the runway. The engines did not stop as a loadmaster jumped off the ramp under the tail. He motioned and twelve Security Policemen deplaned as a loader arrived from the hangar. Six pallets quickly rolled off the C-17 as an Irregular signed the manifest. The loadmaster climbed back on board and the ramp came up. Within moments, the big cargo aircraft taxied out and turned onto the runway. The three officers watched as it took off. "That was quick," Allston said. The big airlifter had been on the ground less than ten minutes.

"And no Major Sharp," Lane said. "We're gonna have to go find her, Boss."

"I was afraid of that. Any suggestions who we send?"

"G.G. speaks Arabic," Lane said. "He talks to the locals all the time. We could always use a little muscle. Maybe Colonel Vermullen could lend us some of his."

"I'll ask him," Allston replied. He turned to Malaby. "Lay on a C-130, ASAP." She spoke into her personal communicator, making it happen. "Dick," Allston continued, "I'd like you to honcho it. Bard Green in your right seat."

"I thought you'd never ask," Lane replied. Allston liked what he heard and he was getting the responses he wanted.

One of the passengers from the C-17 marched up. He was a big and young-looking security cop. He snapped a sharp salute and introduced himself – Master Sergeant Jerry Malone from Dover Air Force Base, Delaware. Allston returned the salute. "Welcome to Bumfuck South," Allston said. "Please tell your men we don't salute in the open. Don't want someone taking pot shots."

"Will do, sir. You don't happen to have a Staff Sergeant Loni Williams here?"

"We do. You know him?"

"In a manner of speaking. We babysat him when he was in our confinement facility."

"What was he locked up for?" Lane asked.

"Barroom brawl. The Air Force dropped the charges and we released him. A few days later, the Dover police produced a warrant for his arrest for striking a cop. But he was over here by then. We're still scratching our heads over how he did that."

"Well, Sergeant Malone," Allston said, "I'd like to keep him here for awhile." Malone didn't understand. "He's useful," Allston explained.

"We got a couple of more just like him on ice back at Dover."

"I can use 'em," Allston replied. As a commander, he had learned a very inconvenient truth. When things got rough, the best men for the job were often in the slammer.

"Can I take Williams along?" Lane asked.

"You got him," Allston said. He turned to Malone. "Is there anything else, Sergeant?"

"I need someone to sign for two-hundred side arms."

"Sign for what?" Malaby blurted.

"For two-hundred Colt .45 semi-automatic pistols with holsters, belts, and ammunition," Malone replied. "As requested."

"Is that the Colt they call the Peacemaker?" Lane asked.

"No, sir," Malone answered. "That was the old Colt .45 six-shooter, sometimes called the Single Action Army. These are the Colt 1911A, forty-five caliber, semi–automatics. These puppies may be old but they've got stopping power. You either love 'em or hate 'em, depending on which end of the barrel you're looking down."

"Better to be the peacemaker than the target," Allston added. "Sergeant Malone, get everyone trained and issue them a weapon."

"Colonel," Malaby protested, "someone will shoot their foot off."

"Not after I train them," Malone promised.

Abyei

BermaNur reined his horse to a halt slightly behind Jahel at the top of a low ridge overlooking the village a mile to the west. The teenager imitated Jahel as he leaned on his saddle's pommel to wait. A few minutes later, Jahel straightened up and pointed to the north. "There." Three helicopters hugged the ground as they over flew the horsemen and converged on the village. The Janjaweed tensed as the three Russian-built MI-24 attack helicopters bore down on their target in a vee formation. Jahel turned to BermaNur. "Is your family still there?"

"No, sire. They left with most of the others." He failed to mention that his mother and sister had flown out on a C-130 with the UN refugee workers the day before. A trail of smoke reached out from the helicopters as they emptied their rocket pods into the village. A series of explosions echoed over the horsemen as the rocket barrage tore the huts apart, killing and maiming the tribesmen who had not escaped.

The helicopters circled to reposition for a strafing run. Jahel sneered at the ugly machines as the burring sound of their 12.7mm Gatling guns split the morning air. "They have no honor, but we are no match for their guns and rockets."

"But sire," BermaNur protested, "they are only killing vermin."

"To have honor, you must face your enemy and look him in the eye when you kill him. There is no honor in this." He watched dispassionately as the helicopters made repeated passes over the big village, leveling it with high explosive rounds. When there was nothing left to shoot at, they circled over the empty refugee camp and raked it with gunfire. On command, they disengaged and settled to the ground. Jahel reined his horse around and cantered towards the waiting machines. BermaNur followed behind.

Major Hamid Waleed climbed out of the lead helicopter and shoved his thumbs in his web pistol belt as he struck a pose. Rivulets of sweat coursed down his cheeks from under his aviator sunglasses and sweat strains spread across his tight uniform shirt. He stared at two Baggara as they approached. Jahel reined to a halt, but did not dismount. It was the first time the two men had met and they stared at each other, each taking the others measure. Jahel leaned across his pommel. "Salem."

"And you are?" Waleed demanded in Arabic.

Jahel came erect with a dignity beyond Waleed. "I am Sheikh Amal Jahel of the Rizeigat. I am a cavalier of the Fursan and lead the Janjaweed." He smiled as if he couldn't be bothered with Waleed's credentials. "How may I be of service?"

Waleed caught the implied insult. "And I am Major Hamid Waleed of the Army of the Sudan" – his right hand swept the helicopters – "and commander of these falcons. We finish what you cannot."

Jahel's Arabic was not good enough to continue the verbal sparring. "We are not armed to fight the French legionnaires, and we cannot move as swiftly as the Americans."

"What is your problem?" Waleed replied.

"Because of the Americans, the legionnaires ride the wind. If we are to be your sword and cleanse this land, you must control these infidels."

Waleed smiled. "The Americans will be punished. Their leaders have no stomach for a fight and they will leave. Without their airplanes, the French will not be able to reach out to harm you."

"*Insh' Allah,*" Jahel replied.

Waleed pulled a folded chart out of his hip pocket. "It is truly as God wills," he said, unfolding the chart. He pointed to a village one hundred miles to the south. "Can you be there in two days?" Jahel nodded and Waleed smiled. "We will be waiting for you."

"*Insh' Allah,*" Jahel said. "Be careful, commander of falcons. These infidels know how to fight." He reined his horse around and headed to the south.

Malakal

A volley of small-arms fire echoed from the makeshift firing range the security cops had built on the far side of the compound and woke Allston. He turned over and tried to go back to sleep. Another volley echoed outside his tent-trailer. Automatically, he checked his watch. It was 6:30 Sunday morning and he had slept in. He sat on the edge of his bunk and slowly came to life. What was he going to do about Jill Sharp? Dick Lane had returned empty-handed, and she was still missing after ten days. As best Lane could learn, Jill had interviewed the UN Head of Mission in Addis Ababa about the rescue of the Legionnaires at Wer Ping, and then taken off for Djibouti where she had contacted the US Air Force detachment operating from the airfield. From there, she had disappeared. Where the hell are you? Allston raged to himself.

A knock at his door brought him to his feet. "Colonel!" it was G.G. "A UN supply truck just rolled in with Major Sharp."

That particular problem went up in smoke only to be replaced with a simmering anger. "Where is she?"

"Waiting in Ops."

"On my way." He quickly dressed and pulled on his boots as his anger flared. G.G. was waiting for him outside. Together, they headed for the hangar offices as another volley echoed from the firing range. He noticed that G.G. was wearing a web belt with a holstered .45 automatic and an ammunition pouch. "I see you qualified."

G.G. shifted the weight of the .45 further back on his hip. "Yep" was all he said as he tilted his bush hat forward. He wore the hat and sidearm with pride.

The woman waiting for him was a far cry from the neat and impeccably uniformed officer he had last seen. Her ABUs and boots were filthy, her hair grimy and matted down, her fingernails broken, knuckles scraped, and a vicious bruise on her right cheek. Only her face and hands were clean. She drew herself to attention and braced for a reprimand. "You've been through the wringer," Allston said, fighting the urge to shout. "What in hell happened?"

She didn't answer. Instead, "I need five hundred dollars."

Allston exhaled, his relief obvious. "My second wife always opened a conversation like that."

"I need to pay off the truck driver. I had to bribe him to get here."

"You really need a bath, Major. You're way past your expiration date." She didn't reply. "One question. You came in on a UN truck, right?" She nodded. "So why do you have to bribe the driver?"

"Because his load was never meant to get here." She smiled at the confused look on Allston's face. "Corruption. By the way, that was two questions. Bath time. Please take care of my driver."

Allston watched her leave. "Please take care of my driver," he groused. But for some reason, he didn't really mind. "G.G. go hit up the APO for five hundred, my account." The postal clerk was also the unit's paymaster and informal bank.

*   *   *

"Colonel," Jill said, "I need to get my report off soonest. It's way overdue." A much different Jill stood in front of Allston and Vermullen. She was dead tired but squeaky clean and fresh in a clean set of ABUs. Her hair glowed, framing her face, and her blue eyes were clear. Allston was stunned, for in her own unique way, she was beautiful. He got a grip and chalked his reaction up to the 'only woman available' syndrome. Jill plugged her computer into the detachment's system and the report was on the wires within seconds. "That's going to stir up a hornet's nest," she said. An explanation was in order. She typed a command into her computer and spun it around for Allston to read the report.

"Ah, shit," he moaned. "Idi, you need to read this." The big Frenchman read the report without comment. Allston motioned her to a chair. She sat down gracefully, her wide hips almost filling the seat. He stifled an inward groan and looked away. She was too full-figured to meet the beauty standards demanded by Hollywood and fashion magazines, but she was incredibly alluring and he was suddenly aware of an aching void in his life. He forced himself to concentrate. "Okay, what happened?"

Jill related how she had interviewed the UN head of mission and his two cohorts, the Zulu chief and Nigerian general, who she called the three stooges. They had talked around her in French and Swahili, assuming that she was a typical American and only spoke English. Fortunately, she was fluent in both languages. Based on what she heard, she filled in the gaps and was certain the three men were selling UN supplies to the highest bidder on the black market. Her problem was proving it. "From Addis," she continued, "I went to Djibouti where all UN supplies arriving by ship are offloaded. The Air Force detachment there is a study in frustration and the UN won't allow them to airlift even a toothpick into the Sudan. It's all got to go by truck, so I bribed my way onto a UN truck convoy that was destined for Malakal. That's when it got interesting."

She recounted how the fourteen-truck convoy was never meant to reach its destination and had lost five trucks in the first two hundred miles. By the time they reached the Sudan border, they were down to three trucks. Two of the trucks disappeared that night and the only way she was able to continue was by paying more bribes. But she ran out of money and had to promise the driver she would pay him even more when they reached Malakal. It had been touch and go and at one point she was certain he was going to abandon her. "It got a little physical, but I convinced him otherwise. Based on what I overheard from the drivers, about one truck in ten reaches its destination. I don't know how much the three stooges are skimming off the top, but it's substantial. You should see their homes and cars in Addis."

"Not to mention their women," Allston grumbled. "It sounds like the African version of the Iraqi 'Oil for Food' scam is alive and well."

"That's the good part," Jill said. "Apparently, the three stooges promised the Sudanese government that the UN peacekeepers would not react to any incident by the Janjaweed as long as they get their kickbacks."

"Well, we certainly have been reacting lately," Allston said. "Which is contrary to their game plan."

Jill nodded. "According to the jungle telegraph, the three stooges popped a few hemorrhoids when you rescued the crew that crashed at the refugee camp."

"So you heard about that even when traveling in the outback," Vermullen said.

"The jungle telegraph," Jill replied, "is very efficient." She didn't mention the rumor of a deal cut between the UN commissioners and the Sudanese government over oil.

G.G. knocked at the door. "They're back," he sang. "The honorable Major Hamid Waleed and crew."

"What the hell does he want now?" Allston groused, still angry from the last time they had met.

"The supply truck Major Sharp came in on," G.G. answered.

Allston jammed on his hat and ran out of his office. "No fucking way." Vermullen, Jill, and G.G. were right behind him.

"We're due for re-supply," Vermullen said.

"If what's on the truck is yours, you'll get it," Allston promised. He slowed when he saw Waleed. "G.G., translate for me. Tell him to get the fuck off my base."

G.G. spoke in Arabic and greeted the Sudanese major, carefully following the established rituals. After a lengthy reply from Waleed, the two men babbled on for a few minutes. It was enough for Allston to cool down. They finally reached an end and G.G. turned to Allston "He says he must confiscate the truck as it is smuggling contraband."

"What contraband?" Allston demanded.

"Weapons," Waleed answered in English.

Vermullen headed for the loaded truck, which was still parked in front of the hangar. He ripped off the tarpaulin covering the load. Over half of the crates were clearly marked for the Legion. Vermullen fixed Waleed with a hard stare. For a moment, it was a contest of wills. Then the Frenchman relaxed and looked away. "Let him have it."

"Why?" Allston demanded. Vermullen jutted his chin towards the hangar. Over a hundred Sudanese soldiers were scattered around the perimeter, their weapons at the ready. In his anger, Allston had lost situational awareness. It was a mistake he would not make again. Waleed shot a look of contempt at Allston and Vermullen, turned and barked a command. Within moments, the loaded truck was moving away as the soldiers followed on foot. Allston burned with anger. Slowly, he regained control and forced himself to calm down. "How are you doing on munitions?" he asked Vermullen.

"We're getting low," Vermullen admitted.

"They're probably taking it to the Sudanese Army dump at Bentiu," Jill said.

"How do you know that?" Allston asked.

She shrugged. "The truck driver. Some men can't keep their mouth shut around women."

Allston pulled a face. "And I thought that only applied to American males."

"It's a universal affliction," Vermullen added. "Leave it for now." He wasn't ready to take on Waleed and the Sudanese Army.

NINE

Malakal

Allston stood in the operations office attached to the big hangar and wondered how long the creaky air conditioner in the window had to live. It still managed to keep the temperature down to a relatively reasonable eighty-four degrees but was making ominous sounds. He made a mental note to requisition a new one before the machine's demise, which was long overdue. A man's voice crackled over the UHF radio behind the scheduling counter. "UN Flight Ops, this is Dumbo One." Since he was alone in the office, Allston stretched his arm across the waist-high counter for the remote mike, but couldn't reach it. "UN Flight Ops," the voice repeated, now more insistent, "I say again, this is Dumbo One."

"Don't get your knickers in a bunch," Allston muttered. He did an easy arm lift and swung his legs over the counter, landing on the other side.

"You'll break your neck, Colonel," Jill called from the doorway. Her voice was cool and reserved as always, the dispassionate observer.

Allston wished he could read her better. He smiled as his slightly misshapen jaw offset to the right and his hazel eyes flashed with amusement. "Piece of cake," he told her, playing to his fighter pilot image. It normally impressed the ladies, but not Jill Sharp. He scooped up the mike as Captain G.G. Libby finally returned from the latrine. Allston mashed the transmit button. "Dumbo One, UN Flight Ops, go ahead."

"Roger, UN Flight Ops. Dumbo One is inbound, fifteen minutes out, with a code three. Request priority handling." A code three was a distinguished visitor equivalent to a four star general or admiral, a cardinal, or a special assistant to the President, someone less than God but much more than a regular passenger.

Allston shot G.G. a look. "Sorry, Colonel," G.G. replied, "no Dumbos are on the schedule." Allston tossed the mike to Libby, an unspoken command to deal with it. Since Malakal didn't have a control tower, Libby checked the meteorological display and keyed the mike. "Dumbo One be advised the wind is calm, altimeter 30.10. Recommend Runway Two-three for landing, no other reported traffic."

A relieved pilot answered. "Roger, Flight Ops. Request minimum time on the ground for offload and transportation for five passengers."

"Well," Jill said, "no code three travels alone."

Allston gave her chain a little tug. "I think I knew that, Major." Jill never blinked. "I suppose we should go howdy those folks," he said. "They won't appreciate walking in, not in this heat."

"I'll get the two six-pacs," Jill replied. "Their air conditioners are still working and they've got room to haul any baggage." She picked up the phone, spoke a few words in Dinka, and listened to the reply before hanging up. "They'll be here in five minutes." For reasons beyond Allston's understanding, when Jill was involved the locals who worked for the Americans were not on African time, which otherwise meant jacking up the time required by a factor of five. True to her word, the two four-wheel drive pickups with their big crew cabs were waiting outside the hangar in four minutes. Allston and Jill walked out and climbed inside for the short drive to the parking apron. She told the drivers to keep the engines running and the air conditioners on.

The two Air Force officers watched in silence as the C-17 entered the pattern and turned onto the base leg. Allston's eyes narrowed as the big airlifter came down final and he gauged the approach and landing. "Not bad," he allowed, paying the pilot a rare compliment.

Libby's voice came over Allston's handheld UHF radio. "Dumbo, roll out long and taxi to the parking area at the far end. Transportation is waiting for your code three." Again, they waited in silence while the C-17 taxied in and a ground crew turned and marshaled it to a stop next to a C-130. The engines spun down and the crew door flopped down. A lone figure deplaned, looked around, and walked towards them.

Allston ran his hand through his short dark hair in frustration. "That's not the code three. That's Brigadier General Yvonne Richards."

Jill was surprised. "You know her?"

"Oh, yeah. She hates my guts and wants my head bad enough to fly sixty-five hundred miles to serve it up."

Jill was fully aware of his reputation and that Richards was an extremely attractive woman. She gave him the look he couldn't read. "Tell me you didn't."

"Make a strafing run on her? I only met her once, eight weeks ago in the Pentagon. I'm not suicidal, Major."

"Sorry, sir." She sat up straight, her eyes wide when she saw the other four passengers step off the C-17. "Is that who I think it is?"

The Dinka driver immediately recognized the actress. "Yes, mum. She comes here many times. She is loved in Africa."

"So that's our code three." Allston shook his head and groaned. "We got better things to do than baby-sit a Hollywood star with White House connections and a clueless one-star. Why would anyone in their right mind come to Malakal?"

Jill opened her door to get out. "It may have something to do with why we're here." She paused. "Or maybe it's about Abyei."

Allston climbed out of the six-pac to greet Richards as she walked in from the C-17. But he couldn't take his eyes off the beautiful actress following the general. "Don't get distracted," Jill warned. "Richards is all business. Let me handle her as much as I can."

"Sounds like a plan," Allston replied. He raked his bush hat to the right angle and walked with measured stride towards Richards. He stopped six feet short and threw her a sharp salute. "Welcome to the 4440th and Malakal," he said. She returned the salute as Jill joined them. Jill snapped a salute, which the general returned with a little smile.

Richards turned to the actress. "Tara, may I introduce Colonel Allston, the commander of the detachment, and Major Sharp, the detachment's Intelligence officer."

Tara Scott was one of those celebrities who truly needed no introduction. She had won two Academy Awards and spent the majority of her fortune on African relief. She was a petite five-foot-four with dark blonde hair, startling green eyes, and a magnificent figure. She extended her right hand to Allston, instantly captivating him as her ever-present cameraman recorded the scene. "General Richards has told me all about you," she purred. She introduced the four men with her. Only the cameraman was unarmed and the other three were bodyguards.

Allston gestured at the waiting pickups. "Why don't we get out of the sun? It's cooler inside." Tara smiled at him as she took his hand and climbed into the crew cab. He turned in time to see Richards staring at him. What is she up to? he thought. He held the door for her. "General?" She climbed in for the short drive to the hangar.

The Irregulars were a tight-knit group and word of the actress's arrival spread like wildfire. Within minutes, everyone who could think of an excuse was gathered in the hangar and craning their necks to get a glimpse of Tara Scott. Vermullen arrived in his battered Panhard utility truck and pushed through the crowd with Hans in tow. Even the old German wanted to meet her.

Richards sucked in her breath when she saw Vermullen. Nothing had prepared her for the shear physical presence of the man. Allston made the introductions and Vermullen snatched off his blue beret. "Mademoiselle Scott, this is indeed a rare privilege. My wife and I were enchanted by your last movie, 'Flying Blind,' and your work in African relief has made a difference."

Tara keyed on his French accent and replied in that language, thanking him for his kind words. Unexpectedly, she turned to G.G. and read his nametag. "Do you go by Gigi?"

The portly captain managed a very lame "Yes, ma'am" and became an instant fan.

"Well, folks, we need to get organized," Allston said, taking charge. He turned to Richards. "General, I assume we need to talk." She nodded in answer. "Major Sharp, Captain Libby, please escort our guests to the mess tent and find them billets. The ladies can use my quarters and I can move in with Major Lane." Within moments, the office had cleared out and he was alone with Richards. He cocked an eyebrow. "How may I help you, General?"

"General Fitzgerald sent me here to evaluate the situation on the ground and report back with recommendations as to our continued involvement. Needless to say, your conduct of operations has raised quite a few concerns."

"I can live with that. I'll detail Major Sharp to escort you and run interference. She's very good at that. But I do have a concern. Why is Scott here? This is a very dangerous part of the world."

"Colonel, the world has changed and image is everything. We are here in a humanitarian role and Tara reinforces that image. She wants to visit the refugee camp at Abyei."

"General, Hollywood stars with bullet holes in them are as dead as anyone else." It was obvious Richards hadn't heard the news. "The Army of the Sudan wiped Abyei off the face of the earth two days ago. Luckily, we got most of the refugees out the day before." He waited as the reality of where she was finally registered. "You'll have to excuse me, but I've got to see a very good pilot about a flight. I'll have someone escort you to the mess tent."

Wun Kwel, Warab, Sudan

Marci Jenkins tried hard not to think about her copilot, but it was like trying to ignore a five-hundred-pound gorilla sleeping in your bed. Allston was sitting in the right-hand seat and seemed content to be the perfect copilot even as he marked every word and move she made. Her fellow pilots joked how Allston often walked out to a C-130 that was about to start engines, kicked the copilot off, and settled into the still warm seat. It was a very informal test of the pilot's ability to command a C-130 and carry out their mission, and she accepted it as something a good commander did. There was none of the paperwork that went with a formal evaluation and only a verbal "Good job," or the dreaded "Ah shit," which was the last thing the pilots wanted to hear. Marci was brutally honest with herself and admitted she was having an "ah shit" moment. The village where they were scheduled to land and drop off five pallets of food and supplies simply wasn't there.

"Check the GPS coordinates," she told Allston, working to keep her voice matter-of fact and calm. Allston gave her a plus mark and double-checked the coordinates loaded into the GPS. He gave her a thumbs up and waited to see what she would do next. "Then we're here," she said as she entered a racetrack pattern anchored on the GPS coordinates Allston had just verified. She flew one orbit and disengaged the autopilot to descend to a thousand feet above the terrain. She leveled off and smoothly transitioned into a right pylon turn so Allston could see the ground out his side of the C-130. "It's the burned-out area next to the road," she told him. The road was little more than a dirt track and nothing was standing in the blackened area.

"Not much left down there but hot hair, teeth, and eyeballs," Allston replied. It was one of his expressions that many of the younger pilots had picked up, imitating their commander. Marci chalked it up to a male thing and running with the pack.

"RTB?" Riley, the flight engineer, asked.

"Too soon to go home," Marci replied. "We got fuel, let's look around before we head for home plate." Allston gave her another plus. That was exactly what he would have done. "There's a rest house about fifteen miles north," Marci explained. "It's next to a watering hole along the road. It should be easy to find." Allston gave her high marks for doing her homework before they flew the mission. "What do you think happened to the village?" she asked.

"Janjaweed," Allston replied. She smoothly rolled the Hercules out of the turn and climbed to 2000 feet above the ground. She reengaged the autopilot and the flight deck fell silent as they headed north. A few minutes later, Allston saw it. "On the nose. Lots of folks around the watering hole."

"I got 'em," Marci said. "I don't see any huts or animals. How many do you think there are?"

"Couple of hundred," Allston replied.

"Let's go howdy the folks," Marci said. Riley smiled. That was definitely an Allstonism. Marci hand flew the plane as they slowed and descended to a thousand feet above the people clustered around the only water source within miles. Again, Allston gave her high marks for judgment and flying ability. She was one of those true rarities – a natural pilot that became better with experience. "There's enough room to land on that straight section of road. Before landing checklist." Allston called out the checklist as they configured for landing. Marci flew a smooth approach and firmly planted the main gear on the hard earth. She rode the brakes and reversed engines, coming to a stop less than thirty yards from the watering hole. The mass of people ran towards the C-130.

Marci called the loadmaster, "MacRay, lower the ramp. We need to backup for takeoff." It seemed to take forever for the loadmaster to lower the cargo ramp under the tail to the horizontal and raise the door.

"Scanner's on the ramp," MacRay called. "All clear in the rear."

The desperate, starving refugees were almost to the C-130 as Marci backed slowly down the dirt track, away from the mass of people, and gaining the distance they needed for a takeoff roll. They stopped. "Everyone listen up," she said, her tone changing. "We're gonna keep the engines running and make this a fast off load. We're talking Guinness Book of Records. Go-go-go!" She climbed out of her seat and checked out the cargo deck. About a dozen tribesmen had crawled on board at the back and were ripping at the end pallet, desperate to get at the sacks of sorghum. She didn't like what she saw and bolted for her seat, reaching for her headset.

"Captain Jenkins!" the loadmaster shouted over the intercom. "We're taking hostile fire! Sounds like an AK-47."

"Time to get the hell out'a Dodge," Marci replied. Her words were clear and distinct with no signs of panic. "MacRay, dump the pallets. We gotta lighten up to takeoff."

"I can't go forward!" the loadmaster shouted. He was at the rear of the aircraft and the quick-release lever for jettisoning the pallets was forward, just aft of the flight deck.

"I'll get it," Riley yelled as he unstrapped from the flight engineer's seat. Now they heard the rattle of a submachine gun. Riley jumped off the flight deck and was back in seconds. "Got it."

"MacRay, hold on," Marci said over the intercom. She ran the engines up and released the brakes, accelerating. The pallets rumbled out the back.

"All clear!" MacRay shouted.

"Ah shit!" Marci roared, stomping on the brakes. A mass of people were running onto the road in front of them, blocking their takeoff roll. "MacRay, what's happening back there?"

"Small arms fire still coming from our six. They're shooting at the refugees. Jesus H. Christ! They're butchering 'em!"

Marci made a decision. "Get everyone you can on board. We're taking them with us."

"Will we have enough runway to takeoff with a load?" Allston asked.

Marci didn't hesitate. "Yeah."

"You sure?" he replied.

"Colonel, I think we do. If you don't, then kick me out of this seat and make the decisions. But as long as I'm sitting in the left seat . . ."

Allston released his seat belt and shoulder harness, and, for a split second, Marci was sure he was taking command of the aircraft. "Come on Riley," Allston called. "Let's get 'em loaded." Riley jumped out of his seat and scrambled down the steps to the cargo deck and opened the crew entrance door to let refugees board from the front. He passed a child up to Allston's waiting arms who dumped the infant on the crew bunk at the rear of the flight deck. Within seconds, twelve more children were crowded onto the flight deck. The track in front of them cleared.

"Button it up," Marci ordered. "Let's go."

Riley pulled the crew entrance door shut and locked it. He pushed his way through the children packed onto the flight deck, finally reaching his seat. The stench was overpowering and he smelled fresh urine. He strapped in and gestured to the rear. "It's a sardine can back there."

"MacRay, ready to go back there?" Marci asked over the intercom.

"Give me ten seconds," MacRay replied. They waited, feeling the mass of people on the cargo deck shift around. She ran the engines up, holding the brakes. The C-130's nose came down, digging into the dirt. "We got 'em all!" MacRay called from the rear, his voice triumphant. "Ramp's up and locked." Marci released the brakes and the Hercules started to move.

A man on horseback with an AK-47 slung across his back galloped up on their right. For a moment, he raced ahead of the accelerating C-130 before starting to fall behind. He looked directly at Allston, and, in that instant, the two recognized each other. "It's that crazy kid from Abyei!" Allston shouted. It was BermaNur and his mouth worked furiously as he cursed the Americans. He reached around for his AK-47, never breaking eye contact as he lost ground and fell back under the wing. His horse stumbled and he pitched forward, tumbling along the rocky ground. "Shit hot!" Allston roared. He hoped the kid broke his neck in the fall.

Marci felt the tail grow heavy as the passengers shifted around. "What the hell is going on back there?"

"They're climbing onto the ramp to get some room," the loadmaster answered.

"We're running out of runway," Allston said. The road ahead took a sharp bend to the left.

Marci kept forward pressure on the yoke and held the Hercules on the ground as long as possible. "Rotate . . . now," she said, pulling back on the yoke. They lifted off as the road turned and barely cleared a rock and low scrub. "Gear up."

Allston's left hand flashed out and lifted the gear handle. A hard silence came down on the flight deck as they climbed out. "Gear's up and locked," Allston said. He took a deep breath. "We almost got hosed down and I didn't think we were going to clear . . ." He couldn't finish the sentence.

"Piece of cake," Marci told him. It was exactly what Allston would have said. "MacRay, how many folks we got on board?"

"Standby," the loadmaster answered. "I'll come forward and get a head count." Five minutes later, MacRay tried to climb onto the flight deck, but it was too crowded with children for him to move. He counted heads. "Two-oh-four," he announced from the ladder.

Marci couldn't believe it. "How many?"

"Counting the thirteen ankle biters on the flight deck," MacRay said, "two hundred and four. They're all standing and jammed in like sardines. I've got 'em stuffed everywhere, storage racks, up in the empennage under the tail roosting like chickens, everywhere. I had to crawl along the side of the aircraft above their heads to come forward."

A single gunshot rang out. "Who's shooting?" Marci demanded.

MacRay climbed the steps onto the flight deck, shoving the children aside. He stood and bobbed his head around the corner looking aft. "Two guys are bulldozing their way foreword. I can't tell who's shooting." He drew his .45 semi-automatic.

"Riley," Marci said, "help him."

The flight engineer unstrapped and tried to stand, but a child was in his way. He picked the little girl up, stood in her spot, and dumped her into his seat. He picked up another child and shoved him into his seat. With enough room, he bulldozed his way to MacRay. He drew his semi-automatic and knelt beside the loadmaster. He chanced a look into the cargo compartment and quickly pulled back. "Got 'em," he said. "They're almost here. Both are armed."

"Take 'em out," Marci ordered. Allston started to protest. He didn't like the idea of gunfire on any aircraft, but they were out of options.

"You take the guy on the right," MacRay told the flight engineer. "On three. One, two, three." Both men leaned around the corner and fired a single round. "I got mine," MacRay said.

"Ditto," Riley said.

Two more gunshots and loud screaming echoed from the rear of the cargo deck. "What the hell!" Allston yelled. MacRay and Riley peered into the cargo hold, but couldn't see anything. More screams and shouts reached them.

"It's coming from the rear," MacRay said. "But I can't see anything to take a shot."

"Colonel," Marci said, "raise the door and lower the ramp. Put a little blue sky in their face. That should calm 'em down." Allston didn't hesitate. He reached for the control box on the flight control pedestal and hit the toggle switch. The open light came on and Marci sawed on the rudder pedals, yawing the C-130. "Anyone fall out?"

"I can't tell," MacRay replied. "But it's quiet back there. Hold on." He jumped down onto the cargo deck and talked to a woman. "I've got a woman here who speaks English. She says there are six or seven Janjaweed at the rear who snuck on board. They've killed some people to get room. Standby." Again, the passing seconds seemed like an eternity. "They're throwing bodies out the back and raping a couple of women."

"Not on my aircraft," Marci said. She slowed and put the C-130 into a nose up attitude and again sawed at the rudder pedals, whipping the tail back and forth. "That ought'a make a few pricks to go limp. Colonel, advise Outhouse of our situation." Outhouse was the radio call sign the Irregulars had given C-130 Ops.

Malakal

G.G. was in his normal position behind the scheduling counter in operations – rocked back in his desk chair, feet up on the counter, and practicing a card trick when the radio call came in. "Outhouse, Dondo Four," Allston radioed. G.G. acknowledged the call, relieved that the last mission of the day was inbound and that his commander was back. "Outhouse," Allston continued, "we're twenty minutes out with two hundred plus refugees on board. We are experiencing gunfire on the cargo deck and will require armed security police to off load."

G.G. came to his feet, not believing what he had just heard. "Dondo Four, say again."

"Dondo-Four has two hundred plus refugees on board and experiencing gunfire on the cargo deck. Have the security police meet us on the ramp."

"What the hell is going . . ." He regained control. "Say nature of emergency."

"Janjaweed are on board armed with knives and guns. Exact number unknown. We require armed intervention and medical aid on landing."

"Copy all," G.G. replied. He sprang into action and within thirty seconds had sounded the alert and the security police were headed for the parking ramp. Dick Lane was the first to arrive and G.G. explained the situation. He took a deep breath. "Sir, getting a hundred passengers on board a C-130 takes some hard packing, but over two hundred? You can't do it. It just can't be done."

"Yeah, it can, standing up," Lane replied. He grabbed the mike. "Dondo Four, say status." He wanted an update. Malaby, Jill, and Master Sergeant Jerry Malone, the recently arrive security cop, skidded through the door in rapid succession.

Allston's voice was cool and matter-of fact as he again described the situation. He paused. "Standby one, the loadmaster's talking to Captain Jenkins."

Jill was confused. "Why is he talking to Marci and not the Boss?"

"Because she's the aircraft commander," Lane explained, "and in command of the aircraft. The Boss is giving her a check ride."

"That's one hell of a check ride," G.G. muttered.

Allston was back on the radio. "Outhouse, Dondo Four. The loadmaster is talking to the refugees. They say there are eight Janjaweed at the rear and they have one AK-47."

"I really needed to hear that," Malone said under his breath.

"Outhouse," Allston radioed, "The Janjaweed can't get to the flight deck because of all the people in the way. We can make them offload out the back, but they'll probably come out shooting." He quickly outlined what he was thinking.

Malone liked what he was hearing. "We'll be waiting for them," he promised. The sergeant bolted from the room, issuing commands into his communicator.

"This is going down fast," Lane said, wishing Allston was there to make the decisions. "Get all the troops who are weapons qualified out to Malone to augment the cops. Two of the Herks on the ground are good to go, so let's get them airborne and out of here ASAP. Tow the Herk that is down for maintenance over to the civilian ramp." Malaby hurried out to make it happen. Lane thought for moment. A decision made, he said, "G.G. you've got the stick here. Contact Vermullen and get some firepower over here. I'll get two crews out to the Herks that are good to go." He bolted out the door.

Twelve minutes later, the two Herks were airborne and Lane focused on the emergency coming his way. He keyed his communicator and issued his last instructions. Now he had to wait. It seemed to take forever to tow the broken C-130, and he breathed a sigh of relief when it finally cleared the runway and turned into the civilian parking area.

Allston's voice came over his handheld radio. "Dondo Four, ten miles out."

Lane looked to the west, but he couldn't see the C-130. He counted to ten slowly. Then he saw it. He keyed his communicator. "Dondo Four in sight. Backstop, are you in place?"

"That's affirm," Malone answered. The security cops and the Irregulars who were weapons qualified were hidden in defensive firing positions around the ramp. Each of the sandbagged foxholes held three troops and provided overlapping fields of fire. The plan was to hide their muscle until needed. Lane's eyes tracked the C-130 as it entered the downwind leg.

He keyed his communicator. "Outhouse, any word from the French?" G.G. replied in the negative. "Where the hell are they?" Lane asked aloud. The C-130 turned onto a base leg, the aircraft still in a nose high attitude with the loading ramp lowered to the trail position. The C-130 came down final in a steep rate of descent with the aircraft's nose high in the air for a short field landing. Lane murmured his approval when the ramp lifted into the closed position, insuring it would not drag on landing.

Marci planted the C-130's main landing gear hard on the runway, 1500 feet short of the turnout to the parking ramp, and well past the civilian terminal at midfield. She slammed the nose down and immediately reversed the four props, dragging the Hercules to a crawl. The aircraft taxied in, swerving, accelerating, and then braking, creating a rough ride for anyone on board and not strapped in. A crew chief marshaled the C-130 as it turned into position, its nose facing the runway and tail towards the hangar. The crew chief gave the sign to run the engines up, kicking up dust and dirt, creating a smoke screen as the ramp lowered, this time to the ground. As planned, the crew chief ran for cover.

A wave of refugees flooded out the back of the C-130, only to sit down in a big group and cover their heads against the bellowing dust. "What the hell?" Lane grumbled. "Dondo, is everyone off?"

"That's an affirmative," Allston replied.

"Fast taxi to the runway and takeoff," Lane ordered. The big aircraft leaped forward as Marci applied power, blowing even more dust over the refugees sitting on the ramp. A man with an AK-47 stood up in the center of the refugees and fired a short burst after the moving C-130. Fortunately, the blowing dust spoiled his aim. A single shot echoed from the far corner of the hangar and the gunman crumpled to the ground. "What the . . ." Lane mumbled, searching for the shooter. A legionnaire was crouched in a firing position in the shadows sighting down a sniper rifle. "About fucking time," Lane growled.

Vermullen materialized out of the shadows and ambled towards Lane as if he were strolling down the Champs-Elysées. "A fine mess you've gotten us into, Laurel," he said with his best American accent. "My father was a Laurel and Hardy fan." He leaned across the hood of Lane's pickup and studied the refugees. "Cool the situation down. Time is on our side."

Lane keyed his communicator. "Backstop, weapons cold, repeat, weapons cold. Do not fire unless fired upon."

"Copy all," Malone answered

"Outhouse," Lane continued, "what happened to Dondo Four. I don't see them."

"They didn't takeoff and turned into the civilian parking area," G.G. replied.

Lane took a deep breath, relieved that Allston would soon be there to take command. He knew when he was in over his head. "Colonel Vermullen, what do you make of all this?"

Vermullen shrugged. "They have hostages, we have them surrounded, and nothing will happen until it is dark." The big legionnaire checked his watch. It was two hours to sunset. "Now what is this?" A man was standing in the midst of the refugees waving a makeshift white flag. "I believe they want to negotiate."

"What do we negotiate for?" Lane asked.

"For time," Vermullen replied. "Send an American. They hate the Legion."

Lane keyed his communicator. "I need a volunteer who speaks the local lingo to establish contact with the gunmen."

"I'm on it, Boss," G.G. replied. It was the first time anyone had called Lane 'Boss' and he liked it. A few minutes later, a pickup pulled up and

G.G. got out. "I'm your man," he announced. He motioned to the rear of the truck that was filled with cases of bottled water. "I figured this might help to get things moving."

"Good thinking," Lane replied. "I know you speak Arabic, but . . ." His words trailed off, his uncertainty showing.

"I've picked up quite a bit of the Nuer language," G.G. countered. "It's the most widely spoken language in this part of Africa." He rattled off a few phrases of the Nilo-Saharan language.

Vermullen replied in the same language and listened carefully to G.G.'s response. "You are very good."

A pickup slammed to a halt and Allston got out. "Okay, where are we?" A very relieved Lane rapidly filled him in, explaining how G.G. was ready to take a load of water under a white flag out to the refugees and try to open negotiations with the gunmen. Doubt nagged at Allston and he temporized, searching for a better option. "Those bastards shot at least a dozen or so on the aircraft and threw the bodies overboard. I'm guessing it's only a matter of time before they start shooting again." One of the six pacs pulled up and its doors swung open. Tara was the first out, followed by her cameraman. Jill and Richards were right behind him. Allston glared at the women. "You're in the wrong place, ladies."

Tara shook her head. "We will stay back and out of the way."

"Tara." Richards said, "Colonel Allston is right. We should leave."

The actress was accustomed to having her way and not about to change. "Yvonne, I know it is dangerous. But I have been to Africa many times and been in much worse situations. We did not come here to be pampered or to be safe. I also speak Nuer, so let me help." She spoke a few words and G.G. replied in some length. "I am impressed, Captain G.G."

Tara Scott was not a typical Hollywood celebrity and Allston sensed he was dealing with an immovable force. "Take cover over there." He pointed to the side of the hangar that was in the shade. "Be ready to beat feet if the situation heats up, but I think we're going to be here for a few hours before anything happens." He waited until Tara and Richards were in the truck and headed for the hangar. "Okay, I'm not so sure about this negotiations thing."

"Captain G.G.'s command of the Nuer language is excellent," Vermullen said.

G.G. waved his hand in a broad gesture, taking in the hostages. "At least I can get some water to them."

Jill urged G.G. to stop well short of the refugees and wait for their spokesman to meet him in the open. "They don't respect white flags," she warned.

"You've done this before?" Allston asked.

"In Afghanistan." The memories came surging back. She had spent a year in Afghanistan interacting and negotiating with local tribal chiefs in the vain hope of bringing stability to that torn land, but in the end there was little to negotiate. Still, this was not Afghanistan. "It might buy some time," she offered.

Reluctantly, Allston conceded. "Okay, G.G., you've got it. But only go halfway."

G.G. snapped a salute hopped into his loaded truck. He unrolled a makeshift white flag and stuck it out the driver's side window. He started the engine and drove slowly out to the refugees who were still huddled in a large, amoeba-like group in the sun. He stopped fifty yards short and got out, holding the white flag. Soon, two men stood up in the middle of the refugees and kicked their way through the mass of people. They sauntered out to G.G.

"I don't like this," Allston said in a low tone. He watched as G.G. talked while motioning to the cases of bottled water in the back of his pickup.

One of the Janjaweed examined the water and turned to G.G., saying something. G.G. turned his back on the second Janjaweed to answer. The man at G.G.'s back threw an arm around his neck in a strangle hold and pulled him to the ground. The other Janjaweed ran up, and his knife flashed in the sun as he drove the blade into G.G.'s stomach. The other assailant holding G.G. drew his knife and slashed at the navigator's neck. Four shots rang out from the side of the hangar where the legionnaires were hiding. "Fuck!" Lane roared. "G.G.'s truck is in the way!"

Allston keyed his communicator. "Backstop, have you got a shot?"

"Negative," Malone replied.

Vermullen raised his FAMAS 62 and sighted. "No shot," he said, lowering the assault rifle.

Something inside Allston snapped. "Shit-fuck-hate!" he roared, jumping into Lane's pickup. He hit the ignition and the engine roared to life. He shifted into gear as he mashed the throttle and wheeled it around. He sped towards G.G. as the two Janjaweed looked up from their grisly work. They were on their feet and running for G.G.'s truck. One pulled his semi-automatic pistol as the other ran around to the driver's side. The shooter knelt in a firing position and emptied his clip into the truck charging down on him.

Allston pulled his head down and laid across the passenger's seat as five rounds smashed into the windshield. Glass shards rained down on him as he steered blindly with his left hand. The left side of his head felt warm. The gunfire stopped and Allston reared up. The Janjaweed in front of him was coming to his feet as he reloaded. He pulled the slide on his weapon back, chambering a round, as he raised the weapon to fire. He was too late, and Allston smashed into him going over forty miles per hour. Allston hit the brakes, dragging the pickup to a crawl. Inertia did its thing, and the man crumpled across the grill flew forward and rolled on the ground.

Allston mashed the accelerator and drove over the Janjaweed. He hit the brakes and dragged the rear wheels over the man, grinding him into the asphalt. Without glancing back, Allston accelerated as he spun the steering wheel and headed for G.G.'s truck, which was now racing towards the mass of refugees still sitting in the boiling sun. Allston never hesitated and crashed into the truck's left rear, causing it to spin out and stall. Both trucks came to a halt. Allston leaped out, drawing his .45. He thumbed the safety off as he sprinted for the other truck. He reached the passenger's side window and fired point blank into the driver's head. He pulled the trigger again.

Allston's rounds echoed across the field, unleashing chaos. Allston ran straight for the mass of people as three men in the center of the refugees stood up. One raised an AK-47 in Allston's direction. Allston never slowed and fired wildly as he closed the gap. At the same time, the refugees started to run in all directions, effectively shielding the gunman and denying him a shot at Allston. Frustrated, the gunman emptied his clip into the backs of the fleeing refugees. Allston fell to the ground and reloaded as the hostages ran for cover. He rolled on the ground, trying to find a clear field of fire through the refugees. The rattle of the AK-47 rang out again, still cutting into the escaping refugees.

The mass of bodies in front of Allston suddenly cleared and he had a clear shot at the shooters. Still in a prone position, Allston drew down on the shooter and squeezed off a single shot. The Janjaweed fell to the ground. The remaining two Janjaweed dropped for cover. Now all Allston could see was a pile of bodies. One of the Janjaweed stood, holding the AK-47. A hail of gunfire from Allston, the security police, and the legionnaires tore the man apart. Allston was vaguely aware of the AK-47 falling to the ground with an arm and shoulder still attached to the sling.

Vermullen ran across the ramp, his FAMAS 62 against his side in a firing position. He shouted in Nuer, ordering everyone to stay on the ground. "David!" he yelled at Allston, "stay down!" Legionnaires erupted from the side of the hangar, running in groups of three as they converged. Vermullen was beside Allston. "Are you okay?" Much to his surprise, Allston was alive, but the side of his head was bleeding profusely, cut by flying shards of glass from the windshield.

Two more shots rang out, this time from the legionnaires who had found the last gunman. An eerie silence ruled the parking ramp. Allston came to his knees and touched the side of his head, finally aware of the blood. Tara Scott was running straight towards him, her cameraman right behind, recording as he ran. She reached Allston and ripped open the first aid kit she was carrying. "Lie down," she commanded. Her fingers probed the gash. She slapped a compress bandage against his head. "You'll live. Hold this." Then she was gone, running for the wounded and dying.

Jill pulled up in a pickup and jumped out. She knelt and quickly examined him. "Thank God," she whispered. She tied the bandage in place.

Allston struggled to his knees, a little dizzy. He surveyed the carnage around him. Tara Scott was in the middle of it all, organizing everyone around her and performing triage on the wounded and dying.

Vermullen walked through the bodies, looking for the Janjaweed. At one point, he stood and drew his semi-automatic pistol. He turned and aimed at Tara's cameraman. "Turn your camera off and lay it on the ground." The cameraman did as he was ordered and stepped back from the camera. Vermullen spoke a few words to the wounded man on the ground. The man snarled an answer and Vermullen squeezed off a single shot, striking the asphalt inches from the prostrate man's right ear. Vermullen repeated his question. The man spat at the big legionnaire, hitting his pants leg. Vermullen shot him in the head. "You can pick up your camera now."

Tara was a woman possessed as she commandeered everyone she saw and turned the hangar into a makeshift dressing station, hospital, and morgue. She was everywhere, making sure the wounded were cared for and tending to the children. To get what she needed, she ordered her three bodyguards to rip into the pallets of cargo waiting for delivery to refugee camps and took what she needed. Malaby started to protest but thought better of it. Tara Scott had taken charge and kept at it until order reigned. Only then did she walk into the air-conditioned offices and slump into a chair with her ever-present cameraman still filming. She was not a pampered Hollywood star, but a caring and dedicated human being. She was fatigued to the point of exhaustion, and it was a rare photo op for her cameraman. He swung the lens on Allston when he entered the office. "Thank you," Allston said. It was not enough, but it would have to do.

"Your bandage is much too big," Tara told him. She made him sit in her chair and gently removed the compress. "You'll need a few stitches." She nodded at her cameraman who went in search of a first aid kit. "Twenty-nine innocent people died out there today and another thirty-eight were wounded because you over reacted."

"Did I?" he replied.

"General Richards agrees with me."

"Why am I not surprised?"

Jill was standing in the doorway. "Those monsters killed and wounded over two dozen on the airplane and threw them overboard, dead or alive."

"I didn't know that," Tara said, her voice softening. Tara's cameraman was back, carrying a first aid kit. Without a word, Tara cleaned Allston's wound and stitched it closed.

"Ouch!" Allston protested.

"You'll live," Tara told him. "Regardless of what they did, you caused the bloodbath here."

Jill wasn't having any of it. "What about the women they raped on the C-130?" She didn't wait for a reply. "At least five, maybe more. Two of them were little girls, eight and nine years old. Don't they count?"

Susan Malaby burst into the room at full-throttle, her standard mode of operation. "Vermullen's found something he wants you to see."

Jill's stare riveted the actress. "You never answered the question."

Tears welled up in Tara's eyes. "Yes, they count." She stood and followed Malaby into the hangar. Allston and Jill were right behind.

They found Vermullen in the corner that had been turned into a morgue. Ten bodies were stretched out in a row. Without a word, Vermullen pointed to a pile of weapons and boots. Jill picked up a 9mm semi-automatic pistol and checked its markings. She looked at the boots and her head came up. "They're not Janjaweed."

"*Oui*," Vermullen said in a low voice.

TEN

Malakal

*T*he whine of a turbo prop engine cranking to life echoed through the walls of the trailer where Richards was sleeping and jolted her awake. She glanced at the travel alarm clock on the nightstand beside her bed – 6:10 in the morning. She sat up and pulled back the curtain over the small window. Outside, the morning twilight was yielding to the new day and she was vaguely aware of the air-conditioning kicking in. She shook her head, getting her bearings. She was in the spare bunk in Allston's sleeping quarters, and she glanced at his bed where Tara had dropped her bags. It had not been slept in.

Richards showered and quickly dressed in a tailored set of ABUs. She rolled the sleeves up as she had seen the others do and examined her image in the mirror. She liked what she saw. She stepped outside and the heat hit her, wilting the crisp image. She walked through the compound, surprised by all the activity; the sun was just breaking the horizon and everyone was at work. She walked into the big mess tent and was surprised to see the food line closed. A lone cook asked if he could get her anything. She settled for her usual breakfast – two pieces of toast, a glass of juice, and a cup of coffee. She found a seat and nibbled at the toast. "May I join you?" a voice said. Richards looked up to see Susan Malaby.

"Please do," the general said. Malaby sat down. Instinctively, Richards knew the lieutenant colonel wanted to talk, and she studied the small, intense woman. Malaby was the new Air Force, totally at home with integrated management and information flows, and an excellent manager. "How's the assignment here going?"

"We have problems," Malaby answered. Richards nodded, encouraging her. Malaby stared at her hands. "We're too fly-by-night . . . seat-of-the pants decision making . . . hopelessly old-fashioned. Allston treats Air Force directives as points of discussion to be disregarded at will. Look at the silly hats they wear. And everyone is wearing a side arm like we're in some wild-west movie."

Richards knew she had an ally. "I see you don't wear either."

Malaby shook her head. "It's not professional. Our mission is to deliver relief supplies for the UN, not play cowboy. Do you know what Allston calls the base?" It embarrassed her to talk about it and a pained look crossed her face. "He calls it Bumfuck South, and we're the Irregulars." Richards was truly shocked. Like Malaby, this was not her vision of the Air Force. Malaby was in full flow and warmed to the subject. "I don't like everyone carrying a side arm. That's asking for trouble and we're setting ourselves up for a suicide or someone going postal."

Richards finished her coffee. "I need to see what you're seeing."

"You don't want to see the inside of the hangar," Malaby said. "You'd think it was a slaughterhouse after yesterday." The two women walked outside.

"After the carnage here yesterday," Richards said, "I'm surprised it's a normal work day. Your people were traumatized after seeing so many killed and wounded. They need a down day for counseling." She checked her watch. She had been at Malakal less than twenty-four hours, and like a good manager, had a programmed response to violence she assumed was good for all situations and circumstances. "How many were killed and wounded?"

Malaby ran the numbers. "In addition to Captain Libby, twenty-nine Nuer were slaughtered on the tarmac and eight Janjaweed gunned down. I heard that another twenty-five Nuer or so were killed on board the C-130 along with two of the Janjaweed. At least thirty-eight Nuer were wounded and are in the hospital." She paused. "It was a blood bath." They walked towards the hangar. From inside, a woman's voice sang out in Nuer and a chorus replied.

"That's singing," Richards said, not believing what she was hearing. A small door leading into the hangar was open and they looked in. It was empty except for a group of women scrubbing the floor and singing. Tara Scott was standing in the interior doorway leading to the offices and waved for them to join her. "What happened to the refugees?"

"We moved them," Tara explained. "I went through those big tents out back, the ones with all the relief supplies, and took what I needed. After that, it was easy to get organized. We're setting up a tent city on the road leading to town. All very temporary until we find a better place." She paused. "There's only 142 of them," she added, as if that explained everything.

Richards chose her words carefully, not wanting to offend the actress but determined that she understood the rules. "I believe those supplies were the property of the United Nations."

Tara laughed. "They're being used the way they were meant to." Richards' body language signaled it wasn't the answer she wanted to hear. Tara tried a different track. "This is Africa, Yvonne. The rules are different here." She turned to the women who had finished cleaning the hangar. "They are magnificent singers. And so resilient. Excuse me, we've got to go." She called out in Nuer and the women followed her out of the hangar.

Jill came out of Allston's office. "Good morning. May I help you?"

"We need to talk," Richards replied. Malaby excused herself and left the two women alone. Jill led the way into Allston's office where she was working, and Richards closed the door. "I assume Allston has told you why I'm here." Jill nodded in answer. "Good. Under the circumstances, I think it would be most productive by starting with the incident at Wer Ping." Without a word, Jill called up her report on her computer. She spun the screen around for Richards to read. Richards scanned the report, her anger mounting with each sentence. "I hadn't seen this. This isn't a report, it's a whitewash. Allston must have used some type of nerve gas."

"It's not a whitewash," Allston said from the doorway.

Richards' head came up. She hadn't heard the door open. "This is a private conversation."

"And my office," he answered. He walked in and sat down. "Major Sharp, please excuse us." The Intelligence officer shot him a grateful look and beat a hasty escape. "Please close the door." He thought for a moment. How did he explain combat to an officer who had never flown an airplane, dropped a bomb, or been shot at? "Ma'am, if you're interested, I can detail what it would take to employ an airborne-delivered gas or nerve agent of any type." Richards tried to stare him down. It didn't work. "First, assuming the Air Force still had chemical weapons in the inventory, which it does not, it takes a special weapons pylon and canisters for aerial delivery. Those pylons and canisters were destroyed at the completion of testing."

"And how do you know all this?" she demanded.

"Because I was one of the crews who did the testing and I certified their destruction. Second, if I had used a gas or nerve agent of any kind, we would not have been able to land without MOPP, which neither we, nor the legionnaires have." He assumed she knew that MOPP, Mission Oriented Protective Posture, was the special clothing and equipment needed to operate in a chemical or nerve gas environment. "I dumped jet fuel on the Janjaweed to create the impression that it was a nerve gas and scare them away. It

111

worked. You can interview every swinging" – he almost said "dick" but caught himself in time – "every crew member who was on board my C-130." He reached for the phone to make it happen as the unmistakable sound of a C-17 taxiing in echoed in the office.

"That's not necessary," Richards conceded, "at this time."

"Please excuse me, ma'am, but I've got an important matter to attend to." He stood up. "We're sending Capt. Libby's body home. Please join us." She heard the pain in his voice and followed him outside where Tara and her cameraman were waiting.

* * *

The C-17's engines were spinning down as the men and women of the 4440th gathered at the tail of the huge aircraft. Without a command, they formed up in two ranks, creating a corridor leading from the Globemaster's loading ramp to the hangar. Tara's cameraman raised his camera as a tug drove slowly out of the hangar, pulling a maintenance cart bearing a wooden coffin covered with an American flag. Staff Sergeant Loni Williams walked behind, holding G.G.'s bush hat in his hands. Allston walked to the head of the corridor and came to attention. "Squad – RON" - he drew the word out, his voice firm and in command, concealing the pain that was tearing at him – "ten – HUT!"

As one, the Irregulars came to attention. "Pre – SENT . . . Arms!" Tara's cameraman panned back and forth as the Irregulars saluted their fallen comrade. The tow motor reached the waiting aircraft and stopped. "Or – DER . . . Arms!" The Irregulars dropped the salute but remained at attention. "Pa – RADE . . .Rest!" The two ranks shifted to the formal at-ease, their feet apart, hands clasped behind their backs, their heads up.

Loni Williams slowly paced the distance to Allston. He dropped his left hand to hold G.G.s bush hat against his thigh and gave his commander the best salute of his career. Allston returned the salute, "Sir," Williams said, "if I may."

"Carry on, Sergeant." Allston said, not sure what Williams had in mind, but instinctively trusting him.

The sergeant walked over to Tara Scott and held out G.G.'s hat. "Ma'am, please accept this. Captain Libby would want you to have it."

Tara took the hat and held it to her breast. "I know what these mean to you, but why? I've done nothing . . ." Her voice trailed off as tears rolled down her cheeks.

"You're one of us," Williams said. He snapped a salute, did an about face, and marched over to the waiting coffin where six security cops were waiting as pallbearers. They carried the coffin on board as a gentle breeze ruffled the silence. Captain Marci Jenkins was the last to board. She would take G.G. home.

* * *

Richards sat in Allston's office and read the two reports on the massacre the day before. The OpRep, or Operations Report, had been up-channeled to AFRICOM and the National Military Command Center in the Pentagon within an hour after the shooting had stopped and the base secured. The IntRep, or Intelligence Report, had followed six hours later and was much more detailed. The general dropped the two printouts on the desk, and stared at Allston and Jill. "Unacceptable." She tapped the reports. "Too many unanswered questions. Who drafted these reports?"

Allston glanced at Jill. "Major Lane drafted the OpRep and Major Sharp the IntRep."

"I need to speak to Captain Jenkins about what happened on your airplane," Richards replied.

"Captain Jenkins is escorting Captain Libby's coffin. She'll be made available the moment she returns."

"And when will that be?"

Allston thought for a moment. "Two weeks at the most."

"How convenient," Richards snapped.

"Major Lane and I debriefed Captain Jenkins before she left," Jill said. "It's all in my report." Richards gave her a hard look and didn't respond. "The gunmen were not Janjaweed," Jill continued. "They were soldiers. SA – Army of the Sudan."

"Really," Richards snapped. "Do you have any proof to substantiate that claim?"

"First," Jill explained, "they were all armed with 9mm Glock semi-automatic pistols and Russian-made combat knives. The SA only issues those to its elite forces. Second, counting the two killed on board the C-130, there were ten of them, the exact number of an SA squad. Third, they were all carrying booklets of sayings from the Koran and Hadith that urge the faithful to become martyrs, also issued by the SA. Finally, they were all wearing standard issue combat boots. Janjaweed won't wear boots like that. It's a cultural thing to do with the honor of being horsemen. Those ten men were a death squad out to kill anyone they could. Further, the Janjaweed participated in the attack, which indicates they are acting with the SA."

"And how did they get on board in the first place?" Richards asked.

Allston answered. "We were off loading supplies at a refugee camp and came under small arms fire. To say the situation was confused is an understatement. The SA were there and exploited the opportunity. Captain Jenkins was sitting in the left seat as the aircraft commander. I fly as a copilot with all my aircraft commanders from time to time, mainly to see how they are handling the stress, and was the copilot."

Richards interrupted. "And to blame them if anything goes wrong, which it did."

Allston ignored the allegation. "The refugees were blocking our takeoff, and rather than leave them to the tender mercies of the Janjaweed, Captain Jenkins loaded them all on board and we took off."

Richards scanned the reports, finding what she wanted. "You allowed Captain Jenkins to take off grossly overloaded for the takeoff conditions and endangered everyone on board."

"With 204 passengers. She set a record for the Hercules."

"And you let her do it," Richards charged.

"She was in command and we made it. Her judgment was correct. That's why she's an aircraft commander."

Richards dropped the reports into her briefcase. "I need to incorporate these into my report."

"No problem," Allston said, "just sign for them." The reports were classified confidential and required special handling. Richards scrawled her signature across the bottom of a transmittal slip and flung it at him. She closed the briefcase and stormed out the door. "Major Sharp," he said loudly, making sure the general heard him. "Please take a letter." Richards stopped, her back to him. "Dear Mr. Lockheed, in regards to your C-130, thank you."

Richards spun around. "Flippancy isn't called for." Allston didn't respond and let her have the final word. She turned and left, her footsteps echoing down the hall.

"We haven't seen the last of that lady," Allston said.

"You were right," Jill replied. "She wants your head on a platter."

"She'll probably get it. But in the meantime, we've got work to do." Jill nodded, her face not revealing what she felt. She would follow this man anywhere he asked, which he promptly did. "Let's go see if Tara needs some help."

"Yes, sir," Jill said. Seeing Allston and Tara Scott together was the last thing she wanted.

* * *

Richards' right index finger beat a relentless tattoo on the table as she quickly rifled through her notes. She glanced at the sergeant sitting patiently opposite her and started to ask a question about Allston. But she knew the answer and didn't want to hear it. She had quickly sorted out the incident at Wer Ping and the alleged use of nerve gas and concluded there was nothing there for her. It had gone down as reported. Frustrated, she turned her investigative sights on the loss of the C-130 when it crashed on landing and the crew almost captured by the Janjaweed. That had led her to Staff Sergeant Louise Colvin who she had grilled for over an hour. Again, nothing. An idea came to her and she almost smiled. It was so simple and had been out there all the time. "Thank you, Sergeant Colvin. I believe we've covered everything." She closed her notebook. "That will be all."

Louise Colvin stood, relieved that the interview was over. It was the first time she had ever spoken to a general, much less been subject to an intense questioning by any officer. She hoped her nervousness wasn't too obvious. "Yes, ma'am." She turned to leave.

"Oh," Richards said, stopping her. "One last thing." The tone of her voice changed, much friendlier. "Do you go by Louise?"

"I prefer Lou, ma'am."

"Lou, is it difficult being the only female loadmaster here, among so many men?"

The young woman brightened. "Oh, no. Not at all. I do my job. That's what counts."

"So no one has made, ah, improper advances? Of a sexual nature? No higher ranking NCO or an officer?"

"No ma'am. Colonel Allston would" – she searched for the right words – "cut their balls off if they did."

That wasn't what she wanted to hear. "Really? He said that?"

"Oh, no, ma'am. He'd never say that. But he'd do it."

Richards' lips disappeared in a straight line. "You may go." She watched the young sergeant make her escape. The general ran her mental abacus, adding up all she had learned about Allston. The one over-arching constant in every interview had been the high regard for Allston, which in a few cases, amounted to hero worship. A change in tactics was called for.

* * *

It was late in the evening when Richards entered the mess tent. The food line was still open and a savory aroma drifted over her. She was suddenly hungry and joined the queue. Laughter and cheering echoed from the far end of the tent that served as a small lounge. She looked around. Everything seemed so normal with none of the signs of stress and depression she expected. "Ma'am," one of the cooks said, catching her attention. "Did you hear that we made the news in the States yesterday?"

"No I haven't. Thank you for bringing it to my attention."

"It was all over the TV," the cook said. "They're running it again in about an hour. That's what all the noise is about. Everyone wants to see it."

"I'll be sure to catch it." Richards moved down the line and looked for a table. Allston was eating alone in a corner. She decided it was an opportune time to switch tactics and walked over. "May I join you?"

Allston looked up from the manual he was reading and came to his feet. "Please do, General." He waited while she sat and then joined her.

Richards tasted the food. "This is excellent," she said. He smiled an answer. "It has been years since I went through a chow line."

"A lot has changed," Allston said. He raised a hand, gesturing at the big tent. "This is very much part of the way we do business these days. So we try to get it right."

"There's something we must discuss." His look seemed receptive so she pressed ahead. "I've interviewed twenty-four of your officers, NCOs, and enlisted over the last three days, and talked to numerous others informally. The high level of morale I've seen is outstanding. I have heard a few complaints, but that's to be expected."

"Ah, the dreaded ten percent," Allston said. "One of General Fitzgerald's favorite warnings is that if everyone who works for you is happy, you aren't doing your job and he'll fire you."

"After what happened Tuesday, I thought you should take a down day for counseling to deal with the trauma your people experienced." Allston explained that he didn't have the trained counselors available. "At least it would give everyone a chance to call home," she added. He assured her that was not a problem and they were in constant contact via satellite communications. In fact, he talked to his kids two or three times a week. She switched topics. "Those hats everyone wears are in violation of Air Force directives."

"General, I learned a long time ago that morale and mission identification go hand-in-hand. That's what those hats are all about."

"I am also very worried about the pistols everyone carries."

"We carry side arms for a reason, ma'am. We were able to rescue those refugees because Riley and MacRay were armed and shot the two goons who stormed the flight deck."

"But they will be misused, and because a weapon is present and available, a suicide attempt will be successful or an argument will turn deadly."

Allston didn't answer immediately. "I'll deal with that if, and when it happens. But for now, they'll carry weapons."

"I understand being armed when you fly, but on the ground? How can you justify that?"

"This is not a peacetime base. General. We're on the front line in a very nasty little war with real bullets. Earlier, you mentioned standing down for counseling. This is the military, ma'am. We handle the hurt and stress of losing our comrades by honoring them, getting on with the job, and never forgetting who we are and why we're here."

"It looks like you're playing cowboys and . . . " She cut her words off in mid sentence.

Allston gave her his lopsided grin "And Indians," he said, completing her thought. "It's okay to be politically incorrect here. In fact, I rather encourage it."

The General's head snapped up, her eyes filled with disapproval. "And why is that?"

"Because the last thing any politically correct asshole wants to do is fly the mission and get their politically-correct ass shot off. The Irregulars are committed to the mission because they believe in what we're doing, and they are willing to put their lives on the line every day. That gives them the right to be as politically incorrect as they want." He gave her his lopsided grin. "Besides, it's good for morale."

"And if I should tell you that I believe we can accomplish the mission and still be politically correct?"

"Tell me that after you've flown with us, after you've seen starving children, babies impaled on stakes, women raped and mutilated." He stared at her, waiting for her to take him up on the offer. Her reply surprised him.

"You are a passionate man, Colonel Allston, and it seems you have filled your people with the same passion."

What is she up to? he wondered. He glanced at his watch. "It's time for that TV special. Want to see it?" She nodded and he escorted her to the end of the tent that held a large LED TV screen and a huge set of loudspeakers. They sat in the front row as Jill walked to the front and stood beside the screen.

She held a microphone to her lips. "This news story made every major network in the States yesterday. The Armed Forces Network is re-broadcasting it, commercials and all. Please remember we have a very important guest with us tonight, Brigadier General Richards." A polite round of applause broke out as the screen came to life.

The program opened with a commercial promoting a hemorrhoid cream. "Yep," a voice at the rear called, "it's all about us." Laughter rippled through the Irregulars. They fell silent as an aerial view of the Sahara filled the screen and Tara Scott's voice explained she was aboard a C-17 inbound to an American airbase in the Sudan. "I love you," another voice called. The audience quieted as Malakal came into view and Tara explained this was her eleventh visit to Africa. The scene shifted to the cockpit as the C-17 landed and taxied in.

"Lieutenant Colonel Allston and Major Gillian Sharp met us on landing," Tara said as the camera zoomed in on Jill. Loud whistles and cheers filled the tent as Allston came alert. Jill was extremely photogenic. He glanced at her standing to the side of the TV, her face bright red. She gave him a helpless shrug. Her mouth formed a silent 'I didn't know.'

"Within hours of our arrival," Tara continued, "all hell broke loose." The scene transitioned to the Nuer hostages huddled on the tarmac. Urgency filled Tara's voice as carefully-edited and blurred images recorded G.G.'s death and Allston's reaction. Silence ruled the tent as the camera documented the killing and fighting. The scene transitioned to Tara standing in the hangar filled with the wounded and dying and the tone of her voice changed again, now soft and caring, as she led the camera through the aftermath and to Jill who was examining the weapons and equipment of the gunmen killed in the fighting. "Who were they?" Tara asked.

"It appears they were a suicide squad," Jill answered. "Fortunately, the French peacekeepers arrived in time, or it would have been a total massacre."

The scene shifted to the ramp as the Irregulars lined up under the tail of the C-17. "Captain G.G. Libby was the only American killed," Tara explained, "and the 4440th honored their fallen comrade." Only Allston's voice could be heard as he called the Irregulars to attention. The camera focused on Loni Williams as he followed the coffin, saluted Allston, and then presented G.G.'s bush hat to Tara. The scene cut to Tara wearing G.G.'s hat. In the background, a C-130 was taxiing out. "For the men and women of the 4440th, it was business as usual the next day, delivering food and medicine to thousands of starving Africans. They are often called 'trash haulers' by the more glamorous fighter pilots, but they call themselves 'the Irregulars.'

The Peacemakers

"They are led by an unusual man they call 'the Boss.' It would be a mistake to think they are like your neighbors next door. They are not. They are warriors who wear this hat with pride, and they want nothing more than to bring peace to this troubled land, and I am honored to wear their hat."

The TV screen went dark, and for a moment the tent was silent. Then it exploded in applause, whistles, and cheers. Jill waited patiently for it to subside. Her eyes glistened as she looked directly at Allston. He gave a little nod in return. Slowly the pandemonium died away. "Well, that's it," Jill finally said. "I hope your loved ones at home see it."

Richards caught it all and ran her mental abacus, adding it all up. She stood and walked back to her sleeping quarters, deep in thought. A note was slipped under the door.

> *Yvonne,*
> *We moved the refugees to Mission Awana, about twenty miles east*
> *of here. We're going to stay at Awana and build a camp that*
> *really works and is safe. Thanks for all the help and come see us*
> *if you get a chance.*
> *Tara*

"We'll just have to do that," Richards said in a low voice. She hummed a tuneless melody and went to bed. But she couldn't sleep as she scripted a new scenario.

ELEVEN

Mission Awana, South Sudan

*T*ara was waiting on the wide veranda that surrounded the mission's guesthouse when Jill wheeled the big six-pac pickup around the corner and coasted to a stop. She jumped out and held the rear door open for her passengers. Richards was the first out, closely followed by Allston. He sucked in his breath as Tara came down the steps, dressed in a wrap-around modeled after the sarongs the local women wore. The cloth seemed to take on a magic of its own and shimmered and changed color when she came into the full sunlight. The effect was stunning. "Welcome to Mission Awana," Tara said, extending her hand. "I'm so glad you could make it."

They exchanged greetings, and Jill followed the three onto the cooler veranda, feeling very much out of place. The two women were beautiful by any standard and complemented by Allston's rugged looks. As usual, Tara's cameraman was recording the event. Jill was about to mention it when Tara motioned at the camera and said, "It's all about publicity and promotion. Our special was number four in the ratings, and the network wants a follow-up. There's a rumor that Sixty Minutes is interested."

"We saw it," Richards said. "You were very complimentary."

Allston grinned "No joke. You should see my e-mail. So far, I've gotten three marriage proposals." He pulled a face, as if he were considering it. "One's very pretty, one says she's wealthy, and the other I can't repeat the offer." He laughed. "And my kids had to change their cell phone numbers."

Tara guided them to comfortable chairs on the veranda, and poured them a cool drink from an unusual ceramic pitcher. "I didn't know you were married."

"Divorced. But I've got two great kids." The three women were very attentive, all for different reasons, as he told them about Lynne, his tall and beautiful twenty-one-year-old daughter, and Ben his gangly sixteen-year-old stepson. "Lynne's in college and Ben is currently with his mother in Los Angeles. But he prefers to live with me." The loud drone of a single-engine airplane caught their attention as it flew low over the mission compound. Automatically, Allston looked up and searched for the aircraft. He quickly found the plane, a high-wing, single-engine turbo prop Pilatus Porter. Tara and Jill studied his face as he took the measure of the pilot, looking for the telltale clues that marked an eagle.

Tara never took her eyes off Allston, sensing something was very different about the man. Then it came to her. He was a raptor, only truly at home in the sky, hunting on the wing. "That's Dr. Tobias Person," she said, breaking the spell.

"Toby Person?" Allston asked, suddenly alert. "Short, red-hair, pudgy, early forties, nice guy. He used to be in the Air Force."

"He's not pudgy," Tara said, "but that does sound like him."

Allston watched as the light plane circled to land at the airstrip located a half-mile to the east of the mission. "I'll be damned," he murmured. From the looks on the women's faces, an explanation was in order. "Toby was the best Weapons Systems Officer that ever strapped on an F-15 Strike Eagle. He was teamed with Gus Tyler, one of the finest officers and pilots in the Air Force. Talk about putting bombs on target."

Tara couldn't believe it. "Dr. Person? He's the most gentle soul I've ever met." She checked her watch. "Why don't we go meet him?"

"I'll drive," Jill said, feeling marginally useful. She wheeled the six-pac through the compound that radiated out in spokes from Mission House at the hub. "Mission Awana," she explained, "is one of the oldest and most successful missions in Africa, all thanks to Dr. Person. Unfortunately, it is located in the disputed border area. So far, Khartoum has ignored it, but how much longer that will happen is anyone's guess."

"It certainly looks prosperous," Allston said. Within minutes they were at the airstrip where three men were pushing the tail dragger into a hangar. A short, wiry man with red hair waved and walked towards them. Allston got out to meet him. "Toby Person," he said. "It's been a long time." The two men shook hands. Person's hands were gnarled and calloused, his grip strong.

A big smile split Toby's leathery features. "Mad Dawg Allston, I heard you were in country. Upsetting any apple carts?"

"No more than usual." The two men laughed, sharing the memories of when they were young.

122

"Reverend Person has invited us to lunch," Tara said, interrupting the two old friends.

"Reverend Person?" Allston said.

Toby laughed. "Well, it sounds better than Parson Person."

"I thought you were a doctor, like in M.D."

"That too. Let's go to lunch. We can talk and get caught up."

* * *

After a light lunch, they took refuge in a large open room inside Mission House, sheltered from the cresting heat of the day. "Reverend Person," Richards asked, "exactly how stable is the political situation here?" Jill mentally shifted gears into the intelligence mode. She gave the general high marks for probing the area where they were the most vulnerable.

"Not very, General," Toby replied. "We're caught in a civil war between the Arab north and Africans in the south. It's been going on over fifty years and I don't see it ending soon."

"I thought that ended when the South Sudan gained its independence and made
Juba the capital." Richards said.

Toby shook his head. "They may have signed a so-called treaty of independence, but they never agreed on the border." He unfolded a map and spread it out on the table. He pointed to the mission. "We're here, on the south bank of the Al Bahr Al Abyad, the White Nile, which Juba claims is its northern border. The Sudanese Army is operating on the north side of the river, and along with the Janjaweed, consolidating its hold."

"Which is in our area of operations," Allston added.

"And the prize is oil," Jill said, leading the conversation in the direction she wanted.

Toby gave her a long look before answering. "Exactly. And the Sudanese want it all." He used a pencil as a pointer to indicate large areas of land blocked in with squares and rectangles, all in Allston's area of operations. "These are the oil concessions where oil has been discovered. The reserves are not huge like the Middle East but they're nothing to sneeze at – about the size of Columbia and Venezuela. The government in Khartoum parceled the concessions out to foreign consortiums, mostly Chinese, and takes eighty percent of the gross. We never see a bit of it down here, and as far as the government is concerned, the Africans are *kafirs* – unbelievers – and not entitled to a cent. To solidify their position, they've used the Janjaweed and the Army to systematically drive the Africans out of the concessions and created an African Diaspora."

"Enter the United Nations Relief and Peacekeeping Mission, Southern Sudan," Jill added. "A testimonial to corruption, greed, and sheer incompetence." Richards shot her a warning look. Jill was to be seen and not heard.

"But the Army and the Janjaweed have left you alone," Richards said, again asking the very questions Jill wanted to ask.

"So far," Toby replied. "There's been some trouble around Malakal, thanks to Major Hamid Waleed. He's the only Sudanese Army outpost on the southern side of the White Nile. For the most part, he just bullies the Africans, otherwise Juba might get involved, and they know how to fight."

"I met him twice," Allston grumbled. "That was twice too many."

"Unfortunately," Toby continued, "a Canadian exploration team discovered a large oil reserve in block five, here." He tapped an odd-shaped, penciled-in area on the map located a hundred miles south of the mission. "Khartoum wants it but Juba has served notice it belongs to them, which is why Khartoum called for jihad against the Africans. Juba" – he pointed to the large town 300 miles south of the mission – "wants to make the White Nile the de facto boundary and Juba their capital." He pointed to the large town 300 miles to the south of the mission. "The good news is that we're on the south side of the river, on Juba's side. The bad news is that we're caught between the Army and the new oil discoveries."

Jill put it all together. "Which is why you invited Tara to the mission."

Although Toby lived in central Africa far removed from the main currents of world opinion, he was a realist. "Publicity works every time."

"I want to be here," Tara added. "We've got to make a stand somewhere, and I can't think of a more worthwhile place."

"I'll give you the tour," Toby said.

"I'll drive," Jill said, hoping to learn more.

Toby sat in the front seat as Jill drove slowly through the compound, following Toby's directions. "The mission is really a plantation," he explained, "but a very modern one. Thanks to the Nile, we've over 4000 acres under irrigation and export food, mostly a type of disease-resistant sorghum. We also have some cottage industries that could be commercially successful. But more important, we have the best schools and the largest medical station in sub Sahara Africa. Our hospital has six doctors, two operating rooms, a hundred beds, and a training school for nurses and midwives. Our medical teams vaccinate over 10,000 children a year. It's taken five generations to create the mission and I'm just the current caretaker."

Near the end of the tour, Jill asked a key question. "Why doesn't the United Nations stop the fighting?"

Again, Toby gave her a long look, considering his answer. He shook his head and there was no doubt the missionary knew she was probing for operable intelligence. "And violate Sudanese sovereignty? If the UN got involved simply because the Sudanese were engaged in a little genocide in their own country, what country would be next?"

Allston changed the subject. "How long is your airstrip?"

"We've got 4000 feet of macadam and a 1000 feet of hard-pack at the western end and 1500 on the eastern end. An Airbus made an emergency landing once. No problem." Allston slumped in his seat, deep in thought. It was more than enough for C-130 operations.

*   *   *

A gentle evening breeze caressed Mission Awana and held the pillaging insects at bay. Allston and Jill sat alone on the veranda of the guesthouse and savored the night air. "My favorite time of day," Allston said. Only the rattling chirps of an unknown bug disturbed the tranquility. "It's amazing what Toby has done here."

"He has made a difference," Tara said from behind him. She pushed through the screen door carrying a tray with the same unusual crock pitcher that gleamed with condensation. She had showered and changed into another, even more beautiful wrap. This one was made of a finer material and flowed over her body, outlining every curve. For a brief moment, a light from inside outlined her figure, leaving little to the imagination about what was not underneath.

A primal urge shot through Allston and he was thankful for the dark. "I was just telling Major Sharp this is my favorite time of day." An animal call echoed through the night. "That sounds canine."

Jill heard a tone in his voice that sent tingles down her spine. There was nothing provocative or unusual in what he said, but it was the call of an eagle reaching out in the dark and her body responded. But she knew the call was not meant for her. With a will that surprised her, she said nothing.

"That's a spotted hyena," Tara answered. "They really own the night." She sat the tray down and poured them a drink. "I love this drink," she told them. "It's non-alcoholic and so refreshing. In the right hands . . . it could be a commercial success."

Jill bit her tongue. It was not what Tara said, but an undertone in her voice combined with the way her body moved that left little doubt the actress was responding to Allston. "That stone pitcher is most unusual," Jill said. "The way condensation forms."

"It is unusual," Tara said. "Some consider it a work of art, and it definitely cools
. . . the drink. With the right approach . . . well, who knows?" She sank into a chaise lounge opposite Allston as the night captured them. Again, the call of a hyena split the night, this time farther away. "She won't be happy until she finds her mate," Tara explained.

"Do you think so?" Allston asked.

Tara sipped her drink, her eyes fixed on him. "Oh, yes," she said. They sat in silence as the chirping resumed. "Hyenas run in large packs and are led by a female."

"So that explains why they are so vocal," Allston said.

Richards joined them and sat down. "Why who is so vocal?" she asked.

"The leaders of a hyena pack," Tara answered.

"Who is always a female," Allston added. "I just learned that."

"You do have a lot to learn," Tara said. "About females."

Allston laughed. "Oh, I hope so." Jill felt her face flush. There was no doubt they were engaging in verbal foreplay, sophisticated, low-keyed, and beyond anything she had experienced. She was jealous and stifled a sigh. "I'm bushed," Allston said. "Time to hit the sack. Good night, ladies."

The three women watched him as he disappeared through the door and turned left toward his room. Tara made conversation for twenty minutes or so and then bid them good night, claiming it had been a long day. Jill's eyes followed her as she entered the guesthouse and turned left. "Her room is on the other side," Richards said. "Next to ours." Her words were clipped and hard. The echo of a faint knock on a door reached the veranda. A long silence came down. Then, "Major, don't even think about it." It was a clear warning that Allston and Tara were free to engage in whatever relationship they chose, but not Jill.

"Pardon, ma'am? Think about what?"

"Sleeping with Allston. Do I need to remind you of his reputation and the differences in your rank?"

"I'm well-aware of his reputation and the prohibitions on fraternization," Jill replied. "His conduct has always been above board and proper."

"I'm not talking about his conduct, but yours."

"General, I have done nothing . . ."

Richards interrupted her. "Nothing indeed."

The Peacemakers

* * *

Tara was on her second cup of coffee the next morning when Richards joined her. A young and very pretty Nuer took the general's order and moved gracefully away, giving the two women a cone of privacy. "They do have a sense of style," Tara said, admiring the way the girl dressed and carried herself.

"Have you seen Colonel Allston this morning?" Richards asked. Tara shook her head. It was not exactly the truth for Tara had left his room just before sunrise.

"Tara, I do apologize, but may I discuss a personal matter?" The actress nodded, not sure what was coming. "Colonel Allston has," Richards continued, "shall we say, a certain reputation in regards to his personal relationships with women. Many women." Tara arched an eyebrow but didn't take the bait. "I just wanted to be sure you understand who you are dealing with."

"Oh, I understand." The two women smiled at each other. Richards was aching to know if Allston was true to his reputation, but was afraid Tara would give her an honest answer, which judging by the actress's quiet response, she certainly didn't want to hear. Richards had a fine-tuned ability to read an individual's emotions that she used in her arsenal of weapons to advance her career. It had worked well with all her superiors except one, General John Fitzgerald, the Air Force Chief of Staff.

Jill burst into the room, her face flushed and damp with perspiration. "General, there's a problem at Malakal, and Colonel Allston is flying back. He needs to speak with you before he leaves."

"May I join you?" Tara asked.

"Certainly," Richards answered. "Let me get my hat." She hurried to her room and was back in seconds.

"General," Jill said. "Colonel Allston asked that you wear this." She handed Richards a holstered .45 automatic and belt. Richards hesitated. The weapon was an overt symbol that she was in combat. "The situation has gone critical," Jill added. The general strapped the weapon around her narrow waist.

The women clambered into Jill's six-pac and she drove quickly to the airfield where the mission's Pilatus Porter was waiting on the ramp, its engine running. Allston hurried over to meet them and stuck his head in the passenger's side window. "I got a call from Major Lane. Waleed and his goons have sealed off the airfield with roadblocks and closed the fuel dump. The UN has ordered us to turn over our C-130s, equipment, everything, and the Legion to surrender their heavy weapons, including their Stinger and Shipon missiles." He let his anger show. "Jesus H. Christ! Our C-130s can't defeat a Stinger and the Shipon can kill any tank in the world. The last thing we need is for those fu . . . " – he caught himself in time – "is for the Janjaweed to get their hands on a Stinger." The capability of the US-made missile was well known and the Israeli-developed, shoulder-held Shipon had a dual mode warhead that was deadly against tanks, fortifications, and personnel. "Waleed's given us until noon tomorrow to comply and evacuate Malakal."

Richards touched the automatic on her hip. "Did these precipitate this?"

"Waleed could care less about handguns. He wants those missiles. Our Herks can jam the hell out of any surface-to-air missile they've got, but not the Stinger." He reached out and touched Tara's hand. "Please stay here. It's safer and you can tell the world what's happening." Tara nodded. "I gotta go."

"I'll stay here and coordinate with AFRICOM," Richards said.

"Yes, ma'am," Allston replied. "Major Sharp, it's gonna get ugly and you can stay here."

Jill shook her head. "My assignment is with the Irregulars." She ran after him.

"Stupid woman," Richards said under her breath.

"I'd follow him," Tara replied.

"But you're staying here."

"Because he gave me a job to do," the actress replied. Richards didn't understand.

*   *   *

Toby was sitting behind the controls of the single-engine utility aircraft when Allston and Jill climbed on board. Allston sat in the copilot's seat, Jill in the back. Allston jammed on a headset as Toby turned into the wind. Without bothering to take the runway, he gunned the turboprop engine and took off from the parking ramp. They were airborne in less than four hundred feet. "Twenty miles to Malakal," Toby announced. "Less than ten minutes." He leveled off at two hundred feet above the ground and turned to the west, flying along the Nile. "I'm guessing Waleed won't close the runway because of commercial traffic. We should be okay."

"And if they shoot at us?" Jill asked.

"Not to worry," Toby answered, "we'll be in and out before they get a clue."

"Stalwart fellow," Allston mumbled.

Malakal

Toby dropped down to a hundred feet above the ground and slowed as they approached the airport. "They haven't blocked the runway," Allston said. Toby didn't answer and concentrated on the landing. He started the flaps down and slowed as he flew along the runway towards the C-130 ramp at the western end. Allston counted all four of his C-130s and did not see any of the familiar Sudanese Army trucks. "I can see a roadblock at the main gate," he said. "That's all." Toby grunted an answer, dumped the flaps to full down and landed the taildragger in less than 300 feet. He turned onto the parking ramp, spun around, and hit the brakes. Allston unlatched the door and was out before the Porter was fully stopped. Jill was right behind him. Allston closed the cargo door and stepped back. Toby gunned the engine and took off at an angle across the ramp and the runway width. "Well done," Allston allowed.

"That was exciting," Jill allowed as they walked in.

Vermullen and Lane were waiting in operations. The Frenchman explained that the orders to turn over his weapons had come directly from the UN Peacekeeping mission in Addis Ababa. "In their infinite wisdom, they only ordered us to leave, not where to go."

"What's your government telling you?" Allston asked.

"To negotiate what I can but in the end, do as ordered. Are you going to turn over your aircraft?"

"That will be one cold day in hell," Allston replied, his words etched in stone.

The satellite phone buzzed and Jill answered. "It's the AFRICOM duty officer. He's talked to Richards." She handed the phone to Allston.

Allston quickly briefed the duty officer on the situation. His eyes went cold when the duty officer ordered the 4440th to stand down while AFRICOM coordinated with the NMCC and the State Department. "I will not turn my aircraft over to anyone under any circumstances," Allston told him. Again, he listened as the duty officer told him not to make the situation worse. Allston sensed he was dealing with a staff officer who did not have the authority, nor the balls, to make a decision. "Thank you, sir." He punched at the phone, hard, breaking the connection. "Fuckin' clueless wonder." He handed the phone to Jill. "Can you get in touch with Toby?"

She punched at the buttons, frustrated by the delays in establishing a link while Allston talked to Vermullen. Finally, she handed Allston the phone.

He quickly updated Toby on the situation. "I'm not turning the Herks over and I'm going to evacuate."

Richards came on the line. "Colonel Allston, I'm in contact with AFRICOM. You were ordered to stand down and not make the situation worse."

"General, a commander never loses the right of self defense. As I read the situation, my only defense is to cut and run. Further, AFRICOM is not in my chain of command."

"Not your formal chain of command," Richards replied, not willing to concede the point. "If you insist on evacuating without clearance from AFRICOM, go to Ethiopia."

"We need to stay in country. If I read this right, once the Legion is gone, there's going to be a bloodbath. We need to relocate as many of the Dinka and Nuer as we can out of the oil concessions, and there is no way Ethiopia will allow us to mount a cross-border airlift."

"We've got the space and a fuel dump," Toby said.

"How about the legionnaires? Okay to bring them?"

"Knowing Waleed," Toby said, "the Legion is the only thing that will keep him away."

Richards interrupted. "Colonel Allston, I say again, stand down while I coordinate. You are making the situation worse by your precipitate actions."

"Copy all," Allston replied. "Standing by." He broke the connection. "Precipitate action, my ass." He drew his .45 automatic and fired a round into the satcom. "Damn, we've just gone com out. I guess we're on our own."

TWELVE

Malakal

Major Hamid Waleed woke with a jerk. It was still dark and he patted the bed beside him. The girl was gone, which was good. As his adjutant had promised, the fourteen-year-old Dinka was a virgin, but she was worthless now. He checked his watch, pleased that he had woken in time for *Fajr*, the first prayer of the day. He quickly dressed and stepped outside his tent to insure the three privates standing guard at the main gate leading into the American compound would see him at prayer. They would talk of his piety and add to his reputation as a faithful member of the *Umma*, the universal Islamic community.

His anger flared when he saw the guards were sound asleep. He drew his prized 9mm automatic and crept up on the sleeping men. For a moment, he hesitated before singling out the oldest, a twenty-year-old private from a village south of Khartoum. The private came from a family without connections or honor, and was less than a man. Because he knew these things, Waleed considered himself a good officer, and, more importantly, knew what to do with guards caught sleeping on duty. He slapped the private awake and waited, ensuring the other two guards were fully conscious. He pulled the slide of his Browning back, chambered a round, and shot the private in the forehead. He pulled the trigger again.

The two guards groveled in the dirt and begged for mercy. Waleed questioned them, anxious to learn if there had been any activity among the Americans during the night. Assured that all had been quiet since the small single-engine plane had landed the previous morning, he let them live. What harm could one small aircraft do? he reasoned. He made a show of checking his expensive Rolex. "My ultimatum expires in seven hours," he announced. "The Americans have no honor, they have no courage. They are pigs and bend to my will." He returned to his tent and knelt in prayer, certain that letting the two guards live would add to his honor as a just and honorable man – and a warrior.

* * *

Master Sergeant Jerry Malone crouched low and held his holstered Berretta to his thigh. The security cop moved silently toward the defensive firing position, DFP for short, which served as an observation post on the main gate and used what concealment he could find. He broke radio silence and spoke low into his radio, using the single word to warn the DFP that he was coming. It was the only radio transmission he would make. Twenty feet away, a woman issued a soft challenge and he whispered the recognition code of the day.

"Advance," Staff Sergeant Louise Colvin said. The loadmaster was an augmentee posted with a security cop in the DFP. Malone slipped silently into the sandbagged foxhole.

"Sum' bitch, Sarge," the security cop whispered. "You got lucky they didn't see you."

"What was the shooting all about?" Malone asked.

Lou Colvin handed him her high-powered night vision scope. "An officer shot one of the guards when he caught them sleeping."

Malone's eyes adjusted as he swept the scene in front of him. The officer in question was praying in front of his tent while the two guards bundled the body in a ragged blanket and carried it to the far side of the road to wait for burial. "So they haven't got a clue."

"It seems that way," Lou replied.

"Good work," Malone said. He watched as the officer disappeared into his tent as two orderlies carried in cloth-covered trays with his breakfast. Malone handed Lou the scope and disappeared into the dark.

* * *

Jill was waiting in operations when Allston arrived. He didn't turn on the lights, anxious to maintain the blackout and the appearance the compound was asleep. Even in the early-morning dark, he could tell she was exhausted. "Any trouble getting through the gate?" he asked.

"A little. The guards were very upset. I bribed my way through and gave them each a Krugerrand. They do like gold."

"An officer, I'm guessing it was Waleed, shot one of them earlier for falling asleep on duty."

"That would explain why they were so antsy," Jill said.

"So how did it go?"

"I found the truck driver from the Djibouti supply run. He says he can arrange for seven trucks. They should arrive around nine this morning."

"It's all in the timing," Allston allowed.

"They're on African time," she replied.

"Cover story?" Allston asked.

"All in place. The driver says they regularly haul cargo for the Sudanese Army. I gave them the loading manifests for what they're to pick up here, all signed by Walced." She gave a disgusted snort and quickly related how she had bribed a Sudanese sergeant to type the loading manifests that gave the SA the right to confiscate whatever they wanted from the Americans. "Waleed actually signed them. The bastard thinks he's got a license to steal."

"Which he does," Allston replied. "But we're going to steal it right back. I want you and the women on the first C-130. It's gonna get ugly if we have to fight our way out."

"No way, Colonel. I can speak for all of us. We do our job like everyone else."

Allston heard the resolve in her voice. He wanted to tell her that he couldn't accept the risks the women were willing to take and at the same time, give her a hug for her bravery. But an inner voice told him nothing he could say would change their minds. And a hug was out of the question. "I still need you on the first C-130. If it all falls apart here, you'll have to play it by ear at Awana. I need some one there with a clue." Jill nodded, understanding. "You've got time to take a shower and eat. Be on the aircraft before the sun comes up."

She pulled herself to her feet and left him alone in the dark. He sank into her chair, still warm from her body heat. He closed his eyes, running through every detail. The four C-130s were loaded and ready to go, everyone had been briefed, and the legionnaires ready to do their part and create the distraction he needed to get the C-130s launched. But would they do it? Vermullen wanted to fight, but, in the end, he had been ordered by his masters in Paris to turn over the Legion's heavy weapons and missiles to the Sudanese. While Vermullen didn't have a choice in the matter, no one had told him the weapons had to be serviceable. His men had removed the battery packs from the missiles, pulled all the fuses from the mortar rounds, and kinked the ammunition belts so they couldn't feed. What have I forgotten? Allston thought. All the doubts were back. Should he have simply loaded his birds with what he could and escaped under the cover of darkness? Waleed had unwittingly cooperated by leaving the runway open for incoming civilian flights. But that would have left the Legion holding the bag. Was he overreaching and trying to do too much? But if they pulled it off, the 4440th was still in business. Had he underestimated Waleed? Only time would tell. He closed his eyes and fell asleep for the first time since arriving back at Malakal from Mission Awana.

* * *

Lieutenant Colonel Susan Malaby barged into Allston's office. "Colonel, this sucks! Why in hell are we hanging around? The runway is open. Let's just crank engines and go!"

Allston let her vent and she quickly spun down. "Are all your troops on board?" he asked.

"Yes, sir. And sweating like pigs. You have any idea how hot it is inside those airframes just sitting in the sun?"

"Shit," Allston said, realizing what he had overlooked. "We need to show some activity on the ramp. Cycle 'em in and out like they're doing routine maintenance on the birds. Make sure they know to get on board the moment a prop starts to turn."

"Yes, sir." She hurried out to make it happen.

His personal communicator buzzed. It was Jill. "The trucks are here," she told him. It was 10:17. "Sooner than I expected."

"Get 'em loaded," he told her, breaking the connection. Now he had to speak to Master Sergeant Jerry Malone, the NCOIC of his security police. It was not a conversation he wanted to have. He hit the transmit button. "Backstop, rendezvous at Outhouse." He had just told Malone to come in.

"On my way," Malone replied.

Allston was still considering what to say when Malone arrived in operations. Rather than temporize or make it sound better, he came right to the point. "What's the minimum number you need for the rear guard?"

Malone spread out a hand-drawn chart of the compound and circled fifteen defensive firing positions. "Seventeen cops and thirteen augmentees. Counting me, thirty-one." He tapped the DFP guarding the taxi path leading to the runway. "I'll use this one for a command post."

Allston paused, hating what he had to say. "You've got to hold the base until the C-130s get airborne."

Malone's face was impassive. "We figured that out a long time ago, Colonel. I think we can put down enough firepower to discourage the bastards until we make it out on our own."

134

The Peacemakers

Allston snapped a salute. "Good luck, Sergeant."

* * *

The legionnaires were standing by their trucks, ready to roll. Vermullen paced back and forth by the lead truck, his anger slowly growing. Allston's pickup coasted to a halt and he got out. Vermullen whirled on him, and, for a moment, Allston feared the big Frenchman. "The Legion does not surrender its weapons without a fight!"

There was no doubt in Allston's mind that the legionnaires were going to fight. He had to change their minds, but how? His mind raced. Then, "Colonel Vermullen, there's a battalion out there waiting to jump on us. We're talking at least a thousand men against your two hundred. This is not Camerone."

As one, every legionnaire within earshot turned to Allston. The myth and mystique of Camerone is at the heart of the Legion. The battle happened in Mexico, on April 30, 1863, when two officers and sixty-two legionnaires under the command of Captain Jean Danjou held out against 2,000 Mexicans at the farmhouse of Camerone. The farmhouse was of no tactical value and the legionnaires were caught up in a political squabble in which they had no stake or interest. But Captain Danjou decided to fight rather than surrender, and his men swore an oath to do the same. And fight they did, for they had given their word to the Legion. Only a handful lived to tell the story and they brought Danjou's artificial wooden left hand back to the Legion. Vermullen didn't move and Allston had no clue what emotions were rippling through the man. "The Legion needs you to fight and die another day."

It was enough. "When do we start this charade?" Vermullen asked.

"Right now. The supply trucks are loaded and ready to go."

Vermullen gave the command and the 200 legionnaires climbed onboard their trucks and moved out, heading directly for the Sudanese roadblock at the main gate.

Allston drove slowly to the seven loaded supply trucks waiting behind the big supply tents. He parked where he could see the main gate. He double-checked his radio, ensuring he was on the same tactical channel as the Security Cops. Louise Colvin broke radio silence. "The legionnaires have cleared the gate and stopped." Allston's mouth compressed into a tight line. The loadmaster was in the defensive firing position closest to the Sudanese and he wanted her out of there. But Lou had protested that "I can shoot better than any swingin' dick here." Malone had confirmed it, and as all the

135

augmentees were volunteers, Allston gave in. Now he was having second thoughts.

He scanned the activity with his binoculars. The French had driven through the main gate and pulled their trucks to the side of the road and stopped in a long line. Vermullen had walked to the last truck and was talking to Waleed. At first, it looked like the two men were arguing. Vermullen waved his right hand and six legionnaires started to slowly unload the last truck. It was time. Allston gave the signal and the seven heavily loaded supply trucks headed for the main gate. Again, there was a delay as the trucks stopped short of the gate and handed over their manifests for inspection. At the same time, Vermullen demanded that Waleed personally verify the number of mortars that were unloaded and now lined up in a neat row on the side of the road. Frustrated, Waleed waved the supply trucks through and walked back to the weapons. Allston keyed his radio. "Start engines." The seven trucks rumbled through the roadblock as the distinctive whine of turbojet engines coming to life reached him.

Again, Allston scanned the front gate with his binoculars. Vermullen and Waleed were arguing about something as the supply trucks rumbled past, laying down a cover of dust and sound. Behind Allston, more engines came on line. Allston knew it was only seconds before Waleed heard them and reacted. Chance intervened when an old Russian-built Antonov An-12 aircraft entered the landing pattern. The four-engine turboprop aircraft was the Russian answer to the C-130 and bore a strong resemblance to the Hercules. This particular one was painted silver and green and painted with markings in what looked like Arabic script.

"What the hell?" Allston said to himself. Was it military or civilian? He scanned the aircraft as it passed overhead. The military version of the An-12 had a tail gunner and the tail of this An-12 was clean. It was a civilian aircraft. Allston kept his binoculars glued on the scene at the main gate as the last of the supply trucks passed by. Vermullen and Waleed glanced at the An-12 as it landed and went back to whatever they were arguing about. The legionnaires handed down the last of the ammunition crates and started to break them open for inspection.

Waleed bent over one of the crates and did not see the trucks turn left at the nearby intersection, away from town where the Army was billeted. Allston swung his binoculars onto the two guards who had seen the trucks make the wrong turn. Allston held his breath. One guard shook his head and deliberately looked away, towards the body of his dead comrade still lying beside the road. They had gotten their second break.

The An-12 was adding to the distraction and Allston made a decision. He keyed his radio, calling the security cops. "Backstop, we got a window here. Start pulling in your troops and load 'em up." He trusted Malone to understand that no plan lasted the first thirty seconds of combat. "Dondo One, Two, and Three, go!"

The sound of the C-130s taxiing out reached him. The first C-130 with Jill aboard started its takeoff roll as the second taxied into position. Twenty seconds later, the second C-130 rolled down the runway. The third Hercules turned onto the runway and took off. Allston shifted his pickup into gear and drove as slowly as he could, careful to not draw the attention of the Sudanese. Once around the corner of the hangar and out of sight, he sped towards the parking ramp and the last C-130. Malone was waving a group of cops up the ramp of the last C-130. Allston accelerated across the ramp and slammed to a stop by Malone. "How many on board and who's left?" he yelled.

"Ten on board," Malone answered. "Twenty-one, counting me, still left."

"Colvin?"

"She's still with her buddies, sir."

Allston's face flushed. "Does she know what will happen if they capture her?"

"She knows," Malone said. "I told her. Sir, you got to go."

Allston didn't move. "Everyone goes."

Sporadic gunfire echoed from the main gate and immediately stopped. "I think it's too late, sir." Malone spoke into his radio. "Say situation." The two men listened as Lou Colvin, still in the forward DFP, answered. The shots had been fired by the Sudanese and while there was plenty of shouting and confusion, there was no movement towards the airfield. "Sounds like they're screwing up their courage," Malone said.

Allston keyed his radio. "What's the Legion doing?"

"They're long gone," Lou answered. "I can't even see their dust now. Hold on, it looks like the SA is setting up one of the French mortars and breaking out a machine gun."

Malone didn't hesitate. "Pull everyone in. Now!"

Allston breathed deeply. "Good call," he muttered, calculating how long he had before the Sudanese attacked.

Malone pointed to the civilian terminal halfway down the runway. The An-12 was taxiing out to takeoff. "You got some cover there, sir. Use it. We ain't got time to get everyone here before it takes off, and I'll be damned if I'm gonna leave two or three of my people behind. We can escape and evade out of here on the ground." Malone cracked a grin. "Besides, I can use your truck to play arsonist."

It was the nudge Allston needed. "We'll get you out." He ran up the ramp and the C-130 taxied for the runway. He worked his way forward around the pallets and passengers crowding the cargo deck. He counted heads and ran a mental tally. Everyone was out except Malone with the rear guard, and, with a little luck, they would be gone before the Sudanese figured and tumbled to what was going on.

On the flight deck, Major Dick Lane sat in the left seat, commanding the Hercules. "Boss, I don't know where that Antonov came from, but talk about dumb luck."

Allston gave the command. "Go."

Lane advanced the throttles and taxied out. He stopped on the runway, set the brakes, and ran the engines up as the An-12 taxied into position to takeoff at midfield. Lane released the brakes as the An-12 started to roll. The two aircraft lifted off at the same time. Lane leveled the C-130 off at 100 feet above the ground, raised the gear and flaps, and immediately turned out to the left, towards the Nile and away from the soldiers on the far side of the field. "Son of a bitch!" Lane roared. The green and silver An-12 with its Arabic markings was turning out in the opposite direction, to the right, and over flying the soldiers still clustered at the gate at low level. It was the perfect distraction.

"Damn," Allston muttered to himself, angry that he had not fully exploited the unexpected arrival of the An-12. He should have slowed down and got all the Irregulars out. He cursed silently. "Dick, I need to talk to Mission Awana." The flight engineer handed his headset to Allston, while the copilot dialed in a VHF frequency. He raised Mission Awana, and gave Allston a thumbs-up. "Mission Awana, Bossman. Request your Porter is engine running and ready for takeoff when I arrive."

Lane turned to the right and flew along the northern side of the Nile. The copilot twisted in his seat and looked back at the rapidly receding airfield. "Whoa! Look at that. Bumfuck is on fire big time." Allston handed the headset back to the flight Engineer and squeezed into the space on the right side of the copilot. He could see smoke and flames billowing from the big hangar and the supply tents.

"I need to get on the ground ASAP," he shouted at Lane.

Lane pushed the throttles up and checked the GPS. "On the ground at Awana in five."

Mission Awana

Major Dick Lane turned his C-130 onto the hard-packed earth near the three other C-130s parked on the hardstand. "Not enough room for all four Herks," he told Allston. He taxied as close to the concrete parking ramp as possible and stopped near the Pilatus Porter. As requested, the engine was running and Toby Person was sitting in the pilot's seat. Richards was standing between the C-130 and the Porter. Allston scrambled down from the flight deck and out the crew entrance door. The loadmaster was standing between him and the engines to ensure he wouldn't run into the spinning propellers as Allston ran for the Porter.

"Colonel!" Richards yelled over the roar of the Hercules's engines. "We need to talk. Now!"

"Sorry, General," he shouted. "I haven't got time."

"Oh, yes you do!" She ran after him. Much to his surprise she was a fast and graceful runner. She caught him at the Porter. "Where are you going?"

"I'm getting my people out of Bumfuck."

"The UN Secretary General in New York called on the satcom and ordered you to turn over your aircraft to his representatives in Malakal."

"I never got that message. We'll talk when I get back." He pushed past her only to face Staff Sergeant Loni Williams. The short and muscular sergeant was standing by the Porter's right cargo door holding a M-249 SAW, the venerable Squad Automatic Weapon with a 750 round per minute rate of fire. Two plastic boxes, each holding 200 rounds of 5.56mm ammunition, were at his feet.

"What the hell are you doing with that?" Allston shouted.

"Going with you," Williams answered. He held the fifteen-pound weapon up. "We're talking industrial-strength intimidation, Boss."

"Get on board," Allston said. He motioned Toby out. "You can't go, Reverend. Some people are going to die and you can't be part of it." Toby understood and climbed out of the seat. Allston jumped into his seat and quickly strapped in as he scanned the instrument panel. He had never flown a Porter but the airspeed indicator had the green and yellow markings he needed. He glanced back at Williams who was sitting against the aft bulkhead and holding onto a strap attached to floor rings. The right cargo door was still open.

Allston advanced the throttle and was surprised by the power surge. "How about that," he muttered. He spun the taildragger around and headed for the runway, leaving a furious general in the prop wash. He turned onto the runway and carefully advanced the throttle to get the feel of the aircraft under power. The Porter was airborne in 600 feet and Allston headed west. Ahead, a towering pillar of smoke marked his destination.

THIRTEEN

Malakal

"*B*ackstop, Bossman. How copy?" Allston asked over the Porter's VHF radio. He waited for Malone to reply. Ahead, he could see Malakal's runway and the towering smoke billowing out of the big hangar. Unfortunately, the supply tents were only a smoldering ruin, and the fire in the hangar was dying down. "Come on," he muttered to himself.

After what seemed an eternity, Malone answered. "Go ahead, Bossman."

"Say status."

"We've withdrawn to the runway side of the hangar. We were taking sporadic gunfire from the main gate, but that's stopped. They seem confused. No organization that I can see. They might be waiting for the fires to die down."

Allston's situational awareness kicked in. The threat was still at the main gate, a quarter-mile behind the burning hangar, and the security cops were near the runway with the hanger in between. But the fire was dying out so how much time did he have? He keyed his mike. "Backstop, did the fuel dump go up?"

"Negative, Bossman. I couldn't get to it. Too close to the bad guys."

"Maybe I can do something. Be ready to board when I land."

"I have you in sight, Bossman. That's a pretty small plane."

"Leave your gear behind. We'll make like a sardine can."

"Copy all," Malone replied, ending the transmission.

"Loni," Allston yelled. "I'm going to climb and try to keep the smoke from the hangar between us and the Sudanese. When you see the fuel dump, pump a few rounds into the fuel bladders. Then hold on while I take evasive action."

"Will do, Boss."

Allston nudged the stick forward and descended to ten feet above the ground. He inched the throttle forward, wringing every knot he could out of the Porter as he flew down the runway. The aircraft was not built for speed and the airspeed indicator bounced around 130 knots, or 150 MPH. Once past the civilian terminal at midfield, he angled slightly to the left and headed directly for the burning hangar at the far end of the field. "Hold on!" he warned Williams when they reached the parking ramp. He pulled back on the stick and immediately entered a tight climbing spiral to the right, keeping the open cargo door on the inside of the turn as he climbed above the parking ramp. He coughed when they darted in and out of the towering column of smoke rising above the hangar. The altimeter read 200 feet when he caught a glimpse of the fuel bladders through the smoke.

"I got 'em in sight!" Williams shouted.

Allston leveled off but continued the pylon turn to the right. They were on the outside of the turn, away from the burning hangar and over the parking ramp when Williams fired a short burst through the smoke over the hangar. Nothing. "We're too low," Williams told him. "I'm hitting the berm around the bladders. Gimme another fifty feet." Allston continued the turn, again flying through the smoke from the hangar. The rising air currents lifted the Porter. Again, Allston coughed from the smoke. Why wasn't Williams coughing? Allston chanced a quick look into the rear. Williams had tied a water-soaked red bandana over his mouth and nose. They came out of the smoke and Allston checked their altitude – 280 feet. He held the turn as Williams fired another short burst. One of the big bladders erupted, sending a pillar of fire shooting into the sky. Allston pulled the throttle to flight idle and tightened up the turn as he dove for the ground. Something heavy rolled across the deck of the cargo bay and bounced against the back of his seat. The second fuel bladder erupted like a huge Roman candle.

Allston dumped the flaps and flew a curvilinear approach to land on the runway. But he landed across it and used the taxi path leading to the parking area to roll out. He spun the taildragger around and pointed the Porter's nose back towards the runway. The security cops broke from their DFPs and converged on the Porter, shedding their equipment as they ran. Allston turned to his right and looked into the cargo area. He couldn't see Williams. "Damn, Colonel," Williams said, "that hurt." He was crumpled up behind the pilot's seat.

Staff Sergeant Lou Colvin was the first to reach the Porter. She dropped her heavy web equipment suspenders, but held onto her M-16 as she dived through the cargo door. She scrambled into the copilot's seat. Eight security cops were right behind her, each dropping their equipment and ammo belts, but holding onto their weapons as they climbed in. Lou reached around and pulled a cop onto her lap. Six more cops squeezed in behind them. "We're full, Boss!" Williams shouted.

"We got six more to go," Allston replied. "Stack 'em in like cord wood." The Porter rocked on its landing gear as five more cops piled in. Finally, only Malone was left. Malone shook his head, indicating there was no room, and motioned for them to leave. Allston turned to the mashed-in bodies behind him. "Troops, we're gonna sit here until you drag Malone on board. So get with the program." Again, the Porter rocked as the cops rearranged themselves in three layers. Two pair of hands reached out to pull Malone in. The sergeant's legs were still dangling outside as Allston ran the engine up and taxied onto the runway. He released the brakes.

They were airborne in less than a thousand feet.

Mission Awana

A very angry Brigadier General Richards paced back and forth as Allston taxied the Porter in. He deliberately parked on the far side of the ramp to make her walk before he cut power and climbed out the small pilot's door. He walked around the long nose to wait for the general while willing hands pulled security cops out of the cargo bay. The four-bladed prop was still spinning down when Richards reached the aircraft. "Just what do you think you're doing?" she said, her voice low and threatening.

Allston ignored her and did a quick head count. Lou Colvin was there with twenty security cops. Williams was the last to climb out of the Porter, the wet bandana still around his neck. "Any water left?" Allston asked. He couldn't believe how thirsty he was.

Williams laughed and tossed Allston a hip flask with brandy. "I soaked it in this. Seemed like a good idea at the time." Allston took a swig and tossed it back.

"Answer my question," Richards demanded. "What were you doing?"

"Getting my people out of harm's way, General."

"You disobeyed a direct order to turn your aircraft over to the UN."

Allston looked at her calmly. "I never got that order."

"I gave it to you!"

"General, for the record, we are under the operational control of the UN Relief and Peacekeeping Mission Southern Sudan. You are not in that chain of command. I did not have the time, much less the communications, to verify any such order with the UN."

Her eyes narrowed. "Colonel, don't play the barracks lawyer with me. You violated a direct order, and I'm relieving you of command."

"Again, ma'am, you are not in my chain of command," Allston replied. He fell silent as Toby drove up in his battered Land Rover.

"We'll see about that," Richards snapped. "Who's the senior security cop here?"

"That would be Master Sergeant Jerry Malone." Allston pointed to the group huddled around Malone. "He's over there." He watched as Richards stormed across the ramp, her rage building.

"That is one angry lady," Toby said from behind him.

"Indeed she is. Can I catch a lift to the guesthouse?" He climbed in and didn't look back.

* * *

Jill was waiting on the veranda of the guesthouse when Allston and Toby arrived. The large house was alive with activity. "Your new headquarters," Toby said. Allston climbed out of the Land Rover and Toby drove away. Jill ran down the steps to meet him. For a fraction of second, Allston thought she would throw her arms around him, but the major skidded to a halt and saluted.

"We were worried," Jill said. He returned the salute, and she handed him a new satellite phone. "I thought you might need this."

"Thanks. I will now. Any word on the trucks and the Legion?"

"Colonel Vermullen radioed in. They ran into a roadblock that had also stopped the supply trucks. Luckily, the Legion arrived in time or the trucks would have been hijacked. He convinced the guards it wasn't a good idea." Allston laughed, imagining Vermullen in a cold rage. "The Legion is escorting the trucks in," Jill continued, "and should arrive in thirty or forty minutes." She paused. "Your staff is all here."

Allston nodded. He couldn't ask for four better officers to serve on his staff, and that included the irascible Malaby. "Super. We need to sort things out and settle in."

"Settle in?" Malaby asked. "Aren't we pulling out? Everyone seems to think we are."

"Not at this time," Allston replied. "We're going to set up operations right here. We're back in business."

Jill finally understood. "So that's why you needed the supply trucks. What about the Legion? Will they stay?" They both knew the presence of the Legion was the only thing that would keep the Sudanese at bay.

"I believe so. Idi wants to settle some outstanding debts. Speaking of which, send some one to pick up General Richards and Sergeant Malone at the airstrip, then join us."

E-Ring

The colonel giving the briefing was enjoying himself as the high-definition image appeared on the big computer-driven screen. He was the project officer for the latest version of Eagle Eye, an unmanned aerial vehicle developed for reconnaissance, and it had performed beyond all expectations. "Eagle Eye had been on station above Malakal for thirty-six hours when these images were captured" – he checked his watch – "sixty-four minutes ago."

"Altitude?" Fitzgerald asked.

"Ten thousand feet," the colonel answered. Fitzgerald stared at him, waiting for an explanation. The colonel caught the unasked question. "We're testing Eagle Eye's daylight stealth capability, as well as its communications monitoring capability. The Sudanese Army talks incessantly over the radios, and at no time did we detect a transmission indicating they had detected Eagle Eye's presence. Based on that result, we believe we can operate as low as five thousand feet at night." Again, the colonel keyed on Fitzgerald's look and quickly added, "But only in that environment, sir." He cycled through the images. "We believe the man you see here setting the fires is Master Sergeant Malone." The images cycled and stopped. "The Pilatus Porter you see here circling in and out of the smoke belongs to Mission Awana, and was piloted by Lieutenant Colonel Allston." He hit the advance button. "In this frame, you can see rounds being fired from the Porter and striking the earthen berm surrounding the fuel dump. In this sequence, the Porter is climbing and again firing into the fuel bladders. The results were quite spectacular." The image of the fuel dump fireballing lit up the room.

The image changed to the Porter landing on the ramp. "Colonel Allston used the burning fuel dump as cover to land and extract the remaining security police, one of whom was a woman. Her identity is unknown at this time. The aircraft recovered safely at Mission Awana, twenty miles from Malakal."

"Twenty-one bodies in a Porter?" Fitzgerald asked.

"Actually, twenty-three counting the pilot and gunner. We think it may have set a record for the Porter."

Now Fitzgerald was enjoying himself. "Please inform the Guinness Book of Records. Colonel, why did the 4440th relocate so close to Malakal?"

The colonel knew better than to wing it. "I cannot answer that question, sir, nor could anyone I talked to when I asked the same question. We're working it."

Fitzgerald considered his options. "Recall General Richards and Major Sharp. Get them here ASAP, no later than twenty-four hours." He thanked the colonel, giving him high marks for the briefing, and stood to leave. The Secretary of Defense had summoned him and the Chairman of the Joint Chiefs of Staff to his office. It was not a meeting he was going to enjoy.

Mission Awana

Allston huddled with his staff in a corner of the guesthouse's lounge. The major in charge of Facilities was talking. "The Reverend Person said we can use the mission's communication center in Mission House for flight ops. I've got a team there now, setting up our radios and plugging into their net. The guesthouse has a large kitchen we can use and enough room for a dining hall, plus ten bedrooms." He unrolled a large-scale chart of the mission. "We brought in enough tents on the trucks to billet everyone else behind the guesthouse. But it is going to be crowded, and we're going to have to build latrines to handle the overload."

It was Susan Malaby's turn. "Maintenance can use the two small hangars at the airstrip, but I'll need a couple of tents." She looked at Allston. "Colonel, we're down to four airframes and I have more people than I need. Can I send some of them home?"

"The same is true for the aircrews," Dick Lane said.

"Good idea," Allston said. "Everyone, identify your essential personnel and they stay. Everyone else can go." He thought for a moment. "We're on the frontline, folks. Make sure everyone gets the word that it may get very sporting around here."

"Sporting?" the major in charge of logistics asked.

"Like in real bullets and real danger," Allston told him.

"Oh, that kind of sporting," the major replied, totally unfazed.

Lane's personal communicator buzzed. He glanced at the message. "The com center has a message for General Richards and Major Sharp. They've been ordered to report to the Pentagon ASAP. A C-17 has been diverted into Addis Ababa to pick them up."

"Dick, lay on a Herk to get them there," Allston said. "Okay, folks, let's go to work." He stood and walked out to the veranda to wait for the Legion to arrive. So where are we? he thought, re-evaluating the situation. The Herks made the mission a target for the Sudanese and Toby knew it. So why did he invite the 4440th to use the mission as its base? Was the missionary simply acknowledging the inevitable and fighting for time? Vermullen and his legionnaires were a deterrent, but they had surrendered their heavy weapons to the Sudanese. If they could rearm the Legion, that would make the mission a very hard nut to crack. So how did they do that? He collapsed into a wicker chaise lounge and closed his eyes. Jill's image emerged from his subconscious and he dozed.

* * *

Richard's voice was there, hard and sharp-edged. "Colonel, stand up when I'm talking to you." Allston's eyes snapped open and he came to his feet. Richards was standing in front of him with Jill and Malone immediately behind her. "I'm formally relieving you of your command." She motioned at Malone. "Take Colonel Allston into custody."

Malone didn't hesitate. "Without authorization from AFRICOM, I don't have the authority to do that."

"Then get it," she replied.

"The mission's communications center is in contact with AFRICOM," Allston said. He couldn't help himself. "There's a message waiting for you, ma'am. Sergeant Malone, please drive General Richards over. It's too hot to walk." He motioned for Jill to join him as Malone escorted Richards to the waiting six-pac truck. He waited until Richards was sitting in the truck and out of earshot. "We need to talk. When Waleed confiscated the weapons on that supply truck that brought you back from Djibouti, you mentioned a Sudanese Army supply dump. Where was that?"

"Bentiu." Like a good Intel officer, she was ready with the details. Bentiu was a large town located 153 miles west of the mission and under Khartoum's control. It was also in the heart of an oil field and was a combination of an oil boomtown replete with bars and prostitutes, a shantytown filled with refugees, and a Sudanese Army garrison. It also housed a large concentration of Chinese soldiers masquerading as private security guards and pipeline construction workers."

"Any chance that's where the Legion's heavy weapons will end up?"

"I'd say there's a good possibility they will. The Stingers and Shipons are high-value weapons, and Bentiu is the most secure facility the Sudanese have in the area. Why the interest?"

"Just curious." He changed the subject. "You need to pack your bag. I imagine the General is reading the message recalling you and her to the Pentagon as we speak." He sensed she needed some encouragement. "Not to worry, Merlin's on top of it."

"I don't want to go."

"It's not like you've got a choice. Hurry back."

"There's the Legion," she said, pointing to the first of a long line of trucks rolling into the mission.

E-Ring

The Secretary of Defense motioned the two four-star generals to the leather couch in the far corner of his huge office overlooking the Potomac and let them stew for a few moments while he signed paperwork and memos. Satisfied the delay had made it clear just how angry he was, he joined them and sat in a big overstuffed chair opposite the couch. He puffed on his cigar, enjoying the aroma, but not what he had to do. "Hal, Fitz, I assume you know what's got me pissed off." Although protocol dictated that the Chairman of the Joint Chiefs of Staff, General Harold Misner, United States Army, answer, Misner hesitated and nodded at Fitzgerald to answer.

"Mr. Secretary, I assume you're concerned with recent developments in the Sudan," Fitzgerald said, stepping up to take the heat. The Secretary nodded and Fitzgerald continued to talk. "Specifically, I assume you are concerned by the landing of a NSA high-value reconnaissance asset at Malakal." He had assumed correctly and the Secretary asked how Admiral Chester A. Bellows, the brilliant and irritable head of the National Security Agency, got involved without his knowledge. Bellows was famous for his short fuse and total inability to put up with fools, bureaucrats, and politicians. His temper was legendary, as well as the results his agency achieved. "We're field testing Eagle Eye," Fitzgerald replied, "and I asked Chester if he could have one of his platforms monitor the same activities to see if we are missing anything. He happened to have an An-12 in the area and obliged."

The Secretary puffed on his cigar, laying a smoke screen between him and the two generals. "So why did it land at Malakal just in time to create a diversion for the 4440th to evacuate?"

"I imagine it was maintaining its cover," Fitzgerald replied. "Did you ask Chester?"

"I did. He gave me the same load of crap. Talk about perfect timing. Just how much coincidence do you expect me, or for that matter, the President to believe?"

The two generals tried to look innocent. "Coincidence does happen," Misner allowed. He had mentioned the situation at Malakal to the vice admiral over lunch, certain that the crusty old salt's fangs would come out. Misner then dropped the subject, for what he didn't know couldn't hurt him. Like many flag rank officers, he was very adept at playing CYA – cover your ass – with politicians. He didn't like it but it went with the job.

The Secretary puffed harder on the cigar. "Apparently, that clown you appointed to run the show at Malakal doesn't understand the tightrope the President is walking with world opinion, the UN, and the Government of Sudan."

"Lieutenant Colonel Allston," Fitzgerald replied, "is delivering more relief in the Sudan than all the NGOs" – NGOs were nongovernmental organizations – "and UN agencies combined. In my book, that counts. Because he is effective, his aircraft are being shot at." He cocked an eyebrow. "I certainly hope the President still allows his commanders the right of self defense."

"There's a pack of lawyers at the DOJ nipping at my heels," the Secretary replied, "who believe self defense is another form of aggression and want Allston's hide nailed to a wall."

"That would be a mistake," Fitzgerald replied. He clasped his hands and leaned forward. "Sir, we've conditioned our officers to avoid aggressive action for fear of retroactive punishment dished out by those same lawyers. Those lawyers couldn't lead a pack of Boy Scouts to a latrine and have never been on the receiving end of an AK-47 or a surface-to-air missile. They've never seen the atrocities that Colonel Allston's people deal with everyday, nor do they intend to. I gave Allston a job to do and he's doing it. He's one of the few commanders I have who isn't afraid to act out of fear for their careers. A fear, I might add, that is well justified. Just what message would we be sending if we fired him now?" He administered the coup de grace. "Especially considering the media attention he's getting."

The Secretary had seen Tara Scott's TV special, and understood the power of the media and what it could do in the upcoming election. He ground the cigar into an ashtray and stood. The meeting was over. "Allston stays . . . for now." The two generals came to their feet but the Secretary wasn't quite finished. "Fitz, I want your resignation on my desk today. Don't date it." Fitzgerald was living on borrowed time.

The two men walked in silence back to their offices. "How much longer do I have?" Fitzgerald finally asked.

"He's bluffing," Misner answered. "He called you Fitz. They just want you to toe the party line."

"I will as soon as my people are out of harm's way."

FOURTEEN

Mission Awana

The three men were gathered around Allston's laptop studying the satellite images of Bentiu. The photos were recent and sharp, detailing signs of recent construction, and the large number of cars and trucks left little doubt it was a boomtown. "This is good stuff," Dick Lane conceded. "I can't believe it's in the public domain." Both Allston and Vermullen agreed with him. The quality of the images was superb, good enough for targeting. "Did Jill know the location of the ammo dump?" Lane asked.

Allston shook his head. "The truck driver just told her it was at Bentiu. She said there's an Army garrison there along with quite a few Chinese soldiers posing as security guards and construction workers." He was frustrated and wanted a threat assessment; unfortunately, he could only make a few assumptions, none of which had a high level of confidence. "I'm guessing the ammo dump will be isolated and near a runway." Allston clicked on the zoom slider and zoomed out. He followed the main road leading north out of town to the Bahr el Ghazal, a tributary of the White Nile, where a bridge led onto a wide riverbed. From the bridge, the road crossed the riverbed to a second bridge that spanned the main channel. "It's at low stage but there's still plenty of water in the river." He pointed to the second bridge. "That's a choke point." He finally found the runway and an airport a mile north. "Tallyho the fox."

Vermullen pointed to a road that led from the airport to a rectangular-shaped compound west of the runway. "There. At the end of the road."

"Damn," Allston muttered. "Where's Jill when we need her?" Her quiet competence was a rock he depended on. He moved the cursor over the compound and measured the distance to the airport. "Three quarters of a mile." He zoomed in on the compound. "Okay, assuming that's the place, what are we looking for?" He hit the print button and the printer spat out a glossy color print.

Vermullen studied the printout and circled the two shacks at the entrance. "Guard posts, one on each side of the gate." He circled two big buildings. "These barracks are company-size. Up to 150 men could be billeted there." He pointed to three buildings separated by earthen berms on the other side of the compound. "These are weapons storage bunkers."

Lane voiced what they were all thinking. "But are the missiles there?"

Vermullen gave a classic French shrug – shoulders hunched forward, his lower lip pushed out, eyebrows arched, head cocked to the right, hands raised – "Who knows?"

"That's reassuring," Lane groused. "We need to ask someone."

"Yeah," Allston replied, "but who? Jill could backdoor her sources and get an answer, but all we can do is query Intelligence at AFRICOM. That would send a signal, and if they've got anyone worth their paycheck like Jill, they'll figure out what we're doing in a heartbeat. We don't need some staff weenie ratting us out so a general can tell us no."

"I can tap the jungle telegraph," Vermullen said.

"You can do that?" Allston asked.

"Certainly," the big Frenchman replied. "We are, as you Americans are fond of saying, wired in. It can be a good source of intelligence, but you must know how to listen. Your Major Sharp also listens to it."

"She never told me," Allston said. How long has she been talking to the French? he wondered. Then it hit him. Who else was she talking to?

"Would you have believed what she heard?" Vermullen asked.

"Probably not," Allston replied. "Okay, assuming the compound is our objective, how do we hit the puppy?"

"We will need trucks," Vermullen answered. "And a diversion." He mulled over the possibilities as his right index finger tapped the photo. His adrenaline started to flow and he smiled, his finger resting on the bridge between the airport and the town.

E-Ring

Jill sat at the far end of the first row of seats in the small auditorium as Richards started her briefing to the air staff. She gave the general high marks not only for her appearance and the cut of her uniform – both were Madison Avenue quality – but for her skills as a briefer. Jill was honest and admitted to herself that the general simply excelled at whatever she did. She studied the men in the audience and wondered if they were more interested in what the general had to say or her legs. A brief image of Richards and Allston in bed flashed in her mind, which she quickly squashed.

"The details of the crash at the refugee camp near Wer Ping," Richards said, "that resulted in the loss of the C-130 are in Appendix B of my report. As no Accident Investigation Board was convened, I relied on the testimony of the aircrews and concluded that the most probable cause of the crash was asymmetrical thrust when the propellers were reversed on landing." She recreated the aftermath of the crash and the attack on the crew. Again, Jill had to admire her for the accuracy and brevity of her report. The image on the big screen cycled and the ramp at Malakal came into sharp focus. It was the opening shot of the video of the hostage crisis involving Marci Jenkins's C-130. "I had just arrived at Malakal and witnessed the massacre of twenty-nine Dinka by ten Janjaweed who had slipped on board an evacuation flight."

Jill sat upright. What was going on? Richards knew the killers were a Sudanese Army death squad and not Janjaweed. The video, recorded by Tara Scott's cameraman, gave full play to the actress and Richards. It looked like they were in the thick of the battle and G.G.'s death was barely mentioned. Jill's anger flared when she realized what Richards was implying; Allston had made the situation worse by over-reacting to a bunch of inept thugs. It was clever and indirect, never stated, but there for all to see. "In the end," Richards said, "the Janjaweed were summarily executed."

Jill's mind raced. Everything shown on the screen was accurate but carefully edited to give it an entirely different spin. The reaction of the men in the front row indicated Richards had made her point. Jill had to set the record straight. But how? The highest-ranking officer present was the three-star Deputy Chief of Staff for Manpower and Personnel, and she didn't have access to Fitzgerald. She couldn't barge into his office and say, "Excuse me, sir, but one of your generals is lying through her teeth." She flipped open her laptop computer and called up her briefing. Her fingers flew over the keyboard, changing her presentation. She finished just as Richards reached a conclusion. "After witnessing and investigating this incident, I was forced to conclude that the 4440th over-reacted to the Janjaweed to the detriment of its mission. Are there any questions?" Grudgingly, Jill gave her high marks for the way she fielded every question, never straying from the charge that Allston had made the situation worse by his actions.

It was Jill's turn but before she could take the podium a voice called out, "Room, ten – HUT!" The audience came to its feet as Misner and Fitzgerald entered the briefing room.

"Please be seated," Misner said.

Jill stepped to the podium as Richards sent her a warning look. The intelligence officer couldn't believe the sudden turn of events. What had drawn the two generals to the briefing? The lanky three-star who headed Manpower and Personnel deliberately held his personal communicator in full view as he turned it off. "Welcome back, Major Sharp," Fitzgerald said. "What do you have for us?"

"Sir, the situation in the Sudan is chaotic at best and rapidly deteriorating." She clicked the remote control and a chart appeared on the screen showing the locations of the UN refugee camps and the boundaries of the oil concessions. "The mission of the 4440th is to deliver relief supplies to these camps. Ninety percent of the camps are located in the oil concessions." Click. The camps that had been attacked burst into flames. "Every camp that has been attacked is in an oil concession." Click. An image of a destroyed village filled the screen. "Based on the attack on Abyei, we are now certain the Janjaweed and the Sudanese Army have integrated their actions in order to drive the Dinka and Nuer from the oil concessions. Further, the Janjaweed are operating in much larger numbers. We go where the refugees are. Unfortunately, so does the Sudanese Army and the Janjaweed."

Fitzgerald interrupted her. "Who's the 'we,' Major?"

The briefing was going where Jill wanted. "Sir, I consider myself an Irregular." Click. A photo of the 4440th at work on the parking ramp with the sign that announced 'Bumfuck South' visible in the background cycled onto the screen. Click. "This table lists the tonnage of relief supplies delivered by date and place."

General Misner scanned the numbers. He was not impressed. "Is this all?"

"We're delivering what we receive. Based on what I witnessed, I estimate eighty to ninety percent of all relief supplies are stolen en route from the port of Djibouti."

Misner was angry. "What's the UN doing about it?"

"Nothing, sir. But I can only speak to the problem in Addis Ababa."

"That's a serious charge," Richards said. "Any proof?"

"I bribed my way onto a convoy of fourteen trucks carrying supplies from the port at Djibouti to Malakal. Only one of the trucks made it." Click. A video of the convoy and Jill interviewing three truck drivers in Swahili played on the screen. She translated for the audience as the drivers laughingly related how they pilfered their loads while diverting them to black marketers. A second video played, this one of Jill interviewing a disgusted warehouse manager in Djibouti. This conversation was in French, and, again, Jill translated for the audience. "'You Americans are so stupid. This is nothing but another Oil for Food scam like in Iraq. Nothing changes with the United Nations. People starve while you make three men rich.'"

"What three men?" Misner asked.

Jill's tone was matter-of-fact. "The three commissioners heading the relief mission in Addis Ababa." Click. Photos of three opulent mansions sequenced across the screen. "These are their homes in Addis Ababa." Click. A photo of a well-dressed African walking into a hotel with a beautiful woman appeared. "The Head of Mission and his receptionist in the Hilton Hotel in Addis Ababa. Their affair is an open secret in Addis Ababa, and many Africans admire him for his corruption and many mistresses."

Richards started to question her but thought better of it. The videos and Jill's multilingual abilities had established her bona fides. The Intelligence officer had not contradicted Richards, but focused attention on the bigger picture.

"Besides the corruption, what else are we dealing with?" Misner asked.

"As you know, the UN ordered the French peacekeepers to turn over their heavy weapons to the Sudanese Army. Those weapons included Stinger and Shipon missiles, which pose a significant threat to both our C-130s and the French if given to the Janjaweed. We are worried the Sudanese Army cannot, or will not, properly secure and control them."

Every person in the room understood how dangerous the missiles would be in the wrong hands, and what that meant for the peacekeepers. "Will we have to withdraw?" Misner asked.

Click. A photo of Vermullen and six of his legionnaires in full gear filled the screen. "The Irregulars and French Peacekeepers have formed an effective team. Without the C-130s for rapid response, mobility and supply, the French will also have to withdraw, most likely to Ethiopia. The result will be a bloodbath for the Dinka and Nuer caught in the refugee camps."

"When the 4440th evacuated Malakal," Fitzgerald asked, "why did they move to Mission Awana, twenty-some miles away?"

"First, Mission Awana is in a no man's land between the Republic of the Sudan and the Republic of South Sudan. It is on the southern side of the White Nile, which the Jubans claim is the boundary, but the Sudanese claim it is in the Sudan. Second, Khartoum has benefited from the lack of public attention. As the mission has a high profile in the world's media, any attack on the mission would make instantaneous news with far-reaching consequences. It is a firebreak the Sudanese will hesitate to cross. Also, the mission provides us a good base to continue relief operations."

"The 4440th stays at the mission," Misner said. "For now."

"Thank you, Major Sharp," Fitzgerald said. "Please stay on top of the situation. Again, welcome back. I'm looking forward to your morning briefings." The two generals stood. The briefing was over.

Jill threw caution to the wind. "Sir, I would prefer to return to my unit." Her simple statement stopped Fitzgerald in his tracks, and everyone in the room froze. She had violated protocol and stepped over the line. Fitzgerald turned and fixed her with a hard look. "They're my buddies," she said, her eyes pleading with him.

Fitzgerald's opinion of Major Gillian Sharp went over the moon. "Go. File a daily update."

* * *

Fitzgerald sat at his desk, his fingers slowly moving over the keyboard. He stopped occasionally, reread the e-mail, and made corrections before continuing. Finally, he was finished.

> Our girl did good today. She is on the way back to you. Richards is still a problem, and definitely has the ear of the Speaker of the House. God only knows where the Administration is on this. Relocating to Mission Awana was a good move. You and the Legion are all that is keeping Khartoum and Janjaweed in check.
>
> The French are leading a coalition supporting South Sudan. Their goal is to make Juba a viable counter to stop Sudanese expansion. They believe that is the only way to stop the genocide and stabilize that part of Africa. You've got to hold on until that happens. Unfortunately, the loss of the missiles to the SA may make your position untenable.
>
> Further, the 4440th may become a political hot potato come the November elections. All bets are off if that happens.

The general reread the message one last time, hit the encrypt button, and sent it out. He kicked back in his chair, disgusted with the situation. A ragtag group of C-130s and legionnaires was all that was sparing the world of another round of genocide, and he was a co-conspirator in a game of nation building. He hadn't joined up for that and had enough pressing matters just running the Air Force to fill his days. For a moment he considered resigning, but just as quickly, dropped it. That wasn't the way he played the game, but he would if he had no other choice.

Mission Awana

Allston sipped at his water bottle in a vain attempt to drown the butterflies fluttering in the lower regions of his abdomen. When that failed, he reread the message for the third time, hoping it would be a distraction. There was no doubt that Fitzgerald wanted him to continue operations as long as he could, but it didn't help with the butterflies. He hit the 'secure delete' button. His laptop whirred for a moment, forever shredding the message. What a shitty way to run a railroad, he thought. But he was pleased that Jill was returning. They needed the Intel officer. He checked his watch and locked the computer in his safe. It was time. He stepped outside, onto the veranda of the guesthouse. Tara Scott was sitting in a chaise lounge, enjoying the evening breeze. She gave him a dazzling smile that set another rabble of butterflies into action. "Hi there," she said. Her hand reached out and touched his. Slowly, their fingers intertwined. "Can you stay a moment?"

He smiled back. "I wish I could. Some business to take care of."

"Nothing serious, I hope."

He shook his head, lying. "Operations stuff. By the way, Jill's coming back. Not sure when she'll arrive."

"You know she's in love with you."

He laughed. "Sure she is. I'm her boss and she's a good staff officer. That's all."

"Seriously, she is." Tara tilted her head and studied his reaction. She laughed, enchanting him. "Men! You are so thick at times."

Sergeant Loni Williams drove up in a battered pickup he had resurrected from oblivion. "It runs good," he called. He waited for Allston to join him.

Reluctantly, Allston pulled his hand free. He bent over and brushed her forehead with his lips. "I'll be back."

* * *

Vermullen was dressed in civvies when he arrived at the two waiting C-130s. He got out of his Panhard P4 utility vehicle, pulled on a heavy jumpsuit, and strapped on a parachute harness while talking to his officers, Major Herbert Mercier and Captain Paul Bouchard. They were all in full battle dress and ready for an airdrop. "If anything goes wrong," Vermullen said in French, "you will not wait for me. Is that understood?" The two men reluctantly agreed. "Good. What do the Americans say, *mes amis?* Let's do it!" He laughed, enjoying the moment.

Allston joined them. "We're loading the last truck. I hope four is enough."

Vermullen assured him that four would do. "Where is Sergeant Williams?"

Allston pulled a face. "On the other side of the plane, puking his guts out. He's never jumped before."

Vermullen was worried. "Can he do it? He will be strapped to me."

"He'll be okay." Allston hoped it was true. Williams had eagerly volunteered for the mission, claiming that only he and Vermullen were the right color and spoke the right language. Vermullen was ready to go. "You sure about all this?" Allston asked.

Vermullen shrugged. "One is never sure."

"Let's do it," Allston said. His butterflies were gone.

FIFTEEN

Bentiu, Unity, Sudan

The flight deck was bathed in red light when Allston leveled off at 28,000 feet. He checked the navigation display- thirty miles to go - and retarded the throttles, slowing to drop airspeed. He looked around the flight deck. Everyone was wearing an oxygen mask and breathing easily. He keyed the intercom. "Oxygen check." His voice sounded tinny, but he credited that to the microphone in his mask. The crew checked in. The loadmaster was the last, verifying the forty-one heavily clothed legionnaires in the rear were all on oxygen and okay. "Depressurizing, now," Allston warned. He gave the high sign to the flight engineer. A whooshing sound filled the flight deck and he felt the change in pressure.

"Five minutes," the copilot said. In the rear, the loadmaster motioned for Vermullen and Loni Williams to stand. They shuffled into position and stood together, back to belly with the short and stocky American in front. Vermullen snapped the sergeant's harness to his. The loadmaster tugged at the connections, making sure they were secure. He double-checked their masks and portable oxygen bottles. At their altitude, their time of useful consciousness was less than thirty seconds without oxygen.

"Jumpers ready," the loadmaster said over the intercom.

The seconds ticked down. "Two minutes," the copilot called. "Lowering the ramp." His hand moved over the right console, lowering the ramp to the trail position. At the same time, the flight engineer turned the cargo compartment and flight deck heat to full on. But they could still feel the bitter cold invading the aircraft. "One minute," the copilot said. Vermullen and Williams shuffled to the edge of the ramp.

"Jumpers on the ramp," the loadmaster said. They waited as the seconds ticked down, their eyes riveted on the red jump light at the rear door. The jumpmaster watched as Vermullen lifted Williams. The red light blinked to green and Vermullen stepped into the night. "Jumpers away," the loadmaster said, stepping back from the ramp as it raised into position, sealing them in from the cold. The aircraft pressurized as they waited.

* * *

The two men plummeted earthward, reaching a terminal velocity of 120 MPH. Vermullen checked the altimeter strapped to his left wrist. They had to get out of the freezing cold and to a lower altitude before their oxygen bottles were depleted. He had practiced high altitude jumps before, but never with a passenger strapped to his harness. At twelve thousand feet they dropped through a layer of clouds and the world spread out below them in a beautiful panorama of sparkling lights and darkness. They were west of the town, exactly where he wanted to be. He pulled the ripcord. The big parafoil, a parachute-like fabric wing developed for special operations, deployed with a slight jerk. The Legionnaire looked up and scanned the canopy with a red-lens flashlight. He grunted in satisfaction. It was not a traditional round parachute but a highly maneuverable airfoil that resembled a mattress.

But something was wrong. Vermullen checked his GPS. They had encountered a wind-shift below the cloud deck and were drifting to the south, not the way he wanted to go. He had deployed the canopy at too high an altitude. He tugged at the risers and spiraled down to get out of the wind. He tugged his thick gloves off and let them dangle from wrist straps. Next, he pulled his oxygen mask free and let it hang around his neck. He pulled the NVGs, night vision goggles, on his helmet into place and turned them on. He tapped Williams on the top of his head to see if he was conscious. "You can remove your oxygen mask. But don't drop it." There was no response. "Are you okay?"

"Yeah, I think so."

Vermullen checked the GPS strapped to his right wrist, and again tugged at the risers, trying to turn northward, but they were still too far south of their desired landing point. He released his equipment bag and let it dangle from a ten-foot lanyard. "Release your FAMAS and be ready to use it," he told Williams. He felt Williams move as he freed the stubby, eight-pound assault rifle strapped to his chest.

Williams swung the FAMAS to the ready position, its sling around his neck and over his left shoulder. He charged a round. Like Vermullen, he snapped his NVGs into place. "Ready."

"The wind is stronger than expected," Vermullen told him. "It's blowing us to the south." He searched for their original objective, the bridge on the north side of town leading to the airport a mile to the north. He found the river and followed it, finally seeing the bridge. His GPS confirmed they were still drifting to the south. He checked his altimeter – 4500 feet. With the unexpected wind out of the north and their rate of descent, they would never make it. He pulled a riser, and they cut a huge swooping arc around the town as he searched for a new place to land.

* * *

"Do you have Bard in sight?" Allston asked his copilot. The two C-130s were stacked in a racetrack pattern twenty miles north of Bentiu. At 28,000 feet, they were still above the cloud deck but it was starting to break up and he caught an occasional glimpse of the ground. It always amazed him how many lights marked the barren land at night. But he couldn't see the second C-130 piloted by Bard Green, which should be stacked a thousand feet above him. For a moment, he wondered if he had misjudged the first lieutenant. No way, he told himself. After Marci Jenkins and Dick Lane, Green was his best aircraft commander. But where was he? For a moment, Allston considered breaking radio silence but discarded that as premature. He forced himself to wait for the one-word radio call from Vermullen that would set the next phase in motion.

It was a quiet moment and, like so many, thoughts of home captured him. He hoped Ben, his sixteen-year-old stepson, turned out as well as Bard. As for Lynne, his beautiful daughter, he was sure she would set the world on fire, much like Marci. What happened to Marci? he wondered, coming back to the overwhelming reality of his life. The pilot had been gone fifteen days and was due back. The raw hurt of G.G. was still there and he would never shake a feeling of responsibility for his death. He forced it aside, promising that he would always remember. He was grateful that Marci had volunteered to escort G.G. home. In the quiet lull, he mused how the Air Force had changed. Twenty-years ago as a second lieutenant, he never would have believed he would be relying on two women so much. Make that three, he told himself. His chief of maintenance, the difficult and irritable Susan Malaby, was indispensable. He laughed out loud over the intercom.

His copilot looked at him. "What's up, Boss?"

"I was just thinking about the 'indispensable woman theory,'" Allston replied.

"Colonel Malaby?"

"Yep. It amazes me how she keeps these crates flying." Ahead and above them, a rotating beacon flashed in the night and then disappeared. Bard Green had just announced his presence and then went back to running with lights-out. "Good man," Allston murmured. It was time to pay attention to business. He called the loadmaster. "MacRay, how the jumpers doing?"

"They're ready to go. Getting kind of antsy."

"I can't blame them. Are the trucks still leaking?" The two rattletrap trucks they had on board were leaking gasoline and oil.

"We got the gas leaks stopped, but the fumes are still pretty heavy. It's venting. Not a problem."

"Stay on top of it," he told MacRay. He checked his watch. Vermullen should have checked in. Is this turning into a goat rope? he wondered.

* * *

Vermullen forced himself to be calm as he searched for a place to land. The original plan called for them to land in the riverbed a mile south of the runway and destroy the bridge to seal off the airport and create a diversion. That could still happen, if they could land close enough to the bridge. He scanned the terrain through his NVGs, wishing the greenish image allowed better depth perception. Then he saw it. A branch of the Bahr el Ghazal cut around the southern side of the town, effectively making the town an island during the flood stage in two months. Fortunately, the branch was dry. Unfortunately, the town and another bridge was between them and their original objective. He pointed to a spot in the dry riverbed. "We land there." He tightened up his turn and spiraled down.

"Relax, relax," he told Williams, his voice barely above a whisper. He waited to hear the equipment bag dangling ten feet below his feet strike the ground. When he heard the soft whump, he pulled on the risers and stalled the parafoil. It would have been a near perfect, standing touchdown, except they landed on the equipment bag and stumbled, falling to the ground as the canopy collapsed behind them. Williams groaned under Vermullen's weight. "I'm sorry," Vermullen said as he stood. He pulled Williams to his feet.

"*Pas de tout*," Williams replied. He gathered up the canopy as Vermullen shouldered the heavy equipment bag.

They hunched over and ran for the bank, finding cover in the heavy brush. They quickly shed their heavy jumpsuits and buried them along with the parachute and their harnesses. Vermullen checked his GPS. They were exactly 2.32 miles from the bridge. "Merde," he breathed. It was further than he had hoped but he wasn't going to quit. He motioned Williams forward, to the edge of the riverbed. Ahead of them, loud music he had never heard blared from a CD player and grated on his nerves. The two men stopped at the base of the steep bank the river had down-cut during flood stage and caught their breath. Vermullen silently crawled up the bank and got his bearings.

They were on the edge of an open area with brightly lit buildings on the other side. A tanker truck was parked in the open area. They watched as a car drove out of the town and stopped beside the tanker. A man got out of the car and pulled a hose from the side of the tanker. Within a few minutes, he had refueled his car and banged on the door of the truck. A hand came out the window and the man pressed a wad of money into the open palm. He walked back to his car and drove off, leaving the hose on the ground. Because of the angle of the hose, Vermullen realized they were on high ground and the terrain sloped down and northward, away from them and into town. He smiled. It was almost too easy.

Vermullen stood up, handed his FAMAS to Williams. "Cover me," he said. He ambled towards the buildings and looked around until he found an open sewer. He hid in the shadows as another car drove up and went through the refueling routine. Again, money exchanged hands with the sleepy driver in the cab. The car drove off. They had found an ambitious entrepreneur selling stolen petrol. Vermullen pulled the fuel hose out as far as it could go but it didn't reach the sewage ditch. He thought for a few moments, drew his knife, and walked back to the truck. He pounded on the door. This time, the sleeper stuck his head out and slurred a fine curse in Chinese about chicken-legged whores mothering misbegotten black bastards. Vermullen's hands flashed. His right hand came up, driving his knife into the soft skin under the man's jaw as his left hand slammed the man's head down onto the blade. Vermullen jerked hard and severed the man's thorax before dragging him out the window.

He dropped the twitching body on the ground and rolled it under a wheel. Without a word, he got in and backed the tanker up twenty feet, rolling over the man. He got out and fiddled with the hose nozzle before getting it to lock on. He laid it in the open sewer and watched for a few moments. Not satisfied with the rate of flow, he went back to the tanker and started the engine. He played with levers and valves until fuel gushed out of the open nozzle and into the ditch.

A small pickup drove up for fuel and the driver got out. The man looked around, confused, and then followed the hose, picking it up as he went. He reached the nozzle and shut it off. He dragged it back to his car and jammed the nozzle into the filler neck, cursing loudly. Vermullen ghosted through the night and closed on the man from behind. His hands flashed as he grabbed the man's jaw, jerked back, and cut his throat. He threw the body under the pickup. He grabbed the nozzle, this time disconnecting it. He dropped the gushing hose into the sewer, and walked back to the waiting Williams. "What happens now?" the American asked.

"We wait," Vermullen replied. He checked his watch. "The tanker is full so it will take at a few minutes to empty. By then, the sewer should be full."

"What happens then?" Williams asked. Vermullen didn't answer. It was a dumb question. "Oh, I get it," Williams finally said.

* * *

Allston checked the time: 0243. Three hours to daybreak, and they were running out of time. The sun comes up quickly in the tropics and he wanted to be as far from Bentiu as possible when it did. But it all hinged on Vermullen blowing the bridge, sealing off the operation. The big Frenchman had delighted in explaining how he would fall back on the airport leaving a string of explosive booby traps behind to discourage any pursuers while his legionnaires parachuted in and secured the airport in the confusion. But Allston had serious doubts that he was going to hear the radioed codeword from Vermullen initiating the attack, much less see the explosion. He decided to give it a few more minutes. If he didn't hear the codeword soon, he would break radio silence and call the mission off. Vermullen and Williams would have to escape and evade out of Bentiu but that shouldn't be too difficult. They could make their way to a refugee camp where a C-130 could pick them up. The plan was simple enough in concept and, as any plan had a life expectancy of thirty seconds in combat, easy to modify. Allston wasn't ready to give up. Not quite yet.

"Anti-collision light on," Allston said. "Ten minute warning." He checked the GPS and broke out of orbit, heading south for the airport. Bard Green checked in with two clicks over the UHF radio, followed by two more quick clicks. "Anti-collision light off," he ordered. He was certain Green was behind him. He felt the aircraft shift slightly as the legionnaires in the back stood and shuffled aft. In front of him, a little box appeared on the navigation display. It was the computed air release point where the legionnaires would bail out. "Thanks, G.G.," he said half aloud. The navigator was still very much part of the mission. He descended to 20,000 feet and checked the radar warning receiver. No radars were active.

"Five minutes," the copilot called.

"Five minute check completed," MacRay answered from the rear. The legionnaires were all standing, equipment checked, and ready to go.

"Depressurizing now," Allston said. Again, he could feel the aircraft depressurize. He slowed the Hercules to jump speed. It was almost decision time. He would either hear the codeword and give the green light to jump or cancel the mission.

* * *

"It's time," Vermullen said. He scrambled over the edge of the riverbank and sauntered over to the tanker. The engine was still running but the tank was empty. He reached in and shut off the engine. He tapped the tank and slapped a small magnetic limpet explosive device against the outer hull. He set the timer and continued walking towards the buildings. When he reached the open sewer, he stood and casually lit a cigarette. He didn't smoke and it was all show, just in case someone was watching. He dropped the burning match into the sewer, and walked casually away. For a moment, nothing happened. Suddenly, a wall of flame erupted out of the sewer. It moved with a will of its own and raced into town, feeding off the petrol-filled sewage ditch. He fell to the ground and rolled into a shallow depression. The tank truck exploded, sending a shower of flaming debris over the buildings and setting roofs on fire. Running figures emerged from the buildings, scrambling for their lives. Cars and trucks raced for safety, adding to the confusion.

Satisfied that he had a diversion in play, Vermullen unclipped the UHF radio on his belt and hit the transmit button. But the radio was dead. Because of the long fall and extreme cold, a drop of moisture had formed when it thawed at lower altitudes and shorted out the transmit circuit. He motioned for Williams to join him as he ran for the small pickup truck.

* * *

"Two minutes," Allston's copilot said, warning the crew and jumpers of the time to go. Allston peered into the night, willing the cloud deck below them to break apart. His left thumb hovered over the radio transmit button. He gave it thirty more seconds before he aborted the mission. "One minute," the copilot said, giving the last warning.

"Jesus, mother of God," Riley, the flight engineer said. "Look at that." The cloud deck below them parted, and they could see Bentiu. It was lit up like a Christmas tree as fire spread through the town. A fireball lit the sky and shot skyward like a roman candle.

"Looks like an oil tank," Allston said. He made the decision. It wasn't the product of a logical, carefully reasoned process. It was just there, the end result of years of experience and training. Something had gone wrong and Vermullen was not able to establish radio contact. Instead, the fire was the signal and the diversion. Allston mashed the radio transmit button. "Picnic time, repeat Picnic time." The raid was on.

The copilot counted the seconds down as the triangle, which marked their position in the navigation display, moved over the box in the center of the screen. "Green light," Allston said over the intercom. The copilot hit the toggle switch on the right console, and, almost immediately, they felt the C-130 change attitude as the forty legionnaires bailed out.

"All clear," the loadmaster called.

"Close her up," Allston ordered as he trimmed the Hercules and turned to the left to enter a racetrack pattern high above the airport. Halfway through the turn, he saw Bard Green's C-130 as another forty jumpers bailed out. He followed the plummeting bodies as they fell. It would be another high altitude jump with a low opening. While hazardous, it minimized the exposure of the legionnaires and insured they landed on their objective. Allston reached the end of the outbound leg and turned to the south, heading back for the airport. Ahead, he could see the town. The fire was generating so much heat that it had created a whirlwind and sparks and burning embers were showering the northern part of the town and setting it on fire. At the end of the leg, he turned again back to the north, hoping to see Bard's C-130. On cue, the young pilot flashed his anti-collision light and promptly turned it off. As planned, he was still stacked in the same pattern, a thousand feet above Allston. "Lights out," Allston ordered. He snapped his NVGs into place, and turned them on.

Again, they had to wait.

* * *

Vermullen dropped the equipment bag into the bed of the pickup. He unzipped it and pulled out two bandoliers of ammunition, a bag of hand grenades, and an old Russian RPG-7. The fourteen-pound warhead on the rocket grenade could take out any vehicle that might get in their way, but he wished they had their Shipons, the Israeli-designed and built, shoulder-held anti-tank weapon that could destroy main battle tanks, fortified targets, and bridges. The lack of Shipons was a deficiency he hoped to correct in the next few hours. "You drive," he told Williams.

The short American climbed into the driver's seat. "Where to?"

"The bridge of course." He pointed to the town, directly into the spreading inferno.

"Now I know why my momma told me never to volunteer," Williams muttered. He banged the truck into gear and headed into town, laying on the horn to clear a path as they raced past burning compounds and fleeing people.

* * *

The legionnaires led by Major Mercier from Allston's C-130 landed in an open field 200 yards from the southern end of the runway. In less than four minutes they were out of their parachutes, formed up in squads and running for their objectives. They rapidly cleared the shacks that served as the airport's terminal and operations building, secured the runway, and set up defensive fire positions on the road leading to town. Only then did Mercier radio the code word that the airfield was secure. "Bastille, repeat, Bastille."

The second wave of legionnaires, led by Captain Bouchard, from Bard Green's C-130 landed 180 yards north of their objective, the weapons storage area. They had to dodge low scrub as they touched down and a few were scratched and cut up but nothing serious. Within minutes they formed up, moved on the compound and deployed around its northern perimeter. Bouchard scanned the heavy concertina-wire fence around the compound with his NVGs looking for gaps. There weren't any. He motioned a squad forward and followed them as they moved along the perimeter until they flanked the two guard shacks on the road leading to the airport. Again, Bouchard scanned the area. Only one man at the gate guarded the army compound, and he was standing in the road, looking at the flames and smoke belching from the town. Bouchard keyed his radio but movement in the compound caught his attention and he broke the transmission.

Soldiers ran from the two barracks inside the compound and quickly formed up. Shouted commands carried into the night as the soldiers mounted their trucks. Within minutes, the convoy rumbled out the gate and towards the airfield and town. The French captain broke radio silence and warned his compatriots that company was coming their way. Again, he studied the compound. It looked deserted and he conferred with his sergeant. "Apparently, they left one guard at the gate. We need to get in without him raising the alarm." The sergeant had an idea. He motioned for his men to form up on the road and quick marched them straight for the compound, hoping the guard would think they were returning soldiers. He hoped right. They were ten feet away when the gate guard realized they were not Sudanese and promptly surrendered. Bouchard ordered four of his men to guard the gate while he led the rest on a sweep through the compound. Within minutes, it was secured and they had reached the storage bunkers. But heavy steel doors barred their entrance. He radioed the code word indicating the compound was secure. "Verdun, repeat, Verdun."

* * *

On the darkened flight deck, Allston tensed, waiting to hear what was happening at the airfield. It seemed like an eternity before he heard Major Mercier's voice on the radio. "The trucks did not stop and are headed for town. Guests are welcome."

Allston didn't hesitate. They had momentum, and he radioed the code words that set the next phase in action. "Remember the Alamo, repeat, remember the Alamo." The C-130s were going to land. For a moment, he wondered if Vermullen and Williams were still alive and how critical blowing the bridge was to their success. But it was too late to engage in second-guessing. The Monday morning quarterbacks at AFRICOM and the Pentagon would do that from the safety and security of their offices. He banked the C-130, reduced power, and circled down, certain that Bard Green was following him. He called for the before landing checklist, configuring the aircraft. He studied the terrain and finally found the darkened runway. It was clear for its entire length of 7000 feet. He wanted to minimize their approach time and opted for a steep approach typical of a short field landing. But this time he would not reverse the props and would roll out long to keep the noise to a minimum. He turned and came down final.

Thanks to his NVGs, he had a visual on the runway but his depth perception left a lot to be desired. His copilot called out their absolute altitude, the actual feet above the ground. They banged down. "Shut down one and four," he told Riley as they rolled out to the far end. He turned off the runway and onto the large earthen parking area. Riley cut the inboard engines as Bard Green touched down. "Cock this puppy," Allston told his crew as the ramp came down. The copilot called the checklist from memory and they readied the C-130 for a quick engine start and takeoff. In the rear, the two battered trucks rumbled off. Bard Green's C-130 taxied to a halt next to Allston's and within minutes, offloaded its two trucks. The four trucks raced for the weapons storage area, three quarters of a mile away.

Allston lifted his NVGs and checked his watch – 03:32. Two hours and thirteen minutes to sunrise. They were running out of time. Major Mercier climbed onto the flight deck, and Allston offered him a bottle of cold water that was gratefully accepted. "Any word from Colonel Vermullen?" Allston asked.

"Nothing," the major replied.

"He should have let someone else do it," Allston said. "He's needed here."

Mercier shrugged. "The Colonel trains us to act independently. Compared to what he does to us in training, this is what you American's call a piece of cake."

"Actually, that's British."

Mercier gazed into the night. "Colonel Vermullen is where he belongs, doing what he does best."

* * *

The legionnaires at the guard shack pointed to the bunkers as they waved the four trucks into the storage area. Bouchard snapped an order and the lead truck backed up against the nearest steel door. A soldier connected a chain to the door and shouted at the driver to gun the engine. He did and let out the clutch. For a moment, it was a stalled tug-of-war. Then the truck inched ahead, its wheels spinning. Suddenly, the entire wall popped out. "That's one way to do it," Bouchard said. "Open up the others." He ran down the aisle trying to make sense out of the markings on the crates. As best he could tell, each crate was labeled in Arabic and Chinese. He could read the Arabic but it didn't make sense. "Does anyone read Chinese?"

The youngest of his men, a nineteen-year-old private, came forward and translated the markings on the crates. "These are all Claymores," he announced. The Claymore's were an anti-personnel mine about the size of a laptop computer. A pair of short legs extended from the bottom edge so it could be set up in the vertical and pointed at the enemy. A light infantryman could not ask for a better defensive weapon.

"Load them all," Bouchard ordered. The men worked like demons and within minutes, the first truck was loaded. They went to work on the second truck.

The teenager was back, carrying a Stinger surface-to air missile. He pointed to the second bunker. "They're all there! In the back."

"Show me," Bouchard ordered. The two men hurried down the darkened aisles. The teenager stopped and handed him a Shipon. They had found what they came for. The captain didn't hesitate and ordered his men to load the Stingers and Shipons. Within minutes, the four trucks were loaded and headed for the airport. Bouchard searched the last bunker and struck gold. There were over 400 wooden crates of landmines. He ran outside and keyed his radio. "Send the trucks back."

SIXTEEN

Bentiu

Williams sawed at the steering wheel cutting between frantic people fleeing the fire as they sped down the main road leading to the first bridge they had to cross. Twice, they had to pull over to let trucks carrying soldiers careen past, heading towards the fire. Then they were moving again. "They could use a fire department," Williams said.

Vermullen shook his head. "In this part of Africa, the firemen would steal the trucks." They sped across the first bridge and were less than a hundred yards from the second one, their original objective, when Williams stomped on the brakes. A makeshift roadblock barred their way. The truck skidded to a stop, and Williams shifted into reverse. Vermullen's huge left hand clamped down on Williams right hand and shifted the transmission to neutral "No. We're too close. They're SA."

"Where the fuck did they come from?" Williams blurted.

Vermullen ignored the outburst. "I count one on your side, two on mine."

"I count the same," Williams answered.

"Drive forward and stop a few feet short. Take your man out when I tell you."

"Got it," Williams said as he let out the clutch and moved forward. He drew his Colt .45 and thumbed off the safety. He switched it to his left hand and lowered the weapon to hide it between his seat and the door. He stopped the pickup short of the roadblock and waited for the soldiers' reaction. They held their AK-47s at the ready and walked to the truck. The soldier on Williams' side shone a light into Williams face and laughed at the short American. "A dwarf is driving," he called in Arabic. He dropped his AK-47 and let it swing from its strap. He pointed at Williams. "Get out,"

"I don't speak Arabic," Williams said in Nuer.

"He wants us to get out," Vermullen replied in the same language. He got out and faced the two soldiers on his side, blocking the first soldier's view. In the dark, the two men didn't see the knife in Vermullen's right hand held low next to his thigh. One of the soldiers lowered his AK-47 and stepped forward to search Vermullen. The Frenchman held up his left hand and let him see his Rolex watch on his wrist. The soldier reached for it. "Now," Vermullen ordered. Williams swung his door open, raised his Colt, and fired without aiming. It was a wild shot but so close in that it hit the soldier in his right side. The striking power of a .45 at close range is deadly and the man spun around and fell backward.

At the same time, Vermullen grabbed the soldier stealing his watch by the wrist and twisted, forcing the man around and in front of him. The Frenchman's right hand flashed, rattlesnake quick, as he cut the soldier's throat. In the same fluid motion, Vermullen pushed the dying soldier into his comrade, spoiling his aim. Williams scrambled around the front of the truck and fired three rapid rounds at the third soldier. The first round grazed the soldier's right shoulder, throwing him back. The last two rounds missed. "Aim," Vermullen ordered. Williams did and squeezed off another round. It hit the wounded man in the jaw, blowing it away.

A hail of gunfire split the air and kicked up the dirt around them. Four slugs slammed into the front of the pickup truck, puncturing the radiator. Williams fell to the ground and rolled under the pickup. Vermullen ran to one of the dead soldiers and jerked his AK-47 free. He thumbed the selector to semi-automatic, leaned across the pickup's hood, and fired three rounds. The gunfire stopped.

"Where's it coming from?" Williams asked.

"From the bridge," Vermullen answered. "Get the equipment bag." Vermullen moved forward in short bursts, taking advantage of what cover there was, with Williams right behind. They drew up short of the darkened bridge and hid behind a low earthen dike. Vermullen chanced a look and raised his head. He quickly pulled back. "Four soldiers are retreating across the bridge. There's a roadblock on the other side. Give me your FAMAS." Williams handed him his assault rifle. The colonel knelt in a shooting position and laid the FAMAS across the top of the dike to steady his aim. "The 'Bulge' is much more accurate than the AK." He squeezed off three carefully aimed rounds and waited.

"They're still moving," Williams said.

"The angle is bad and I can't see them," Vermullen said. "I'm aiming at the roadblock." He fired another three rounds. This time the men at the roadblock reacted to the incoming rounds and sprayed the dark running images on the bridge with gunfire, killing them. "Much better," Vermullen allowed.

"What now?" Williams asked.

The Colonel shook his head in frustration. He had to explain everything to the American. "Most of the SA are on this side of the bridge, which is where we want to keep them. Unfortunately, the SA also control the bridge from the other side, so we do what we came for. We blow the bridge."

* * *

The four heavily loaded trucks rattled to a stop behind the two waiting C-130s. The original plan had called for them to simply drive on board with their loads. But Captain Bouchard had radioed for them to return. Allston's eyes narrowed as he ran the numbers. How much time did they have left? He checked his watch and made the decision. "Off load," he ordered. "The trucks go back." The legionnaires tore into the packed trucks, pushing and dropping the crates out the tailgate as the trucks inched forward. The trucks were offloaded and headed back in less than three minutes. "MacRay," Allston called. "Load Bard's Herk first." The loadmaster directed the legionnaires to carry the crates littering the ground onto Green's C-130. They ran up the ramp as the two loadmasters spread the load down the center of the cargo deck, keeping the aircraft's center of gravity within fore and aft limits.

Allston climbed back onto the flight deck of his C-130. "Any word from Vermullen?" he asked. His copilot shook his head then pointed to the east. The darkness on the far horizon was yielding to the new day.

* * *

Williams lifted the flap of the canvas bag and shook his head. "I've never seen one of these before." It was an explosive charge with a remote control detonator.

Vermullen pointed to the detonator fuse box. "It is very simple. Turn this dial to the arm position, lift this guard and throw the switch. Then press this button. Once you have pressed the button, do not touch it. It has an anti-tamper device and too much movement will detonate it."

"What's too much movement?" Williams asked. Vermullen answered with a shrug. "Okay," Williams said, picking up the two explosive packs by their shoulder straps. "So where do I place them?"

Vermullen scanned the bridge with his NVGs. "We need to drop the center span. Fix a charge to the pier on each end."

"Colonel, those piers are in the water. You ever hear of crocodiles?"

"It's the dry season. I doubt if the water is knee deep."

Williams was even less convinced. "It's pretty open out there. What happens if they see me and start shooting?"

"I'll convince them it's a bad idea. Go."

"Should've listened to my momma," Williams grumbled. He took a deep breath and rolled over the dike where they were hiding and scampered for the bridge. He reached the concrete embankment and caught his breath, not believing his luck. Then he was moving again, into the riverbed.

Vermullen shifted his position thirty yards up stream to a better vantage point. Thanks to his NVGs, he could make out Williams as he made his way under the bridge. He swept the area in front of Williams. "Bastards," he muttered. Two soldiers on the opposite side of the river were making their way towards Williams. For a moment, he lost them. They are good, he thought. He fitted a silencer to the muzzle of his FAMAS and adjusted its night scope before lifting his NVGs. It took a few moments for his eyes to adjust to the scope. "*Merde*," he whispered. Williams had waded out to the first pier and was strapping a charge to it. He methodically set the detonator, totally unaware of the two men stalking him from the far bank. Vermullen aimed and squeezed off a single round. Thanks to the silencer, the muzzle blast sounded like a loud sneeze. The man closest to Williams keeled over and screamed as Vermullen fired again. Williams looked up at the sound in time to see the second soldier go down. He turned towards Vermullen and gave him a thumbs up.

Williams swam to the next pier and quickly attached the second charge just above the water line. He activated the detonator and swam back. Just as he waded ashore, gunfire from the far bank drove him to the ground. Vermullen returned fire. Now the gunfire concentrated on him as he hunkered down. The clatter of a 12.7mm heavy machine gun opened up, zeroing in on his position, and blowing huge gaps in the dike. Vermullen crawled for safety, dragging the equipment bag. The gunner kept hammering at the dike, methodically forcing Vermullen away. Out of ideas, and lacking any place to go, Vermullen pulled the remote detonator off his belt, lifted the guard cover, and pressed the detonate button.

* * *

The Peacemakers

The sound of distant gunfire echoed over the parked C-130s. Allston stood under a wing and strained to locate the source, but he was getting an echo effect from the big aircraft. He moved away, towards Mercier who was standing in the open. Now the sound was crisper. "It is coming from that direction," Mercier said, pointing to the south and the bridge. "Maybe two kilometers." The heavy rattle of a machine gun added to the growing din. "Large caliber," the Frenchman added.

"Is it ours?" Allston asked. Mercier shook his head. Allston made a decision. "Recall. It's time to get the hell out of Dodge. Call everyone in." Mercier spoke into his radio and repeated the code word three times. Bouchard at the weapons storage area acknowledged as the legionnaires holding the airfield pulled in. Within minutes, they had re-established perimeter security around the parked aircraft. Allston turned to climb back on board when he heard a heavy explosion. He turned in time to see a red glow die down. "What do you think?" he asked Mercier.

"It's the bridge. The Colonel is at work."

"But we can't be sure," Allston added.

"No. We cannot."

Now they heard the laboring sound of the first truck returning from the storage area. "Get it loaded," Allston ordered. The second truck was right behind it, also fully loaded. "What in the hell did they find?" Allston wondered. He checked the time. "Sunrise in ten minutes."

* * *

A heavy dust cloud from the explosion rolled over Vermullen. He buried his head in his arms until it settled. He raised his head and squinted into the settling dust. A soldier on the far bank was clearing away rubble in front of the roadblock and he could see the muzzle of the machine gun. Vermullen pulled the RPG-7 out of the equipment bag and laid it across the top of the dike. He had never fired one before but it was simplicity itself. He carefully sighted and squeezed the trigger. It was a hard pull. The first stage of the rocket ignited and it streaked for the roadblock. The rocket homed with deadly accuracy and the roadblock disappeared in a fiery explosion. He was surprised to see four men crawl out of the debris, dragging the machine gun. But its barrel had a decided bend and it was out of action.

Williams rolled over and came to his knees, surprised that he was still alive. He shook the dust off and looked at the bridge. It was still standing. "You mutha fucker!" he shouted, surprised that he couldn't hear his own words. Again, he shook his head, trying to clear his ears. Nothing. A big

175

hand clamped down on his shoulder. His head came up and he was looking at Vermullen. The colonel's mouth was forming words but nothing was coming out. "I can't hear," Williams said. Vermullen picked him up and set him on his feet.

Two army trucks on their side of the river drove up to the bridge and stopped. An officer got out and studied the bridge in front of him. He issued a command and the first truck moved slowly forward, onto the bridge. Vermullen pushed Williams towards the main channel. He made a swimming motion and waded in, still carrying his FAMAS and a bandolier with hand grenades. "Don't you believe in crocodiles?" Williams yelled. He added a respectful "Colonel." Vermullen was now swimming. "Momma, you warned me," Williams muttered, plunging into the water. Adrenaline pumped through Williams and he swam like a madman, quickly reaching the shore where Vermullen was waiting. "What now?" His words were drowned out as the center span of the bridge collapsed under the weight of the truck.

Vermullen slapped a fresh magazine into his FAMAS, charged a round, and handed Williams the bandolier with the grenades. "Run!"

* * *

The legionnaires tore into the trucks, manhandling the heavy crates and running them onto the C-130s. Most of the crates required two men to carry, and the loadmasters estimated their weight as they came up the ramp, keeping the weight evenly distributed. The last two trucks pulled into the parking area, closely followed by Captain Bouchard's raiding party. The men were exhausted from the long run but they pitched in, offloading the trucks. The props started to turn, adding dust and even more noise to the seeming confusion. When the last crate was onboard, the French officers did a head count, ensuring all were accounted for. Mercier climbed onto the flight deck and told Allston everyone except the perimeter guards were onboard.

Allston keyed the radio. "Bard, go." He watched as the C-130 taxied onto the runway and took off in the rapidly growing light. Allston turned to Mercier. "Call the perimeter guards in."

* * *

Vermullen scrambled over the top of the riverbank, less than twenty yards from the destroyed roadblock. But the men in it were far from dead and started shooting. Vermullen swung his FAMAS around, emptying a clip into the pile of debris and sandbags. Williams was right behind him and lobbed a hand grenade over their heads in the general direction. It fell short and rolled back towards them. They both fell to the ground as the grenade rolled into a slight depression. The concussion was deafening, but the wrinkle in the dirt was enough to direct the explosion over their heads. Vermullen pulled Williams to his feet. "Go!" the colonel yelled as a Sudanese soldier stood, dazed and confused.

"You muthas!" Williams yelled as he lobbed a second grenade. This time, it reached the roadblock. Again, the two men fell to the ground as the grenade exploded with deadly effect, killing or wounding the four men hiding in the rubble. Now gunfire from the opposite side of the river split the air. The two men scrambled forward, getting a little cover from the roadblock. Vermullen came to his feet and ran. Williams was right behind him. "Shit!" Williams roared. In the rapidly increasing light, a C-130 was climbing out to the north, its tail to them.

"Faster!" Vermullen yelled, putting on a fresh burst of speed.

* * *

Allston released the brakes and taxied forward, turning onto the runway as the sun broke the eastern horizon. His eyes followed Bard Green's C-130 as it climbed into the clear sky. He set the brakes and waited. "MacRay, you ready?" he asked over the intercom.

"Gimme two or three minutes to get everything tied down," the loadmaster answered.

"You got it. Get shooters on the ramp to clear our six."

"Will do," MacRay replied. The copilot raised the ramp at the rear but kept the door in the up position. "Two shooters on the ramp," MacRay said. He went back to work, securing the load. Then, "All secure in the rear. We're good to go." Allston ran the engines up and released the brakes. Even with the forty men in the rear and the load of weapons and ammunition, the Hercules accelerated smartly. Allston pulled the yoke back and they came unglued. "Colonel!" MacRay shouted over the intercom. "Mutt and Jeff in sight."

"It's gotta be them," Riley said.

Allston agreed. "Where are they?"

"Running down the runway," MacRay replied.

"Hold on," Allston ordered. He climbed to 150 feet and banked sharply to the left, circling back around. "Short field landing," he said. "MacRay, the moment we land, get shooters in the jump doors and on the ramp."

"Will do."

Allston flew a short downwind and located the two men on the runway. They were stopped and looking in his direction. "Keep going," he urged, wanting them at least a thousand feet further on. But they were exhausted from the long run from the bridge. Allston climbed to 300 feet and circled to land. He touched down on the first fifty feet of the runway, slammed the nose down, and raked the throttles aft and over the detent, throwing the props into reverse. The airspeed indicator needle descended through fifty knots as they passed Vermullen and Williams.

"It's them!" the copilot shouted.

"We're taking fire!" MacRay shouted. "Six o'clock,"

"Hose the livin' shit out of 'em," Allston said, his voice amazingly calm. He left the props in reverse and backed down the runway, into the gunfire, as the shooters in the rear opened fire. The din was horrific as every legionnaire who could get to the ramp helped lay down suppressive fire. The smell of cordite flooded the flight deck.

"Stop!" the copilot shouted. He saw Vermullen lying on the ground but no Williams. Allston stomped on the brakes and moved the throttles forward, bringing the props out of reverse. The nose of the Hercules lifted high into the air as the rear skid hit the ground. The nose banged down. Vermullen was up and running. Much to their surprise, Williams was right behind. The Frenchman had covered Williams's body with his, giving him what little protection he could from the hostile gunfire. Allston stomped on the brakes and ran the engines up as the legionnaires kept firing.

Vermullen was the first to reach the rear parachute door of the C-130. He grabbed Williams and pitched him on board. Willing hands grabbed the colonel and pulled him through the open door. "We got 'em!" MacRay shouted. "Go! Go! Go!"

Allston released the brakes and the Hercules surged forward. The gunfire in the rear slowly trickled off and stopped as they rotated, climbing into the bright clear morning. Allston leveled off at fifty feet and cleaned up the aircraft, flying low and leaving the threat behind. "All secure in the rear," MacRay announced.

"Check for battle damage," Allston said. The copilot and flight engineer checked their instruments and systems.

"A-okay," the flight engineer announced.

"A-okay," the copilot repeated.

"We got holes in the ramp," MacRay said.

Allston reduced power and climbed to a thousand feet. "Controllability check," he ordered as he gently cycled the controls to see how the Hercules responded. They were lucky that a round had not nicked a propeller blade. "It looks good," he announced.

"We might want to take it easy," Riley said. "Just in case."

"Sounds like a plan," Allston said. "MacRay, have the good colonel come forward whenever it's convenient."

"Will do, as soon as his men stop hugging him and kissing him on the cheek."

"That's the French," Allston replied. A smiling Vermullen climbed onto the flight deck. Allston turned around in his seat. "Well, Colonel, that was a piece of cake."

"Indeed it was, *mon ami*."

SEVENTEEN

E-Ring

The click of Richards' high heels echoed down the quiet and almost deserted corridor announcing her presence. She liked late Saturday afternoons in the Pentagon as it gave her chance to savor the building for itself and all that it meant. The aura of contained power that was part of the walls rejuvenated her, filling her with a sense of purpose and resolve. She was surprised that the doors to Fitzgerald's offices were open and he was alone. He waved her to a seat. "Have you read the latest OpRep?" he asked, assuming that was why she was in his office.

He assumed right. "Yes, sir, I have. We have a problem."

"Which is?"

The brigadier pitched her voice to match the seriousness of the situation. "The raid on Bentiu was not authorized – not by the UN, not by the NMCC, nor by AFRICOM. We definitely have a loose cannon on our hands."

"Any reaction from the other side of the River?" In Pentagon-speak, the 'other side of the River' meant Congress and the White House. Supposedly, the Office of Military-Political Affairs was created to facilitate communications between the two sides of the river but Richards had leveraged her office into policy role. While Fitzgerald didn't like that arrangement, it was one beyond his control. But Richards was not.

"I received a query from the Speaker's office," she replied. The 'Speaker' was the Speaker of the House and Richards' sponsor. "I related what I knew and said I would get back to them." She anticipated Fitzgerald's next question and hastened to add, "I confined my answer to what is in the OpRep." It was a blatant lie but there was no way he would ever learn of the private conversation she and the Speaker had the night before.

Fitzgerald nodded in approval. "We should have a better handle on what went down by Monday."

"General, my sources are telling me that the Speaker will talk about the Bentiu raid on Meet the Press Sunday morning. Apparently, it's the hot topic of the day and he's promising that heads will roll in the Pentagon."

Again, Fitzgerald nodded, masking his reaction. "Get back to them and confirm they know all we know. Make sure they understand there are still many unknowns and that we'll forward any new information the moment we receive it. Stay on top of this. You may have to burn some midnight oil but I don't want our political masters claiming we blindsided them." The meeting was over. "Thanks for coming in."

Richards stood. "It's my job, sir."

Fitzgerald leaned back in his chair and watched her leave. He folded his fingers and rubbed his chin with his thumbs. He wasn't a happy man. His Air Force was caught in a no-win situation because his political masters on the other side of the River wanted to cuddle up to the UN, and the diplomats in the State Department had convinced the President that placing the 4440th under the operational control of the UN Peacekeeping Mission was critical in stroking the UN's fragile ego. However, the end result was that the 4440th was caught in a no-man's land, vulnerable to the marauding Janjaweed and hamstrung by a corrupt UN relief mission. He also suspected Richards was kicking the 4440th around like a political football to curry favor with the Speaker. He hoped to solve that problem by Monday evening.

He turned to the computer screen and keyboard on the right side of his desk. He called up his secure line and sent Richards a memo recapping all they had discussed. Satisfied that he had covered his backside, he composed another message to Allston, this one much longer.

Mission Awana

It was late Sunday afternoon before Allston finally returned to his office and had a chance to check his e-mail. He snorted when he read Fitzgerald's message. "The games we play," he muttered to himself. He hit the secure delete and consigned the message to electronic oblivion.

"What games?" Dick Lane asked. Allston looked up to see his Ops Officer standing in the doorway.

"I just got a magic-gram from Merlin. He's playing Puzzle Palace games over Bentiu and needs more info."

Lane was perplexed. "We covered Bentiu in detail in the OpRep; the time line, personnel and aircraft involved, exactly what weapons we recovered, even burning the town down."

"I know," Allston said. "You did good work getting that out. Specifically, Merlin needs a copy of this." He handed Lane a single page document. "I can't make the damn scanner work."

"Not a problem." Lane glanced at the document and looked at Allston, his eyes wide. "I hadn't seen this. Sum-bitch." He showed Allston how to scan the single page and encrypt it for transmission.

"Our masters in Addis Ababa laid this on me the second day I was here," Allston explained. "It's our get-out-of-jail-free card." He changed the subject. "How's it going with Sixty Minutes?" Thanks to Tara, they had made the world news and CBS had sent a film crew and a reporter to interview the actress for the Sunday news show. Allston had detailed Lane to take care of the film crew while he and Vermullen dealt with the Bentiu operation. The major had done a good job but Allston sensed Jill would have done it better. He wanted her back, the sooner the better.

"Tara has them eating out of her hand," Lane answered, "and they can't get enough of Toby. Sixty Minutes is running a special Sunday afternoon, New York time, devoted to the Sudan. The producer wants to end the show by doing a segment from here. They're going to broadcast Toby's evening church service live," he checked his watch, "which starts in an hour. Tara asked for you to be there."

"Do I have to?"

"It might be a good idea, Boss." Allston nodded. Tara had pulled some powerful strings to make it happen and he owed her. "Good call," Lane said.

Air House, Fort Myer, Maryland

It was a rare Sunday for the Air Force Chief of Staff. He was kicked back in his den and enjoying the basketball games on TV. His wife had not seen him so relaxed in weeks and protected the moment, determined to make it last. She was used to him watching two games at once but was surprised that he also kept replaying the clip from the early Sunday morning Meet the Press talk show. In her estimation, it had been a disaster for the Air Force but he wasn't upset in the least. The TV program had triggered a conference telephone call with the Secretary of Defense and General Misner, and he had replied with calm and reassuring words. "No need to disturb the President prematurely on this," he counseled. "We'll sort it out in the morning in the situation room. The President can decide then how he wants to respond after he's seen all the facts."

Frustrated, his wife waited until commercials were playing and asked him a direct question, wondering why he was taking it all so calmly. Fitzgerald only smiled as his fingers played on the remote control and the clip from Meet the Press replayed. The Speaker of the House was responding to a question about the raid by the UN peacekeepers on the town of Bentiu in the Sudan. "As you know," the urbane and handsome politician said, "we are in the Sudan to support the UN Relief and Peacekeeping Mission. The raid on Bentiu by the 4440th was not authorized. Not by our National Military Command Center, not by AFRICOM, nor, according to my sources, by anyone in the UN. It appears we have a loose cannon on our hands."

The general pounded the arm of his chair, which was much closer to his normal self. "I know where that came from!" He let the clip play out.

"I intend to get to the bottom of this," the Speaker continued. "I assure you, the right questions will be asked, and" – Fitzgerald joined with him in chorus – "heads will roll in the Pentagon."

Fitzgerald gave his wife a hungry look. "He's not going to like the answers."

"But you will," she replied.

"One can always hope."

She wasn't convinced. "Some idiot will screw it up."

"Not to worry." He reached for the remote. "Isn't it time for that Sixty Minutes special?" He touched her hand and changed channels.

Most of the program had been pre-recorded at Mission Awana, and played exactly as he had been briefed. The TV reporter started by recapping the genocide and violence in the Sudan with scenes of destroyed villages and wounded Africans. He then introduced Tara as a one-woman tour de force, forcing the world to take note of the ongoing tragedy. She led him on a walking tour of the mission leading to the hospital where Toby was tending patients. "This is the largest and most successful hospital in this part of Africa," Tara explained. After a tour of the wards, Tara led the reporter to the runway where a C-130 was landing. They watched as it taxied in and discharged 128 refugees.

"In the last forty-eight hours," she explained, "the Irregulars of the 4440th have flown over a thousand refugees to safety here. Their aircraft is the venerable C-130 Hercules, the workhorse that has served the Air Force for over fifty years." She handed her bush hat to the reporter. "The men and women of the 4440th wear these hats with pride. For them, it is the symbol of what they do." The reporter asked her what they did with the refugees and she continued on the tour, showing him the large camp outside the mission where the refugees were housed and fed. "As soon as we can," Tara explained, "we transport them to refugee camps in the south where they are safe. But it's a slow process."

The reporter asked about the French peacekeepers. Footage of the legionnaires came on the screen as Tara did a voice over. "There are only two hundred of them. They are led by Colonel Pierre Vermullen of the French Foreign Legion. This is the tenth time he has been on a peacekeeping mission in Africa and he's a legend in this part of the world." A scene of the legionnaires parachuting out of a C-130 played on the screen. "The C-130s give the Legion the mobility it needs to be an effective force and Colonel Vermullen always leads the way." A clip of Vermullen with his men played without comment. From the shouting, it was obvious how the legionnaires felt about their commander. "His men would follow him through the gates of hell and most of them say he will ask." She checked her watch. "Sunday evening is my favorite time of the week." She gave him a radiant smile. "Have you ever been to a church service here?"

The screen faded to an announcer in New York. "Our final segment," she said, "is a first for Sixty Minutes. When we return, we will be live from Mission Awana in the Republic of South Sudan."

Fitzgerald hit the mute button as the commercials came on. "Now it gets interesting," he told his wife.

Mission Awana

A reluctant Allston made his way to the rustic amphitheater on the side of a low hill facing north. He found a place on the rough plank benches as a soft evening breeze broke the heat of the day. He spoke to the family next to him and they shared their dinner of bread, cooked vegetables, and a cool drink of herb tea. More families wandered in and found places under the canopy of fronds and tree branches as they unpacked their dinners. Their numbers kept growing and Allston estimated the size of the crowd at over a thousand. Many of them were recently arrived refugees and everyone was talking, laughing and eating. A trickle of Irregulars wandered in and found places on the benches. They pushed their hats back, letting them hang on their backs. Soon, more arrived. "It is nice when you join us," the mother of the family said in heavily accented English.

Allston smiled in answer. "When does it start?"

"When the time is right," she replied. "We're on African time here. Be patient." A song leader stepped to the front and started to sing. One by one, the families stopped eating and joined in, repeating his words. Soon, all were singing and they were a congregation. The woman motioned to the TV camera set off to one side. Tara was there with the reporter. Tara scanned the crowd and waved at them.

Allston was transfixed. "It's beautiful. I wish I understood the words."

"It's a local dialect," the woman explained. She translated, "We give thanks, Oh Lord, we give thanks. We give thanks for our food, we give thanks for each other." A lone man sang out and, again, she translated. "I give thanks for tomorrow." The congregation repeated it and another man gave his personal thanks. Again, the congregation sang back. The song continued for almost ten minutes before it died away and the families went back to their dinners.

"I wonder who wrote it?" Allston asked.

"No one," the woman answered. "That's the way we sing." Another song leader stepped forward and began to sing. Again, the people joined in. "We're singing about our families." The congregation continued to sing until the night wrapped them in safety, temporarily hiding the death and destruction that marked their lives. A rare calm captured Allston, and, for a moment, he was at peace with himself. The TV camera's bright Video Lights came on and every head turned as the camera panned the audience. They were live for the world.

Air House

Fitzgerald and his wife sat transfixed by the scene on the TV. "Their voices," she said, "so beautiful. And look at their faces."

They listened and watched as Tara narrated. "That's Dr. Tobias Person making his way to the front." The camera followed Toby as he made his way down the hill, touching people as they extended their hands to him. He stood in front and spoke for a few moments in Nuer, then Dinka. He raised his right hand and chanted a few words of benediction. The congregation responded and the service was over.

Tara walked over to a woman sitting nearby and picked up a three-year-old girl. The camera focused on the little girl's face and her serious dark eyes. "This is NyaMai. It's a pretty sounding name but can roughly be translated as 'Daughter of War.' Her right arm was shot off by the Janjaweed and her stomach ripped open. Because of the relief efforts of the 4440th, she survived." The camera followed Tara as she carried the child through the crowd, finally finding Allston. "Colonel," Tara called. "This is someone you need to meet." She handed the child over to Allston.

The little girl threw her left arm around Allston's neck and buried her cheek next to his. She whispered the first words of English that she had learned into his ear, "Thank you."

Allston said nothing and only held the child, taking her into his heart.

Tara smiled for the camera. "I hope you remember NyaMai. You met her the first day you were in the Sudan. It was in the village of Abyei when you and your crew delivered a load of food and medical supplies." The camera zoomed back and framed the beautiful actress with Allston and the child.

"You saved her life," Tara said. She turned to the camera and it zoomed in on her face. "This little band of peacekeepers made up of a few Americans and French legionnaires, along with four old and worn-out C-130s, are making a difference in this devastated land. They are all we have sent to stop the killing and destruction. They alone are the conscience of the world."

The camera panned back over the watching Africans, capturing Allston as he held NyaMai. She looked at the camera with hope and confidence as if to announce "I am here."

"I'm Tara Scott and these are the people of South Sudan. They need our help." The broadcast cut to the studio in New York.

Fitzgerald's wife held his hand. "John, you old softie. Don't you try to hide those tears."

"What tears?" the general grumbled. The phone rang and he answered. It was the duty officer from Public Affairs. He nodded and smiled before breaking the connection. "Well, it seems we've got a celebrity in our midst. The media is doing cartwheels over Mad Dawg." He stood and stretched. "I've got to go to work." That was the man his wife knew.

EIGHTEEN

E-Ring

The two generals ambled down the corridor, making the short walk to the Secretary of Defense's office. General Misner, the Chairman of the Joint Chiefs, tried to play it straight. "Fitz, I'm assuming you didn't have a clue about Sixty Minutes yesterday."

Fitzgerald was absolutely honest. "I knew the general format but had no idea what Miss Scott would say."

"Well, I can tell you the Speaker of the House has egg all over his face and is pissed off something mightily. The President is not very happy, which means the Sec Def is even more unhappy. By the way, have you seen the morning news?" He answered his own question. "Thanks to Miss Scott and Sixty Minutes, you'd think we walk on water. Talk about an 'atta boy.'"

"A thousand 'atta boys,'" Fitzgerald cautioned, "are cancelled by one 'ah shit,' especially if it is a political 'ah shit.'"

"Not this time," Misner replied. They reached the Secretary's offices and were escorted into the small adjoining conference room. The head lawyer of the White House's Office of Legal Counsel, OLC for short, the Speaker of the House's chief of staff, and the Air Force's Judge Advocate General, Major General Aaron Forney, were sitting in the conference room. Misner shot Fitzgerald a warning look. "I may have been wrong about the 'atta boy.'" Silence ruled the room as the two generals sat down next to Forney and opposite the two men from across the river.

The Secretary of Defense came through the door and sat at the head of the table. "Well, gentlemen," he began, "it appears we have a problem. If I may summarize, the Speaker of the House claims we have lost control of the 4440th and have a loose cannon on our hands in the person of Lieutenant Colonel David Allston. The White House shares that concern. To that end, the Office of Legal Counsel is trying to determine exactly what laws Lieutenant Colonel Allston violated by participating in that unauthorized raid on Bentiu Thursday night."

The OLC lawyer jumped in. "At this point, you need to immediately recall Allston and place him under house arrest. That will keep him in our jurisdiction until you can bring charges for a court martial. Failing that, Justice will have to intervene."

"To the best of my knowledge," Fitzgerald said, "Allston has not violated any article of the UCMJ, no order, nor any directive. In fact, he was following a specific order from the UN when he supported the French peacekeepers in the raid." He handed Forney a single sheet of paper. "Colonel Allston was given this standing operations order by the United Nations Peacekeeping Mission the second day he was in Africa. That was on April eighth of this year." The silence grew even heavier as Forney read the order.

"If I may quote the relevant passage," the JAG began, "'You are hereby directed to respond to any request for support, to include airlift, by the peacekeeping contingent under the command of Colonel Pierre Vermullen, *La Légion Étrangère*. Further, any such request will be considered as a direct order by this Mission and will take priority over relief airlift.'" He passed the order to the Secretary of Defense. "It is a valid order, duly signed and dated, and it was transmitted, received, and understood." The Secretary passed the order to the OLC lawyer and the Speaker's man.

They read it in silence. "General Fitzgerald," the lawyer finally asked, "has this order been modified or rescinded since it was issued?"

"Not to my knowledge."

"Why hasn't my office seen this before?" the lawyer asked.

"Colonel Allston notified my office the day after he received it," Fitzgerald said. "At the time, I considered it clarification of his status with the UN. In short, it was an internal matter."

"May I add," Misner said, "that the command and control of the 4440th was taken away from AFRICOM and placed under the UN Peacekeeping Mission, effectively removing us from the loop." Every head turned to the Speaker's chief of staff. The Speaker had been instrumental in making that happen.

"That policy was driven by our lack of credibility with the UN," the chief of staff replied. "It was a major step in improving our relations, not to mention legitimacy, with the rest of the world."

Misner was enjoying himself. "We are now living with the results of that decision. In our view, the UN issued that operations order as a deliberate slap at the US by placing the 4440th under a French commander. Further, the UN put every peacekeeper at serious risk by ordering the French to turn over their Stinger and Shipon missiles to the Sudanese Army. The peacekeepers were justified in believing that the Sudanese Army could not, or would not, properly secure them and would give them to the Janjaweed. We concur in that assessment."

The lawyer from the OLC had one last gambit to play. "That does not absolve Allston from following an illegal order. Either you arrest Allston or we will." The Speaker's man nodded in agreement.

Now it was the JAG's turn. He leaned forward, folded his hands, and fixed the two men with the look he reserved for lecturing incompetent lawyers on obvious points of the law. "Command and control is like sovereignty, you either have it or you don't, and it cannot be divided. You cannot expect Colonel Allston to serve two masters. Further, if you wish to bring charges against Colonel Allston, you will have to do so through his chain of command, which means you must first indict the commander of the French peacekeepers. We do not have the jurisdiction to do that. Further, it appears that the French were simply retrieving weapons stolen from them. If it is all the same to you, we would prefer to represent Colonel Allston in this matter." He played his trump card. "Of course, Tara Scott will be one of our witnesses."

"Perhaps you would be interested in this," Fitzgerald said. He handed them a thin folder. "Here are the current airlift stats. In the last twenty-four hours, the 4440th has flown over fifteen hundred refugees to safety, along with nineteen UN relief workers who were stranded and under attack by the Janjaweed." He let the political implications sink in. "Further, our intelligence confirms that a large scale genocide is underway and fifteen hundred is a small fraction of what the Janjaweed and Army of the Sudan have killed in the last few days. The situation has deteriorated to the point that we're flying with armed legionnaires on each sortie."

The lawyer stood. "We will advise the President and the Speaker." The meeting was over.

The two generals walked in thoughtful silence back to their offices. Misner motioned for Fitzgerald to join him in private. "We drove a stake in their hearts on that one," Misner said.

"You can kill 'em but you can't kill 'em dead," Fitzgerald said. "Hal, how do you read the Administration on this?"

"It all depends on how committed the President is to reconciling with the UN. He may decide to hang Allston out to dry to accomplish that." A wry grin split his weather-beaten face. "He may nail our hides to the wall to make it a trifecta. But the political reality is how the public views the situation. Right now, the Speaker appears tone-deaf and the President looks like he's isolated from the facts on the ground. Thanks to Tara Scott, we're out in front on this one, at least for now."

"How deep a pile are we in?" Fitzgerald asked.

"I don't know," Misner replied. "But your General Richards isn't helping. You need to stomp on her."

"I'm waiting for the right moment. No need to piss off the Speaker twice in one day."

Al Ubayyid, North Kordofan, Sudan

Jahel tried to relax into the helicopter's leather-covered seat but wearing a ceremonial robe and holding the gold-plated AK-47 upright between his knees made it difficult. BermaNur sat in the seat opposite and twitched nervously, uncomfortable in his borrowed robe and panicked by his first ride in an aircraft. Jahel gave him a reassuring look. It was the Sheikh's second time in a helicopter; Waleed had invited him for a ride in one of his MI-24s to interrogate a Fursan suspected of spying for the Americans. But the man had protested his innocence so the MI-24 landed with one less passenger. But this helicopter was totally beyond the MI-24, quieter, air-conditioned and much more comfortable. He knew the crew was Chinese, which did not surprise him, but not the make nor type of the aircraft, which was French. He glanced out the window as the pilot circled the capital of North Kordofan.

A flight attendant wearing an exquisite headscarf that accentuated her eyes and beautiful face joined them. She spoke in Shuwa, the language of the Baggara, another mark of respect. "We will be landing soon. Would you like to circle the airfield first to announce your arrival?" Jahel swelled at the compliment and told her to make it happen.

BermaNur could not contain his excitement as they flew over the airport on the southern end of the large town. He tried to count the tanks, artillery, armored personnel carriers, and trucks lined up for inspection. "There's over a thousand men," he said as their helicopter landed next to three MI-24 attack helicopters. The flight attendant opened the passenger door and bowed them out.

Waleed was waiting for them in his dress uniform in the arid heat. He saluted the two Baggara and invited them to join him in the back of a small truck designed for review. Jahel handed BermaNur his AK-47 and climbed up the steps to the truck. Waleed stood beside him as they drove past the men and equipment on review and took the salute. They continued to the northern end of the airdrome where a complex of glistening white tents were surrounded by even more soldiers. The truck stopped in front of the largest tent and Waleed invited Jahel to enter while he waited outside. Inside, four Asian men, all in civilian clothes, were waiting with two Sudanese generals. Aides from both groups hovered in the background, ready to be of instant service. An interpreter stepped forward and made the introductions, his Suwa, Arabic, and Chinese faultless. He ended by escorting the men to a circle of divans and overstuffed chairs arranged on a priceless Persian rug. Jahel was given the seat of honor and BermaNur stood behind him, the AK-47 at the ready.

Refreshments were served before the ranking Sudanese general stood and went through the formal opening statements. He turned the meeting over to the second general who stood beside a large computer-driven screen. "You are all aware of the attack on Bentiu by the French Legionnaires and their American lackeys. It will be avenged." The civilians nodded in approval with hard looks, their faces frozen. The general turned to Jahel, "I will lead the forces you have seen outside." A map came on the screen and he tapped the target, 265 miles to the south. "But we must cross the Al Bahr Al Abyad before it floods. Unfortunately, the floods will come early this year and we must move now. In order to be successful, we must hold the French in place. To that end, it falls to the Fursan of the Baggara to lead the attack and kill this man." A photograph of Allston flashed on the screen.

BermaNur snapped to attention as Jahel lifted his head and spoke. "The honor is mine."

Mission Awana

Jill knocked on the door jam and motioned Marci Jenkins inside. Allston looked up, glad to see the two women had finally returned. They reported in with sharp salutes. "I hear I missed all the fun," Marci said. Allston returned the salute and asked about G.G.'s funeral. "G.G.'s parents almost adopted me," the captain said. "He was their only child and I cannot tell you how proud they are of him."

"I've recommended him for a Silver Star," Allston said.

Marci beamed at him. "His family will appreciate that. Mrs. Libby said they were thankful for the time they had together. She wished it was more, but it was enough." There were tears in her eyes.

"The Libbys sound like wonderful people," Jill offered.

"They are," Jenkins said.

"Well, Captain," Allston said, "I'm glad you're back. See Major Lane and get on the flying schedule soonest."

"Will do, sir." She threw him a salute and hurried out of the room.

He smiled at Jill. "Well, Major, welcome back – finally." He felt better saying the last bit. Jill returned his smile and made no attempt to account for the eight days it had taken her to reach the mission, much less the time she had spent in Ethiopia. "How are things at Fort Fumble?" Allston asked.

"Normal. One third of the troops haven't got a clue, one third don't care, and the other third are confused."

Allston laughed. "Some things never change."

Jill chewed on her lower lip. "Sir, ah, there's something we need to discuss. In private." He motioned for her to close the door. She did and turned to face him. "Colonel, Marci's expecting."

Allston was at a loss for words. "Are you sure?" he finally stammered. Jill nodded in answer. "Any idea who the 'he' is?"

Jill gave him the look she normally reserved for the totally clueless. "G.G."

The answer set Allston back. He blinked. "Why did she come back? She should have asked for reassignment."

"I don't know, sir. You'll have to ask her."

"I will. And I'm really glad you're back. To say the situation here is fluid is an understatement. I'm worried about the threat, so talk to whoever you talk to and get back to me with an assessment."

"Will do, sir." She turned and left, leaving a trace of perfume in the air.

Allston studied the empty space where she had been standing. She does grow on a guy, he thought. He refused to follow that thought and tucked it away. Still, it kept coming back. "Damn," he muttered. He concentrated on Marci Jenkins and G.G. How had he missed that? As a commander, it was his job to be aware of any relationship that might compromise his unit's morale. He had been around the flagpole enough to learn that a pair bonding of any kind chipped away at unit identification and morale. However, they were both captains and had been discreet enough that he was unaware of the affair. Fraternization was never an issue and was a moot point now. Still, Mission Awana was no place for a pregnant pilot. But thanks to Toby, they had excellent medical care. Another thought came to him. How many pregnant women did he see every day working around the mission? He put it aside, called up a file on his computer, and went to work.

He was still at it that afternoon when Dick Lane burst into his office. "Sir, we got a Herk inbound with battle damage and casualties. It's Bard Green. I've scrambled the mission's fire truck and the medics."

Allston came to his feet. "Stay here and handle the radios. I'll be at the airfield." He grabbed his hat and ran for his pickup. Jill was right behind him. The airfield was over a mile away and he had to drive slowly to clear the mission compound. Then he accelerated, racing for the airstrip. "There it is," Jill said, "to the west. It looks like a long straight in approach." Allston was driving and couldn't twist around to see it. He took Jill's word, impressed that she understood what Green was doing.

The truck's radio blared at them. "Bossman, Outhouse." It was Lane calling Allston from Operations. "Be advised there are 128 souls on board and their primary hydraulics are out."

Allston relaxed. The C-130 had two backup hydraulic systems plus the auxiliary power unit in the right wheel well. "It's a precautionary landing," he told Jill. He slowed and glanced at her. "Where did you learn about approaches?"

Without turning, she said, matter-of-factly, "I pay attention."

Indeed you do, he thought. Another stray thought intruded. She did have a lovely profile. "Damn," he grumbled.

"What's wrong?" she asked.

He lied. "I'm thinking about the threat. Any updates yet?"

"It's complicated and I haven't gotten the total picture yet. But it's coming together. I'll brief you later today, if that's okay."

He wheeled the pickup to a stop behind the maintenance tents and they got out. Susan Malaby was standing on the parking ramp watching the damaged C-130 come down final. "Gear's down," Malaby said. They waited in silence as the Hercules touched down and rolled out. Green made it look normal. "The lieutenant did good," Malaby conceded. The aircraft taxied in and shut down. Malaby sucked in her breath. The left side of the fuselage aft of the wheel well was perforated with bullet holes and hydraulic fluid was leaking from under the left wing.

"You call that a precautionary landing?" Jill asked.

Malaby was worried. "Not good," she said. The three walked out to the aircraft as refugees streamed off the back.

"It looks like Bard saved another 100 or so refugees," Allston countered. "In my book, that's good." An inner voice told him they had to do more even though the danger was ratcheting up. The mission's makeshift ambulance arrived and two legionnaires deplaned carrying a litter with the body of a comrade.

Finally, Bard Green got off with his flight engineer. They walked around the Hercules, surveying the damage. "A legionnaire caught a round," Green told them. "During takeoff."

"Where and who" Allston asked.

"Al Araish," Green said. His face turned hard. "I think the shooters were SA, but I can't be sure."

"Major Sharp, your estimate?" Allston asked.

"The good news is that Al Araish is north of the river. The bad news is that Al Araish is only seventy miles away. If it was the SA, they'll probably try to cross the Nile in force and hook up with Waleed at Malakal."

Malaby ignored them and examined the holes in the side of the aircraft. "Small caliber machine gun," she announced. "We got lucky on this one. A heavier weapon with high-explosive rounds would have been fatal." She thought for a moment. "We need to pull some panels off the wing to check the damage, but we should have her back in commission by tomorrow morning." Allston was impressed and told her so.

"Major Sharp, let's go," Allston said. "We got work to do."

"Which is?" Jill asked.

"We need a base defense plan. Like soonest. Get all the players together today." He rattled off a list of names, starting with Jerry Malone, the NCOIC of the security police. "And we need to talk to Idi."

"He isn't here," Jill said. "Most of the legionnaires are training in the field."

"He never lets up," Allston conceded. "Let's make something happen." Another thought came to him. "How did you know that?"

"That's what I get paid for," she replied.

*   *   *

Jerry Malone was on top of it and had the embryo of a defense plan he had been working on since arriving at Malakal. But he had a problem; he only had eighteen cops for day-to-day security. To be effective, they had to augment their number with Irregulars. But that took them away from their normal duties. Another option was to use the legionnaires; however, they were already committed to defending the growing refugee camp and carrying out an intensive training schedule. Mission Awana also had a security force of ten men, but they were used for keeping domestic peace within the mission. They were not trained nor had the weapons for mounting an armed guard.

Allston walked over and studied the chart Malone tacked on the wall showing the minimum defensive posture for the mission. During the day, Malone calculated that six cops could effectively patrol the mission. However, at night he needed twelve cops, augmented by twelve Irregulars, to

196

provide the mission with basic security. "Sir," Malone concluded, "we're asking a lot of the Irregulars to meet their normal duties and post out with us under normal conditions. As we increase our defensive posture, we will need even more help from Maintenance, and that means flying will grind to a halt. If that happens, why are we here?"

"Good question," Allston replied. He made a mental note to talk to Vermullen the moment he got back and work out a way to integrate his legionnaires. "Major Sharp," he said, "we're putting a big monkey on your back on this one." They all knew that it fell to her to warn them of impending danger.

"Toby has a good feel for the situation," she told them. "I'm talking to him constantly."

"Where does he get his information?" Malone asked.

"A variety of sources," Jill answered. "The refugees, his medical teams in the field, local authorities, the jungle telegraph."

Lovely, Allston thought. "Okay, let's make this happen and hope we don't get our . . ." he almost said 'tits in a wringer' but caught himself in time, "sweet young bodies in a wringer."

Jill laughed. "I know what you meant."

* * *

The distinctive clatter of an AK-47 woke Allston from a sound sleep. He glanced at the bedside clock – 0407 – and rolled out of bed. He listened, only to be greeted with silence. "What is it?" Tara asked.

"Gunfire. Don't turn the light on. Get dressed and find Jill." He pulled on his flight suit and boots and ran, holding his web belt with its holstered .45 in his left hand. Jill was running down the hall from the other side of the guesthouse. "You stay here and get everyone to safety," he ordered. He was out the door and running for Mission House and his operations center.

Jill took a deep breath and calmed her raging emotions. She knocked on the door of his bedroom. "Tara, you there?" A burst of submachine gunfire inside the guesthouse shattered the stillness. Jill fell to the floor and rolled against the wall as Tara burst out of the bedroom in full panic. Jill grabbed the actress and pulled her to the floor beside her. Jill drew her .45 semi-automatic and held it with both hands as she sighted into the dark. The soft sound of footsteps reached the two women. A burst of gunfire deafened them as it split the air above their heads. Jill saw a shadow and fired twice. Both slugs hit their target and the shadow collapsed to the ground. Jill came to a standing crouch and moved slowly towards the body, holding the .45 at the ready in front of her. She sensed movement and fired a single round in that direction. A loud scream and the clatter of a dropped weapon rewarded her. Again, she crouched, her back against the wall and her breath coming fast. She held the .45 with both hands in the raised position in front of her. Tara was behind her, touching her in the dark. "Follow me," Jill said in a low voice.

"Believe me, I will," Tara replied. The fear in her voice was palpable.

Jill came to her feet and inched forward. She reached the first body and picked up the AK-47. She handed it to Tara. "Can you use this?"

Tara took the weapon and checked it. It was ready to fire. "I fired one once on a publicity shoot."

"This isn't for publicity." Running feet echoed down the hall. The sound grew louder and Tara came to her feet, firing the AK-47 from the hip Rambo style. The recoil of the assault rifle lifted the muzzle and the shots went wild. Jill methodically aimed and fired. A shriek of pain carried down the corridor. Jill was up and running. She fired as she went, putting another round into the rolling body. Again, the man screamed. Jill paused long enough to fire once more, this time into the man's head. She grabbed his AK-47 and the two women crept down the hall towards the main room and the veranda. A light flicked on and Jill saw two more figures. She raised her .45 and started to squeeze the trigger. Just as quickly, she relaxed and lowered her weapon. One of the men was wearing a bush hat. "Turn out the light," she ordered. She threw the AK-47 she was carrying to one of the men. "There's another one back there in the hall," she told the men.

"Thanks," Bard Green said.

* * *

The loud bark of submachine guns exploded in the night as Allston ran for the Ops Center in Mission House. Most of it was coming from the outskirts of the mission compound, but it was growing louder. Gunfire drove him to cover beside a school building where he caught his breath. He started to move as a burst of submachine gun fire drove him back to his hiding place. He drew his automatic and waited. It seemed an eternity as the minutes clicked away.

* * *

Jill quickly gathered everyone she could find and ordered them to barricade the guesthouse as best they could. She keyed her communicator and called the operations center. Dick Lane answered. "Where's Bossman?" he asked.

"He's headed your way," Jill replied. In the sudden quiet, she heard the beat of galloping horses passing by. "Janajweed," she warned.

* * *

Allston knew movement was life. He had to start moving even though his hiding place seemed secure. He fought the urge to call in on his communicator. Silence is golden, he told himself. Finally, he came to his feet and darted into the night. Now he could hear the sound of pounding hooves. He ran faster. A security cop and an Irregular manning a defensive firing position saw him. "Over here!" the cop shouted. The sound of running horses grew louder. "Run!" Allston put on a burst of speed and ran toward the voice. The horses were bearing down on him. "Drop!" the cop yelled. Allston fell to the ground as the two men unlimbered their M 16s, emptying their magazines. The lead horseman veered off, disappearing into the night.

The second rider and his horse went down in the hail of gunfire and skidded into Allston. The horse kicked in pain and a flailing hoof struck Allston in his left shin. A searing pain shot up his leg. He heard a loud scream and for a moment was confused. Was he screaming? This time the scream was louder. It was the horseman. Allston came to a crouch and fired a single shot into the horse's head, putting it out of its misery. He grabbed the rider and dragged him out from under the horse. "I got a live one!" he yelled. The rider kicked at Allston, knocking the semi-automatic out of his hand. Allston scrambled for his weapon as the rider kicked him in the side. Allston grabbed the rider's ankle and rolled, taking the man down. He grunted in pain when he rolled over his .45. He pushed the rider away as he picked up the weapon. Now the man was scrambling away on all fours. Allston squeezed off a single round, hitting him in a leg, just as he came to his feet. The .45 ACP cartridge fires a big, low velocity bullet with tremendous stopping power, and this particular round passed cleanly through the man's right calf. But it knocked him to the ground and sent him into shock.

The two cops ran up. One rolled the man over and patted him down. "Just a teenager," the airman said.

"I need to get to the Ops Center," Allston said.

"We'll get you there," the cop replied. He made a radio call, reporting they had found Bossman and were bringing him in. "Let's go," he told Allston.

Allston pointed to the Janjaweed lying on the ground. "What about him?"

The security cop thought for a moment. He fumbled with the first aid kit on his web belt and pulled out a tourniquet. He quickly looped it around the teenager's leg, just above the wound and cinched it down. "He's not going anywhere. He'll be here when we get back." The two men moved out and Allston followed. They ran through the night, always using a building or wall for cover. Finally, they reached the darkened Mission House where they were challenged. The cop responded with "Dog poop," the code of the day.

"Thanks," Allston told the two men. He went inside.

Dick Lane was pacing when he saw Allston. He collapsed into a chair in relief. "Thank God . . . I . . . we were worried about you." He gulped, anxious to say more. "You're a mess. Are you okay?" More gunfire echoed from the far side of the mission compound.

Allston took stock of himself. Other than the pulsating ache in his leg where the horse had kicked him, he was okay. "Sorry about the delay, I had a pressing engagement with a horse. So what's going on?" He had assumed command.

"The Janjaweed hit us," Lane replied. "Horsemen are inside the compound. Lots of confusion. I'm in contact with both Malone and the Legion. Vermullen is in the field on a training exercise with most of his men. They are inbound and should be here around daybreak. We have to hold until then."

Allston thought for a few moments. The sound of pounding hooves punctuated his worry. "Dick, get me a status on casualties." While Lane worked the radios, Allston called Backstop, the security police command post, on a landline. "Backstop, Bossman. Say situation."

"Unknown number of hostiles in the compound," Malone replied. "I've ordered everyone to hunker down and stay put."

"Is this a hit and run?" Allston asked.

"Unknown," Malone answered. "I'm treating it like a softening up action for the main attack."

"Boss," Lane said in the background, "we got at least a dozen wounded, some bad. We need to transport 'em to the hospital."

Allston relayed the information to Malone. "We need to move 'em soonest," Allston added.

"Negative," Malone replied. "The Janjaweed are hitting targets of opportunity, anyone they catch in the open. The bastards have got NVGs and are moving fast."

The Peacemakers

The hard calculus of combat pounded at Allston. By moving his wounded, more of his people would be injured or killed. And he couldn't afford that. Until they drove the roving Janjaweed out of the compound, the wounded would have to wait. He made a decision. "Everyone holds for now." The sound of gunfire echoed through Mission House and over the radios. That attack was still in full force. "Are the C-130s covered?" he asked.

"Per the plan," Malone replied. "I've got two fire teams at the airfield and will reinforce them when I can. So far, no activity reported."

"Keep me advised." Allston broke the connection. He pulled into himself, trying to make sense of the raid. Why hadn't they hit the C-130s? Outside, the two DFPs guarding Mission House opened up, driving riders off with well-aimed bursts of overlapping gunfire. Where are the French? Allston raged to himself. Rather than ask Malone, who was up to his ears in alligators, he called the French command post on the landline they had installed the day before between Mission House and the refugee camp. Mercier's gravelly voice answered. The French major quickly explained how the twenty-four legionnaires still at the mission were deployed around the refugee camp. But he was working with Malone to expand that defensive ring to include the southern side of the mission compound. They were improvising and had to move slowly and coordinate the move to avoid a friendly fire incident. Good man, Allston thought as he rang off.

The sharp bark of a machine gun reached inside the com center. "That sounds like a SAW," Allston said. Was it Williams? Now the gunfire tapered off, punctuated with the occasional sharp staccato of the SAW. They waited. More pleas for help from the wounded flooded the radios.

"Is it over?" Lane asked. That one question burned white hot and demanded an answer. Allston remembered what Jill has said about Toby's sources. He made a mental note to set up a liaison between the mission staff and his Ops Center. Lacking any other ideas, he called the hospital and a woman answered. She spoke English with the distinctive accent and lilt of a Dinka. He asked if Toby was there and if they needed help.

"We can take care of ourselves, Mr. Bossman. We have five wounded here, and Doctor Person is stitching one closed now. You must not worry so much about us. This attack is over."

The sharp, distinctive rattle of an AK-47 carried over the telephone, putting a question mark to the woman's confidence. The sudden quiet was deafening. "That's good to know," Allston allowed. Silence hung in the air. Was the attack over? "By the way, have we met?"

"Oh, no, Mr. Bossman. I'm D'Na. Sometimes, I am called Mrs. Person." She broke the connection.

Allston shook his head. You learn the strangest things at the damnedest times, he thought. The radio came alive as reports started to come in from around the mission. The horsemen had vanished and the casualty count was steadily increasing. A security cop burst into the com center. "We're bringing a prisoner in," he said. "He's wounded but conscious."

Allston ran outside as a pickup drove up. Loni Williams got out and and dragged a man out of the back. "Look what I found." He hauled his prisoner to the steps, and held him up by his collar. It was the Janjaweed Allston had shot. Allston hurried down the steps to finally take a good look at the teenager. It was BermaNur.

"I've seen him before," Allston said, turning to the boy. "You were at Abyei. Then you tried to hose us down with an AK-47 at that refugee camp." BermaNur heard the one word he understood – Abyei. He spat at Allston.

Williams slapped the side of BermaNur's head and spoke a few words in Nuer. The boy snarled an answer. "He says you and that whore you were with should have died at Abyei."

"Ask if they are going to attack again," Allston said.

Williams barraged the teenager with questions but got nowhere. "He's being stubborn, Boss."

"Damn. We've got wounded out there we need to bring in."

Williams dropped the Baggara to the ground and stood with his back to Allston. He stepped on the teenager's wounded leg, and slowly applied pressure as he repeated the same question over and over. BermaNur screamed with pain, cursing the Americans.

"What the hell are you doing?" Allston shouted. Williams didn't answer and pressed down even harder. Allston finally realized what Williams was doing and grabbed him by the back of his collar. He jerked hard, pulling him off the Janjaweed. Williams bent over and pulled a knife out of the bloody bandage around the Janjaweed's leg. He handed it to Allston. "He's talking, Boss. He says that Jahel will feed us to the ants."

"I've heard that name before," Allston said.

Again, Williams spoke to the teenager, and, again, BermaNur snarled an answer. Williams stepped forward. The teenager held up a hand and started talking. Williams listened and asked a few questions. Finally, the teenager was finished. Williams spoke quietly. "According to our friend here, Jahel is the leader of the Rizeigat, the finest horseman of the Baggara, and the avenging sword of Allah. He says there were many martyrs today and we

202

will be dead meat when Allah wills. I'm thinking we hurt them pretty bad, so I don't think it's gonna be today."

"We'll find out soon enough," Allston said. But the relief he felt was evident on his face. He keyed his communicator. "Dick, start bringing the wounded in." The iron band of command that held him tight eased. It would never totally go away, but for a few moments, he could breathe easier, gaining a second breath and the strength to continue. It was a hellish burden few men or women could bear, but it was one he willingly accepted. He closed his communicator and turned to the sergeant. "Sergeant Williams, don't ever do that again."

"Yes, sir. But I got you some answers."

NINETEEN

Mission Awana

"*O*uch!" Toby ignored Allston's protest and continued to probe his leg. "What school of medicine did you graduate from?" Allston asked. Toby continued the quick exam, pushing and poking at Allston. It was old-fashioned, hands on medicine because of the Mission's limited X-ray facilities and laboratory. Those were saved for the serious cases and Toby was satisfied that it was only a bad bruise. He told the lieutenant colonel to get dressed. "I didn't know you were married," Allston ventured.

"Sure am. Got one kid, a boy. D'Na keeps everything on track here. It's a cultural thing." Allston wasn't sure he really understood for he thought that women were subservient in Dinka society. Toby laughed, sensing Allston's confusion. "She's my warrior queen and office manager." He washed his hands. "Use ice packs to get the swelling down. Come see me if it starts to feel warm, or if you run a temperature."

Allston's communicator buzzed at him. It was Malone with the news that he had discovered how the Janjaweed had gotten inside the mission compound. "On my way." He broke the connection. "Thanks, Toby." Another thought came to him. "Do you have a casualty count?"

"All told, nine killed, twenty-five wounded, two seriously who I don't expect to make it."

"What about the Janjaweed?"

"Eight of the dead and sixteen of the wounded were Janjaweed. One Dinka was killed and five were wounded. Only four of your troops were wounded, none seriously. It could have been worse, much worse. The jungle telegraph says this was a disaster for them. Sergeant Malone and his cops did a great job."

"I'll relay that to Malone. What about the Janjaweed I shot?"

"He'll make it. The wound was far from fatal."

For a reason he didn't understand, Allston felt better. "Thanks again." He walked to the bunker Malone used for his command center. His left shin throbbed as he hobbled along. Before long, a group of children surrounded him and followed along. One little girl held his hand as two boys mimicked the way he walked. Malone was waiting for him and chased the kids away after passing out some hard rock candy he had received from home. "Whatcha got?" Allston asked.

Malone led him inside where a security cop and a maintenance crew chief were waiting. "This is Sergeant Lee Ford, one of my flight commanders," Malone said, "and Sergeant Wayne Byers from Maintenance. They were teamed last night and posted out for guard duty." He tapped a wall chart that showed the numerous defensive fire positions the security police were digging on the mission's perimeter. "They were assigned to the DFP nearest the river. They fell asleep and the Janjaweed forded the river and slipped past them."

"Who reported they fell asleep?" Allston asked.

"I did," Ford, the security cop, replied.

"Ah, shit," Allston moaned. He sat down, his leg hurting even more. "Call Colonel Malaby. We need to sort this out."

"She's on the way," Malone said. As Byers was assigned to Maintenance as a crew chief, Malone had anticipated Allston would want her involved. As usual, the hyper lieutenant colonel arrived in overdrive. She listened impatiently as Malone repeated how the Janjaweed were able to attack because the two men had fallen asleep on guard duty.

Allston told Ford and Byers to wait outside and out of earshot. They double-timed out. "What do you recommend I do?"

"Nothing," Malaby said. "Look, my people have not let up since we got here. They're turning aircraft, digging foxholes, filling sandbags, and then standing guard duty. They're dropping in their tracks. Just how much more do you expect of them, Colonel?"

"It's the same with my cops," Malone said.

Allston pulled into himself. He was pushing his people to the limit and then asking for more. What right did he have to demand the impossible? How much more could they give? "Call them in," he told Malone. The two men marched in and stood at attention. "I don't have to tell you how serious this is," Allston began. "I also know there are extenuating circumstances, and that we got lucky with only four of our troops wounded. But an innocent Dinka was killed and five were wounded because of you. In your favor, you came forward and blew the whistle, even though that meant incriminating yourselves. Is there anything else you want me to consider in your defense?" He waited to hear what they had to say.

Ford gulped. He came to attention. "No excuse, sir. I'm learning to speak a little Dinka . . . I'll take any punishment you give me . . . just don't send me home."

"Same for me, sir," Byers said.

"Why should I keep you here?" Allston asked.

The cop's answer surprised Allston. "Because my buddies are here and I won't let them down again."

"Same for me, sir," Byers said. He was a man of limited vocabulary but he spoke to C-130s with a rare understanding.

"Give 'em to me, sir," Malone said. "They'll wish you had court-martialed their sorry asses instead."

"Colonel Malaby?" Allston asked.

"Okay by me. I got more crew chiefs than I need, which, by the way, we need to talk about."

"Sergeant Malone, " Allston said, "you got 'em." He stood and hobbled outside, his leg feeling much better. Malaby was right behind him.

"Colonel Allston," she called. He waited for her to catch up, which given her normal state of hustle, took two seconds. "Sir, thank you." Before he could ask what for, she said, "Do you have an extra hat?"

Allston couldn't believe it. "Is mine okay?" He held out his bush hat. She ripped off her blue beret and jammed the bush hat on her short-cropped hair. "Why?"

"That was the right call in there." Her words were matter-of-fact but the way she held her head said it all. "We flew over two thousand Dinkas to safety yesterday. For the first time in my career, I'm doing something that really matters."

"Welcome to the Irregulars, Colonel Malaby." He saluted her.

* * *

Allston sat in Toby's office and flipped through the after action report detailing the raid and what they had learned. It was the second time he had read it and was looking for a specific item. He found it. "Excellent work, Major Sharp. Get this on the wires ASAP." He handed the report to her. "There is one thing that I want to be sure I've got right. You shot and killed the three Janjaweed who made the mistake of breaking into the guesthouse." She only nodded, not wanting to discuss it. "Okay, one last question. Where did you learn to handle a weapon like that?"

Jill's chin came up and she fixed him with a determined look. "Sir, I can't answer that."

"Can't or won't?" he asked. She didn't respond and he tried to stare her into talking. It didn't work. "Let's start over," he finally said. "You took out three of the eight bastards we morted. Further, you fired six times and all six bullets found a target. You did this in near dark conditions." His eyes blinked as he connected the dots. I can't believe I'm so stupid, he thought. "And you are able to run around with the locals all by yourself as if you were a native."

"I do speak Swahili, sir. And I am picking up a little Nuer." The last was an understatement.

"True," Allston conceded. "And you know things. According to Colonel Vermullen, you're wired into the jungle telegraph. You may well be, but I think there is a better reason." He waited for her response. Again, he was greeted with silence. "Major Sharp, I think you know people." Again, no reply, and his frustration level ratcheted up a notch. "There are obviously things I don't know about you and what you are doing that can affect our mission here. I need to know and it's time you came clean."

"I can't do that, sir."

He didn't know what to do. She was a vital member of his staff and he doubted that he could replace her with anyone half as competent. But did he completely trust her? He didn't have an answer and needed to think about it. When he was completely honest with himself, he did like her. But that had little to do with his job. Or did it? "Major Sharp, you puzzle me, and that's a problem. Dismissed." She spun around and rushed out of the room.

She stopped in the hallway, her back to him. Just as quickly, she returned and shut the door. She stood in front of him as tears coursed down her cheeks. "Five years ago, I was recruited by the Boys in the Basement as a special agent." Allston had heard of the Boys and suspected they had a connection to Special Operations and Intelligence. "Part of my training," she continued, "involved extensive weapons training. I was recruited primarily based on my language skills . . . and for other reasons . . ." She took a deep breath and plunged ahead. "African men find my type of figure appealing." She was brutally honest. "Sexually." She paused, her face now hard as stone. "For two years, I was on special assignment in Nairobi."

An inner voice warned Allston to drop the subject, which, like a fool, he disregarded. "You were engaged in humint?" Humint is human intelligence or old-fashioned spying. A little nod answered him. "A Kenyan?" Her eyes said yes. Then he knew. "Why are you telling me all this?"

"Because, I . . ." her voice trailed off. Then, very firmly, "Because I'm ashamed of what I did. I seduced a nice man with a lovely family. Like an idiot, he talked too much, trying to impress me. He was taking kickbacks from OPEC and Iran, supposedly for his tribe. But instead of funneling the money to his tribe, he used most of it to buy off rival tribes so they would cooperate with him in the national government. It was a very dangerous game if his tribe discovered what he was doing. I reported everything he told me. The CIA picked it up . . . I was sent home."

"And the prime minister ended up dead," Allston said. The Kenyan press had reported it as a suicide but there were many rumors to the contrary.

"Then his clan butchered his family." Her voice was shaking. "Because of the money."

Allston didn't know what to say. He managed a lame, "It wasn't your fault."

Jill stood there, now dry-eyed and composed. "Yes, it was. Will there be anything else, sir?"

For the first time, he saw her for what she was, a very attractive, intelligent, and competent woman who got caught up in a situation beyond her control, and was now paying the price for it. For her, responsibility came with the job. "Thank you for your candor, Major Sharp. I hope we can still work together." She spun around and walked out, leaving him alone. "Damn," he muttered. Why did she tell me all that? he thought.

* * *

Vermullen led the tour around the refugee compound with Allston and Malone as he pointed out the defenses the legionnaires had built with overlapping fields of fire. "Great work," Allston said. "Can you work up a plan for us?"

"It would be my pleasure," Vermullen replied. "How many men can you commit?"

"Right at a hundred men and women," Allston said. Vermullen didn't reply at first. He had never used women in a combat role and didn't want to start now. Allston decided the timing was right and ventured, "I was hoping we could integrate our forces into a defensive plan. Again, Vermullen was silent. Allston plunged ahead. "I know the emphasis you put on training, but perhaps now is the time to . . ." He deliberately left the proposal open. Did the Frenchman understand that the time for training was at an end?

"It is not what you think," Vermullen said. "We have been training the South Sudanese."

Allston was shocked. Training the southerners was a direct violation of the UN peacekeeping mandate. "Does the UN know?"

"Of course not," Vermullen replied. "Let me work on a plan. Can I use your Major Sharp and Sergeant Malone?"

"You've got 'em."

* * *

Allston sat in the corner of his makeshift operations center at a small table that served as his office. While he didn't have the privacy he often needed, he was at the heart of all activity and wired in with operations and maintenance. The downside was that he was too available for anyone who came in, and he had to tune out distractions so he could focus on whatever task demanded his immediate attention. "Colonel Allston," Jill said, breaking his concentration. He looked up. She was standing a respectful distance away with a beaming Loni Williams.

"Whatcha got?" he asked in a friendly tone, trying to close the gap that was looming between them.

"The kid you shot is talking," Williams said. "You wouldn't believe what this Jahel guy is like."

"Yeah, I would," Allston replied. "He's a first-class bastard." He kicked back in his chair and interlaced his fingers, tapping his thumbs together. "I hope you're following the Army Field Manual on interrogation."

Jill answered. "Yes, sir, we are. Sergeant Williams is much more fluent in Nuer than me but I monitor the interrogation. His name is BermaNur, and he's seventeen years old. The raid was more than a hit and run. You were the target. That's why they hit the guesthouse."

Allston's stomach disappeared, and, for a moment, he was speechless. "Well, that certainly made my day. Anything else?"

"The SA," Jill continued, "is going to cross the White Nile and reinforce Waleed. Probably in the next week or so."

"How would a seventeen-year-old kid know that?" Allston asked.

"He doesn't," Jill replied. "But he said the SA promised Jahel he could sack Malakal as soon as they found a ford for the SA to cross the White Nile. That fits with what we're hearing on the jungle telegraph. Also, the townspeople are leaving Malakal in droves, and that Waleed's men are deserting in mass. He's down to less than two hundred men." She let him digest the news. "I'm just connecting the dots, sir." She checked her watch. "Colonel Vermullen will be here in a few minutes. He's got a defensive plan worked out, and he asked for the Reverend Person to be here."

"Please call the good parson and the key players," Allston said. More and more, he was relying on her as his second in command.

"Will do, sir."

* * *

Major Mercier tacked a large-scale chart of the mission and the surrounding area on the wall of the big room in Mission House. Vermullen stood beside the chart. "I have walked every meter of the terrain," he began, "and the two most likely axes of attack are from Malakal or from across the White Nile at the ford the Janjaweed used when they attacked the mission. I believe we can successfully defend against one, if we have early warning to position our forces. The plan you see here is based on concentric rings surrounding the mission, but not the refugee camp or airfield. The outer ring is approximately three kilometers out." He touched the small circles that formed the outer ring and extended to the southern bank of the Nile. "I call this Delta Ring. It is made up of manned listening posts, or LPs. The LPs have only one purpose, to warn of any attack. Once we know the axis of the attack, we concentrate our forces accordingly on the next ring, which I call Charlie Ring. It is made up of many defensive firing positions and is our first true line of defense. It is far enough back from the river that we can dig in, at least until the river floods. Then it will turn into a bog. But until then, we must dig as many DFPs as we can. The more we have, the more flexible we can be in reacting to an attack."

Allston got it immediately. "So the listening posts on Delta Ring, where there is no activity, fall back to help reinforce the part of Charlie Ring where the action is. What happens to the LPs that detect an attack?"

Malone answered. "They're on their own." In the hard calculus of combat, the forward LPs were expendable.

Again, Vermullen tapped the chart. "This shaded area between Charlie Ring and the mission compound is a minefield. I call it Bravo Ring." He waited for their reaction.

"I thought land mines were used at the forward edge of the battlefield," Allston said, "and not so close in."

"Normally, that is true," Vermullen replied. "But we don't have enough mines to cover a broad area and must concentrate them where they will do the most good." He tapped the last ring of densely packed DFPs inside the minefield that surrounded the mission itself. "This is Alpha Ring, our last line of defense, that your Sergeant Malone created. The minefield provides a cover for Alpha Ring."

Toby's face turned gray and he felt sick. "If anything makes the case for evil, it's land mines."

"This evil will keep us alive," Vermullen said. "We'll plot where each one is and dig them up later. We've done this before."

Malaby had a question. "How do we get our troops through the mine field to Alpha Ring if we have to pull back?"

Mercier answered . "You are very observant, Colonel. Some of the mines that we captured at Bentiu, over a hundred, are armed by remote control." He sketched in four narrow corridors through the minefield. "We mark these corridors with stakes for everyone to see and place the remote-controlled mines in the corridors. We will arm the mines after we have withdrawn into Alpha Ring."

"But some of our people might be trapped on the wrong side," Dick Lane said.

"It is the best of many bad options," Vermullen replied.

"What about mortar and artillery fire?" Allston's Facilities commander asked.

Vermullen answered. "Without a counter-battery radar, that is a problem. We can suppress close-in mortar fire with ours and our best defense is to dig as many DFPs as we can to rapidly concentrate our men while still protecting them. Reverend Person, I am hoping you can help with this."

The coppery taste of bile flooded Toby's mouth. "I didn't come to Africa to kill people." He paced the floor. "This isn't what I wanted."

"I know," Allston said.

Toby jerked his head yes, finally accepting the inevitability of what he had to do. "I'll have everyone I can here in the morning. " He walked from the room and disappeared into the night.

The reserved and quiet major who headed logistics spoke. "Is there any way we can make the SA more predictable? I was thinking, what if we take out Waleed now? before the SA hooks up with him. That way, they would have to come across the Nile. I hear most of his men have deserted."

"A preemptive attack?" Allston replied. "I don't see how."

"Let me work on it," Vermullen said. He had a few scores he wanted to settle with the Sudanese major.

E-Ring

Brigadier General Yvonne Richards was in a state of shock when the phone call came in and it was not a conversation she was ready for. Suddenly, her career was on the chopping block. "Yes, Mr. Speaker, I'm reviewing the CD you sent over as we speak." The Speaker of the House was adamant about what he wanted done. "Yes, sir, I'll get right on it." She was thankful for the abrupt click ending the conversation. There was no doubt he wanted a blood sacrifice and had banged the phone down with force. She placed the CD in a leather folder and considered her next move. The reality was that she was out of options. She called Fitzgerald's secretary and said that she had a communication from the Speaker of the House and had to see the general immediately.

Twenty minutes later, she was standing in front of Fitzgerald as the CD played out on his computer. "Why does it always hit the fan on Friday afternoon?" he asked. It was an occurrence that happened all too often in the Pentagon. "Have you downloaded this?" She assured him she had. "We need to preempt." The implication was clear; he expected the Speaker to break it to the media when it could do the most harm and they had to be ready when that happened. He hit the direct dial button to the JAG, Lieutenant General Forney. "Aaron, meet me in the Chairman's office ASAP."

He listened for a moment, his lips compressed into a tight line. The JAG was scheduled to deliver the keynote address to the annual American Bar Association convention in three hours. "Cancel or send your deputy," Fitzgerald said. He punched off the number and called the Chairman of the Joint Chiefs. "General, I have a situation that requires your immediate attention." Although they were old friends, formality conveyed urgency and Misner reacted accordingly. Fitzgerald dropped the phone in its cradle, ejected the CD, and handed it to her. "I'll let you brief the Chairman." For a moment, he thought Richards was going to throw up.

Richards followed a half step behind as Fitzgerald quick marched to Misner's office where Forney was waiting. They were ushered directly into the Chairman's office. "This is your baby," Fitzgerald told Richards.

She gulped hard, and inserted the CD into a player. The three men watched in silence as the short scene played out. "The Speaker expects a court-martial," she told them.

"I really needed this," Misner replied. "Aaron, appoint your best legal beagle to head an Article 32 investigation." An Article 32 investigation under the Uniform Code of Military Justice was the military's equivalent of a pretrial investigation and the first step leading to a court-martial. "I don't see how we can avoid a court-martial on this, so play it by the book. No mistakes and no cover-ups. And no leaks. Fitz, lay on airlift and get the lucky lawyer there ASAP. I'll brief the Secretary. Any questions?"

"Sir," Forney said, "the best man I have is a reservist, Lieutenant Colonel Henry Sutherland. Hank was an extremely successful deputy district attorney and now teaches law at the University of California at Berkeley."

"Since Berkeley is the Speaker's hometown, that should set well," Misner replied. He hated the part of his job that required him to play games, but there was no avoiding it. The reality was that appearances trumped logic and reason in the give and take of Washington politics and mattered more than substance.

"It will take a few days to get him there," Forney added.

Misner's fingers drummed a tattoo on the table. The Speaker would interpret any delay on their part as stonewalling or a cover up. "Anybody else you can send?"

"No one half as good," the JAG replied.

Fitzgerald had a solution. "We need to preserve the evidence. I suggest we send an officer, preferably flag ranked, to start the investigation and then turn it over to Sutherland when he gets there."

"Someone who is familiar with the situation," Forney said. The three generals turned and looked at Richards.

TWENTY

Mission Awana

Allston's small staff clustered around his table in the Ops Center for their morning meeting. They were a cohesive team, and because the 4440th was small and well-integrated unit, they were extremely efficient. The meeting didn't take long and they were almost finished when the radio squawked; a Dumbo was inbound with a code six on board. Malaby was worried. "Can a C-17 land on the mission's runway?" Allston assured her it could although turning around might get dicey. "A code six is all we need," she added.

"I'm betting it's the US consul general for the Sudan," Dick Lane said.

"It might be a brigadier general," Malone said.

Allston cut off the speculation. "It's a chance to get some of our folks out of here," he told them. "Who have you got that wants to get out of Dodge?" He went quickly around the table. Malaby had fourteen maintenance personnel, Logistics two, and Facilities six who wanted to leave. Malone shook his head, a satisfied look on his face, as none of the security cops wanted out. "What about the aircrews?" Allston asked Lane.

"No one wants to leave," the ops officer said, "but with only four Herks, I only need twenty-four bodies to make up six crews. I can send sixteen home."

"Make a decision," Allston told him. Then, "Jenkins goes."

"Why?" Lane asked. "Marci's the best pilot I got."

"We'll discuss it in private," Allston told him. "Okay, folks, go tell your troops to pack." The meeting was over and Lane held back as the others left, wanting an answer. "She's pregnant," Allston said.

Lane was philosophical about it. "It happens every time you put healthy young bodies together. Someone will get it on. I always felt sorry for the Navy, turning their surface combatants into love boats. At least, we can fly the lucky little mother out ASAP." It was a quick way to solve the problem, and one that some young women used to escape a hard assignment. But there was more. Breaking up a romantic couple in the forward area was simply the smart thing to do. Both men had been around operations long enough to experience how a pair bonding of any kind undermined unit morale and identification. "By the way, who's the lucky father?"

"G.G.," Allston replied.

"Ah, crap," Lane moaned.

"Yeah, it's a bummer. Well, let's go howdy the code six. With a little luck he's in and out on the C-17."

"We should be so lucky," Lane said.

The two officers drove in silence to the airfield, each caught up in his thoughts. Lane saw a man standing on the ramp with his bags and equipment waiting to leave. "Isn't that Tara's cameraman?" the Ops Officer asked.

"I guess he's leaving too," Allston said. The major in charge of Facilities took care of moving personnel in and out of Awana so he didn't think much of it. They waited while more outbound passengers arrived with their hastily packed bags. "I don't see Captain Jenkins," he said. Lane explained that she was flying a sortie and wouldn't be back in time. Allston walked over to wish the departing Irregulars a safe journey and thank them for all they had done. "You made a difference," he told them. He went around shaking their hands.

One of the crew chiefs shifted his weight from one foot to the other, crumpling his bush hat in his hands. "Sir, Maintenance doesn't need me, which is why I'm leaving. But can I stay and work with the cops?"

"You bet," Allston told him. "They need all the help they can get." The crew chief saluted, picked up his bags, and walked away as the C-17 taxied in. Allston watched with pride as three of Malaby's crew chiefs guided the big airlifter as it turned around, barely keeping its main trucks on the asphalt. The engines spun down as the crew entrance door opened and Brigadier General Yvonne Richards came down the steps.

"Oh, no," Lane moaned. "That's all we needed."

"Tell me," Allston muttered, feeling exactly the same.

* * *

Richards sat behind the desk in Toby's office and clasped her hands on the desktop as she leaned forward. She kept Allston and Jill standing and slowly raised her eyes to fix them with her authority. "I am here," she explained, "in order to conduct a pretrial investigation under Article 32 of the

Uniform Code of Military Justice." Nothing in her tone or face revealed the relish she felt. "I have been appointed by Major General Aaron Forney, the Judge Advocate General of the Air Force." She handed Allston the special order signed by Forney. He quickly read it and handed it back. "Any questions?" she asked.

"It would be nice if I knew who and what was being investigated."

"This is a serious matter, Colonel. Flippancy is not called for. I will get to that at the proper time and place."

He leaned across the desk and intruded on her personal space. She pulled back. "General Richards, cut to the chase and don't waste my time."

"Don't try to intimidate me, Colonel."

Allston didn't move. "Am I under investigation and how may I help you?"

"You may be. My investigation will determine that."

"You're on a fishing expedition. How did you manage that?" He looked up at the sound of submachine gun fire as Richards flinched. "Ours. Practice. You'll learn to tell the difference. Again, what is the purpose of your investigation?"

Visibly shaken by the continuing staccato, and determined to reclaim her authority, Richards came to her feet. "I'm conducting an investigation into the mistreatment of prisoners of war in violation of the Geneva Convention, the Uniform Code of Military Justice, and Air Force regulations. This investigation is in response to a video that has come to our attention." She opened her laptop computer and inserted a disk. She hit the play button and turned the screen towards Allston and Jill. They watched as the scene opened with a telephoto lens zooming in on Sergeant Loni Williams as he dragged the wounded Baggara, BermaNur, out of a pickup truck. Because of the distance, the only sound was sporadic gunfire in the background. The scene continued as Allston and Williams talked and Williams slapped the back of the Baggara's head. Then Williams turned towards the camera, his back to Allston, and stepped on the Baggara's wounded leg. The lens zoomed in, capturing the teenager's face as he screamed in agony. The screen went blank.

"When did that happen?" Jill asked.

"When the Janjaweed attacked the mission," Allston replied.

Richards pressed the stop button. "I assume you now understand the seriousness of my investigation. Torture is a crime under the UCMJ."

"So how may I help you?" Allston asked.

"I'll need a private office and an officer to act as recorder," Richards replied. "This office will do."

"This is Toby's office and not mine to make available," Allston told her. "You'll have to speak to him or we can pitch a tent for you." Richards face blanched at the thought of working in a tent in the heat. "The only officer I have available is Major Sharp." He shot Jill a sideways glance. She glared at him. "Will there be anything else?"

Richards stared at Jill for a full ten seconds. It seemed a lifetime. "Major Sharp is acceptable," she finally said. "That's all for now." The two saluted and beat a retreat, closing the office door behind them.

"Thanks a bunch, Colonel," Jill said.

Allston gave her his best fighter pilot grin. "I knew you'd appreciate that. As your first duty as recorder, I suggest you write a memo for the record on what happened in there. Be sure to show it to Richards and have her initial it."

"Is Loni in trouble?"

"Oh, yeah. Right along with me. What the video did not show was that I stopped Williams."

"But what about the knife Williams took off him? Doesn't that count? So why are you in trouble?"

"Knife or no knife, I didn't pursue disciplinary action against Williams. I am his commander, fully aware of what he did, aware that it could be a serious crime, and I chose to ignore it."

"Why did you do that?" He heard the concern in her voice.

"Because I had more pressing things to deal with, and Williams gave me what I needed to know." Why did I tell her all that? he wondered.

* * *

Tara lay on her side and dragged a finger down Allston's chest. The creaky fan above the bed barely stirred the night air but it provided a curtain of noise that gave them the privacy they desired. She let him talk as she played with the hair on his chest. "I wish I knew where that video came from," he told her.

"It was Glen, my cameraman," she admitted. "He was out filming the attack."

"At night? How did he do that?"

"Infrared," she told him. "I saw the clip and told him to delete it. I thought he had. It's worth a lot of money, and he must have e-mailed it to someone in the States. He wants an Emmy so bad he can taste it."

"Fucking lovely," Allston groused.

"Speaking of which," she murmured, linking a leg with his.

218

"Glen left on the C-17 today," Allston told her.

She came up on an elbow. "I didn't know. That complicates things. Technically, he was working for me and that video is my property." She thought for a moment, considering her options. "I can take care of it. Can you get me to Addis tomorrow? I need to get to the States and sort it out." He nodded, and she cuddled against him. "I don't know if I'll be back."

"We've got a C-130 going to Addis tomorrow afternoon. I'll get you on it. All things considered, it's best you get out of here. I will miss you."

"Not if your major has her way."

"There's nothing between us."

"Really? You like her, but are too stubborn to admit it." She pulled him to her. "Now say goodbye properly."

* * *

The summons for Allston to report to Richards came late the next morning. At first, he considered ignoring it and pleading the press of other duties. On reflection, he realized that would be counterproductive, and he did need to speak to Jill about the countless administrative details that nibbled at a commander's time and attention. It bothered him that it was barely six hours into the day and he already missed her. He made the short walk from the Ops Center to Toby's office where the brigadier was conducting her investigation. Jill was waiting at the office door and ushered him in. She closed the door behind him and waited for the fireworks to start.

Allston reported in and stood in front of Toby's desk while Richards thumbed through her notes. At her nod, Jill started a mini CD recorder and sat down to take notes. "Let's begin," Richards said. "You are aware of my authority to conduct this investigation into the torture of a prisoner of war."

"Alleged torture of an illegal combatant," Allston corrected. Jill dutifully continued to make notes.

Richards ignored his reply. "Major Sharp, please read Colonel Allston his right to remain silent under Article 31 of the UCMJ." Jill did so while Allston continued to stand. "Colonel Allston," Richards continued, "were you present at Mission Awana on early Thursday morning of last week?"

"With all due respect, ma'am," Allston said, "I will be glad to answer your questions when my attorney is present to advise me."

Richards' fingers beat a tattoo on the desk. "Colonel, do you consider that answer worthy of a pro?"

Allston couldn't help himself. "Ma'am, where I come from, a pro is a hooker." Jill suppressed a laugh and turned away so Richards couldn't see the expression on her face. Unfortunately, the general caught it. "Major Sharp, please note that I am reprimanding Colonel Allston for his flippant and disrespectful remarks to an investigating officer."

"Yes, ma'am," Jill replied, dutifully recording the reprimand.

"This interview is terminated for now," Richards continued. "Colonel Allston, there is a related matter we must discuss that concerns the well-being of your prisoner, BermaNur. With the aid of an interpreter provided by the Reverend Tobias Person, I have interviewed him in conjunction with this investigation. The prisoner is fearful of his life while in your custody. I am convinced that his fears are well-founded, and I am ordering you to turn him over to the United Nations Relief and Peacekeeping Mission, Southern Sudan."

"With all due respect, ma'am," Allston replied, "that would be a mistake. You are giving up custody of a witness."

"So noted," Richards replied. "However, the physical safety of the prisoner is paramount. You will do as ordered."

"Yes, ma'am," Allston replied. "Will there be anything else." Richards told him no and that he was excused. "Ma'am, I need to speak to Major Sharp about some administrative details and other matters that do not concern your investigation."

"You may, but only in my presence."

Allston thanked her and huddled with Jill, going over some paperwork. Then, "Any progress on getting Waleed out of Malakal?"

"Colonel Vermullen's working on it. I'll talk to him today and get an update."

Richards interrupted. "What are you up to now? You're not authorized to engage in combat operations."

Allston glanced at the CD recorder. It was still on. "With all due apologies, ma'am, this matter does not concern you." He turned and left.

"We'll see about that," Richards muttered.

Outside, Allston checked his watch. He keyed his communicator and called Malone, telling him Richards had ordered them to turn the Janjaweed over to the UN, and that he wanted BermaNur on the C-130 that was leaving for Addis Abba in two hours.

"I can make that happen," Malone replied, "but that's dumber than dirt."

"I know," Allston said. "Let's get him as far away from here as possible. Hell, I'd send him to the UN in New York if we had a plane going there." Another thought came to him. "Send two escorts with the little bastard and record the turnover to the UN on video. I want it documented we delivered him healthy and in one piece."

"Will do." Malone understood the game of 'cover your ass.'

Allston returned to his desk in the operations center and wrapped up a few minor matters. Finished, he spun around in his chair and checked the latest numbers posted on the boards that tracked the status of the 4440th. Because of the twenty-one Irregulars who flew out the day before, his unit strength was down to 140 people. Thanks to Malaby, all four of his C-130s were operational and flying over twenty sorties a day. But the big numbers were eighteen and 17,892. They had been evacuating every Nuer and Dinka they could find out of harms way and flying them into the mission for eighteen days. Unfortunately, the huge number of refugees had overwhelmed the mission's ability to handle them. Toby was working with the rebels in Juba and moving them out as fast as possible by trucks and buses but the refugee camp was overflowing with humanity.

He wanted to fly the refugees to the main camps three hundred miles south but fuel was a problem as C-130s gulped fuel at over 600 gallons an hour. By keeping sorties short, they were able to rescue more tribesmen from certain genocide. His eyes moved down the status boards to the fuel remaining in the dump. He did the math. They had enough fuel for three days of operations. That reserve had stayed constant and he wondered where the major in charge of logistics was finding the fuel. He suspected the major had tapped into the flourishing black market. But that was a question he would not ask. What he didn't know, he could ignore.

He studied the wall chart that Jill kept current. Every attack by the SA and Janjaweed was marked with a red flag and the date. The frequency of the attacks was increasing and coming their way. How much longer did they have before he had to evacuate the mission and find safety in Ethiopia or deep in rebel held territory? He mentally crunched all the variables, trying to predict the future. There was a high uncertainty but that day was not far off. So what could he do to delay it? If Vermullen could get Waleed out of Malakal, that might give him an extra week. And that meant seven to eight thousand more Africans saved. Could they hold on that long? How much more could he ask of his people? They were working eighteen to twenty hours a day in the stifling heat and dead tired. Still, if he read them right, their morale was high. He closed his eyes.

* * *

Someone was talking to him. Allston's eyes snapped open. He was napping at his desk and Jill was standing in the doorway. "Colonel, we've got to hurry if you're going to see the C-130 off."

He came to his feet and grabbed his hat. "Thanks. Let's go. I owe you one."

She gave him the look he couldn't read. "I'll add it to the list." She drove in silence, racing for the airstrip. In the distance, he heard the sounds of a C-130's engines. Jill put her foot down and accelerated. They reached the ramp just as the C-130 started to move. Suddenly, it came to a halt. The crew entrance door flopped down and the loadmaster hopped off. He held his arms out, a barricade against the whirling props. Tara ran down the steps and towards him. She flew into his arms and held him tight.

"I was afraid I would miss you," she said, yelling into his ear. She kissed him on the cheek and pulled back. "Take care." Then she was gone, running for the Hercules.

Allston watched her climb on board. The loadmaster followed her and closed the hatch. Allston didn't move as the Hercules taxied out. He turned, only to face Jill. "That was sweet," she said.

"Was BermaNur on board?" he asked.

"Oh, yes. With two armed escorts."

"And Captain Jenkins?"

"I haven't seen her."

TWENTY-ONE

Mission Awana

A gentle breeze drifted over the three as they sat under a canopy and enjoyed the evening. The chirping insects softened the ever-present clamor of the nearby refugee camp, and were held at bay by the canopy's netting. Hans Beck, the aging private who served as Vermullen's valet and self-appointed bodyguard, stood back, tending a bottle of chilled wine and ready to be of instant service. A fragrant aroma from the dining tent announced that dinner was ready. Jill looked up from the wine glass cradled in her hands. "No music, Idi?"

"That can be remedied," Vermullen assured her. He gestured at the private. "Hans." Beck disappeared into the tent, and an Edith Piaff CD started to play in the background.

"Ah, gay Paris," Allston offered, trying to do his part. "That's nice," he allowed. "Very Parisian. What is it?"

"It's called *Non je ne regrette rien,*" Jill replied. "There is nothing I regret." Vermullen gave a slow nod, impressed that she recognized the French classic. Jill's eyes danced as Beck emerged from the tent carrying a loaded tray and served dinner. "It smells delicious. What is it?"

"Grilled gazelle with Private Beck's special marinade," Vermullen told her.

"A bit much for the Legion, *ne c'est pas?*" Allston ventured.

"*Parlez-vous francais, monsieur*?" Jill asked.

"That's about it," Allston confessed. He started to eat. "This is really good. Is this the new Legion?"

"The Legion is still the collection of misfits it always was," Vermullen said. "They haven't forgotten how to fight." He didn't tell the two Americans that he paid well for his private mess.

Allston changed the subject. "Major Sharp tells me you have some ideas on how to dispose of our village idiot, Waleed."

Vermullen played with his food as he laid out his strategy and tactics. "Waleed is dangerous, but he is not the enemy I want to fight at this time, in this place." He spoke in a monotone, the cool professional plying his trade, as he laid out his plan. The two Americans exchanged glances as Vermullen's tone changed, becoming clipped and hard. The conflict between the French officer and the Sudanese major had become personal and Vermullen wanted Waleed dead. However, Vermullen knew he could accomplish more by settling for less.

"You really hate that bastard," Allston said.

"Totally and absolutely. He is a disgrace to our profession. He is vermin."

"I don't hate the bastards," Allston said. "I just want them to stop."

"Only the world can make them do that," Vermullen replied. "For that to happen, people need a face so they know who to hate. Only then will they take sides. Such is human nature."

Jill ran Vermullen's plan through her mental abacus, weighing the pros and cons. It was a skillful use of tactics with a political payoff, and a side of Vermullen she had not seen before. She was impressed. "Waleed could be that face, if we do it right."

Allston was intrigued with the plan. "Will the good Reverend do his part?"

"Why not?" Jill replied. "He benefits if we can pull it off."

Vermullen turned to Allston and asked the key question. "This may upset your masters in the Pentagon. Are you willing to take that chance?"

Allston gave them his best fighter pilot grin. "What the hell, they're already pissed off. What are they gonna do? Send me to the Sudan? Besides we can top off our fuel tanks at Juba, which means we recover here with tanks three-quarters full."

"I understand fuel is a problem," Vermullen said.

Allston leaned forward and lowered his voice. "It's a limiting factor. Even with Waleed gone, I'm not sure how much longer we can operate out of here. We need to think about evacuating."

Vermullen didn't answer as he pulled into himself. Finally, "We can cross that particular bridge later."

Allston checked his watch. "Thanks for the dinner, Colonel. It was superb, as always. But tomorrow's a long day." He glanced at Jill. "Major?"

She shot an enquiring glance at Vermullen. "You go on," she said. "I'll catch a ride later."

Allston came to his feet and ambled to his truck. How long has that been going on? he wondered. An image of the two in bed flashed in his mind's eye. "Damn," he muttered to himself. But he was brutally honest with himself. "And just what are you bitchin' about?"

* * *

Jill sipped at her coffee and savored the early morning quiet. She had another hour before the sun split the horizon and the constant buzz of activity, punctuated by the occasional roar of a C-130 taking off or landing, that marked the mission's life would return. The attentive Beck hovered in the background, ready to be of service. "Hans," she called softly, raising her empty cup. He rushed over to fill the cup. "How long have you been with the Colonel?"

The rugged old German was slow to answer and fumbled with his English. "Since he was a *sous-lieutenant* new from St. Cyr." St. Cyr was France's West Point founded by Napoleon in 1802. "Even then, he could fight."

"Is that why you stay with him?"

"For that, and other reasons."

From the way he studied her, Jill sensed that he would cut her throat in a flash if she harmed or betrayed Vermullen. "Thank you, Hans." Vermullen joined her at the table and a huge breakfast appeared as if by magic. She smiled at the way he attacked the omelet. "You are hungry."

"It is your fault," he replied. She fell silent and stared at her coffee. "What is troubling you?" he asked between mouthfuls.

"I don't understand what's happening," she began, not sure she could explain the emotions tearing at her. He continued to eat, waiting for her to go on. "I don't know why I'm acting like this." She looked at him, pleading for understanding. "I am fond of you. But . . ."

"But your mother would not approve," he said. "Neither would mine. But they have never faced the dangers we live with. When life hangs by a thread, when our very existence is in doubt and danger lurks in every shadow, Mother Nature commands us to procreate. We have no choice in the matter. We are genetically wired this way." He laughed. "It is something you Americans do not understand. Don't blame yourself, it is an ignorance in your culture."

For a moment, Jill assumed he was being urbane and witty, and almost laughed. Then the truth of it all hit her like a revelation. "So that's why Tara and . . ."

"I see," Vermullen said, now understanding. "Your colonel and Tara Scott. She is a child of nature and reacts naturally. Your colonel was merely the best available."

"Why does he do it? I mean, why does he, why do you, deliberately seek out danger?"

"Ah, this is not about sex." He thought for a moment. "So why do we fight? It is hard to explain. It is a felt need, something we are driven to do, much like you have experienced, but very different. It is a testing. Every man, I don't know about women, has a secret image of himself. In combat, that image is taken out and tested. Your colonel is the most fortunate of men. His secret image has been held up to the bright light of reality and it was all a normal man could hope for. He has seen himself for what he is. He is a leader, not a posturing egomaniac hungry for power. Because of what he is, men follow him."

"And which are you?" she asked, "leader or egomaniac?"

Vermullen had come to terms with himself years before. "My case is different. I am a throw back to an earlier time. This is all I am. Just ask Hans here."

"It is true, mademoiselle," the old private replied. "He is the ancient warrior."

Vermullen's laughter split the morning quiet. "Nonsense, Hans. I am a misfit like all the rest of you." He drained the last of his coffee. "Come. We have work to do if we are to wink Waleed out of Malakal."

* * *

Richards' fingers danced over the keyboard as she rushed to finish the report of investigation. Jill proofread each page as the general finished it, and her panic grew with each paragraph. Richards was an accomplished staff officer and marshaled her facts with stained-glass logic and a rare expertise, leaving little doubt that Allston was guilty of permitting a subordinate to torture a prisoner and then covering it up with his silence. Richards finished the last page and checked the time: it was just before noon. "Print it out." Jill hit the print command and the printer whirred, spitting out the hundred-page report. Richards scanned it with a smug satisfaction. "Not bad, if I say so myself." She watched as Jill bound it in a report cover. "I hope you learned something from all this," Richards said.

Never trust a vindictive bitch? Jill thought. "I'm quite sure your Colonel Sutherland will be impressed." She glanced at the wall clock. "A Dumbo is landing in twenty minutes." She handed the report to the general. "Colonel Sutherland is on it."

"I've never met the gentleman. I understand he's famous for gaining convictions." She enjoyed twisting the knife and watching Jill's reaction. They walked out to Jill's truck and headed for the airstrip. "I would have preferred that Colonel Sutherland served as trial counsel in a court-martial and not the investigating officer."

"It appears you have done his work for him," Jill said.

"That's why I was sent ahead, to prevent a cover up." They reached the airfield as a C-17 entered the landing pattern. "I'll be glad to get out of here once and for all."

"Yes, ma'am," Jill replied. They watched in silence as the big airlifter landed and taxied in.

Richards got out of the truck and waited for the aircraft to stop. "Stay here and keep the air conditioner running." She walked towards the lone figure who deplaned. From her vantage point, Jill watched them as they talked and headed her way. The lawyer was slender, non-descript, and slightly hunched shouldered. Richards introduced them and they stood talking. There was something about his boyish features and the way he listened that made Jill trust him. Satisfied he had his bearings, Sutherland climbed into the truck. Richards handed him her report. "The investigation to date," she announced.

Jill drove in silence as Sutherland scanned the report and her panic mounted.

Sutherland read at well over a thousand words a minute and had digested the report by the time they reached Mission House. "Very interesting," he allowed. "And very thorough. But there's a problem. I need to speak to Sergeant Malone. Immediately."

Now it was Richards' turn to panic. She called the security cop on her communicator and handed it to Sutherland. The colonel identified himself. "When did you turn over BermaNur to the United Nations?" He listened. "Twenty-four hours ago. At Addis Abba. Got it. Thank you." Without getting out of the truck, he turned to Richards. "This is an excellent report, general. Top notch. You made a strong case. But you gave your prime witness away. Without him, we have nothing, nada, zilch."

"But the video," Richards protested.

"Without BermaNur in the witness box, it can all be explained away in court by any first-year law student. Not only that, Allston, against his own interests, urged you to retain custody and not transfer him to the UN. Does that sound like the actions of a guilty man? Not to me."

"So what do we do?" Richards asked, her voice stretched tight.

"We get him back. How soon can we get to Addis Ababa?"

Jill spoke up. "There's a shuttle tomorrow afternoon."

"They'll damn well do better than that," Richards said. "I'll talk to Allston." She hurried into the Ops Center with Sutherland and Jill in tow. Dick Lane was there, manning the scheduling desk, and shook his head when Richards demanded a C-130 for immediate transportation to Addis Ababa,

"General, I would if I could." He scanned the board. "We got three Herks inbound but they're on hold for another mission and I can't release them."

"So who can?" Richards demanded.

"Colonel Allston. He's flying. I expect him back this evening with the fourth Herk."

Sutherland took charge. "Stay on top of it, Major. It's important that we get to Addis Ababa as soon as possible. But since we have a few hours to kill, I'd like to see the mission."

Jill perked up. "General Richards, if you no longer need me, I can show Colonel Sutherland around."

"You do that," Richards groused.

"Thank you, ma'am." It was her turn to twist the knife. "And I did learn a lot." Richards stormed out. Sutherland thought for a moment and followed her, leaving Jill and Lane alone. "Delay as long as you can," Jill told him. "The longer the better."

"I didn't hear that," Lane said. He lowered his voice. "But if they want out of here before tomorrow, they'll have to walk or drive."

"Thank you," Jill murmured. She ran after Sutherland. "Colonel," she called, "would you like to meet Reverend Person? He's with Colonel Vermullen."

*   *   *

"Very impressive," Sutherland said. Jill had given him a Cooks Tour of the mission and the refugee camp, and was driving west on a gravel road. "Where are we headed now?"

"This is the road to the town of Malakal, but we're only going as far as the outskirts. The Legion has a checkpoint there and that's where I expect we'll find Toby. I imagine he's pretty worried about now."

Sutherland gave her his friendliest look, playing the game. "Okay, Major. Where is all this leading, and why is the Reverend Person worried?"

"Because his wife is shopping," she replied. She slowed and turned into a large open area with a camouflaged revetment and a canopy-covered rest area. A squad of legionnaires sat in the shade and shared cigarettes with four young African men dressed in civilian clothes. "We're there. That's Colonel Vermullen's Panhard over there and his bodyguard, Private Beck. He's the most dangerous man I've ever met."

"That old guy?" Sutherland asked, taking in the legionnaire and the battered utility vehicle. He got out and followed her into the revetment that was also covered with a canopy where Jill introduced him to Vermullen and Person. "My pleasure. Gentlemen," Sutherland said. "If I read Major Sharp correctly, there is something I need to see."

Vermullen took over. "We are trying to coax a Sudanese Army battalion into evacuating Malakal. I'm hoping we can do it with smoke and mirrors."

"Actually, with well-placed rumors on the jungle telegraph," Toby added. "And a little encouragement." From the look on Sutherland's face, he didn't have a clue and an explanation was in order. "The jungle telegraph is Africa's internet. It is word-of-mouth news transmitted by merchants and truck drivers who move about. Market places are the URLs."

"I get it," Sutherland said. "The market places are where information is stored and disseminated. Major Sharp tells me your wife is shopping today, so I assume she is gathering news."

"Not quite," Toby explained. "She's pumping information, actually misinformation, into the system."

"Just like the internet," Sutherland added, understanding the analogy.

Toby nodded. "The mission buys a lot of food and supplies from the local vendors, which creates goodwill. Right now, D'Na is spreading the rumor that the South Sudan's People's Liberation Army intends to attack tomorrow morning, and it's payback time."

"Because the South Sudanese have been losing big time," Sutherland added.

Toby had to make the lawyer understand the stakes. "If you call genocide, 'losing' then they are losing big time."

A high-wheeled pickup loaded with crates of food drove up, and a big, raw-boned woman got out. She gleamed with vitality and, like most Dinkas, her hair was cut short. Toby visibly relaxed. "My wife, D'Na," he announced. She motioned for the four young men dressed in civilian clothes to join her as she came into the revetment. They all gathered around a large-scale map of Malakal as she filled them in. From the concise way she briefed the men and commanded their attention, there was no doubt she was an accomplished and experienced leader.

D'Na's first stop had been at the stall of an old woman, Malakal's most famous fortuneteller and traditional healer. D'Na had whispered the rumor that the South Sudanese were going to attack the SA garrison, and then gone about her business. But she also carefully marked the location of every Sudanese Army checkpoint around the market. By the time she was finished, the market was buzzing with the rumor. "I counted six checkpoints," she told the men. She carefully marked the six locations on the chart and turned to the four young men. "Go," she ordered. "Do not spend time talking to the girls. Make sure the soldiers see you and then leave. Get back here as soon as you can." The four men were all smiles as they left.

"Who are they?" Sutherland asked.

"South Sudanese from Juba," Toby explained. "You can't tell it, but every Dinka and Nuer in Malakal will know they're from a different tribe."

Sutherland understood. "Confirmation of the rumor. So what happens next?"

"We wait," Toby replied.

Two hours later, the young men were back, still smiling. They reported they were seen scouting the Army checkpoints and were as popular as Ebola fever.

"Now the next phase," Vermullen said. He keyed his handheld radio. "Freedom Flight, Freedom Flight, this is Wink One transmitting in the blind. You are cleared to drop. Repeat, you are cleared to drop." He ended the transmission. "I hope the SA monitored that," he said. "Have you ever seen an airdrop from the ground?" he asked Sutherland. The lawyer said he had not. "Then you will find it most interesting."

"Who's being dropped?" Sutherland asked.

"South Sudanese, of course," Vermullen replied. He led the way to his Panhard and climbed in the back with Jill. Sutherland sat in the passenger's seat and Beck drove. "Colonel Allston is flying the C-130," Vermullen explained, "and the parachutists are South Sudanese recruits we have trained. It is what you Americans call a Hollywood jump. They are jumping without equipment." They made the drive to a large open area four miles south of Malakal.

The sun was setting when Sutherland saw a single C-130 approach from the west. It passed overhead as jumpers streamed out both aft jump doors. Within minutes, the jumpers were on the ground and gathering up their parachutes. They quickly double-timed into the brush and disappeared.

"More confirmation of the rumor?" Sutherland asked. It was a rhetorical question and he knew the answer. "So what now?"

"We have dinner," Vermullen replied. "Colonel Allston will be joining us."

"So what happens next?" Sutherland asked.

"We wait."

* * *

Jill relaxed into her chair and cradled her wine glass in both hands. As always, Vermullen was the perfect host and the dinner superb. She was content to listen as the four men talked. They were an odd mixture; the small and wiry Toby, the scholarly and reserved Sutherland, the lanky and edgy Allston, and the dominating presence of Vermullen. There was no doubt they were a band of brothers, complementing each other, yet different. She looked up to see Sutherland studying her. "Major Sharp, there is something I've been wondering about. Why did you show me all this?"

She decided to go with the truth. "Two reasons. First, we need a friend at court. Second, I trust you."

"What a nice compliment," Sutherland replied. "Colonel Allston, you know General Richards and I need to get to Addis Ababa as soon as possible. All your C-130s are sitting on the ground but you won't release one. May I ask why?"

"Because we are going to need them," Allston answered. He checked his watch. "If Colonel Vermullen's plan is on schedule, it won't be too long."

"So we wait," Sutherland said. He held out his wine glass to be refilled.

* * *

Allston's communicator buzzed just after midnight. He glanced at his dinner companions as he listened. "They're here," he announced.

"At the risk of sounding very stupid," Sutherland said, "I'm guessing your guests are Sudanese Army troops from Malakal demanding you evacuate them to safety."

"Very good, Colonel," Vermullen replied. "You have deduced our little plan."

"May I make a suggestion?" Sutherland asked. "Reverend Person, it would be best if you disappeared at this point."

"You are afraid our guests will not arrive safely at their destination?" Vermullen wondered.

"The thought has crossed my mind."

"I did consider it," Vermullen explained, "but this is better."

"I've got to see this," Sutherland said, now totally hooked.

"We better get going," Allston said. Toby stayed behind as they piled into their trucks and drove for the airstrip.

A very agitated Major Waleed was waiting for them. He paced back and forth beside his silver-blue Mercedes Benz sedan. "Do you always ignore the presence of your superior officers?" he snarled.

"My apologies, Major," Allston replied, ignoring Waleed's arrogance. "But we were not notified you were coming and were entertaining our guest, Lieutenant Colonel Sutherland." He went through the formal introductions. "How may I help you?" Allston asked.

"I have been ordered to report to Khartoum and require you fly me there immediately."

Allston looked at the soldiers Waleed had brought with him for muscle. They were all armed and milling around the C-130s. If the Jungle Telegraph was correct, they were all that was left of the garrison. "Yes, of course we can do that. We can also take your men, if you require."

"I demand it," Waleed said. "And my car."

"Yes, we can take your car," Allston said. "But weight will be a problem. You must either leave some men behind or your heavy weapons and much of your baggage. I will let you decide who stays and you can give the appropriate orders to your men. We can start loading immediately." Waleed's left eye ticked nervously. His soldiers wanted out of Malakal as badly as he did and were not in any mood to be left behind, especially when they could argue the point with an assault rifle. Allston offered him a way out. "Perhaps it would be best to let us handle it. I'm sure everything will go smoothly as long as we get everyone on board. And of course, your car."

"Yes, of course," Waleed said, breathing much easier.

Allston made a show of issuing orders and the ramp exploded in activity as aircrews appeared and loadmasters quickly loaded the C-130s. Within minutes all the soldiers and the Mercedes were on board. The ramp was littered with bags, suitcases, machine guns, mortars, and ammunition. Allston escorted Waleed to the first aircraft and ushered him up the crew entrance steps. He made a big show of waving his right arm in a start engines motion before climbing on board as the last passenger.

Sutherland was worried. "Is it safe taking them to Khartoum? Waleed's an arrogant bastard here, what's he going to be like on his home turf?"

"Who said anything about Khartoum?" Vermullen replied. He laughed at the look on the lawyer's face and gave in. "I don't think Waleed will recognize Juba as long as it is still dark when they land."

"I'll be damned!" Sutherland roared. "You're taking them to the South Sudanese. You clever bastards. I would love to see that."

Vermullen motioned at the last C-130. "Please, be our guest." The lawyer ran for the Hercules.

"He's having a great adventure," Jill said. She had read the lawyer right.

"Who will tell your General Richards?" Vermullen asked.

"Frankly, my dear, I don't give a damn."

Vermullen appreciated the use of the famous movie line by Clark Gable. "Perhaps we should tell her in the morning." Jill followed him to his Panhard and got in. He cocked an eyebrow at her.

"Blame Mother Nature," she told him.

TWENTY-TWO

Mission Awana

The far off drone of C-130s woke Richards from a fitful sleep. For a moment, she was back in time when a C-130 had woken her that first morning in Malakal. But this wasn't Malakal and she was sleeping on a chaise lounge on the veranda of the guesthouse at Mission Awana. She pulled on her boots as the sound grew louder. She stepped to the railing just as four C-130s passed overhead in formation, echeloned to the right and a thousand feet above the ground. The roar pounded at her. Her eyes narrowed as she followed the aircraft. They flew over the approach end of the runway and pitched out to the left, in sequence, circling to land at thirty-second intervals. She didn't recognize the classic overhead recovery of aircraft returning from combat. She had no idea where they had been, but was certain where at least one was going in the very near future. She ran for Mission House and the Operations Center. She barged into the center and confronted a very tired Dick Lane. "Where's Allston," she demanded.

Lane posted the arrival times of the C-130s on the scheduling boards with a Magic Marker and marked them all OR, operationally ready. "He just landed and should be here in about twenty minutes," Lane told her. "Can I get you some coffee?"

"You can get me a plane to Addis Ababa," she said, her voice low and threatening. Lane handed her a cup of coffee that she eagerly grasped without a word.

"Thank you, Major," Lane said.

Richards glared at him and stepped outside on the veranda. She didn't have to wait long. The first six-pac truck arrived from the airfield jammed with two aircrews. Hank Sutherland was with them. The lawyer was dead tired and trudged up the steps. "Where have you been?" she demanded.

"Juba," the lawyer answered. "It was the damnedest thing." He followed the smell of coffee into Mission House. "They pulled off one fantastic con job and I was there. Colonel Vermullen came up with a plan to scare the Sudanese Army into evacuating Malakal. Major Sharp rang me in on it." Richards stiffened at hearing Jill's name. The general had a few scores to settle and was going to terminate her career. "The SA commander," Sutherland continued, "a Major Waleed . . . he was the most arrogant bastard alive . . . showed up around midnight and demanded airlift to fly him to safety at Khartoum. But Allston wouldn't do it without taking all of his men. That was why they were holding the C-130s on the ground. They had to do it while it was still dark."

Suddenly, Richards sensed an opening. "You said Waleed 'was.' Did they kill him? Throw him out of the airplane without a parachute?"

Sutherland tried to keep a straight face, but failed miserably. "Not a bad idea, but no, they didn't. They flew Waleed and his men to Juba. Waleed didn't have a clue where they were because it was still dark. You should have seen that arrogant ass deflate when he got off the plane and realized where they were. Allston turned Waleed and his troops over to the South Sudanese, lock stock and barrel. It turns out that the International Criminal Court in the Hague has issued a warrant for Waleed's arrest. He's got a history going back to the genocide in Darfur." He smiled broadly. "The world is gonna love him when he goes on trial."

Richards wouldn't let it go. "Flying the Sudanese Army anywhere is a violation of the UN's peacekeeping charter. Who authorized it?"

"Allston."

"Got him!"

"I don't think so, General. The International Criminal Court was created by the UN and Allston can argue that his job over here is to support the UN."

Another truck arrived and Allston got out with the crew. He hadn't slept in twenty-four hours, and his face was lined with fatigue. Richards went on the offensive and demanded a C-130 immediately fly her and Sutherland to Addis Ababa. "Let's go see what's available," Allston said, trudging inside. Lane was waiting with a cup of coffee and handed it to him. "Thanks, Dick," Allston said. He sipped the strong brew and studied the scheduling boards.

"They're all operational," Richards sneered. "Do you have any other excuses?"

"I've got one damn good reason. I only have two flight crews available to fly. All the rest, me included, are beyond our crew duty day and have to go into crew rest. Hopefully, those two crews will each fly four or five sorties in the next twelve hours. If we're lucky, they can rescue another twelve to fifteen hundred Dinka and Nuer before it gets dark and we have to knock off. Unless you literally have a life or death reason for going to Addis Ababa, I'll have a crew available twelve hours from now to fly you there."

Richards was shouting. "You know damn good and well why we need to go to Addis!"

Allston deliberately pitched his voice to sound reasonable, egging on her anger. "No, I don't."

Richards lost it. "You expect me to believe that bitch didn't tell you!"

"Which bitch tell me what?"

"General," Sutherland counseled, "we need to discuss this, outside, in private." Richards stalked out. Sutherland turned to Allston. "Do you have any idea why we need airlift?"

"Not a clue," Allston told him.

Sutherland wasn't upset in the least. "A flight this evening will be fine. I can use the time to make some phone calls and send a few e-mails. By the way, Colonel, that was one fine piece of work last night. Thanks for letting me go along. "

"You're more than welcome," Allston said. "Major Lane here will make sure you get everything you need. Now if you'll excuse me, I'm gonna hit the sack."

"Not to worry, Boss," Lane said. "I got it here."

* * *

Dick Lane looked up from the report he was working on when Allston walked into the Ops Center after lunch. "Six hours, Boss? You need more rest than that."

"I don't plan on flying," Allston said. In order to fly, he had to have twelve hours of uninterrupted crew rest. It was a lesson the Air Force had learned the hard way. Tired pilots got killed. "Go hit the sack. I've got it here."

Lane cleared his desk and stood. "I got a problem, Boss. Can you speak to Captain Jenkins. She doesn't want to leave."

"Will do. By the way, there's something else. I'm working on your performance evaluation. I'm going to recommend you transfer to C-17s."

"You remembered," Lane said, very impressed. He had mentioned that he wanted to fly C-17s when Allston had first arrived. He tried to remember how long that had been. It came to him – two months ago. It seemed a lifetime. "I changed my mind. I'm going to stay in Herks." He gave Allston his best grin. "I'm just a trash hauler at heart."

"Hey, aren't we all. Send Marci in if you see her." He checked his message file and went to work.

Marci reported in fifteen minutes later. "You wanted to see me, sir?"

"Right." He motioned her to a seat and came right to the point. "Major Lane tells me you don't want to leave. May I ask why?"

She had been expecting this conversation and was ready. "Because my friends are here. Besides, I'm the best pilot you've got."

"Indeed you are." He tried to reason with her. "But right now, you have a higher priority than being a pilot. You need to have a fine, healthy baby."

"There's plenty of time for that," she replied. "I'm not even showing yet and feel great."

"That's not the point. You owe this to G.G., his family, and most importantly, to yourself."

"It's more important to me that I stay here and do my job."

He sensed he was spinning his wheels. "Captain, none of us are going to be here much longer. You won't miss much."

"I don't want to leave, Colonel."

Allston did the one thing he had never done, and had hoped that we would never have to. He gave a direct order. "Captain Jenkins, you will be on the next airplane out of here that is going to Addis Ababa. Is that understood?"

Marci stood. "Yes, sir." She stood and snapped a salute. "Will that be all, sir?"

"That's all," he replied. He watched her march out. "Ah, shit," he moaned. He firmly believed that a commander diminished his authority whenever he gave a direct order. In his experience, it was much better to let authority hover in the background, and remain unused because everyone understood what had to be done and did it.

"Problems, Colonel?" Hank Sutherland asked.

How much had the lawyer overheard? "It's the Air Force. We have to deal with problems that weren't problems when I was a newly minted brown bar."

"Women in the service?"

"Nope. Women in combat."

Sutherland made a mental note to explore the difference. But that would have to wait for now. "Colonel, if you've got a moment, I'd like to go over the Article 32 investigation that brought me here."

"Please shut the door and have a seat," Allston said, wondering what the lawyer was doing. Normally, the commander ordering an Article 32 investigation was the first to see the results. The report was only released if the commander decided to press charges and convene a court-marital.

Sutherland came right to the point. "Colonel, we don't have a case because General Richards gave our prime witness to the UN Peacekeeping Mission."

"So you need to get the little bastard back." Allston leaned forward in his chair. "Why didn't you say so? I'm not trying to cover up anything here." He glanced at the scheduling board. "I've got a C-130 inbound. I'll have the crew fly you to Addis Ababa ASAP."

Sutherland shook his head. "Don't bother. Two reasons. First, that would mean four or five less rescue sorties. Second, it wouldn't do any good." He paused to let it sink in. "I made a phone call to the air attaché at our embassy in Addis and called in a favor. He made some phone calls. It seems the Peacekeeping Mission turned one BermaNur loose within an hour after he was turned over. You ready for this? They even gave him an airline ticket to Khartoum."

"Fuckin' lovely," Allston muttered

"Indeed it is," Sutherland agreed. "Like the man said, my work here is done. Colonel, this was a wasted trip but I wouldn't have missed it for the world." He extended his hand in friendship. The two men shook hands. There is one thing I've been wondering about. How much time did you buy by getting Waleed out of Malakal?"

"Good question," Allston said. "Maybe a week, two weeks at best."

"I hope I can get out of here before then." He chuckled at the look on Allston's face. "Lawyers aren't fighters, not in the real sense of the word. We're great Monday morning quarterbacks as long as we don't have any skin in the game."

"We'll get you out," Allston promised. "But do me a favor. Take Richards with you. She's worse than herpes the way she keeps coming back."

TWENTY-THREE

E-Ring

Admiral Chester Bellows came right to the point. "Get 'em out. Now." Fitzgerald wanted to ask the irascible admiral the source of his information but knew better. Bellows had not made the trip from the headquarters of the National Security Agency at Fort Meade in Maryland out of courtesy, and Fitzgerald suspected that NSA was engaged in humint, short for human intelligence, which was outside of its charter to monitor foreign communications and gather signals intelligence.

"How bad is it?" Fitzgerald asked.

"The Sudanese Army is deploying as we speak. By morning, they'll be on the northern banks of the White Nile, less than ten miles from Mission Awana, and in control of the only ford across the river within a hundred miles that can support mechanized operations. My weather prophet claims the Nile will start to flood early, within five days max."

"So they attack now or wait until the next dry season," Fitzgerald added.

"That's the way we read it," Bellows said. "Second, over a thousand Janjaweed have crossed the Nile on horseback and are operating south of the mission."

"That's new," Fitzgerald said, now convinced that NSA was definitely operating outside its charter. He never suspected that NSA was simply monitoring the CIA's communications.

"My analysts don't expect them to directly attack the mission," Bellows said, "not after the mauling they received the last time. We think they will try to seal off the mission to the south." He stood to leave. "You've had a damn good run. How many have you rescued?"

Fitzgerald knew the numbers by heart. "As of yesterday, 25,324. Hopefully, they'll get another thousand or so out today."

"Your unit strength at the Mission?" Bellows asked.

Again, the numbers were seared into Fitzgerald's consciousness. "We've got 127 men and women on station and four C-130s, all operational."

"Shouldn't be a problem getting them out," Bellows allowed. For the first time since Fitzgerald had known the admiral, he softened. "They did good. You can't ask them to do any more." Given Bellow's nature, there was no higher praise. "You want me to brief the Chairman?"

"No thanks," Fitzgerald said. "I'll brief him." Bellows grunted and left. Fitzgerald immediately turned to his computer and composed an email.

The intercom buzzed. It was his secretary. "General Richards has requested a meeting soonest. The House Select Committee to Study Governmental Operations with Respect to UN Peacekeeping Activities has subpoenaed her to testify tomorrow morning. It's a closed session."

"That's a new committee. I never heard of it."

"The Speaker of the House created it and is the chairman."

Fitzgerald treated it like a tactical problem. Richards was firmly in the Speaker's camp and the new committee was his personal bailiwick. By holding closed hearings, the Speaker could control the leaks and drive its findings. Images of chopping blocks and headhunters played in his imagination. Better to stay totally out of it, he thought. He didn't need any allegations that he had tried to influence her testimony. "Tell her we'll talk after she testifies," Fitzgerald replied.

He reread the message, made a few corrections, and hit the send button. Ten minutes later, he received a subpoena.

Mission Awana

The sun was setting and the last C-130 was inbound for the day when Allston read the message from Fitzgerald. He was sitting at his desk in the Ops Center and Jill was standing at the big boards marking in the latest numbers. Allston read the total; the four Herks had flown nine sorties and airlifted another 1013 Dinka and Nuer to safety for a grand total of 26,337. It was all they were going to get. "Major Sharp," he called. She turned and he spun his laptop around for her to read the message. "It doesn't get much more specific," Allston told her. "Judging by the language, this one is for the record." Without a word, she read the message.

> Consider this an order to immediately evacuate Mission Awana.
> Sudanese Army is moving into position on the north side of the
> White Nile opposite Mission Awana. Expect an attack at anytime.
> Janjaweed are maneuvering in force south of Mission Awana.

The Peacemakers

Estimated strength approximately one thousand (1000).
Reply immediately upon receiving and state intentions.
John M. Fitzgerald, General, USAF
Chief of Staff, USAF

"Have you replied?" she asked. He shook his head. "Play it straight," she counseled. "The bureaucrats in the Pentagon and the crowd across the River will Monday morning quarterback it to death." He spun the laptop around and typed a reply. He showed it to her before hitting the send key.

Your message received and understood. Will commence evacuation
as required immediately after coordinating with Col Pierre Vermullen,
La Legion Etrangere, UN Peacekeeping forces, and Reverend Tobias
Person, Mission Awana.
David O. Allston, Lt. Col. USAF
Commander, 4440th Special Airlift Detachment

She fixed him with the steadfast look he had come to expect. "Keeping your options open?" He gave her his best fighter-pilot grin as he hit the send button. "I always considered an order as a point of discussion. We need to talk to Toby and Idi." He printed out the order.

"They're at the hospital," Jill said.

* * *

Nothing on Vermullen's face betrayed his thoughts as he read Fitzgerald's order. He passed it to Toby who read it twice. "You don't have much of a choice," Toby said.

"Actually, I do," Allston replied. "I will evacuate as many folks out of here as we can. So what are we looking at?" Toby ran the numbers. There were just under two thousand men, women, and children at the mission, and approximately three thousand more in the refugee camp. "Plus two hundred legionnaires," Allston added.

"We're not leaving," Toby said, his voice quiet but sure and unwavering.

"The Legion is also staying," Vermullen announced.

"That's crazy," Allston protested. "It's going to be a bloodbath." But he knew neither man would budge. "At least, evacuate everyone who wants out."

"Certainly," Toby agreed. "But I don't think you have much time."

"What about arming convoys?" Jill asked. "We can move a lot of people in the next twenty-four hours."

Toby shook his head. "Even if we had the trucks and busses it would be too dangerous. A convoy returning from Juba was due in this afternoon and there's been no word. The jungle telegraph says the Janjaweed have cut us off to the south, the same as your message."

Allston made a decision. "Okay, here's the drill. I'm flying the 4440th to Juba tonight. I'll keep a small contingent here and start a shuttle; evacuees out and fly in whatever support the South will give us. The birds can refuel at Juba, and we'll keep at it as long as the runway here is open." The details were quickly arranged. "Major Lane will take the Irregulars to Juba and run the operation from there. I'll stay here and keep the shuttle going from this end." He turned to Jill. "Let's go do it." The two hurried to the Ops Center to set the evacuation in motion.

An hour later, the advance party of crew chiefs and mechanics, along with their baggage, tools, and spare parts, started to load the first Hercules. Lieutenant Colonel Susan Malaby counted heads and sorted out who would shuttle out and who would stay at the mission. She was not surprised when Loni Williams and four crew chiefs volunteered to stay. The two majors who ran Logistics and Facilities conferred and decided which of their troops would stay behind to keep the shuttle going. Like Maintenance they had plenty of volunteers. Master Sergeant Jerry Malone clumped into the Ops Center in full battle gear and caught Allston's attention. "Like Malakal?" he asked.

"Just like Malakal," Allston confirmed. The security cops would be the very last to leave – on board a C-130 if they were lucky.

"Got it," Malone replied. He snapped a salute and left.

Major Dick Lane was next and told Allston that the aircrews were all gathered and ready to go. Did he want to say anything? Allston did. He went into the big room where his pilots, flight engineers, and loadmasters were waiting. For a moment, he couldn't find the right words. Supposedly, these men and women were not the elite, the fighter pilots or the bomber crews, but were trash haulers who moved cargo. They had flown day after day with skill and determination, at the risk of their lives, and had done everything he asked of them.

Now he was going to ask for more and there was no doubt they would give all they could. "You all know the situation," he began, "so I won't try to blow smoke up your backside. The next few days are going to be tough, and most of you are going to get shot at and some are going to be hit. But we've got a job to do and with every sortie you fly, you save innocent men, women, and children from certain death.

"I seriously doubt that the generals and politicians back home give a damn or care about the Dinka or Nuer. But I've seen way too many starving babies, shattered men and women without hope, and mutilated and desecrated bodies not to care."

"That's why we're the Irregulars, Colonel," a voice from the back called. A rumble of approval swept the room and kept growing, and Allston knew, without doubt, that he was in the company of heroes.

"Okay," Allston said, "forget about the twelve hour crew duty day. This is a max effort and fly as long, and as safe as you can. I'm not asking you to fall on your sword and self-destruct, just give it your best shot. Show the world what the Irregulars are all about." He looked around the room, taking them in. Jill stood by the door, her eyes shining. "That's it, folks. Let's make it happen." The Irregulars came to their feet and trailed out the door. He caught a glimpse of Marci Jenkins as she tried to blend in and sneak out.

"Captain Jenkins," he called. "Wait up." He walked towards her, his anger growing with each step. "Didn't I order you to leave?"

"You did, sir."

He pushed his face close to hers, their noses an inch apart. "Then why are you still here?"

"Sir," Jill called, "I have it on the best of authority that a direct order is a point of discussion."

He whirled around and glared at her. She cocked her head and smiled sweetly at him and, for a moment, he was speechless. Then, the irony hit him. Marci Jenkins was doing exactly what he would have done. He turned back to the pilot. "Report to Major Lane and tell him I said to fly your pregnant ass off."

"Yes, sir," Marci said.

"And you," he said to Jill, "be on the first shuttle to Juba."

"Yes, sir," Jill replied.

* * *

Allston kept looking at his watch as he stood on the ramp with Toby. "Any time now," he said. The C-130s had been gone for three hours. The flight time was one hour each way, and with one hour on the ground to turn around at Juba, they should be back at any moment. That meant all four could be turned and launched with a full load of refugees well before first light. He fought the urge to get on the radio and break radio silence, but the SA had to be monitoring their frequencies. "Come on," he urged.

"Did you get all your folks out?" Toby asked.

"We evacuated a hundred," Allston answered. "We got all the spare parts and equipment for the birds and enough tents and MREs to set up shop at Juba." He scanned the dark sky, looking for a telltale shadow moving against the moonlit clouds. He had to talk, anything to break the rising tension. "We got twenty-six folks still here; eight ground crew to turn the birds and eighteen security cops."

"And you," Toby added.

"There," Allston said, pointing to the south. A dark shadow punched through the clouds.

"You got good eyeballs," Toby said.

They watched as the darkened C-130 flew a lights-out approach, the pilots relying on their NVGs. It touched down and taxied in. The rear ramp came down and eight South Sudanese soldiers double-timed off. All were carrying weapons and full backpacks. Private Hans Beck was there to meet them and they quickly climbed on board a waiting truck and sped away. Just as quickly, Loni Williams and one of the loadmasters who had volunteered to stay behind, marshaled over a hundred refugees up the ramp. The Hercules taxied out as the ramp came up.

A lone figure walked towards him. It was Jill. Allston stared at her. "Doesn't anybody understand an order anymore?"

"A point of discussion, sir," Jill answered. Then, "We have a problem at Juba."

* * *

It was a tense meeting as Jill described the situation at Juba. "The South Sudanese closed the airfield and won't let us takeoff. I have no idea why. Major Lane is furious and collected all the money we had to bribe the guards. Then he asked for volunteers to fly a special mission. Marci put a crew together; the copilot was Bard Green, Riley the flight engineer, and MacRay the loadmaster. I asked the soldiers hanging around if any wanted to kill some SA. You saw the eight who took me up on the offer. Colonel Malaby got the Herk refueled, MacRay loaded the soldiers, and Marci just took off, no flight plan, no clearance, nothing. No one stopped them."

"And you decided to come along," Allston said.

"You ordered me to be on the first shuttle to Juba," she said, her voice matter-of-fact. "And I was. You never said I had to stay there."

Vermullen laughed. "You have another lawyer on your hands." He turned serious. "The Legion trained those eight soldiers and they say more want to come."

"Did they say why Juba had closed the runway?" Allston asked. Vermullen shook his head.

"The South Sudanese are split by tribal factions," Toby said. "It's a matter of bribing the right tribe. If we can get D'Na to Juba, she'll find the right people."

"Do we have enough money?" Allston asked.

"The mission has about 50,000 Euros worth of Krugerrands in Juba," Toby replied. "A little gold goes a long way in this part of Africa."

"Reverend, you shock me," Allston said, trying to break the tension. Toby gave him a helpless look, his arms outstretched. Allston's head came up. In the distance he heard a familiar drone. "That's a 130." The sound of the turboprop grew louder. "Let's go howdy the folks. Toby, can you get D'Na to the airstrip ASAP? The Herk won't be on the ground long." Outside, the first light of the new day cracked the far horizon. They ran for their vehicles as the first shrieks of incoming artillery split the air.

TWENTY-FOUR

Mission Awana

Allston floor-boarded the accelerator as he raced for the airfield. Off to his left, dust and dirt mushroomed into the air as another artillery shell exploded. The concussion rocked the pickup as shrapnel cut into the back and shredded a tire. Allston slowed as he regained control. A second round exploded harmlessly further away. "It's not aimed," he shouted.

"Close enough for me!" Jill shouted back. The coppery taste of bile flooded her mouth and she held on, fighting the panic that was tearing at her. Two more explosions pounded at them as they reached the airstrip. Ahead of them, a C-130 came down short final, its nose high in the air. It banged down and reversed its props, roaring to a stop. It turned into the parking area, spun around, and stopped. In the growing light, they could see Marci sitting in the left seat. She gave them thumbs up as the ramp came down. A mass of humanity ran for the aircraft, desperate to escape the hell around them.

Another artillery round exploded. "They're getting closer!" Allston yelled. Two more rounds walked towards the Hercules. "Go! Go! Go!" he yelled, urging the people to hurry. "Damn it," he moaned. "If we had a howitzer with a counter-battery radar we could blow those bastards halfway to Khartoum."

"A howitzer?" Jill shouted, partially deafened by the explosions.

"Yeah. Those sons of bitches are out of range of Idi's mortars. We need something that can reach out and touch them." Jill ran for the C-130. "Where the hell are you going?" he yelled after her. She was the last to board as it started to taxi. Jenkins ran the engines up as she turned onto the runway and accelerated. The nose came up and the big bird lifted into the air. Marci immediately turned out to the right and for a split second, Allston was sure the right wing tip would strike the ground and they would cartwheel in flames. The Herk rolled out, barely a hundred feet above the ground as a shell hit the runway, exploding harmlessly but leaving a nasty crater.

"Cheated death again!" Allston shouted. The C-130 hugged the ground as it disappeared to the south. Another round hit the airfield and Allston ran for one of the freshly dug slit trenches that ringed the airfield. He piled in and covered his head with his arms. A body landed on top of him. It was Williams. A loud explosion washed over them. Then it was silent. Slowly, Williams lifted his head.

"Sorry, Boss," he said, climbing out and standing. Allston stood. His truck was a burning pile of steel and rubber. "Looks like you need another set of wheels," Williams said.

"Well, it did have a flat tire," Allston replied.

Vermullen drove up in his Panhard utility. "Ah, I see you are okay. Your Major, she comes, she goes. Are all your officers like that?"

"She specializes in pissing me off," Allston groused.

"Perhaps you noticed something unusual?" Vermullen asked.

"Other than getting pounded by artillery, not a thing."

"The last few rounds were very accurate," Vermullen said. "If your pilot had climbed out straight ahead, well, do not think about it."

"So what are you saying?"

"They have an artillery spotter on the field."

"Wonderful news," Allston muttered.

"There is some good new, Boss," Williams offered. "We got about a hundred-fifty refugees out."

"Thanks to Marci Jenkins," Allston said.

* * *

"Did D'Na get out on the C-130?" Allston asked Toby. The two men were huddled with Vermullen in the sandbagged bunker the Legion was using as its command post.

"She was with the refugees along with two bodyguards."

"No word, I assume," Allston replied.

Toby shook his head. "The phone line is cut and our radios are all jammed."

"It is the same with us," Vermullen added. "Even our satellite communication frequencies are jammed. It is very sophisticated. Probably Chinese."

"Lovely," Allston groused. A thought niggled at the back of his mind. Then it came to him. "You know, I think we've got one of their satcoms. The last I remember, Sergeant Williams had it." Vermullen nodded at Beck who disappeared out the entrance. "So," Allston continued, "how are we doing on our defenses?"

Vermullen used the wall chart to recap their posture. "We've bunkered about half the DFPs on Charlie Ring, and have eight phone lines strung out to Delta Ring." He touched the eight listening posts on the outer defensive ring that were tied to his command post with landlines. "We placed four where we think the Sudanese will ford the river. The other four are spread out around the perimeter. I have teamed a legionnaire with one of the Juban soldiers to man each one. We have thirty-two more listening posts on Delta Ring and need volunteers to man them. Their job is to warn the LPs with a landline, or the command post here, if they hear or see any activity. They must be very fast runners and know the terrain." Toby said that he would ask for volunteers from the boys and young men at the mission. "It will be very dangerous," Vermullen cautioned. "And if there is an attack, they will be on their own."

"They want to help," Toby assured him.

"They are very brave," Vermullen replied. "That leaves 190 legionnaires to man Charlie Ring. Half of them are pre-positioned, again concentrated where we expect the attack. I'm holding the other half in reserve inside Bravo Ring." Bravo Ring was the minefield that surrounded the mission but not the refugee camp that was closer to the airstrip, over a mile away. "I will deploy them as the attack develops."

"What about the security cops?" Allston asked.

"Their job is to defend the mission," Vermullen said.

"Who activates the mines in the corridors through the minefield?" Toby asked.

"They can be activated either here or by Sergeant Malone in his bunker." The men fell silent and listened as a loud protest echoed from outside. "I believe that is Hans," Vermullen said.

Loni Williams tumbled into the command post followed by Beck. "He didn't understand," Beck explained in French.

"Fuckin' Kraut," Williams muttered.

"Knock it off," Allston said. "Do you remember that satcom you took off the Janjaweed?"

"The guy I morted? I still got it."

"We need it," Allston told him. Williams bobbed his head and hurried out of the bunker. "We're gonna have to work on communications," Allston

251

said. Vermullen filled in more details of his defense plan as they waited. Allston was uncomfortable with the way he relied on his legionnaires to operate so independently in small units, but given their degraded communications, there were no alternatives. Williams was back in minutes and handed over the satcom. Allston turned it over in his hands, examining it. He removed the battery cover and tried to read the markings. "It's Chinese. Why am I not surprised?" He snapped the cover back in place and turned it on. It was not a telephone but a transceiver. He cycled through the channels and found one that was clear of jamming and in use.

"That's Arabic," Toby said. Allston handed him the satcom. Toby listened as his face paled. "The Janjaweed are going to attack the refugee camp after midnight."

* * *

"I wish we had enough mines to protect the refugee camp," Toby said.

Allston cocked an eyebrow at the admission. "When you're on the short end of the stick, mines are the great equalizer." He checked the time. It was midnight. "I hope we've read it right. Otherwise, we've given them a target rich environment." The two men were standing outside the legion's bunkered command post as the last of the refugees from the camp streamed into the mission compound. The shrill scream of an incoming artillery shell arched overhead. They held their breath, waiting to see where it impacted. A dull explosion from the refugee camp echoed over the compound. "How about that?" Allston said. "As advertised."

"I'll be at the hospital," Toby said. There was an infinite sadness in his voice. He knew what was coming. Allston watched the small man make his way through the crowded refugees who were huddled in big groups clutching their meager possessions. Vermullen emerged from the bunker with Beck right behind. Both were in full battle dress. "I'll be at the refugee camp," Vermullen told him.

"I'll be here," Allston replied. Vermullen climbed into his Panhard and Beck drove him slowly through the mission compound.

"You should stay in the bunker with Colonel Allston," Beck told Vermullen.

Vermullen gave a shrug. "As long as they are jamming our radios, it is best I go forward. Besides, Major Mercier can handle it." Vermullen was a master at small unit operations and had turned the refugee camp into an ambush. His natural inclination was to command from the front and that was where they were headed. "Either we are right or we are dead." They drove through the now deserted refugee camp with its empty tents hanging like ghostly shadows in the night. It was deathly silent except for the low rumble of the Panhard's engine. Vermullen keyed his tactical radio and hit the mute button. "The jamming is more intense. Let's talk to the lads."

Beck parked the Panhard near a hardened defensive firing position at the center of the camp that was linked by a field telephone line to the Legion's command post. The DFP was at the apex of a big vee formed by two lines of DFPs that opened to the south, the expected direction of the attack. The four firing positions that made up each arm of the vee created a huge funnel with overlapping fields of fire. The plan was to channel the Janjaweed when they entered the vee into a narrow lane as they passed through the apex and charged into a kill box flanked by Claymore anti-personnel mines. An artillery round drove Vermullen and Beck into the sandbagged foxhole where three legionnaires were hunkered down. Three more artillery rounds walked harmlessly across the camp. "The softening up begins," Vermullen told the men. "Hans, check the men on the left. Encourage them to shoot straight ahead and remember where their comrades are." It was Vermullen's way of telling his legionnaires that he was with them. The old private waited for a pause in the shelling. He bolted out of the DFP and ran into the night.

Vermullen scanned the area with his NVGs. "Waiting is always the hardest part," he told the three men. More artillery shells walked through the camp. Beck was back. The men on the left were ready and relieved that Vermullen was there. "Now tell the ones on the right. Beck grunted an obscenity in German and again disappeared into the night. "Stalwart fellow, Private Beck," Vermullen said. The three legionnaires laughed. The artillery shelling stopped. "Now the attack begins," Vermullen predicted. Beck exploited the lull and piled into the foxhole. The right side was ready.

Sergeant Thomas, one of Vermullen's veterans, heard it first. "Bloody trucks."

"And I promised you Janjaweed," Vermullen replied. "So much the better, is it not? Much more sporting."

"It's not bloody Eton," Thomas replied, his Cockney accent even more pronounced than usual.

Nine trucks charged out of the brush and accelerated straight for the camp. A machine gun was mounted over the cab of each truck and the gunners swept the field in front of them with heavy fire. Sporadic gunfire from the DFPs cut into the trucks, forcing them straight-ahead and deeper into the funnel. A truck was hit and rolled to a stop. The drivers bailed out as the legionnaires unlimbered their assault rifles and shredded the soldiers. The other trucks veered to the right only to encounter concentrated gunfire from the DFPs on that side. A truck exploded as the others cut back. Behind them, a large group of Janjaweed broke from cover at a full gallop and charged after the trucks, heading into the V.

The legionnaires came to their feet and fired, laying down concentrated fire at the oncoming trucks. Another truck fireballed and rolled. The six remaining trucks sped by Vermullen's DFP and into the deserted camp. Vermullen didn't hesitate. He reached for a small green plastic detonator and flipped open the guard on top. He mashed the trigger. The line of Claymore mines behind the DFP erupted, each sending a cloud of over 700 steel balls into the trucks, ripping and shredding the men and trucks. The carnage was absolute.

"Those were meant for the bloody Janjaweed!" Thomas shouted.

Vermullen cranked the phone and called his command post. He ordered Mercier to send Bravo Company, half of his reserve, to the refugee camp to block access to the mission compound. "I estimate over 500 Janjaweed are in the camp," he told Mercier.

"Please save some for us," Mercier replied.

*   *   *

Allston stayed out of the way as Mercier ordered forty legionnaires to the refugee camp. No sooner had they left than all four lines to the listening posts along the river lit up. Mercier listened, his face grim. "Armored vehicles and APCs are fording the river," he told the men in the bunker. "This is more than a reconnaissance in force." He called Captain Bouchard over and quickly identified which DFPs on Charlie Ring to man. "Take every man you can find and hold until we can disengage from the refugee camp and reinforce you," he told the young captain.

Bouchard actually smiled. "That won't be necessary."

"That is very fortunate," Mercier shot back. Bouchard snapped an open-handed salute and ran from the bunker.

"Was the attack on the refugee camp a diversion?" Allston asked.

"Oh, yes. It was a classic maneuver, very well executed. But as you Americans say, we honored the threat." He thought for a moment. "Sacrificing the Janjaweed could have been a mistake."

A teen-age boy burst into the bunker. He was winded from a long run and his eyes were wide with fear. He babbled in Dinka, which neither man understood. Allston grabbed the phone to Outback, the security police bunker. "We need a translator," he told Malone. "Send Williams here ASAP." Now they had to wait.

254

The Peacemakers

* * *

Vermullen emptied his FAMAS at the Janjaweed thundering past his DFP. He jammed a fresh clip into the over-heated weapon and fired another burst. Beside him, Beck lobbed round after round of grenades at the horsemen as they swept by. The ground was littered with bodies and horses but still the Janjaweed kept coming. The green light on the telephone line blinked. In the chaos, Vermullen answered, still firing short bursts as he listened. "Excellent," he shouted, breaking the connection. "Bravo Company is through the minefield and blocking them," he told the four legionnaires. "We have them in the bag. Do we have any more Claymores?"

"Ten," Thomas, the Cockney sergeant, answered.

"Good. You take four and give one to each DFP on the left. Tell them to position them to face south, away from our DFPs, and to only fire at the Janjaweed after they have passed by. Hans, take four and do the same on the right. Go!" Thomas handed Beck four small canvas bags. The English Legionnaire slung four over his shoulder and followed Beck. A storm of small-arms fire echoed from the side of the camp nearest the mission. "I believe the Janjaweed have met Bravo Company," Vermullen said to the two legionnaires still in the bunker. "Place the last two Claymores there and there, facing each other." He pointed to where he wanted the Claymores, one on each side of the kill box. "Go." He didn't have time to explain and the legionnaires reacted instinctively, leaving him alone in the DFP. He cranked the phone to the command post but it was dead, the line cut.

Beck and Thomas were back in time to see their comrades rig the last two Claymores. They snapped open the short legs that held each mine upright and placed the side with the Chinese markings facing outward. Each weighed less than four pounds and were extremely effective killing machines out to fifty yards. The legionnaires attached the detonator wires and ran for the DFP. "Brilliant," Thomas muttered. "The Janjaweed are shitting their knickers and only know one way out, right through here. Those two Claymores are for traffic control and the others will collect the exit toll." The pounding of hooves confirmed his guess.

* * *

Williams kept telling the teenager to talk more slowly. "He's a volunteer manning a listening post," Williams explained. He spoke to the boy and pointed to the chart at the same time. The teenager jabbed a finger at the chart and spoke rapidly. "He says an armored car and ten soldiers are stopped here."

Where did they come from? Allston wondered. "Okay, who have we got left?" "Only your police," Mercier replied. He cranked the telephone and called Malone. He quickly recapped the situation and listened for a moment. Then, "The boy is here and he can show you. We have a Shipon." He broke the connection. "Malone will be here shortly."

Malone and Sergeant Lee Ford made it in two minutes. "We're it," he told Allston. "I think you remember Sergeant Ford. He speaks Dinka and is wide awake now. I've got one guy left manning Outback. Everyone else is posted out with orders to fall back on the hospital. So how do you use a Shipon?"

Mercier opened a case and handed Malone the shoulder-held anti-tank missile. "It is good for 600 meters, but a shame to waste it on an armored car." He went through the aiming and firing sequence. "Beware of the blowback. It can kill you."

Malone gestured at the Dinka teenager. "Tell him to show us the way." Airman Ford spoke a few words in Dinka and the boy nodded. "Let's go," Malone said. The Dinka understood and led the way out.

* * *

The horsemen came directly at Vermullen's DFP, retracing their path through the camp in a desperate attempt to escape. Vermullen waited, trying to determine where they were the most concentrated. Deciding they were massed to his right, he triggered the Claymore on his left. The mine exploded, sending a hail of death into the leading Janjaweed, cutting and tearing into the horses and their riders. Instinctively, the survivors veered away, into their more densely packed comrades on Vermullen's right. Again, he waited. At the last critical moment, he triggered the Claymore on his right. But now the carnage was more brutal as the Claymore's fourteen ounces of C-4 explosive sent a cloud of steel fragments into the densely packed Janjaweed. The unhurt men and horses immediately behind piled into their downed comrades, adding to the chaos as the rest split around the DFP, racing for safety. The five legionnaires in the DFP came to their feet, firing into the retreating horsemen. They fired in short bursts, emptying their magazines and quickly reloading. Still the horsemen surged past, swinging wider and wider to avoid the slaughtered horses and riders.

The last surge of Janjaweed raced past the DFP, the riders frantically urging their horses on and not bothering to return fire. The last Claymores started to detonate as the legionnaires timed their detonations to max effect, cutting into the backside of the retreating horses and men. The sound of gunfire and running horses gave way to the bellow of baying horses and screaming men dying in the night.

Vermullen reloaded, careful not to touch the overheated barrel of his rifle. "An ugly business," he muttered. "Hans, fire a flare." Beck did as ordered and a single flare arced over the killing ground, illuminating the carnage around them.

"What now?" Thomas asked.

"We wait," Vermullen answered. "If I am right, Bravo Company will be needed elsewhere shortly, and is probably withdrawing back into the mission." A few minutes later, another green flare arced over the killing field, this one from Bravo Company. They were withdrawing into the mission. "Now you must mop up," Vermullen said. He climbed out of the DFP and ran for the Panhard with Beck in hot pursuit.

"Bloody hell, what are we supposed to do with the survivors?" Thomas yelled.

"What survivors?" Beck shouted back.

Vermullen was surprised to find the utility truck undamaged. Beck climbed in behind the steering wheel while Vermullen took one last look around. Gunshots echoed over them as the legionnaires went about their work. Vermullen snorted and climbed in. "The command post," he said. Beck slipped the truck into gear as more gunfire split the night air.

* * *

Malone ran through the night, hard pressed to follow the nimble Dinka. Ford, the other security cop, was right behind him, breathing hard. The teenager stopped and knelt, motioning them to do the same. Malone almost ran into him and came down beside him. Ford piled into him. "Sorry," he said, gasping for air. The Dinka pointed into the night. Ford's night vision was superb and he looked to the side, getting the maximum definition. "Sweet Mother of God," he whispered. "There's two of 'em, not one."

Malone turned on his NVGs and waited for the image to stabilize. Slowly, the greenish image came into focus. Two, eight-wheeled armored personnel carriers were parked beside the road with their side hatches and gun ports open. A machine gun was mounted in a turret aft of the driver's compartment. "They look like BTR-80s," Malone said in a low voice. He could feel the Dinka beside him shake from fear. "Tell him to take off," he said to Ford. The cop whispered a few words and the teenager disappeared into the night, running for safety. "When in doubt, run like hell," Malone muttered. Far to their right, towards the river, they heard machine gun fire followed by two sharp explosions. An artillery shell screamed as it cut an arc overhead, striking the mission. "Sounds like things are heating up," Malone allowed. The diesel engine of the lead BTR rumbled to life and most of the soldiers climbed aboard. The second BTR cranked to life.

"There's nothing between them and the mission," Ford said.

"Except the mine field," Malone said, "and us." More explosions from the river echoed over them. "That's different," he said. "How many rounds we got for the Shipon?"

"Just the one in the launcher," Ford told him.

The first BTR started to move, coming down the road straight at them. Malone fumbled with the missile, trying to recall Mercier's hurried instructions. "Give it to me," Ford said, taking the Shipon away from him.

"Okay, take him out. Try to block the road."

"Got it," Ford said. He rolled to his knees and lifted the Shipon to his right shoulder. He dropped the monopod under the muzzle to support its weight and stabilize it. His left hand grasped the monopod while his right hand fingered the fire control lever. He laid his right cheek against the tube and sighted through the eyepiece. Now he waited. He almost dropped the Shipon when the Dinka teenager skidded to his knees beside him. Two more teenagers were right behind him. They were each carrying a FAMAS and one had a bag of hand grenades, which he quickly passed out.

"Welcome back," Malone said, doubting they understood a word he said. The lead BTR was moving faster now, with the second close behind. A few soldiers straggled along behind. Ford laid the crosshairs over the driver's window and rotated the fire control lever to the first detent. "Mercier said it takes less than a second for the sight to resolve and set the aim point," Malone offered. Ford counted slowly to three and rotated the lever full down. The whoosh of the missile and plume of flame shooting out the back surprised them all. The missile tracked true and Malone was certain the soldiers had seen the fiery blowback. "Run!" he shouted. He sprang to his feet and ran to his right, angling away from the BTRs. Ford dropped the launcher tube and followed as the missile hit the lead BTR less than an inch from its aim point. The tandem-shaped charge punched through the relatively thin-skinned armored personnel carrier, allowing the second stage to detonate inside. It was a massive case of overkill and the second explosion shredded the men inside and blew the engine out the back, into the second oncoming BTR.

Malone ran harder with Ford and the three boys still behind. The machine gun on the second BTR raked the night, kicking up dirt around them. One of the boys stumbled as a burst of gunfire cut the air above him. Then he was up and running again. The BTR pushed around the burning hulk as the sharp crack of an M-16 echoed. Ford had fallen into a prone firing position and was trying to draw the gunner's attention so the others could flank the BTR. The gas tank on the burning personnel carrier exploded, coating the moving BTR with burning diesel fuel. It still came on, its machine gun firing wildly as flames washed over its carapace. One of the Dinka teenagers dropped his FAMAS and ran towards the BTR, pulling the pin of a grenade as he zigzagged.

A gun port on the left side of the BTR flipped open and the muzzle of an AK-47 poked out. The shooter mashed the trigger and emptied the magazine in a vain attempt to cut down the running Dinka. He missed and the Dinka reached the BTR. He tossed the grenade through the open gun port and fell to the ground. Nothing happened and Malone swore loudly. The side hatch of the BTR started to open as the grenade exploded, ripping into the men inside and blowing the hatch down. A secondary explosion rocked the BTR. "Son of a bitch," Malone breathed. In the heat of battle, his sense of time had slowed down.

The Dinka jumped to his feet in victory and waved his arms in victory. A burst of gunfire cut into him. "Get the bastards," Ford yelled as he squeezed off round after round. It felt good and he kept firing. Suddenly, a hand clasped his right shoulder.

"It's okay," Malone said. "We got 'em all." They ran for the destroyed BTRs and reached the Dinka teenager. "He's still alive," Malone yelled. "Let's get him to the hospital."

* * *

"LPs Four and Five report tanks are in the water," Mercier told Vermullen. The big Frenchman studied the chart on the wall of the command post and pinpointed the two LPs that flanked the river ford on the southern bank. The telephone line to LP Four buzzed and Mercier pressed his headset against his head to hear. "*Merde!*" he shouted. "Two tanks are across and eight more are in the water." The two Frenchmen were speaking English so Allston and Williams could understand.

"Where's Captain Bouchard?" Vermullen asked.

"The lines are dead," Mercier answered. "He was on Charlie Ring opposite the ford."

"I'm going forward," Vermullen said. He would lead from the front. He picked up his FAMAS and waited as an artillery shell whistled overhead. A dull explosion reverberated through the command post. Then it was silent. Vermullen snorted in contempt. "Harassing fire only." He motioned at Beck and darted out the entrance.

Allston analyzed the frequency and pattern of the shelling. As best he could tell, the SA only had two artillery tubes and, given the sporadic rate of fire, a limited number of rounds to waste on barrage fire. Only the airfield had been subject to aimed fire and only when a C-130 was on the ground. "Their spotter is at the airfield and doesn't appear to be moving," he finally said.

"He must be dug in," Mercier replied. "He's probably waiting for one of your aircraft to land."

"We've got a security police team posted at the airfield," Allston said. "Maybe they can find him before the next Herk lands."

"That will not be easy," Mercier said. The telephone line to LP Four buzzed and Mercier hit the toggle switch to listen. He looked at Allston. "All ten tanks are across the river. If they break through Charlie Ring, I will have to close the corridors through the minefield. Perhaps it would be best if you went to the hospital."

"I got a better idea," Allston said, fed up with being on the sidelines. "How many Shipons you got left?" Mercier replied that he had four launch tubes and sixteen missiles in the command post. "I need one launcher and at least four missiles. Get the rest to the cops." He turned to Williams. "You know how to use one?" Williams shook his head, not sure what was happening. "Time to learn. We're going to give Idi some close air support."

Mercier broke out a launcher, loaded it, and again went through the arming and launch sequence. Satisfied the two Americans had the drill down, he handed them two fiberglass ammo boxes that resembled thick briefcases. "Two missiles are in each carrier," he said.

"Get the rest to the cops," Allston ordered, "and get the word out not to shoot at any low flying aircraft." He picked up the two boxes. "Let's go kill some tanks," he told Williams. He disappeared out the entrance.

"What ever happened to volunteering?" Williams muttered, following his commander.

*　*　*

Beck's NVGs gave him a diabolic appearance as he hunched over the steering wheel and reminded Vermullen of a gargoyle on a cathedral. They had barely cleared the minefield when a mortar barrage walked towards them. Beck stomped on the brakes and the two men bailed. Vermullen hit the ground and rolled under the Panhard. Beck was already there. Explosions rocked the truck. "They're good," Beck allowed. The barrage ended and they quickly crawled out from under the truck as steam poured from the radiator. Shrapnel from a mortar round had cut into the grill but missed them. "Better on foot," Beck grunted. Without a word, he took the lead and Vermullen followed. The logic was simple: in the confusion of combat, recognition by friendlies was a problem and it was Beck's job to take any friendly round.

The private stopped when he saw what looked like a sandbagged foxhole. "*Mistral*," he said in a low voice. It was the recognition code.

"*Alouette*," a voice answered. They were cleared to advance. The two men ran forward and jumped into the DFP as another mortar barrage opened up.

"Where's Captain Bouchard?" Vermullen asked the three legionnaires in the DFP.

One of the legionnaires gestured to his right. "In the next hole. He's wounded." The mortars stopped and the distinctive clank of a tank's track grew louder. One of the legionnaires came to his feet holding a Shipon. He laid it across a sandbag as gunfire raked the night. A slug ripped into his helmet, killing him instantly, and throwing him back into Vermullen.

Beck never hesitated. He grabbed the Shipon and carefully sighted. "Clear," he said, warning them he was about to fire.

"All clear," Vermullen replied, confirming that no one was behind the missile. Beck didn't move as the clanking tracks grew louder. Vermullen and the other legionnaire came to their feet and fired, emptying their magazines into the infantry following the tank bearing down on them. Beck depressed the fire control lever to the first detent, counted to two, and mashed the lever full down.

* * *

Allston gunned the truck onto the airstrip and slammed to a halt behind the shed where the Pilatus Porter was hangared. He motioned to Williams and they pushed the hangar doors back. Allston ran to the aircraft and kicked the wheel chocks free. He slid both cargo doors back along the fuselage and showed Williams where to sit. "When we see a tank, I'll set up a pylon turn like we did at Malakal, and you take it out with a Shipon. Be sure to keep the launcher's breech pointed out the other side or the blowback will fry us."

He rigged a tie-down strap to the deck. "Sit on the floor and strap in with this. It's gonna get rough and we don't need you falling out. Got it?"

"Boss, I ain't got a clue."

Allston gave the sergeant his best grin. "Play it by ear." He climbed into the pilot's seat and cranked the turboprop to life as he adjusted his NVGs. He glanced back at Williams to see if he was ready. The sergeant was sitting Buddha-like sideways on the cargo deck, the tie down strap across his lap, and facing out the left side of the aircraft. The Shipon was clutched tightly to his chest. "You ready?" Allston shouted.

"Do I have to do this?" a very worried Williams shouted back.

Allston ignored him and pushed the throttle forward. The Porter roared out of the hangar straight ahead, across the parking ramp. Allston pulled back on the stick and they broke free of the ground before reaching the runway. They climbed into the night.

* * *

Beck's aim was good and the Shipon hit the tank on the driver's side. A secondary explosion washed over the legionnaires huddled in the DFP as an artillery round cooked off inside the tank. A pillar of flame lit the night. Vermullen snapped up his NVGs, lifted his head above the revetment, and quickly scanned the scene in front of him. He pulled back to safety as a burst of machine gun fire ripped harmlessly into the sandbags above his head. "I count nine more Type 62s," he said. The Russian-designed and Chinese-built Type 62 main battle tank was the mainstay of the Sudanese Army. "Range, 800 meters. The clever devils know they're out of range and are regrouping." Another burst of heavy machine gun fire cut into the DFP. Beck gave him a questioning look. "And you think we should do the same," Vermullen said.

"They know we're here," Beck said calmly as he reloaded the Shipon.

Vermullen made a decision. He keyed his tactical radio but the jamming was still intense. He addressed the two legionnaires by their first names. "Henri, alert the DFPs on our left that we are going to pull back through the minefield when I fire a green starburst flare. Phillip, do the same on the right. Go." The two legionnaires rolled out the back of the DFP and disappeared into the night.

"What about Captain Bouchard?" Beck asked.

"You were trained as a medic. Go take care of him and move him to the hospital as soon as you can. Go." Beck didn't hesitate and followed the other two legionnaires, leaving Vermullen alone. He laid his last missile next to the loaded Shipon. Diesel engines roared, shortly followed by the clanking of tank tracks. His lips cracked in a little smile as he sighted the Shipon and fired.

* * *

Allston inched the Porter down another ten feet and skimmed the ground as they flew towards the river. He pulled up to clear a low tree and bright flames from a burning tank washed out his NVGs. Allston snapped them up as his eyes adjusted to the night. He inched the Porter back down and chanced a look towards the burning tank. A line of tracers cut the night and he followed them back to a moving shadow – another tank. "Tallyho the fox!" he called. "Time to rock and roll. Williams, you ready?"

A simple "Yeah" answered him.

Allston climbed a hundred feet and set up a left pylon turn. Williams fired two seconds later. Allston dove as the missile streaked towards the tank. The tank fireballed.

Below him, Vermullen's missile cut through the night and another tank exploded in flames. "Someone down there can shoot," Allston shouted. "Oh, shit!" He counted seven more moving tanks in the burning light. "We're engaged." He pulled back on the stick and the Porter climbed steeply. He immediately leveled off and set up a left pylon turn around the lead tank. Two lines of tracers reached up and bracketed the slow moving Porter. Williams fired.

* * *

Vermullen reloaded and sighted the Shipon on the lead tank. He depressed the fire lever to the first detent. The sound of the Porter's turboprop engine stopped him and he released the lever, not firing his last missile. The flash of a missile launching lighted the Porter as the missile homed on the tank. Vermullen grunted as the tank disappeared in a bright flash and a thunderous explosion. Flames reached into the night sky and smoke rolled over the other tanks, obscuring them. The air cleared and he saw a burning hulk where four men had lived and breathed moments before. The turret was upside down thirty yards away with its 100mm rifled gun skewered into the ground, canting the turret in an upward angle. The searchlight mounted on the turret was still on, casting a bright light on another tank moving towards him. Not believing his luck, Vermullen quickly sighted on the tank. He depressed the fire lever. The sight stabilized and he mashed the lever. Again, the missile tracked true as more machine gun fire ripped into his DFP. He hunkered down as the tank erupted in a double explosion, deafening him. It was his last missile and Vermullen dropped the tube. He picked up his FAMAS and came to his feet in one fluid motion.

A tank was advancing directly towards him with a squad of soldiers following close behind. He laid a fresh magazine on the sandbag beside him and hummed a refrain from an old song. *"Non je ne regrette rien,"*

* * *

Allston reacted instinctively without thinking, the product of years of training and experience. He had a mental image of the battle around him that few men ever achieve in combat. It was reality, focused and fine tuned, and made the difference between life and death. He was skimming the ground at 130 knots, a snail's pace by his normal standards. But he was so low that the advancing tanks could not bring their weapons to bear. He turned towards them and overflew Vermullen's DFP. "Lock and load," he shouted at Williams. "We're engaged." Again, he ballooned the Porter into a left pylon turn, and two seconds later, Williams fired a missile. Submachine gun fire raked the side of the Porter as Allston dove for the ground.

* * *

Vermullen thumbed the FAMAS to single-shot and fired as Williams' missile hit the tank. The soldiers firing at him disappeared in the tank's fireball. Vermullen kept firing, methodically killing the soldiers around the second tank coming at him.

* * *

Allston flicked on his instrument lights to check for damage. In less than a second, he had scanned the instruments and turned the lights off. Everything was working as advertised. At the same time, he detected movement on the ground in his peripheral vision. He jinked the Porter hard, its wing tips almost hitting the low scrub below him, as he turned into the movement. A tank was less than a hundred yards away from Vermullen's position. "Tank in sight," he told Williams. They had three more missiles and he intended to use them. "Ready."

A very weak "Ready" answered him.

264

"We're engaged." Again, he jinked hard as he turned into the tank. An inner voice warned him that the soldiers knew how he attacked, always turning to the left in a low pylon turn. "No turn this time," he shouted. "Nail him as fast as you can." There was no answer as he closed on the tank.

At four hundred meters, Allston lifted the Porter up to fifty feet and banked hard to his right, turning his tail to the tank. He stomped on the left rudder pedal and yawed the nose to the left as he played with the ailerons and power. The agile Porter skidded sideways, tracking away from the tank. He looked to his left and could see the tank at their eight o'clock position. "Fire!" he yelled. He was answered when the blowback from the missile shot out the right side of the cargo compartment. Allston did a hard reverse and looked to his right in time to see the tank disappear in a bright flash. The concussion rocked the Porter, and an eerie light revealed a scene of death and destruction. He jinked back to his left and his eyes swept the battlefield. The mental picture he held in his mind matched what he saw on the ground. Six tanks were burning in the night. The closest one was less than fifty yards from Vermullen's foxhole. The four remaining tanks were retreating to the river, leaving the infantrymen behind. "You got 'em," he shouted at Williams.

"Boss, I'm hurt," Williams said. Allston could barely hear him and he twisted around. Williams was slumped forward over the launcher as blood spread across the cargo deck. Allston headed for the mission.

* * *

Vermullen jammed a fresh clip into his FAMAS and squeezed off a single round. His face was impassive as he picked off one man after another as they retreated. It was all in a day's work. Smoke from the destroyed tank nearest him rolled across the terrain, blocking his aim. He rolled out of his foxhole and ran towards the burning tank, using the smoke as cover. He skirted the tank in time to see three soldiers running for the river, their backs to him. He thumbed the FAMAS to full automatic and cut them down as he ran. Ahead, he saw a single soldier. Vermullen snapped his short bayonet onto the barrel as he chased the man down. In his panic, the soldier never saw nor heard the killing machine that ran over him, driving the bayonet deep into his back. Vermullen stopped to wrench the bayonet free. A sixth sense tingled in his subconscious and he fell to the ground behind the dying soldier. A long burst of submachine gun fire cut into the soldier's body. Vermullen squinted into the dark, finding the shooter. He lay motionless in the dark, his eyes locked on his target. His right hand moved slightly as he keyed his tactical radio. All jamming had stopped and the listening posts along the river reported in. The tanks were in the water and swimming for safety. "Do not let the stragglers escape," he ordered.

Smoke rolled over him as he came to his feet and moved forward, stalking the man who had shot at him moments before.

* * *

Allston circled the mission looking for a place to land. He picked the road leading to the hospital and flicked on the Porter's landing lights. He buzzed the road to clear off the two vehicles and the two dozen or so people heading for the hospital. He circled to land and stalled the aircraft just as he touched down. He stomped on the brakes, dragging the Porter to a halt in 250 feet. He had to swerve past a truck at the last minute and stopped outside the hospital. He shut the engine down and jumped out, pulling the unconscious Williams out of the cargo compartment. He carried him up the steps and into the waiting arms of a nurse and an orderly.

It was triage in the rough and the nurse quickly checked Williams' breathing as the orderly applied pressure to the wound, slowing the flow of blood. She probed the gaping wound on his left side and made a decision. "He's next. Take him inside." She shined a flashlight on Allston, studying his face. "Your sergeant is a very lucky man," she said. "You're dehydrated. Drink some water." She pointed to an old woman sitting on the veranda and tending a box filled with a hodgepodge of plastic water bottles. Then she was gone.

The woman handed Allston a water bottle and he sat on the hospital steps. He drained the bottle. The eastern horizon glowed with the first light of the new day. Heavy smoke from two burning buildings billowed past as Beck trudged towards him carrying Bouchard in a fireman's carry across his shoulders. He was fatigued to the point of collapse and his steps were faltering. Allston rushed down to help him. "Wounded man!" Allston called. "We need help here." The nurse was there with her orderly. She quickly examined the French officer, impressed with the way Beck had dressed his wounds.

"You, my gorgeous man," she said to Bouchard, "are going to live, but you must wait for now."

"Can I help?" Allston asked.

"Keep him company," the nurse replied. She turned to the next arrivals. It was Malone and Ford with the wounded Dinka teenager. Again, the nurse performed triage. She shook her head and told Malone to take him to the far side of the veranda. "Did you get the armored car?" Allston asked.

"There were two," Malone answered. "We got 'em." He touched the teenager. "Thanks to him." He carried the dying boy to an open spot on the porch.

Allston sat beside Bouchard as the artillery rounds tapered off and stopped. A constant flow of wounded were streaming into the hospital. Bouchard's eyes blinked. He was conscious. "What happened?" Allston asked.

Bouchard's voice was barely audible. "It started with two BTRs probing for a weak spot. We let them go by to lure the others into range." That explained the two BTRs on the road that Malone destroyed. "There were twelve more BTRs. They were no match for our Shipons. It was a turkey shoot. Then a squadron of tanks waded across supported by infantry. Their officers are idiots and they are not very good but their men are very brave. I was wounded and not sure what happened after that. When Beck found me, I knew Colonel Vermullen was there."

"We stopped them," Allston said.

"*C'est bon*," Bouchard answered. He looked at Allston, a half smile on his lips. "My wife's name is Clarice. Please tell her that I love her more than life itself but I had to follow . . . "

"You can tell her yourself," Allston said softly. But he was speaking to a lifeless body. Shaken, he walked to the edge of the veranda. He made no attempt to wipe away the tears streaming down his cheeks.

A giant of a man walked out of the smoke drifting through the compound. Behind him, the first light of dawn cast long shadows, partially hiding and then revealing his gaunt face. Dust and smoke swirled around his feet as he walked towards the hospital, his long strides measured and steady. Two legionnaires followed him at a respectful distance, and even the irrepressible children moved aside and did not walk beside him, imitating his bold stride. Allston watched as the man climbed the steps and did not recognize Pierre Vermullen, the man he called "friend." The American shook his head to clear the cobwebs and saw the man he knew. Yet he didn't know him at all. Vermullen's only allegiance was to the Legion and his men, not to a belief or his country, and for them he would willingly sacrifice his life. Then Allston understood. He was looking at an incarnation of the ancient warrior, the mythical figure who emerges from the mists of time and only lives for combat. And, for a split second, he was looking in a mirror.

"Is this all I am?" he wondered aloud.

TWENTY-FIVE

The Capitol, Washington D.C.

*R*ichards took a deep breath as the door closed behind her. She was standing in a small anteroom off the main committee hearing room, the private preserve of the congressional elite, an inner sanctum where political deals had been cut for generations, careers made and broken, and love affairs consummated. It was a political holy of holies. The door opened and the Speaker of the House marched in followed by his ever-present personal aide. The Speaker was tall, lean, and erect with a mane of salt and pepper hair. His blue eyes sparkled with a rare intelligence, and at sixty-four, he was considered one of the most handsome men in Washington. "Yvonne," he called, his voice rich and commanding. "Thank you for coming."

She laughed. "Did I have a choice?" They embraced.

"You always have a choice, m'dear." His voice changed as he turned to business. "I've scheduled you for last on the agenda, after Fitzgerald and Misner testify. Your job is to drive a spike into the bastards' hearts."

"I can do that," she promised.

He nodded slowly, his eyes closed. Her words were music to his ears. "Thank you, m'dear. We must get together for dinner." He squeezed her hand, the promise of things to come. He spoke quietly to his aide and bolted out the door, surprisingly quick and light on his feet.

The aide opened her planner and called up the Speaker's schedule. "Would tomorrow night be acceptable?" She didn't wait for an answer. "You will be traveling with the Speaker on his private jet, so pack an overnight bag. May I suggest a simple black dress with high-heeled pumps? The Speaker likes stiletto heels. A short black negligee with a low back is preferred."

"Yes, of course," she stammered.

"Excellent," the aide replied. "I'll send a car at six-thirty. Please be ready." She snapped her planner closed and followed the Speaker.

Richards was stunned, not believing what had just happened. She had been rendered like meat on the hoof. She had been in the Air Force twenty-two years and hit on many times, but not once subject to sexual harassment or treated like a commodity plucked off a shelf. She forced her breathing to slow and forced it out of her mind. The Speaker's voice came over a small speaker on a small and exquisite antique Chippendale writing desk in the corner. She sat in the elegant chair and listened. His voice filled the anteroom as he called the hearing to order and announced they were in closed session. She fully expected the intercom to go dead but she could still hear every word. In Washington, information was the currency of power and not to be denied to the inner circle of players who had access to the anteroom. But she was not a member of that group, which meant the Speaker was paying her, in advance, for services rendered. A raging anger swept over her.

She listened as Fitzgerald was sworn in and answered the committee's questions. She gave him high marks for his direct and complete answers. Never once did he spin his relationship with Allston and readily admitted he was in daily contact with the 4440th. When asked why, his answer impressed her. "While the command and control of the detachment was given to the United Nations peacekeeping mission, the welfare of our people remained with the Air Force. However, there is no command protocol in place to deal with this situation, which is why I became personally involved. I was, and remain, committed to the safety of our men and women. This committee has seen the spread of violence in southern Sudan, which is why I ordered the 4440th to pull back."

General Harold Misner, the Chairman of the Joint Chiefs, testified next. After the standard formalities, he unloaded on the committee. "I cannot express my concern over this new policy of placing our men and women under the United Nations without an American general officer heading the chain of command. I believe it is a sure formula for disaster." The committee erupted in bitter accusations and the Speaker was barely able to control the committee until Misner was excused.

The vice chairman of the committee, one of the Speaker's implacable political enemies, called for a surprise witness, Tara Scott. Again, the committee room raged with debate. Finally, the Speaker gave in and allowed the actress to be called. The room fell silent as Tara entered and was sworn in. She concluded her opening statement with, "I would remind you that our Peacekeepers have saved over 26,000 men, women, and children from certain genocide in the Sudan. I was there when they were attacked by Janjaweed militia and had to fight for their lives. I know the price the men and women of the 4440th have paid."

Civility prevailed as the committee questioned her. Upset at the turn of events, the Speaker tried a diversionary tactic. "But the commander of the peacekeepers, Lieutenant Colonel Allston, has been accused of war crimes. Specifically, torturing prisoners."

"That accusation is based on a video my cameraman shot at night," Tara replied. "It was recorded at a great distance, during the attack. I know all of you have seen it, but what you did not see was Lieutenant Colonel Allston's reaction. Nor did you see the savagery of the attack by the Janjaweed. If I may, I would like to show the committee the unedited video." The intercom was silent as the video played and Richards flinched when she heard gasps come from the committee. Then it was over. "Tonight, this video will be part of a special program that I am hosting on CNC-TV. For the first time, the American public will see exactly what it means to be a peacekeeper in that ravaged part of the world." Every man and women in the room ran for political cover. The actress had a cause and the attention of the media. Before she could do further damage, the Speaker excused her.

Richards pulled into herself, and calculated her next move. Tara Scott had changed the political landscape. The door opened and a teenage page, a pretty sixteen-year-old girl, held the door for Fitzgerald. "Please wait in here," the girl said. "General Richards, the committee has requested your presence."

Richards nodded at Fitzgerald as she followed the page into the committee room. She took her place at the witness table. Her heart beat fast knowing that Fitzgerald was listening to every word. The Speaker smiled knowingly at her.

Mission Awana

Beck fought the battered Land Rover he had appropriated from the mission to a stop at the side of the airstrip's parking apron. Allston and Vermullen climbed out in time to see the C-17 turn final. "A most welcome sight," Vermullen said.

"And a total surprise," Allston added. He keyed his handheld UHF radio and called the big cargo plane. "Dumbo, be advised we are experiencing sporadic artillery fire. Exercise minimum time on the ground."

A cool voice answered. "Copy all, Awana. Arriving passengers advised of situation. Min time on the ground."

Automatically, Allston scanned the big bird, checking the landing gear. "Gear down," he transmitted. "Cleared to land." The pilot answered with two clicks. "Must be an old fighter jock," Allston said. The two men watched as the plane touched down and rolled out. It turned off the runway onto the parking apron as its rear door came up and ramp lowered. Two crew chiefs guided the bird as it turned on the small ramp, using every inch. "Jesus H. Christ," Allston swore. "That's Williams. What in hell is he doing here?" The big Globemaster stopped briefly as a self-propelled howitzer clanked down the ramp and onto the tarmac.

"Ah, very good," Vermullen said. "That's your Paladin, with a 155mm howitzer. He stomped a foot. "That rotating antenna bar on top is a counter-battery radar."

The C-17 swung onto the runway as its engines spun up. The Paladin came towards them as the shriek of an incoming artillery round split the air. The C-17 was moving as the Paladin's long barrel swung to the north. It fired a single round without stopping. Vermullen and Allison sprinted for a slit trench and piled in as the incoming round hit the ramp. The Paladin fired again as another incoming round screamed its arrival. Allston's head darted up for a quick glance. The C-17 lifted off as the Paladin fired a third time. Allston buried his head as the round hit the runway. Silence ruled as the smoke and dust cleared. The Paladin's anti-battery radar had tracked the trajectory of the incoming artillery shells and backtracked them to their location. The Paladin's computers had slewed the big cannon and the crew had fired three rounds, taking out both artillery pieces shelling the airfield.

Allston stood and scanned the sky. The C-17 was safely climbing out.

The Paladin spun around on its track and clanked to a stop beside Allston. The commander's hatch flipped opened and a tall and lanky young man stood, the upper half of his body well clear of the turret. He was dressed in civvies but his haircut and bearing were US Marine. He snapped a sharp salute. "Corporal Rickert . . . ah . . . ah . . . sorry, sir. Richie Rickert reporting for duty." He lifted himself out of the hatch and waited. Jill's head popped up and she climbed out. The marine helped her down the side of the turret and onto the ground. "My apologies ma'am," he said. "It is cramped inside."

"And very noisy," Jill added.

"Where did you find them?" Allston asked her.

"Djibouti." She lowered her voice as the gunner, loader, and driver climbed out. Like Rickert, they were wearing jeans and T-shirts. "They're Marines, but think of them as temporary civilians."

"How did you make that happen?" Allston asked. Jill didn't answer. He didn't need to know that the Boys in the Basement were involved and pulling strings. She introduced the four young men.

"Welcome to Mission Awana," Allston said. "You could not have arrived at a better time." He introduced Vermullen and asked what was on the pallet.

"Glad to be here, sir," Rickert said, still uncomfortable in his new role. He pointed to the pallet. "Those are spare parts for the Paladin and forty rounds, a mix of high explosive and anti-tank." A wicked grin played across his mouth and quickly disappeared. "We got two Copperheads on board." The Copperhead was a smart artillery projectile that guided itself to a laser designated target, and was bad news for any tank that came within its range.

"We'll make good use of those," Vermullen promised. "For now, stay and operate from the airfield." The Paladin was a great deterrent but it was also a target that he wanted as far from the mission as possible.

"What do you need?" Allston asked.

"Diesel fuel," Rickert replied. "We got our field gear on the bustle." The bustle was the equipment rack welded on the back of the turret. He shifted his weight from one foot to another. "Sir, we. . . ah. . . were wondering. . . if you might still have some of those hats."

"You bet we do," Allston said. He looked around the ramp. "Williams! Get your young body over here." But the sergeant had disappeared.

The Capitol

The Speaker was hunched forward, his hands folded in front of him on the committee bench, as Richards finished her opening statement. He leaned into the microphone. "General Richards, I'm not sure I understand your point." He was giving her a chance to change her testimony.

"My apologies, Mr. Speaker. I'll try to clarify. When I was investigating the 4440th, I discovered they were in an untenable situation. Their commander was determined to carry out their mission of supporting the UN relief and peacekeeping operation, yet the UN commissioners running the operation are hopelessly compromised and corrupt. For example, they ordered the peacekeepers to turn over their heavy weapons and aircraft to the Sudanese Army, which is engaged in genocide operations against the Nuer and Dinka tribes. That would have been a grave dereliction of duty if Colonel Allston had complied with that order and surrendered his Hercules C-130s. It would have been a moral failure if Colonel Allston had ceased relief operations. As to the alleged charge of torturing a prisoner, the only direct evidence I discovered was the testimony of the alleged victim."

"Then how do you explain the video?" the Speaker asked.

"The video I saw was taken at a great distance without audio. While conducting my investigation, I repeatedly heard a rumor that the prisoner had hidden a knife in his bandages and was attempting to use it. But I could not confirm that rumor."

"But it was at your direction the prisoner was turned over to the UN. Is that correct?"

"Yes, Mr. Speaker, that is correct. The prisoner was worried the Dinka and Nuer at the mission would kill him. I believed that fear was well founded and moved him for his own safety. I never suspected that the UN would immediately release him."

The Speaker was furious. "If there are no more questions, this committee is in recess." He didn't wait for the committee members to reply and banged the gavel.

Mission Awana

It was midnight when the small group gathered in Mission House. Jill spread out eight satellite photos on the table as Allston, Vermullen, Toby, and Malone crowded around. "We're facing a reinforced regiment of over two thousand infantry," she explained, "along with twenty tanks, and at least fifty APCs and armored cars. The good news is that they only had one battery of artillery with two pieces, which, I suspect, the Paladin made short work of. The bad news is that they still have mortars they can use as they come in range. Mortars will be much harder for the Paladin to take out."

"Your source for all this?" Allston asked.

"The Air and Army Attaches at Addis."

"And they arranged for the Paladin?" He was still fishing for an answer.

"Another agency, sir. The marines at Djibouti held a raffle to see who would come. It got pretty hot and heavy."

"You wouldn't happen to know the source of the jamming?" Vermullen asked.

Jill shuffled through the photos and found the one she wanted. "It's a mobile unit, Russian made." She pointed to a big truck with a canvas-covered bed and a tall mast holding multiple antenna arrays. "They have to stop to erect the mast. It takes about five minutes and they can't move with the mast erected. That's when they stop jamming."

Vermullen studied the vehicle. "It is very distinctive."

Allston knew what he was thinking. "It should be easy to identify."

"Especially with the mast up," Vermullen added.

The radio at the Ops desk squawked. "Outhouse, Outhouse, Gizmo One inbound. Fifteen minutes out." It was Dick Lane in a C-130. Before they could answer, the frequency was drowned out by a loud squelch.

"Well, they're not moving now," Allston said. "We need to take that puppy out." He looked around the table. "Let's go move some people." Another thought came to him. "Toby, let's air evac out as many of the wounded as we can."

E-Ring

Fitzgerald's intercom buzzed. It was his secretary. General Richards was on the line requesting a personal meeting. Fitzgerald savored the thought of ignoring her and letting her stew but he owed her another chance. "In thirty minutes. She's got five minutes." His fingers danced over his keyboard as he called up the link to the NMCC. The image in front of him flickered and stabilized as the encryption circuits did their magic.

The duty officer's image appeared on the screen. "Good evening, General. How may I help you?"

"What's the latest on the 4440th in the Sudan?" He waited while the duty officer made the handoff.

A young-looking Army lieutenant colonel appeared. He came right to the point. "All contact with the 4440th is lost but we have satellite imagery of the four C-130s and numerous personnel at Juba. Fighting was reported at Mission Awana but has stopped, and the airfield is open." He checked a computer screen. "We'll have a Keyhole overhead in twelve hours and will have an update then." The Keyhole series of reconnaissance satellites had a high-resolution camera that could breakout individuals on the ground. "The Boys In The Basement inserted a Paladin at Awana, and Special Ops will have personnel on the ground to support the peacekeepers in the next thirty-six hours. The situation appears to have stabilized."

Fitzgerald breathed easier and broke the connection. With a little luck, he'd have the 4440th out of the Sudan by Monday. He called up a file on the quadrennial defense review and shifted his attention to the future of the Air Force. He worked that problem until his intercom buzzed. It was Richards. He took her measure as she entered his office and reported in. "You're here late for a Friday."

"Yes, sir," she answered. "I'm looking for a new assignment."

"There's not much going for flag-rank military-political affairs officers."

"There's a position in Brussels with NATO that's opening up."

"That's an intelligence function."

"Yes, sir. I started out as an intelligence officer."

"But got sidetracked," he said. He sensed that he was talking to a different person. It was testing time. "I don't trust you but I did hear your testimony in front of the committee. What you did took guts. You made a powerful enemy today and you can kiss any thoughts of promotion goodbye."

"I am aware of that. But I need to make a difference, accomplish something worthwhile before I retire. This is my last chance."

"Why the sudden change?"

She knew it was a fair question. "I saw what Allston did in the Sudan. I totally misjudged him." Fitzgerald didn't respond and waited. "All I saw was arrogance and disrespect. He's profane and crude, and, well, a womanizer, but he saved lives."

"And he's aggressive." Fitzgerald waited, almost convinced. "And?"

Richards had to make the general understand. "I've never met anyone like him. I can't stand him . . . he's everything I disapprove of . . . but the way the Irregulars follow him . . ." her voice trailed off.

"It's called leadership." He made a decision. "Don't disappoint me in Brussels."

"Thank you, sir. I won't."

Fitzgerald watched her leave, struck by the irony of it all. Because of Allston, she had been challenged and emerged a better officer. An inner voice told him she had changed. But would she revert to type? He didn't know but the same voice told him it was a chance worth taking. He spun around in his chair and switched on the TV. He settled back to watch Tara's special on his peacekeepers.

An announcer read a news flash. "This just in from the Hague in the Netherlands. The International Criminal Court has issued arrest warrants for the three UN commissioners in charge of the Relief and Peacekeeping Mission of Southern Sudan. The United Nations has pledged to fully cooperate in any investigation and end the corruption that has marked the relief operation in Addis Ababa."

"Yeah, right," Fitzgerald mumbled to himself.

TWENTY-SIX

Mission Awana

D'Na walked down the ramp of Lane's C-130 closely followed by twenty-two rebel soldiers. She hurried over to her husband and stood close. They talked for a few moments as forty-five walking wounded boarded the aircraft. Stretcher-bearers were next as they carried twelve critically wounded up the ramp. Allston keyed his handheld radio but the frequency was immediately jammed. He ran up the crew entrance steps and climbed onto the flight deck. "What's happening at Juba?" he asked Lane.

Lane turned around in his seat. "D'Na bribed the right folks and got the field open." He looked at his watch. "Another Herk is inbound in about forty minutes. There should be one arriving about every forty to fifty minutes."

"Any more reinforcements coming?"

Lane shook his head. "That's it. I'll keep the Herks coming as long as the field is open."

The loadmaster stood on the flight deck's ladder. "We're loaded and good to go," he shouted over the engine noise.

Lane gave the sergeant a thumbs-up and extended his hand to Allston. "Thanks, Boss."

Allston was puzzled. "For getting your ass shot off?"

"Naw. That goes with the job. You're the best man I've ever worked for and I've done things here I never knew I could do." They shook hands.

Allston bolted down the ladder and out the crew entrance door. He ran for the battered Land Rover where Williams was waiting. "You should be in the hospital," Allston told him.

"I'm okay. I just got a gash in the love handle on my left side and lost a lot of blood. They gave me a transfusion. No way I'm gonna hang around a hospital when I can walk." He drove slowly through the night towards the mission. "Are we gonna make it, sir?"

Allston caught the 'sir,' which was not like Williams at all. The sergeant had to be very worried and Allston went with the truth. "I don't know. Look, you should be in a hospital, not here. I'll get you out on the next bird."

"If it's all the same to you, sir, I'll go when you go."

Allston didn't have a reply.

* * *

Daybreak was less than an hour away when the third C-130 landed, lights out. Williams and a crew chief used lighted wands to guide the pilot through the turn. The aircraft's ramp was already down and refugees streamed on board. Allston ran on board to speak to the pilot. "Where's Jenkins?" Allston asked.

"She's flying the next bird," the pilot replied, "with Bard Green. We're taking gunfire on final and the jamming is getting pretty damn bad. We could sure use radios to warn the next Herk." Williams was still standing in front of the Hercules and gave the pilot a thumbs up. Another 145 refugees were on board. Allston clambered off the Hercules and ran clear as the pilot released the brakes and taxied out.

The rattletrap Land Rover drove up and Jill motioned to him from the driver's seat. "The listening posts are reporting tanks in the water. Idi is on Charlie Ring running the show from there."

"Are we still in contact?" Allston asked.

Jill shook her head. "Jamming and the landlines are cut. We'll probably be in mortar range in a few minutes." She was very worried. "Colonel, this could be a final effort."

"If it's a do-or-die, they'll be doing the dying. Williams! Get your body over here." He ran for the shed where the Porter was parked.

Williams moved slowly, unable to catch Allston. "Get in," Jill ordered. He did and she drove after Allston.

"I'm not going to like this," Williams complained.

Allston was pushing the doors of the shed back when they arrived. He checked the Porter's cargo compartment as Williams crawled out of the Land Rover. "We need Shipons and weapons," Allston yelled. Jill gunned the Land Rover and headed for the mission. The rumble of explosions echoed in the distance and the two men hit the ground when the Paladin's cannon roared. Before they could move, another mortar round hit the ramp. The Paladin fired again and it was quiet.

"Damn," Williams cursed. "Now we gotta fill in the hole."

Allston was worried. "Right where the C-130 stopped. They've got the range." They pushed the Porter out of the shed and Allston did a careful preflight, checking if there was any major damage. Other than numerous bullet holes in the left side of the fuselage, the aircraft was undamaged. He turned to Williams. "You good to go?"

"Boss, do I really have a choice?"

"Sure you do. I can always get Major Sharp."

"Yeah, right," Williams groused. "She's back."

The Land Rover slammed to halt beside the Porter and Jill motioned to the Shipon and Stinger in the rear seat. "You've got two rounds for each one. That's all I could find," she told them. She crawled out and handed an M-16 and two clips to Allston.

"Well done," Allston said. He handed her the flare pistol from the Porter. "A Herk is inbound. Stay here and don't let it land. They've got a spotter directing mortar fire on the air patch. We gotta take out the bastard to get the field open." He climbed into the pilot's seat and hit the starter button, spinning the turboprop to life.

* * *

Vermullen peered into the early morning dark, trying to make sense out of the attack coming at him. Judging by the gunfire and mortar rounds the Sudanese were throwing at them, they were softening up the left for a flanking maneuver. Jamming had made the Legion's tactical radios useless but he knew where his men were posted and could rely on them to operate independently. He mentally calculated how long the sixty legionnaires he had deployed on that section of Charlie Ring could hold out. He had trained them and knew what they could do, and Claymores and Shipons did make a big difference. The Sudanese might break through, if they were willing to pay the price. Beck piled into the DFP beside him, and loudly sucked air, catching his breath.

"Getting too old for this, Hans?" The private didn't answer. "Everyone is briefed?" A nod answered him. Each fire team had been briefed on how Vermullen expected the attack to develop. He was certain the Sudanese would concentrate their attack on one part of Charlie Ring rather than a broad frontal assault. His plan called for that section to pull back and let the Sudanese move forward to present a flank to the other legionnaires.

Beck removed his NVGs and peered into the early-morning dark as the distinctive mix of diesel engines and clanking tracks grew louder. "Tanks," he said. "Coming at us." A missile from their right streaked through the night and a tank exploded. Another tank pushed around it, its turret-mounted machine gun firing. The tank commander's head was barely visible above the open hatch as he directed the driver. Vermullen raised his FAMAS and carefully aimed. He estimated the range at 125 meters and squeezed off a single shot. The top of the tank commander's head disappeared in a red haze. "Nice shot, Colonel," Beck said.

A red flare arced over them from their left. The Sudanese had broken through that side of Charlie Ring. Beck centered the Shipon's crosshairs on the driver's side of the tank charging at them and fired.

* * *

The Porter hugged the ground and popped over a low stand of trees. "It's getting pretty rough back here," Williams shouted as he held on for dear life in the open cargo compartment. Bright flashes off to their left confirmed they were flying over Charlie Ring and approaching the river. "The Legion is taking a beating down there," Williams yelled.

Allston didn't answer and concentrated on clearing the ground rushing by fifty feet below. He jerked the Porter to the right, barely missing a tree. Now he could make out the dense green vegetation that marked the marshland bordering the White Nile. Again, he darted around a tree, using it for cover. Below him, he made out the river's main channel. Less than a mile ahead, a long line of trucks was stopped on the road paralleling the northern side of the river. He caught a glimpse of a tall mast with the distinctive antenna arrays that marked his target. A line of tracers reached up from the road. Instinctively, he loaded the Porter with a three-*g* turn and dropped to ten feet off the deck as a line of tracers cut the air above them. "Fuckin' ZSUs!" he shouted, venting his anger. The 23mm, four-barreled ZSU-23-4 was an old, but very deadly anti-aircraft artillery that he wanted nothing to do with. But he was out of options and had to challenge the ZSU in order to get at the jammer. He circled to the north, trying to get behind the weapon. "Lock and load!"

"Ready." Williams was still firmly strapped to the cargo deck and aiming the Shipon out the left side.

"We're going after a APC with a radar antenna on top and four barrels sticking out the front. You gotta be quick on this one." Allston firewalled the throttle and turned towards the road. He had lost sight of it but knew where it was. He displaced his heading thirty degrees to the right of the ZSU. A line of tracers cut back and forth in front of him as the gunner fired wildly, hearing the Porter's turboprop but not able to find it in the dark. Allston's eyes followed the tracers back to the ZSU. "Ready, ready," he shouted at Williams. "Pull!" They were less than 200 yards from the ZSU when he pulled on the stick and popped to eighty feet above the ground, enough to set up a pylon turn. He turned to the left as ZSU's radar found them and the line of tracers swung around. Williams fired.

Allston rolled out, wings level, as he bunted the stick forward. The agile Porter hit the ground and bounced, the big tires and landing gear struts absorbing the shock. The tracers cut above them. One round grazed the top of the Porter's vertical stabilizer, taking off the top nine inches but not exploding. The ZSU fireballed as the Shipon found its target. Allston fought for control, finally leveling off at thirty feet. He turned towards the road. Ahead, he could barely make out the tall mast sticking out above the low scrub. "Ready?" he shouted.

"Reloading," Williams yelled. It seemed an eternity as the mast loomed larger with each passing second. "Ready!" Williams shouted just as Allston put the stick over to turn away. He jerked the stick back, snapping three gs in the opposite direction. Williams let out a loud "Oomph!"

"We're engaged," Allston shouted. This time, he half turned and half skidded the Porter around, giving Williams the angle he needed. Williams fired and the missile tracked true. Allston turned away as the jammer disintegrated in flames and smoke. The concussion rocked the Porter, sending it out of control.

* * *

Vermullen fired a green starburst flare to signal his left flank to fall back. Beck reloaded the Shipon and lifted the launcher over the edge of the DFP in time to see two tanks coming right at them. "Which one?" he asked. Vermullen pointed to the one on the right. The private sighted and fired. The missile hugged the terrain as it homed on the doomed tank. Unfortunately, the rocket motor's plume left a very visible path back to them for the other tank to follow. Both men rolled out the backside of the DFP as the tank disappeared in a fiery cloud of death and destruction. They scampered for the next DFP as the second tank's cannon traversed towards them. Before it could fire, another missile reached out from their far right and found the seam between the tank's turret and hull. The explosion blew the turret off. Overlapping fields of fire had saved the two men.

Vermullen rolled into the foxhole and came to his feet and scanned the battleground. At the same instant, his radio came alive. The jamming had stopped and his teams were reporting in. Their luck was holding and the Sudanese were not pressing the attack as the legionnaires on his left flank fell back onto Bravo Ring in good order. They weren't dead yet.

* * *

The Porter's left wing tip grazed the ground as Allston regained control. "You okay?" he shouted at Williams.

"Do they serve cocktails on this flight?" Williams asked. He was fine.

Allston circled back, looking for another tank. He saw the road and turned, crossing it on a southerly heading. He popped up and could see for over a mile. The river was dead ahead and burning tanks littered the ground on the far side. The legionnaires had given a good account of themselves. "Boss!" Williams roared. "Helicopters coming at us!" Again, situational awareness made the difference. Allston knew that Williams was looking out the left and he turned to the left, bringing the threat to the nose. Three Russian-built MI-24 attack helicopters were bearing down on them in a loose vee formation.

"Oh shit!" Allston yelled. "Hinds!" The nimble 25,000-pound helicopter had a top speed of 205 MPH and an awesome array of weapons under its stubby wings. He wanted nothing to do with one, much less three. But they were headed straight for Mission Awana. "Hold on!" Years of training and experience paid dividends as he firewalled the throttle and pulled into the vertical. He never took his eyes off the helicopters as he rolled over the top inverted. Automatically, he checked their armaments and only saw rocket pods for ground attack under the short wings. The Hinds were not carrying air-to-air missiles, which only left the 12.7mm, four-barreled Gatling gun under the nose chin. It was an awesome weapon with a 4000 rounds per minute rate of fire. Fortunately, it only held 1470 rounds and was limited to a forward-looking cone of aimed fire. It was a ground attack weapon and the Hinds would have to turn into him to fire. He watched to see how they maneuvered. "Shit hot!" he roared. The pilots were turning after him in level turns to the left and not using the vertical. He marked that up to fear of the ground and poor training. In Allston's very specialized world, it was their death warrant. The difference between a normal pilot and a fighter pilot kicked in and his fangs came out. "Lock and load a Stinger," he shouted at Williams.

The trick was to stay above the helicopters and keep their noses off him, which was no small feat. He shot out in front of the low-flying helicopters, which were 500 feet below him. The gunners tried to follow the Porter but their weapons hit the up stop at fifteen degrees of elevation. The lead Hind's nose came up, finally bringing its machine gun to bear. Allston ballooned the Porter and immediately ruddered the Porter to his right, skidding away from the Hind. A line of tracers cut through the night well behind him. He circled back to the left, calculating the Hinds would keep turning. "Ready?" he called, his voice calm and controlled.

"Ready," Williams answered.

Allston did a wingover and sliced into the Hinds. His timing and positioning were perfect. The helicopters were at their nine o'clock position at 500 yards with their tails to them. Williams fired. The Stinger is an incredibly fast missile and tracked true, homing on the exhaust of the tail end Charlie. The helicopter fireballed and pitched forward. Allston pulled into the vertical, again using the cloud deck for cover. "Reload," he ordered.

"This is the last one," Williams told him. Then, "Ready."

But where were the two Hinds? They were scattering the last time he had seen them, and were probably panicked by the fate of their comrade. But he knew where to look.

* * *

Vermullen had lost track of the battle. As best he could tell, his left flank was withdrawing to the minefield in good order, making the SA pay dearly for every foot of ground it gained. Far to his left, a pillar of flame shot skyward, again proving how lethal a Shipon was in the right hands. But what about his right flank? He hunkered down in the DFP and pressed the earpiece deeper into his ear, trying to make sense out of the radio calls. Slowly, a picture emerged. The tanks were concentrating their attack on his left and his right flank was falling apart as APCs and infantry opened up a corridor. "Colonel," Beck said, gaining his attention. "A tank with infantry." He laid the Shipon's crosshairs on the tank. "This is the last one." Vermullen chanced a glance as Beck fired their last missile. The missile barely had time to arm before it struck the tank's carapace, easily penetrating the T-62's seven inches of armor. The secondary charge detonated inside, shredding the four-man crew. An oxygen bottle cooked off, adding to the carnage.

* * *

Jill instinctively covered her ears as the Paladin raised its cannon to the near vertical and fired. The high angle indicated the target was very close and the projectile was arcing high into the air, trading range for altitude. She sank back against the sandbagged revetment and read the manual for the laser rangefinder/designator Corporal Rickert had given her. She picked up the small device and peered through the rangefinder. It was easy to use but surprisingly heavy at six pounds. She gingerly laid it in her lap as the Paladin fired again. Malone's voice came over her radio. "Janjaweed horsemen are in the refugee camp. Repeat, Janjaweed in the refugee camp." She switched frequencies to the channel the legionnaires were using. Mercier was trying to raise the four legionnaires still guarding the refugee camp. There was no answer.

"Close the corridor through the minefield," she mentally urged. Her head came up when she heard the unmistakable drone of a C-130. She switched frequencies to the operations channel in time to hear Marci Jenkins voice announce she was on short final for landing. "Do not land, do not land," Jill radioed. "The field is closed, repeat, the field is closed due to mortar fire."

"Going around," Marci said, her voice cool and calm.

Jill stood and watched as the Hercules leveled off twenty feet above the ground and started to climb. But before Marci could turn out, a mortar shrieked overhead and hit the runway in front of her. The Hercules flew through the explosion and cartwheeled into the ground. The cargo plane's fuel tanks exploded and a pillar of fire reached skyward. Jill forced her eyes away, remembering what Allston had said about a spotter directing fire on the field. But what did a spotter look like? She climbed into the Land Rover and drove slowly around the airfield, determined to find the spotter. At the far eastern end, a flash of light from a low tree caught her attention. Flames from the burning C-130 had reflected off the lens of a spotting scope. She breathed deeply as her heart raced. In her excitement, she stomped on the brakes and stalled the Rover. She quickly raised the laser range finder and zoomed in on the tree. A woman was hidden in the branches, holding a radio to her lips, her body jerking with excitement, and her other arm pointing at the flaming wreck.

"You are history," Jill whispered as she laid the crosshairs on the woman's head. A killing rage swept over her and she forced herself to calm down. She keyed her radio and called the Paladin. "I've found the spotter," she said. "It's a woman in a low tree maybe a quarter of a mile to the east of the airfield." Rickert was over a mile away at the western end of the airfield and did not have a visual on the tree. He asked her for the coordinates. "I haven't got a clue," she replied. "We got to get her before she moves."

"Can you designate with the rangefinder?" Rickert asked.

"Can do," she answered.

"Say your location."

"I'm on the eastern end of the runway," she told him. She pressed a button. "Designating now."

"On the way," Rickert said. The Paladin roared and a Copperhead arced high into the sky and homed on the reflected laser energy. The tree came apart as the shell exploded, shredding it into matchwood.

She radioed Malone. "The airfield will be open as soon as we fill in a crater."

"Copy all," Malone replied. "Be advised horsemen broke out of the refugee camp. Whereabouts unknown. Also, all corridors through the minefield are closed and are hot." Mercier had activated the mines in the corridors, sealing the mission and cutting off the legionnaires – and the airfield.

* * *

Allston found the two Hinds hovering over the river, a few feet off the water, poised like stalking tigers and ready to pounce. He almost flew over them before he could turn away and circle behind them. There was nothing chivalrous or heroic in what he intended to do. He was going to sneak up behind them and kill at least one with their remaining Stinger. "Ready?"

"Go for it," Williams replied. They had welded into a team, and Williams was reacting instinctively.

Allston turned back towards the river where the Hinds were still hovering over the river. He displaced thirty-five degrees to the right and simply flew behind them. "Coming under the left wing now," he told Williams.

"Got 'em," Williams said. He fired the Stinger and Allston turned hard to the right, escaping to the north. They never saw the missile fly up the helicopter's right exhaust nozzle but the bright flash lit up the night. "Scratch that fucker," Williams shouted. Allston turned hard to the left as a burst of tracers cut behind them. Again, he pulled into the vertical and did a wingover, desperate to gain a visual on the last helicopter. Nothing.

"He's underneath us!" Williams shouted. He had done his work well and found the Hind, keeping them alive. The nose of the Hind sliced towards them and came up, bringing its machine gun to bear. Allston pulled into the vertical and pirouetted, spinning the agile Porter on its tail as he pulled the nose back to the ground.

The Hind was still below him and turning, keeping them in sight. "M-16!" Allston shouted, communicating in shorthand.

"Got it," Williams said as he dropped the Stinger tube and picked up his M-16. The Hind's nose was almost on them and the helicopter's gunner slewed the machine gun towards them as he fired.

"Fire!" Allston yelled, certain they were dead. Williams mashed the trigger and emptied the magazine, still firing out the left side of the Porter. Both Williams and the Hind's gunner were firing wildly, making no attempt to aim their weapons. The Hind's pilot saw the bright muzzle flashes coming from the Porter and accelerated, trying to avoid the gunfire. The nose of the Hind came down as the helicopter moved, throwing the machine gun's muzzle down, harmlessly raking the ground.

Fighter pilots call it the "Golden BB," the magical bullet that hits the target because of blind luck. The last round out of Williams M-16 was the Golden BB and it hit one blade in the Hind's rotor, shattering it and throwing the helicopter out of control. The helicopter spun violently to the right and hit the ground in a flat spin. The big blades flexed down and came apart, cutting into the fuselage. But the fuel tanks did not explode. Allston circled the wreckage. He felt no jubilation or pride, no sense of accomplishment. They had just killed two more men. He watched as the flicker of a flame grew and engulfed the right engine. It quickly spread and the fuel tanks finally erupted, cremating what was left of the men inside.

"Boss," Williams said. "Can we go home? I'm hurtin'." Allston twisted around in his seat. Williams was hunched over holding the bandage on his left side. "I think I ripped a stitch."

"Home plate it is," Allston said. He had asked all he could from the sergeant. "You did good."

"How come I'm not feeling good about it?"

Good question, Allston thought. He radioed Malone. "Backstop, Bossman inbound with one wounded. Can I land in the mission?"

"Negative, Bossman. Be advised the airfield is open but the mission is sealed off. The minefield is fully activated."

"Say situation," Allston replied.

"The Legion is holding on Bravo Ring but can't withdraw through the minefield. Janjaweed are reported operating near the airfield and refugee camp."

"Rog. I'll check out the area." He hugged the ground and flew a big arc over what had been Charlie Ring. Burning tanks cast eerie shadows as flashes of small arms fire punctured the dark. He climbed to a hundred feet and clearly saw the mission. Below him, a soldier raised his AK-47 and fired. It missed. He banked hard and dove, heading for the airfield.

* * *

Vermullen's tactical radio was alive with shouts and pleas for a medic as the battle seesawed back and forth. "The left is holding," Vermullen told Beck. His left flank had successfully collapsed to the minefield and was holding, thanks to the Shipons. Beck bobbed his head up and peered into the dark. "Our right flank has been wiped out." Vermullen knew it was his fault. He had held the eighty men on his right in place as his left side pulled back in the hope the advancing SA would present a flank for the legionnaires to attack. But he had miscalculated and his men had been isolated and encircled, including him and Beck. But they had extracted a terrible price and stopped the Sudanese.

"Colonel, I hear a diesel." Beck strained to hear. "It's an APC." Again, he chanced a look. "Maybe ten-twelve infantry following." The diesel engine raced and Beck looked again. "It's stuck. The men are digging it out. They have mine detectors."

An inner voice warned Vermullen that the APC marked the SA's final effort. But they were out of Shipons and low on ammunition. "It will be trouble if they get it moving," Vermullen said. "It must not break through."

"Colonel, I never wanted to die like a rat in a hole." Beck held up their last bandolier with four, thirty-round magazines. "I have two grenades."

"Give me one." Vermullen clipped the grenade to his equipment suspender and shoved two of the magazines into his thigh pocket. Beck did the same. "It has been an honor to know you," he said.

Beck squeezed off three short bursts, emptying his magazine at the APC, which was now moving. They could clearly hear the tracks and the sound of the laboring engine. Beck ejected the magazine and methodically reloaded. "The pleasure has been all mine."

The two men looked at each other. "Now," Vermullen said. He rolled out his side of the DFP as Beck did the same. Both came to their feet and charged the APC and the advancing men, firing from the hip. "CAMERONE!" Vermullen bellowed at the top of his lungs.

* * *

Jill coaxed the Land Rover down the runway, inspecting the surface as she went. Ahead of her, and off to the side, the C-130 was still burning. She stopped and examined the mortar's shallow crater. It wasn't very big, slightly over four feet across and eighteen inches deep. Still, the blast had been deadly when Marci's C-130 had flown through it. She remembered seeing some quick-setting cement in one of the sheds. It wouldn't be too difficult to patch. She stood in front of the Rover, listening. It was eerily quiet, no echoing gunfire and the dull reverberations of mortars were silenced. Was it over? A sudden weariness washed over her and she leaned against the fender.

Her radio squawked. It was Rickert in the Paladin. "Major! Horses! Behind you! We're coming your way."

Jill turned and looked back. Two riders were coming at her at a full gallop down the runway. She jumped into the Land Rover and twisted the key. But it wouldn't start. She ground the starter. The engine coughed to life and she jammed it into gear, only to stall when she let out the clutch. The Janjaweed were almost on her. She drew her automatic and emptied the clip. She missed. The two riders split as one circled around to her left, the other to the right. Her radio blared. "We threw a track! " Rickert shouted.

She glanced at the disabled Paladin that was over a mile away. Its long barrel traversed and fired a round, more to distract the horsemen than to kill them. It missed and she could see the tall horseman on her right laugh. He was not the typical Janjaweed and rode his horse with a rare confidence. Even at thirty yards away, she could see his ornate saddle. Who the hell are you? she thought. Then she knew. She had seen his photos many times and briefed numerous generals on his activities. He was Sheikh Amal Jahel of the Rizeigat, the leader of the Fursan. He reined his horse around and came at her, bending over, his head against the horse's neck. A jolt of fear and awe immobilized her as he bore down. How many times had she described him as a cavalier, not really understanding what that word meant? She raised her Colt .45 and squeezed off a single round. Again, she missed. Was it deliberate? She would never know but she would always remember the look of excitement and joy on his face.

The Porter flew by, cutting between Jill and the charging horse and rider. Allston pulled up and ruddered the Porter around, again coming at Jahel. The stalled Paladin fired again, deliberately missing but adding to the confusion. It was enough to drive both horsemen away from Jill. Again, Allston pulled up and ruddered the Porter around, still chasing Jahel. Jill turned around at the sound of hooves pounding on the runway. The other rider was less than twenty yards away and coming directly at her. It was

BermaNur. Her anger flared, shattering the fear and awe that had bound her tight in a burst of anger and hate. "You fucking bastard!" she roared as she fired twice. BermaNur veered away unhurt and raced for safety. She let him go and turned. Jahel was cutting back and forth as Allston closed. The Porter's left main gear touched the runway as Allston turned after him. Then he reversed and the right gear briefly touched. Jahel turned and fired his AK-47 from the saddle.

Round after round tore into the Porter and Jill saw a red mist paint the left side of the aircraft. The Porter pulled up and came back down, bouncing off the runway as it ballooned into the air. The turboprop engine roared as Allston fought for control. He slammed the Porter down and the prop hit Jahel. His head disappeared in a red cloud and the frenzied horse bolted to the right, still carrying its dead rider.

The Porter bounced out of control and tumbled down the runway, finally coming to a halt upside down. Allston hung from his harness as his hands moved automatically, shutting off the battery and twisting the fuel cocks closed. He passed out before he could hit the quick release on his harness.

BermaNur raced for the Porter and reined his horse to a halt. He dismounted and looked down the runway at the disabled Paladin. Men were running towards him but they were too far away to arrive in time, if he acted quickly. His eyes squinted in hate when he saw Jill running towards him. He would deal with her shortly. He jammed a fresh magazine in his AK-47, thumbed it to single-shot, and methodically aimed, firing a single round and hitting Williams in the left shoulder. He turned to the unconscious Allston. "Insh' Allah." He raised his weapon.

He didn't see Jill as she closed on him. She raised her Colt and fired on the run. "No way!" The slug tore into BermaNur's back and spun him around. He fell to the ground and she kept pulling the trigger. The Janjaweed jerked violently as she emptied the clip. She reloaded.

"He's dead, luv," Allston mumbled.

Jill fired twice more and dropped the Colt. She ripped open the pilot's door. Allston was still hanging upside down, half out of his harness as blood gushed from wounds in his head, chest, and left leg. She reached inside and applied pressure to the wounds as Rickert ran up. Tears coursed down her cheeks. "Help me!" she shouted.

* * *

The early morning light cast a long shadow down the row of beds and makeshift cots in the hospital's main ward. Allston blinked, getting his bearings. He tried to move, but his body wouldn't respond. A heavy bandage clamped his chest and his head hurt. He was vaguely aware that his head was bandaged and he could not see with his left eye. He managed to move his head enough to see who was sitting beside him. It was Jill. She was asleep, slumped over her right arm that was stretched out on the bed beside him. His left hand moved ever so slightly and his fingers found her hand.

She woke up. "You're awake. Water?" She reached for a water bottle but he wouldn't let go of her hand.

"The Herk?" his voice was barely audible. "Who was it?"

"Marci Jenkins," she told him. "With Bard, Riley, and MacRay. I didn't warn them off in time."

His voice was stronger. "They knew the risks. Don't go blaming yourself." He squeezed her hand. "Williams?"

A little smile. "The nurses like him."

"Casualties?"

"The mortars were terrible before the Paladin finally silenced them. We were lucky, only five cops were wounded, but there are over three hundred dead and wounded at the mission." She gestured down the ward at the long line of beds. "Toby's been in surgery for over three days."

"The Legion?"

"They held and died in front of the minefield. Over half were killed and all but two were wounded. Special Ops is reinforcing the mission. It's over – for now."

"Idi?"

A slight shake of her head. "They found Beck's body in front of a burnt out APC with fifteen dead SA. His rifle was empty. But there's no trace of Idi. They're still looking. He's a true missing in action."

"He'd want it that way."

She held his hand and wouldn't let go.

EPILOGUE

Arlington National Cemetery

The long cortege of cars wound through the cemetery, following the four horse-drawn caissons, each bearing a flag-draped coffin. Jill glided their car to a stop. "We'll have to walk from here. Can you make it?" Allston assured her he could as he got out of the rear seat. Ben, his lanky sixteen-year-old stepson, hurried around the car to help him with his crutches. Jill turned to Lynne who was sitting beside her in the front seat. She was still struck by the sheer beauty of Allston's daughter. "I'll meet you back here." She pointed to the large group of Irregulars clustered around Susan Malaby. "I'll be with them."

Lynne took her hand. "Thank you for everything. May I ask you a question? It's very personal and you can tell me to mind my own business." She lowered her voice. "Are you going to marry him?"

Jill smiled gently. "Maybe. But he's going to have to work for it."

Lynne beamed. "Yes!" Jill got out of the car and walked towards the Irregulars while Lynne joined her father and Ben. "I really like her," Lynne confided in a low voice.

"So do I," Allston replied.

Ben was much more enthusiastic. "Works for me, Colonel."

Allston suppressed a laugh at the echo of himself.

Lynne gave Allston her serious look. "Dad, don't blow it this time, okay?"

They walked slowly to the gravesites. Allston had to stop and catch his breath. He took it all in; the April sky, the ordered rows of crosses, the structured dignity and predictability of a military funeral that bound his universe. They joined the families sitting by the graves and found seats in the second row. A low murmur swept over the mourners when General John Fitzgerald followed the honor guard. He stood with them as Master Sergeant

Jerry Malone called the Irregulars to attention. Six Irregulars carried each coffin and they placed their fallen comrades over the open graves. "Parade Rest," Malone called. The chaplain read the service and stepped aside for Malone. Again, Malone called the Irregulars to attention and asked the mourners to please stand for the rendering of honors. His "Present arms," echoed in the quiet. The honor guard fired three volleys and the bugler played taps. "Order arms," he called. "Please be seated."

The pallbearers stepped forward and folded the flags into the time-honored shape of a tri-cornered cap. The head of Marci's detail presented the flag to Malone who passed it to Fitzgerald. The general knelt in front of her parents. "On behalf of the President of the United States, the Department of the Air Force, and a grateful nation, we offer this flag for the faithful and dedicated service of Captain Marci Louise Jenkins." He repeated the presentation three more times and came to attention as three C-130s approached from the east out of the sun, in a vee formation.

Allston looked up. "Dick Lane," was all he said.

Ben responded to his father. "Dad, do you think I could be a trash hauler? Like them?"

"That's your decision, son. But it would make me very proud."

Fitzgerald's eyes followed the C-130s. He slowly turned to the families to offer his condolences. "Thank you for allowing us to join you today. I cannot express how proud the Air Force and all who serve their country are of your loved ones. I know there is little any of us can say to comfort you in your loss but may I offer this: Captain Marci Jenkins, First Lieutenant Bard Green, Technical Sergeant Leroy Riley, and Staff Sergeant James MacRay truly made the ultimate sacrifice, not only for their country but for humanity. They were a crew and they served and died together, and it is entirely fitting and proper that we should inter them together. I want to thank you for your understanding and allowing this day to happen.

"They didn't hesitate to risk their lives to save others, and helped stop the genocide that has cursed a troubled land. Your children were our conscience as they strove to right a terrible wrong. By fighting and dying for a people they hardly knew, they made it possible for us to create a better peace. They are the true Peacemakers of our world." He came to attention and saluted the coffins. It was over.

Allston paid his respects to the family, and alone, made his way to the coffins. He stood there, proud of them beyond measure, and their faces were seared into his very being – Marci, Bard, Riley, and MacRay. And G.G. was there, standing with them. Their images glowed with life and the promise of what could have been. But they were lost because he had failed them. "I'm sorry," he said aloud. A hand slipped under his arm. It was Jill.

"Don't blame yourself," she said softly, holding him tight.

"I didn't get them out."

"You got everyone else to safety. And how many Africans did you save? You started on that very first day with NyaMai – remember her? And you never stopped. It's not an equation a human being can solve, so stop beating yourself."

An inner voice told him that she was right. He let the quiet wash over them, not sure what to say. "I have to deliver a message to Captain Bouchard's widow in France. Her name is Clarice. He said to tell her that he loved her more than life itself, but he had to follow. I guess he meant he had to follow Vermullen. You speak French and I can use some help." Jill nodded in answer and stood quietly, waiting. "Is there a future for us?" he finally ventured.

"I hope so." She looked at him, her eyes misting. "What do you think happened to Idi?" The legionnaire would always be a presence in their lives.

"I don't know." Allston looked up. High scattered clouds scudded across the Spring sky reaching for the horizon. "But if we need him again, he'll be back."

Jill looked at the man she loved, knowing him for what he was. "No, he won't. But you will."

The End

ACKNOWLEDGMENTS

Because of the advent and growth of e-books and print-on-demand, every morning seems to bring a new dimension to the world of writing and publishing. But writing is still a lonely business, and few writers work in a vacuum. I am no exception and owe a debt of thanks to a few friends. James L. Kenny introduced me to the reality of flying C-130s in the Sudan. Val Herman and Judy Person performed wonders in copy editing the manuscript. Gretchen Ricker did yeoman labor in taking me through the complexities of designing and formatting a manuscript for electronic publication, which is no small task.

As always, William P. Wood, the co-publisher of Willowbank Books, offered countless suggestions and endless encouragement, and without the patience and gentle support of my wife, Sheila Kathleen, I would have never started my first novel, much less finished *The Peacemakers*.

Made in the USA
San Bernardino, CA
20 March 2019